BAD BOY SEDUCTION

"You're playing a dangerous game," Troy drawled into her ear, his breath hot and way too close. "Never do what you did again, unless you want to reap the consequences of such actions."

She turned her head to tell him off. It was just the move he needed. He slammed his mouth against hers, demanding she open her mouth to receive him. She groaned, her hot spot growing hotter against her will, every fiber of her being wanting this man inside her. A surge of energy rushed to her core, causing a wetness that had nothing to do with sweat. The same arm that had tried earlier to push him away now wrapped itself around his neck and pulled him closer. All she could think about was being with this man, in the most intimate way imaginable, and as soon as possible. . . .

Also by Zuri Day

Lies Lovers Tell

Body By Night

Lessons from a Younger Lover

What Love Tastes Like

Lovin' Blue

Love in Play

Heat Wave (with Donna Hill and Niobia Bryant)

The Morgan Men Series

Love on the Run

A Good Dose of Pleasure

Bad Boy Seduction

Published by Kensington Publishing Corp.

Bad Boy Seduction

A Morgan Man Novel

ZURI DAY

Dafina BOOKS

Kensington Publishing Corp.

http://www.kensingtonbooks.com

DAFINA BOOKS are published by

Kensington Publishing Corp.
119 West 40th Street
New York, NY 10018

All Kensington titles, imprints, and distributed lines are
available at special quantity discounts for bulk purchases for
sales promotions, premiums, fund-raising, and educational
or institutional use. Special book excerpts or customized
printings can also be created to fit specific needs. For details,
write or phone the office of the Kensington Special Sales
Manager: Kensington Publishing Corp., 119 West 40th
Street, New York, NY 10018, Attn: Special Sales Department,
Phone: 1-800-221-2647.

Dafina and the Dafina logo Reg. U.S. Pat. & TM Off.

ISBN-13: 978-0-7582-7513-4
ISBN-10: 0-7582-7513-7
First Kensington Mass Market Edition: April 2014

eISBN-13: 978-1-61773-025-2
eISBN-10: 1-61773-025-4
First Kensington Electronic Edition: April 2014

10 9 8 7 6 5 4 3 2 1

Printed in the United States of America

Bad Boy
Seduction

1

He's my protector,
and I love how he makes me feel.
Strong arms, charm, and sex appeal.
No hurt to my heart, his love heals.
The real deal . . .
He's my protector.

"Wipe that smile off your face, fool," Troy Morgan said, pushing his top employee's feet off the desk before taking a seat. "She's not talking about you."

Alex reached over and turned down the number one song in the country. "I wish she were. This chick is the truth!"

"What? Somebody knocked Beyoncé off the throne?"

"Man, Gabriella is getting ready to be my wife."

"As soon as you meet her, huh?"

"No doubt! I've even put her on my iPad screen saver." Alex fired up his notebook. "Check this babe out."

Alex turned his iPad toward Troy, who checked out the newest pop and hip-hop sensation, Gabriella Stone, known to the world simply as Gabriella. Alex was right. The triple threat performer was definitely a stunner: doll face, hourglass shape, and creamy brown skin. Her naturally curly hair gone wild was very unlike the sleek weaves and wigs worn by her counterparts. But her sexy image and deep, raspy voice was the stuff that stars were made of.

"She's hot, I'll give her that," Troy said, with a nod of his head. He turned the iPad back toward Alex.

"Man, I'll give her whatever she wants!"

"Ha! Well, son, you might just get that chance."

"How so?"

"It's not a done deal yet, but we might get the security contract for the West Coast leg of her world tour."

Alex straightened up so quickly he almost upended his chair. "Word?"

"Calm down, man. We're probably one of at least a dozen firms that put in a bid."

"Oh, man! I'd take five or ten years off my life to guard that girl."

Troy chuckled. "I think you're serious."

"As a brain tumor. Troy, I'd give up my pay and guard her for free! Promise me, man."

"Promise you what?"

"That if we get the contract, you'll give the job of being her personal bodyguard to me."

"You'll definitely be on the detail, Alex. The job will call for at least five guards working various points around the venues. Maybe more."

"I'm not talking about working somewhere in the building, man. I'm talking about personally guarding my girl!"

"I don't know, dude. The last thing my company needs

is a sexual harassment lawsuit, and I don't know if you'd be able to restrain yourself."

"You might be right about that!" Alex clicked on a link and began scrolling through images of his idol. "Damn, this chick is fire."

"Enough ogling, my brother. It's time to go to work."

"What do we have?"

"For me, a Saudi prince arriving in town by private plane. For you, your favorite rapper with the death wish."

Alex rolled his eyes. "Great. I ask for the babe and get the bonehead. When?"

"Late tonight." Troy handed over a file. "Here's the workup on him: itinerary, bio, you know the drill."

"Man, how can you get me excited about possibly guarding Gabriella and then hand over the manifesto on this fool?"

"That fool is responsible for your paycheck this week, Alex. Don't bite the hand that feeds you."

"You get that contract with Gabriella and I'll be biting something, all right."

"Ha! Too much info, man. I don't need to hear your fantasies."

"More like prophecy. Get that contract and give me a shot."

"You know there's no fraternizing with clients, right?"

"I sure do. That's why as soon as I get that first date with baby girl, I'll be turning in my resignation."

"Damn! You are wide open!"

"No shame to my game, man." Alex reached for the file on the temperamental hip-hop artist Sho'Nuff and began flipping through it. "Give me your word, Troy. If we get that contract, I get to guard her person."

"I'll give you my word to think about it," Troy said,

rising from the chair and heading to the door. "Until then, *as-salaam alaikum*."

Alex laughed at Troy's use of the Arabic greeting—which meant "peace be unto you"—one that he'd soon be using with his client. He nodded and responded, *"Alaikum as-salaam."*

Gabriella Valencia Stone leaned against a floor-to-ceiling window, gazing dispassionately at a stunning view that ninety-eight percent of the world would never see—New York City from seventy-five stories up. Penthouse suite. Twenty-five thousand dollars a night. One of those "if you have to ask the price you can't afford it" kinds of places. She was dressed in couture and flawless, having just finished the last interview of the day. Since her latest CD had dropped, the media frenzy had been relentless. She'd been in New York for a week—TV shows, radio interviews, photo shoots—all leading up to the Stone Cold Sexy tour's kickoff performance at the Barclays Center in Brooklyn. Seven shows at the nineteen-thousand-seat arena had been sold out for six months. Scalpers were getting rich off those who'd pay anything to see their favorite star. Rumor had it that tickets were selling for as high as five g's. Apiece. Pretty heady stuff for an average twenty-five-year-old. Except for one thing. Gabriella was nobody's average. This pop star princess had experienced such luxuries for more than half her life.

Stunning suite, startling views, stocked bar, and whatever she wanted at her fingertips—and Gabriella was straight up bored out of her gourd.

"Why are you still wearing that gown?" Carol Robbins's

voice oozed attitude as she entered the living area of the suite, carrying an iPad and an oversized bag. The cell phone that Gabriella swore was glued to Carol's ear was in place. "I'll call you back," she said into the phone. She placed down the bag and threw the phone and iPad on a nearby chair. After noting that Gabriella's stylist and dresser was nowhere in sight, she asked, "Where's Melanie?"

"Probably meeting with the fashion editor for tomorrow's shoot and interview."

"Have you been standing here all this time just waiting to be unzipped? Girl, turn around," Carol said with a shake of her head. At her former classmate, former girl group member, and current best friend turned personal assistant's command, Gabriella dutifully complied. "I don't know how you do it, day after day. This tour hasn't even officially started and I'm already tired."

"Calm down, Carol." Gabriella slipped out of the dress and reached for the silk robe that had been retrieved from the master bedroom. "The magazine people just left. I'm surprised you didn't see them in the hallway."

"How was it?"

Gabriella shrugged. "Like all the others. I'll just be glad when it's over. You're right in saying our schedule is a whirlwind. I'm ready to go home."

"Okay?! You haven't even done the first concert and you're ready to go, too. But then again, thousands of women would give anything to be in your shoes."

"They'd change their mind if they knew how much my feet hurt." Carol gave her friend a look as Gabriella sat and rubbed her toes and heels. "I know I shouldn't feel that way. I need to adjust my attitude."

"We both do." Carol walked over to where she'd

tossed the iPad, sat in the chair, and fired it up. "I think we've got a couple of hours before you have to leave for dinner."

"Please, don't tell me the day isn't over. I'm ready for room service, a bubble bath, and bed."

"Sorry, chickie. You're meeting . . ."—she paused, scrolling down the iPad screen—"Leonardo diRossi. The jeweler."

"We're going to have to cancel that."

"Can't do that, honey." Both women turned toward the sound of Gabriella's father and manager, Gary, coming into the room. "He's flown over from Italy just to meet us. If we want this jewelry line designed in time for the holiday shoppers, we've got to meet tonight."

"Daddy . . ."

"One hour, little bunny," Gary said, walking over to give Gabriella a kiss on the cheek. "Then you can leave."

Three hours later Gabriella was back in her suite and, finally, in her bed. Unfortunately insomnia had lain down with her.

"Great . . . this is just great," she mumbled, throwing back the covers and standing. She padded barefoot into the kitchen, poured herself a glass of grapefruit juice, and picked up a copy of the tour schedule on her way back to the bedroom. Sitting against the plush backboard, she silently scanned the cities: Boston, Philly, Atlanta, Miami, a couple cities in the Midwest, and then on to the West Coast. Gabriella's smile was bittersweet as her finger ran over the words: Los Angeles. Memories flooded her. Crazy beautiful yet conflicted thoughts about her whirlwind romance with a mega-rapper California native, hip-hop artist Marlon "Mr. President" Simmons. Her very first boyfriend and second heartbreak.

The relationship that at her father's insistence ended almost before it began.

Gabriella put down the schedule and, with a sigh, turned off the light and pulled up the covers. These were the hardest moments. When the crowds were gone and the lights had faded; when the nights were quiet and she was alone. This was when the superstar receded and the little girl emerged. The one who in a New York minute would give up the fancy suites, international travel, and world adulation for that one thing that she wanted to experience most: true love.

2

Three weeks and counting and it had been grueling: New York, Newark, Boston, Philly, Richmond, Charlotte, Memphis, DC, Atlanta, Chicago, Dallas, St. Louis, and now . . . sunny LA. Except the weather was pretty much the only thing about the day that was shining. After back-to-back performances and PR jaunts and photo shoots, Gabriella's mood was dark and stormy.

"I don't care who you hire, Daddy. I don't feel like meeting anybody right now!"

This wasn't Gary's first time witnessing a Gabriella tantrum, and it showed. He continued to text on his phone, not one feather ruffled, as he answered. "You say that now, but we've got two weeks here in LA. So if I choose the man who guards you, without one iota of your participation, I don't want you to come whining to me later on because he has an eye in the middle of his forehead or garlic breath. And one more thing. Watch your tone."

"Sorry." It was her show, but the fact that the security firm they'd hired on the East Coast couldn't continue on in the West was, to Gabriella, not her problem. "But don't you think you're being overly dramatic?"

Gary's brow arched. "So stated by the woman who could have invented the word. I'm just mindful of how well things went with Edward and company on the East Coast, and was very disappointed that because of personal obligations, he couldn't continue for the entire tour."

"Yeah, Ed was cool. It would have been nice to keep the same company."

"But that isn't the case. So if you want me to, I'll conduct these interviews and make the decision myself. Or I can work with Carol to find an hour where you can spend a few minutes with each of the final candidates. It's up to you."

Gabriella sighed. "Well, considering the fact that the only place I like to smell garlic is in my pasta and not on someone's breath, I guess I'll have to make some time."

Gary laughed at the reference to the security guard they'd hired for the family's Long Island estate, who ate raw garlic "for good health." He always smelled like he'd just eaten an entire bulb of the stuff, but he was a top-notch protector. So the family grinned and bore him.

"Good girl. I've already pared it down to three firms, so it shouldn't take more than one brief meeting to decide. I'll get with Carol and see you tomorrow."

Gabriella told Carol that she'd meet with the security guards the next morning following their visit to a juvenile detention facility. So the next day, emotionally drained after a two-hour sit down with girls who'd been locked up for years, some from as early as when they were nine years old, Gabriella walked into a meeting room. She wore black leggings, a long yellow T-shirt, and sneakers. Her hair was tied back in a ponytail and she was devoid of makeup. She was forty-five minutes late and because the first appointment had arrived thirty minutes early, he'd already been waiting more than an hour when she arrived.

Gary, obviously chagrined, gave her a look as she walked into the room, but Stewart, the well-trained, thirty-something former police officer who'd been waiting, was on his feet in an instant.

"Ms. Stone, it's a pleasure." He held out his hand.

"Ms. Stone?" she asked, a slight frown marring her blemish-free skin as she engaged in a handshake.

Stewart looked from her to Carol to the dad and back. "That is your last name, correct?"

"Yes, but nobody calls me that. I'm simply Gabriella, as any preliminary research done on me would have told you."

"Of course, Ms.—uh, yes, I understand that . . . Gabriella. I just didn't want to be presumptuous."

"So instead you chose to be rude?"

"Gabriella." Gary's voice of warning caused his head-strong firstborn to replace the scowl on her face with a friendlier expression.

"I'm just messing with you . . . Stewart is it?"

"Yes, ma'am," he replied, as he visibly relaxed.

"Stewart comes very well qualified, Gabriella." The firmness in Gary's voice was indicative of his no-nonsense mood, and left no doubt that he wanted to get back to the seriousness of the task at hand.

"Before becoming a bodyguard, he was LAPD for fifteen years. Most recently, he worked for Shawn Deele."

This information elicited a raised eyebrow from a woman for whom impressing was hard to do. But Shawn was a standout among Hollywood actors who'd joined the incredibly small and elite group of African-Americans by winning an Oscar just last year.

"I take my job seriously, Gabriella," Stewart said, his confidence returning on the wings of Gary's accolades.

"I'm sure you do." Gabriella gave the compact, muscular man a once-over before taking the bottle that Carol offered and drinking a sip of water. "Thanks so much for coming, Stewart. We'll be in touch."

"He's a good, solid candidate," Gary said, after he'd shaken the man's hand and walked him to the door. "No nonsense. Plus, he's a family man. We won't have to worry about where his focus is while we're out on the road. He's got something and someone to live for. I like him."

"He's all right," Gabriella said, motioning to Carol to hand over her cell phone. "Where's the next guy?"

Gary looked at his watch. "He should be here in five minutes. When you were so late arriving for your first appointment, we called him and moved back his time."

"That couldn't be helped, Dad. Nobody could bring cell phones into the detention area. Not even me."

"How did that go, by the way?"

Gabriella's mood shifted. "There are so many heartbreaking stories in there—girls in gangs, others who had to raise themselves and did whatever to survive. I hope I helped."

Five minutes later, Walter walked in. Five minutes late. He sported black diamond studs in his ears, a platinum cross around his neck, and Gabriella thought that he wore enough cologne to douse her whole band.

"Gabriella," he said, strolling over and, after offering his hand, raising hers in a kiss. Had he been as astute as someone protecting her needed to be, he'd be trying to dodge the daggers that Gary aimed at his back right about then. As it was, he was too busy making doe eyes at his potential employer. "I just want you to know one thing. I was put on this planet to protect you."

Now, Gabriella thought, *I can upchuck for real.*

He was handsome enough, she'd give him that. Smooth chocolate skin, bald head, big lips, and a body that alluded to too much time in the gym. Gabriella appreciated swagger and this man had enough to bottle and sell. In her industry, a certain amount of arrogance could be effective, and cocky confidence backed up by a well-trained aim could save a person's life. But there was something about him that rubbed her wrong. Not the way he looked at her with unabashed lust in his eyes. A man who was digging her sexually could work in her favor. No, it was something else. She couldn't put her finger on it, but she could recognize that her intuition was talking and that she should listen.

"We'll be in touch," she said with a shy smile. He gave her a knowing "I got this" nod and strolled out the room.

"My God," Carol said, giving Gary an exaggerated roll of her eyes. "I thought he'd bend down and kiss Gab's feet!"

Gabriella giggled. "He was pretty pathetic, huh? But he was also kind of endearing with those puppy dog eyes."

"Don't sound so full of yourself," Gary said, with slight annoyance. "Millions of dollars in one's bank account will make anybody attractive."

"I don't see why you didn't put up the 'no fraternizing' roadblock," Gabriella countered, making air quotes. Her smile turned to a pout in a New York minute. "Like you always do."

"That would have happened before we signed contracts. But he has a solid work history."

"Yeah," Carol said, thumbs once again flying over her phone screen, "and a bunch of solid platinum jewelry around his neck."

"He is rather shiny," Gary acknowledged.

"Shiny?" Gabriella repeated, humor in her eyes.

"Yeah, you know, flashy."

"Oh."

"But he comes highly recommended. He's literally kept a couple rappers alive. Plus he's clean: no drugs, no alcohol, no criminal history."

A knock on the door signaled the arrival of their third interviewee. Gary went to the door and seconds later turned the corner with Troy in tow. "Gabriella, Troy Morgan."

Gabriella, who'd been busy texting, looked up and then immediately focused her eyes back on the screen. The average person watching would think it one of her dismissive maneuvers, used on many of the service personnel who helped her world turn. But it was actually so she could Google a mask of indifference and put it on her face to replace the one of admiration, interest, and unabashed lust she felt sure was now showing.

"Gabriella," her father repeated, his patience all but gone.

She looked up, first at her father and then at Troy. "Hi," she said curtly. She was sure that later her father would again reprimand her rudeness. But she was tripping on her body's immediate reaction to this walking turn-on. If Gary Stone knew the thoughts running through her head, he'd throw this guy out on his beautiful behind. Now! Because there was something about her panties becoming moist while her daddy was in the room that seemed wrong on every level of this Four Seasons Hotel.

"Hey," Troy replied, giving only as much warmth as he'd received.

This brought Gabriella's head back up. *Yes, get me angry. If I'm mad at you, then maybe I'll stop feeling like you're the man that I've waited for since before I was born.* Her eyes narrowed and she prepared to say something, but Troy had already turned his attention from her to her dad. Complicating her overwhelming physical attraction to him, Gabriella experienced the rare occurrence of being dismissed. He was as fine as baby hair, but she didn't like his attitude, and planned to tell the cocky cutie just what she thought, right before she excused his ass, and right after he shut up the walk with her father down memory lane!

Troy laughed at something Gary said about his short stint as a crooner. His reply about Gary's father— Gabriella's grandfather—however, was sincere. "My mother was superexcited when I told her that we were meeting. She grew up listening to your dad's group, the Starlights, said they were as popular as the Temptations, the Miracles, and the Four Tops back in the day."

"They were definitely one of the top groups, that's true," Gary said with a nod, his eyes reflecting that he was impressed with the man standing before him. "I see you've done your homework."

"It wasn't hard. The group's information is all over the Internet. And once my mom waxed on about them, I downloaded all of their songs, and her favorite from your heyday—'Directions to Your Heart.'"

Gary was clearly enjoying the conversation. "That was a good one."

Without being invited, Troy sat in a chair close to Gary and got comfortable. "You know, I can see that song being updated, given a hip-hop remix, and released right now."

His presumptuous air was too much for Gabriella to take. Even more so was his seeming disinterest in her and ability to focus on someone else. "Are you here to get a job with my father, or with me?!"

Troy looked over as if for a moment he'd forgotten she was even in the room. *Arrogant asshole. Albeit the cutest one I've ever seen.* "I thought you were here for an interview, not to take a walk down memory lane."

"I was waiting until you finished," he retorted with a nod toward her phone, acting as cool as an icicle hanging from a snow-covered roof. "When I entered, you were obviously preoccupied."

"Well, in that case you should have waited quietly until I was finished."

His chuckle was genuine, ingratiating, and sexy as hell. "Is that so? I'm a multitasker, Gabriella, able to handle many things at once. I'm also not a rude human being, and would never ignore someone I respect—someone like your father." He gave Gary a nod and then turned to face her, a copy of his company's resume—the same one that he'd earlier sent over electronically—in his hands.

"Everything about Morgan Security is laid out succinctly in the resume that was sent over, but I'd love to answer any questions that"—he looked from Gabriella to Gary—"either of you might have."

"How many singers have you guarded?" Gabriella

asked, while once again returning to the text on her cell phone.

"Not many," was his easy answer. "There's usually too much drama associated with music-oriented tours . . . and I'm not one to deal with much foolishness." She looked up to glare at him. He met her stare without a flinch. She finally looked down and resumed texting on her phone. "As the resume shows," he continued smoothly, "we mostly deal with affluent businessmen and corporate executives, along with a few politicians, professional athletes, and a couple hip-hop artists."

"What athletes?"

"The Nighthawks' Kelvin Petersen, Tony Johnson with the LA Sea Lions, Shayna Washington-Morgan—"

"Is she related to you?"

"My sister-in-law." Troy gave her a few more names.

"What other musical artists?"

"It's all there, on the resume."

"I'm asking you!" Gabriella snarled.

Troy looked at Gary as he stood. "Look, Mr. Stone, I think you might need to find someone else to guard your daughter." He headed for the door.

"Wow, that was easy," Gabriella drawled. She looked at her father. "He's a lightweight."

Screech! Troy turned on a dime and had nine cents change for anybody needing it. "What did you just say?"

"You heard me."

Troy leaned against the door. "Is that right?"

Gabriella smiled, slow and sexy, as she nodded toward a magazine. "Hand me that magazine."

One second passed.

Two.

Ten more.

"The job I came to interview for was that of protector, not patsy." He turned to Gary. "Good-bye, Mr. Stone." Troy tipped his head in her direction. "Gabriella."

Gary didn't even look at his daughter as he followed Troy out the door and down to the elevator. "Don't pay any attention to Gabriella and her antics."

"Don't worry. I won't."

"I'm responsible for who guards Gab and have the final say in the matter. You're well qualified, come with stellar references, and aside from the subtle flirting I picked up on—behavior that in the future would not be tolerated—I think you would be a perfect choice."

"I appreciate the vote of confidence, Mr. Stone—"

"Call me Gary."

"Okay. I'm happy to have met you, Gary, but honestly don't think I'm the man for the job."

"Why don't you let me decide that," Gary said with the merest hint of a smile. He held out his hand. "When can you start?"

3

Troy walked into his office, loosening his tie as he entered. "Alex!"

"In here!"

"Well, son," Troy said as he entered the break room and leaned against the counter. "You got your wish."

"We got the Gabriella contract?" Alex's smile could have lit up New York City during an electrical malfunction. "And I get to guard her?"

Troy nodded. "I will be guarding her person, per their firm request," he hurriedly added when Alex would have argued. "But no worries. You'll be a part of the overall detail and as such will get to meet your dream girl."

"Close enough. Thanks, bro!" Alex said, giving Troy a bear hug.

"Yeah, you say that now, but wait until you deal with her. She's obviously read her press, believes the hype, and thinks the world revolves around her."

"It doesn't?"

The men laughed. Alex stepped back, his eyes twinkling with excitement. "I really appreciate it, man."

"You're welcome, bro. But you'd better work quickly. You'll have less than two weeks to impress her into accepting a marriage proposal. That's the length of the West Coast tour."

"Man, I'll be happy if she just accepts a date!"

"Alex . . ."

"I'm not going to harass her," Alex quickly replied, knowing the direction that Troy was headed. "I'm just going to win her heart and spin her head around with my charm."

"Good luck with that. It's a pretty big one."

"I know how to handle divas like her. When do we get started?"

"We'll have orientation tomorrow," Troy explained, walking over to his desk and reaching for his laptop "Gary and I have worked out some logistical details, but there are still a few loose ends to tie up. Plus, I'm still deciding on the right personnel mix for our team. Your being enamored I can handle. You talk crazy, but at the end of the day, when it comes to work I know you're going to come correct. Everyone wants to work this job, but we still have other clients to protect. He nodded toward the printer. "Her schedule is coming out now. The first arena concert is this Friday, at the Staples Center. Make sure you're ready."

"Cool."

Troy snorted. "You say that now. But you haven't met her yet. Gary Stone is cool, but I can't stress this enough. Her Highness," he emphasized by using air quotes, "is a major piece of work, squared."

"Hey, she's got it going on and knows it. You just have to come at her with the right touch."

"And I guess you think you've got it."

Alex wiped nonexistent lint off his shoulders, standing up to his full height of six feet. "I think I do."

"Well . . . good luck, my brother, and handle your business. I've got my hands full with a certain sexy Southern chocolate drop."

And he did. Troy had been spending the past few months in the rare position of being off the market, having met a shrewd, smart, prosecuting attorney named Delores Atchison. There was nothing docile about Dee, as she was known to close friends, though many a man had let her shy smile and petite frame fool them. Truth be told, she chewed up defense attorneys for breakfast and spit them out for lunch.

Their paths had crossed when Troy went to the courthouse with one of the rappers he was guarding, one who epitomized the drama that he'd spoken to Gary about. The nouveau rich kid had basically torn up a nightclub, then got the charges dropped by paying for the damage and lining both the owner's and his attorney's pockets with lots of cash. Troy's compensation, besides the check containing a number and several zeros following, had been meeting Delores. She was independent and drama free, just as Troy liked it, and their busy schedules prevented them from getting on each other's nerves.

"What time and where?" Alex asked, all of his focus on what he clearly felt was the most important security job of his life.

"Ten o'clock," Troy responded. He reached into the fridge for a bottle of sparkling water. He gave Alex the name of the hotel where he'd be meeting Gabriella and Gary. "I know I don't need to tell you to bring your A game."

"You're right," Alex said, grabbing a drink as well and

heading out of the break room. "I'm getting ready to meet the love of my life. So I'm going to be poised, professional, and prepared."

He ducked the wadded up paper towel that Troy threw at him and walked out of the room.

The next morning, at 9:55 sharp, Troy and Alex knocked on the door to the suite where the Stones were staying. Carol answered and was immediately impressed. She spoke to Troy before taking in the man beside him: six feet of butterscotch goodness, with close-cropped dark brown hair, a groomed goatee, and dimples in both cheeks. What?

"Good morning," she said flirtatiously, with an uncharacteristic batting of the eyes. Between the two of them, Carol was most definitely the serious, pragmatic, and no-nonsense one over Gabriella. She was the one with both feet on the floor and her head beneath the clouds. Until now. Right about now she found herself fairly swooning over the fantasy in front of her, the way she'd read women did in fairy tales or romance novels. Before, she would have rolled her eyes at any woman who claimed a man had taken her breath away. Yet here she stood, wondering where the air went. "And you are?"

"Alex Worthington," he said with hand outstretched. "What is your name?"

"Carol," she replied, shaking his hand, and trying not to think too much about the strength she felt in his fingers, or how at a mere innocent touch, a spark of electricity had flown up her spine.

"I hope you don't mind my saying that it is a pretty name for a pretty lady."

"Thank you. I don't mind at all." She noted Troy's

subtle glance over at Alex and became all business at once. "Gary is expecting you. Please, come in."

She watched as Alex straightened his shoulders, inhaling and exhaling purposefully and slow. An inward sigh was allowed as Carol gave a sympathetic smile. He'd tried to hide it, but she saw it anyway. For a perceptive soul such as herself it was too much of a red flag to miss. The way he'd taken a breath to calm himself, the way his eyes looked beyond her trying no doubt to see the sexy Stone. Something simple, done over and again, was enough to let Carol know that Alex was like all the other men she'd met who had stars in their eyes for Gabriella. However she hadn't missed the sly wink he gave her as they entered, or the scent of his cologne as it tickled her nostrils. It was musky and manly . . . just how he looked. Carol had seen her share of bodyguards and, while many had flirted, none had made her feel like Alex had . . . all nervous and shy-like and girly inside.

"Right this way," she said, turning her back to lead them. She tried not to think of the riveting man behind her, tried not to imagine his eyes on her booty, highlighted by the form-fitting skirt and halter she wore. "Gary," she called out once they reached the living area. "Alex and Troy with Morgan Security are here."

Alex looked around, trying not to appear anxious. Most upscale suites he'd been in held an air of opulence and wealth. This one was no different. What it didn't hold, much to his disappointment, from what he could see so far, was his dream girl, Gabriella.

Gary came from around the corner, hand outstretched. "Hello, Troy."

"Hello, sir."

He turned to Alex. "Gary Stone, good morning."

"Good morning, sir." Alex offered a firm grip. "Alex Worthington."

"I understand you'll be working closely with Troy in the guarding of my daughter."

"Yes."

Gary eyed Alex speculatively. "Besides the fact that you're with one of the top security firms in the state if not the country, what qualifies you to protect the most talented and successful pop star that the world has ever seen, one for whom paparazzi, overzealous fans, and even stalkers have presented problems in the past?"

"Eight years military, sir. United States Marines. Sharpshooter, presidential medal, honorable discharge. Not that I like to talk about myself, sir. I'd rather let my work, my record, and my employer speak for me."

"Troy spoke very highly of all his employees, and your stellar records are comforting. Welcome aboard." The two men shook hands again and then Gary looked at his watch. "Gab should be here any minute."

Carol spoke up. "Can we get you something to drink? Orange, apple, cranberry juice, or sparkling water maybe?"

Troy declined. Alex nodded, as Gary excused himself to take a call. "Sparkling water sounds nice."

"My favorite, too. Be right back."

Troy pulled out his phone. "I'm going to step over here and check my e-mails." He walked away and within seconds Alex's phone pinged with a text message. From Troy.

I see how you're checking that sistah out. Watch yourself. :)

Carol walked to the dining area of the open-concept space and within a minute was setting a crystal goblet of sparkling water in front of Alex, along with a bowl of nuts. As she did so he ignored Troy's teasing and took the opportunity to really look at her. He liked what he saw, from her graceful ladylike movements to her smooth brown skin to her silky long hair. And there was something else. His brow furrowed as he tried to remember. Then it dawned on him.

"Hey, weren't you one of the Haute Coutures?"

The wispiest of smiles as she answered, "Yes."

"I thought you looked familiar."

Carol took a seat on the love seat facing the chair where Alex sat. Gary was still on a phone call in another part of the suite.

"It was you, Gabriella, and . . ."

"Latoya . . ."

"Yeah, the little girl with the long braids and big voice."

"Yes, that's her," Carol said, laughing. "And then Brandi and Brianna, the twins."

"Right; I'd forgotten that they were sisters. Wow. You guys were young to be so good. You were what, ten, twelve years old?"

"I was ten when we started and sixteen when the group disbanded and Gabriella went solo."

"How did that make you feel, the fact that she went on without y'all?"

Carol shrugged. "It was inevitable, really. She always was the real star. From the beginning, she was the one who came up with the idea for the group, who pushed us to practice and work hard, and who treated it like it was her life from day one. There are times when Latoya, the twins, and I just wanted to be regular kids: hang out at the mall, eat pizza, play video games, and watch movies. But not Gab. She always knew this"—Carol waved her hand across the room—"was what she wanted. She focused on getting it twenty-four/seven. Those were some fun years, but it's also a grueling existence. I don't need the limelight. I'm happy where I'm at."

"You're her assistant?"

Carol nodded. "And best friend."

"Cool."

There was an easy camaraderie between Alex and Carol as they continued chatting. When she saw Alex look at his watch, she commented, "Don't worry. She's usually on time. And that's even with the whirlwind of a schedule her publicist has created."

"No worries," Troy said as he rejoined them in the sitting area. "This is LA. You're not late until an hour has gone by."

Gary reentered the room as well. "Sorry about that," he stated. "Overseas business call. Couldn't be helped." He looked at Carol. "She's still not here?"

Just as he asked the question they heard the door open. "That's probably her now," Carol said, rising and heading to the foyer. "I'll be right back."

Gabriella walked in looking larger than life, and not just because of her mammoth five-inch heels. She oozed class and confidence and a starlike charisma, with perfect makeup, flawless hair, and a body-hugging jumpsuit.

Alex and Troy joined Gary, who was already standing.

"Gab," her dad said, seconds after she'd strolled into the room. "Of course you know Troy. This is Alex, his number two man at Morgan Security."

"A pleasure to meet you," Alex said, with hand outstretched.

"Hello." Gabriella blessed Alex with one of her signature smiles as she shook his hand, even while surreptitiously glancing over at the man who'd been the star of her fantasies the day before and played the lead role in her dreams the previous night. Not that she had to see him in person to remember what he looked like. After placing his name in a search engine and hitting almost every available link, she could almost write a biography on the man.

"Hello, Gabriella," Troy said.

Damn his voice feels like a cashmere blanket on a snow-filled day. "Hello, Troy."

Greetings and intros out of the way, they all sat down. Gary and Gabriella occupied the couch while Carol sat on the love seat and Troy and Alex sat in the two chairs facing the sofa.

"As I explained to you earlier, honey," Gary began, "we've hired not only Troy and his firm, Morgan Security, for the West Coast leg, but we've expanded the contract to also cover the European and Asian tour. Some of his men will guard our house as well."

"Mommy's here?" Gabriella asked, momentarily forgetting to be cool and sexy for her audience as her voice filled with childlike glee.

Gary clinched his jaw. "Yes, and I just now remembered that this was supposed to be a surprise, so later on when I take you over there, act like it." Carol tsked and Gary offered a sheepish grin. "I know—can't keep a secret. Anyway, Gab, Troy, Alex, and the rest of his team will be joining us Friday. Troy will be handling the overall security and this fine young man and ex-military personnel, Alex, will work concert detail as well as help to oversee those guarding the house."

"You have nothing to worry about under our protection, Gabriella," Troy said. "We take our jobs very seriously. I'll guard you with my life."

Something about the way he said that, all professional and thugish at the same time, made her kundalini tingle. She cleared her throat, forcing herself to stay casual and relaxed under Troy's unflinching gaze and her father's probing stare. "I'm sure you will." She'd tried not to sound flirty, but if Gary's narrowed eyes were any indication, she hadn't been totally successful.

They finished the meeting. Troy and Alex left for their cars while Gary went down to the front desk for a brief meeting with the manager. As soon as all of the testosterone had left the room the women began talking at once.

"Did you see—"

"Girl, I almost—"

They laughed, then Gabriella joined Carol on the couch where they put their heads together and whispered like teenagers about to share secrets with pinkie finger promises not to tell.

"Did you see that?" Carol gushed. "Did you see that walking ad for fine-as-hell looking at me? Girl . . ."

Gabriella grabbed and hugged a decorative pillow. "It's a crime for two men to look that good."

"But what is it, Gab? We've seen fine brothers before."

"It's more than their looks. It's their attitude, their swagger. They're intelligent and suave and, heck, after we've been forever surrounded by jeans sagging and thick gold chains, they seem like grown-ass men!"

"I saw you checking out Troy. You tried to be slick . . . but I saw you."

"I know, and so did Daddy. He's already suspicious, so I have to be cool. One wrong move and he'll be all over my ass, and looking for a new security team."

"And you'll be looking for another assistant, because if Alex leaves, then I'm going with him."

Gabriella laughed. "Look at you, all smitten and everything. I hope something does work out. I haven't seen you this excited over a man in a while."

"I haven't seen you so smitten either," Carol shot back. "You might be able to fool Gary, but you can't fool me. When it comes to Troy Morgan you are totally sprung."

"I am not. He's fine and all, but I'm not really interested. I'm focused on my career."

"Yeah, well, according to where I saw your eyes as Troy walked out the door, your career must be somewhere near his strong-looking long legs and firm behind."

The women laughed, then went their separate ways to prepare for the next appointment. But their thoughts were similar—Carol's on Alex, Gabriella's on Troy. The Stone Cold Sexy tour had just gotten very interesting.

4

Troy navigated his powerhouse black Ferrari along La Cienega Boulevard, headed for Beverly Hills. It was only four o'clock in the afternoon on a Thursday, but the streets were jam-packed. He was an impatient driver on his best day and, right now, after missing out on a night of loving due to his demanding new job and her early morning case, his nerves were on edge. A face instantly came to mind as he thought of how he could feel better and it wasn't that of his newest conquest, the lawyer-Delores. It was that of his newest client—the one who was high maintenance, the one he'd decided to leave to his starry-eyed associate. The one who'd grown incensed upon learning that his world didn't revolve around her. The one who her father had pointedly said was off limits, no matter how much Troy's body and mind objected to this truth.

Even when she was satisfied with his company, as she seemed to be upon meeting Alex, Gabriella still acted the control freak. She'd demanded to meet any and all security personnel who'd have backstage access. Troy's response

had been simple: "Okay." Heck, she wasn't the only one
who wanted to make demands. Troy did, too. But no, he
wouldn't come at her—the no-fraternizing rule and all.
She was Alex's wet dream and Troy wouldn't interfere.
He had no shortage of sexy, beautiful women at his fingertips. He was cool with letting Alex go for the gold. Or
for the Gabriella, as the case may be. Alex may have
been smitten, but he was also the consummate employee.
Troy knew that when it came to his lead security man's
professional decorum, he had nothing to worry about.
His meandering thoughts were interrupted as his phone
rang. He turned down the sounds of Tupac rocking on
his car stereo, and pressed the hands-free device on his
wheel. "Morgan."

"Hey, man."

"What's up, Alex?"

"Gary called in to the office. There's been a change in
plans. Instead of the hotel, Gabriella is visiting her parents' new crib. I'm here now."

"No problem. What's the address again? I've got it on
my phone, but I'm driving." Alex gave him the Bel Air
address and Troy keyed it into his GPS system.

"What are y'all doing now?"

"Just chilling by this amazing piece of work called an
infinity pool. Carol is working with her personal trainer
in the water. Gab is getting some sun."

"Sounds like cushy guard duty, dog. Why do you
sound so sad?"

Alex was already speaking low, but his voice lowered
even further. "Old girl has showed me no action whatso-
ever. I might as well not even be here."

"I won't say I told you so, man, but I tried to warn you."

"You did indeed, Troy. I can't even be mad."

"Please don't. Because when you see the size of your paycheck, it will be smiles all around."

"That good, huh?"

"Even better. Besides, we're just two days into this job. We have a couple weeks here before heading to Europe and Asia."

"Whoa, wait! You didn't tell me that our job would extend beyond the two weeks."

"We discussed it at the meeting. Gary wants us to continue working with them when they travel internationally."

"Right. He did say that."

"So don't be so quick to throw in the towel."

"That's real talk, bro. I appreciate it."

"But no playing footsies until the tour is done."

"Right, until she's pulled me from your team and put me on her payroll."

"Oh! Is that how it's going down? She's going to steal my best employee?"

"A woman can't steal what already belongs to her."

"Aw, man, dude. You're so gone."

"A brother can dream. Are you on your way?"

"I will be shortly. Before your call I'd already agreed to personally escort the Saudi prince on his last day of business here in America." Troy turned off the major thoroughfare onto a residential street with ridiculously large houses and perfectly manicured lawns. "He has appointments with a couple businesses, and a high-end masseuse."

"Translated: call girl?"

"Let's just say the visit will probably have a happy ending."

"Man, those Middle Easterners love their honeys."

"No doubt. And they're generous, too." Troy looked at the phone's face, displayed on his dashboard screen. "Look, Alex, I have another call. Check back later." He switched calls.

"Mama!"

"Hello, son. Are you working?"

"Yes, but I've got a couple minutes. I'm on my way over to pick up a client."

"The Stone family?"

"No, Alex is handling that detail right now. I'll be there in a couple hours though, and beginning with the first night of her concert tomorrow will probably be sticking closer to her than her shadow."

"The way she looks that won't be too hard." Troy laughed. "Did you tell her daddy what I said? About loving both his and his father's music?"

Hearing the excitement in her voice, Troy asked, "Does Robert know about this thing you have for another man?"

"Don't mess with me, boy!" The command was delivered sternly, but the mention of her gentleman friend of two years added to the smile in her voice. "Robert knows he doesn't have anything to worry about. In fact, he's sitting right here."

"Tell him I said hello."

Jackie conveyed the message. "What did Gary say when you told him how I was once enthralled with the Starlights and his father, Otis Stone? And that I had pictures of him from *Ebony, Jet,* and other magazines plastered on my wall?"

"He seemed impressed that I knew so much. Especially when I mentioned how much you loved his biggest hit single, and that I'd downloaded it to my own rotation."

"Did you also tell him my idea of their coming out of retirement, him and his father? I bet there are millions of women who still remember them, as I do. While not as successful as Otis's group, Gary's star burned out quickly, but while here it still burned bright."

Troy cleared his throat. "I must tell you, Mama. I kind of made your suggestion my own."

"What does that mean?" she asked, with a hint of chagrin.

"I told Gary that I thought it would be a good idea to do a remix of your favorite song . . . with a hip-hop twist."

"How are you going to take credit for what used to be my jam?!" Jackie started singing the chorus of "Directions to Your Heart," the seventies classic that was still a favorite in old school stations' rotations. "Turn left. Go right. I'll hold you tight . . . directions to your heart."

"Sing it, Mama!" Jackie's joy in reliving her glory days brought sunshine to Troy's heart.

"Slow down. Now, merge. I'm on the verge . . . directions to your heart."

"Girl, you're singing that song like you know something about that?"

"You and your brothers wouldn't be here if I didn't!"

"Ha! Well said. I can see you and Daddy now, pulling out the hits and memories on a warm summer night. Which one of us do you think was first conceived on it?"

"Okay, son, you're getting just a little too much in my business."

"You started it!" Troy laughed, thinking about the woman he loved more than life itself. Thrust into the world of single motherhood while still in her thirties, she flawlessly assumed the role of both parents while keeping alive the memory of their late father, Samuel Morgan. Troy also prided himself on the fact that occasionally, like today, he could get her to let down her guard and be a woman instead of just his mother, to remember what it was like to lose herself in laughter and love.

"Okay, Mom. I'm almost at my destination. Is there a particular reason for your call?"

"It was about Sunday dinner, but with this new job . . ."

"I'll be busy. You already know."

"Yes, I do. Well, have fun, baby. Who knows? Maybe you and Gabriella—"

"Ah, here we go. My mother has receded and the matchmaker has emerged."

"I'm just saying. She's a beautiful young lady, successful, seems to have her head on straight."

"You're just thinking about having a former Starlight singer in the family."

"Worse things could happen," Jackie smoothly replied, surprising Troy with both her candor and the playful sexiness she put into her voice.

"I gotta go. Love you, Mom."

"Love you, too."

Jackie wasn't the only one thinking about two beautiful, successful people hooking up. Across town, Gabriella tossed and turned on her chaise by the pool: bored, restless, and unable to get one fine bodyguard out of her mind.

"Carol!" she called out, jumping up from the chaise with hands on hips. "Let's go."

Carol had finished her water exercises with the trainer and was now chilling on a floating chaise. "Where are we going?"

"Shopping. And grab the girls. They're coming, too."

"Gab, why are we shopping? We bought out half of Fifth Avenue before we left New York!" Carol ran her hands through the water to bring her chaise to the side of the pool. She reached the stairs and climbed out. "And Melanie and her team bought out the other. What's the matter?" she asked, once they'd reached the guest room where they'd changed into swimsuits. Not that Gabriella needed a reason to spend money, but Carol knew that shopping was her friend's number one medication for whatever ailed her.

"Just bored."

"Seriously? You're going to use that excuse and think I believe it?"

"Believe what you want to; I know how I'm feeling."

"And I know who you want to be feeling, and who you want to be feeling you."

"Who?" Gabriella asked, all innocence and charm.

"Who?" Carol parroted, as she headed to the shower. "His first name starts with a T, the last name with an M, and he'll be here tomorrow. And you can't wait."

"Forget you, heffa. I don't even know what you're talking about."

"You're such a bad liar."

"And you're such a pain. Hurry up and shower. And text Melanie, Dana, and Li to see if they want to come with us."

"Girl, please. All of the assists will join us. Who's

going to turn down a shopping spree where someone else is paying?"

"And tell them to hurry up, too. I'm ready to get out of here. And I'm hungry."

"Uh-huh. And I know just who'd like to assuage your appetite." She ran into the bathroom before there could be a response.

Gabriella smiled. She'd tried to deny it, act as though she were just playing, but there was no use trying to hide her true feelings from one Ms. Carol Robbins. The two had been friends since kindergarten; there wasn't one secret they hadn't shared.

Yes, I'm thinking about Troy Morgan. Yes, I think he's a fine specimen of a man and simply amazing. For a nanosecond, she allowed herself to dream that they could be together.

But then Gabriella remembered something else. Her father, and how he reacted the last time she tried her hand at serious dating. He reminded her of the promise, threw a conversation from years ago up in her face. She'd tried to reason her way out of it, citing her inexperience, naïveté, and youth, but her father would have none of it. Gabriella knew that she had to be careful. One slip, one wrong move that alerted her father to this interest, and Troy would be sent packing. Just like what happened with Marlon. But even as she thought this, she knew it wasn't so. Without so much as a decent conversation, without a kiss or a touch, Gabriella was sure that being with Troy Morgan would be nothing like being with Marlon, and nothing like her first puppy love. In her soul, she knew Troy was a man's man and that any liaison with this man would be one not easily broken.

Surprisingly enough for someone so young, someone

so famous, and someone so inexperienced at matters of the heart, this prospect didn't scare Gabriella. Rather, it spurred her on. Because no matter what came with the territory, Gabriella Stone wanted Troy Morgan. And this woman had gotten what she wanted . . . all her life.

5

Morning came quickly. Gabriella waved away the housekeeper who'd awakened her and rolled over for another thirty minutes of sleeping. A knock on her door let her know that this was not to be.

"Get up, Gab," Melanie said as she entered the suite's master bedroom.

"Leave me alone," Gabriella mumbled before pulling the sheet over her head.

Melanie walked over and opened the blinds before heading to the bed and yanking the covers off Gabriella's face. "Don't shoot the messenger," she said, calmly walking to the closet and looking at the clothes. "You're the one who asked Carol to have me wake you at seven-thirty, who wants to be all glammed up for breakfast with Troy."

"I do not." Gabriella had pulled the covers back over her head.

"Okay. I'll just call and let him know that you've canceled and to meet us at the arena instead." Melanie walked toward the door.

Gabriella jumped out of bed. "Pick up that phone and you're fired."

"Jeans or dressy," Melanie asked, laughing at how fast Gabriella had lost all sleepiness. "You have thirty minutes."

"Jeans," Gabriella threw over her shoulder before going into the master bath. "I'm not trying to impress anybody."

Melanie chuckled as she reached for a pair of skinny jeans that she knew fit Gabriella to a tee and showed off what she was working with in a respectable way. She paired it with a tank top that had an image of Trayvon Martin across the front. "Oh, Gab?"

"Yes?" She came back to the master bath doorway.

"Should I send Tiana up for hair and makeup?"

"Naw, I think I'll go au naturel."

"Thank God that you've got it like that, girl." Melanie reached for the tote containing the costume jewelry. "And thanks for yesterday, too."

"You're welcome." Gabriella went over to the shower and turned it on. "I know I can be demanding sometimes, but y'all know I appreciate you." She began doing vocal warm-ups in the shower. "Melanie!"

This time it was Melanie who closed the distance between them. She stuck her head inside the master bath. "Yes?"

"How's your grandmother?"

"Much better, thank you. Now that she has the proper type of wheelchair she's almost getting around like she used to. Hardly a day goes by that she doesn't mention you, and she plays your music all the time."

"Ha!"

"If you knew how much of a stretch it was for Nana

to play anything but gospel, you'd know how funny that truly was." Melanie finished laying out the morning's wardrobe. "Do you need me to stay and help you get dressed?"

"No, I'm cool," Gabriella said, having ended her quickie shower and now entering the bedroom as she finished toweling off. "I can take it from here."

"You sure?"

"Yeah."

"Okay, call me if you need me."

Carol entered moments after Melanie had left. "Good, you're almost ready," she said by way of greeting. "I told the chef to have breakfast served exactly at eight-fifteen." She looked at the simple, casual outfit that on Gabriella looked as if it had cost a million bucks. "Interesting choice of outfits."

"You don't like it?"

"No, you look great, as always. I'm just surprised you didn't go for something a little dressier."

"It's breakfast, Carol. That's all."

Carol raised a brow as she texted on her phone. "If you say so."

"Has Troy called?"

"He's on his way."

"Why didn't he call my phone?"

"Oh, you want this regular-nothing-special-I'm-not-interested employee to have your cell number?"

"No. I want the bodyguard who is responsible for my personal safety, in fact my life, to have it."

"No problem."

The two women chatted casually until 8:10 a.m., when a knock on the door interrupted them. Gabriella couldn't resist a quick look in the mirror before she walked from the living area into her master suite. A sistah needed to make an entrance, even in her hotel room.

She heard Carol greet Troy before her light steps and his heavier ones sounded against the marbled foyer entrance. Gabriella walked into the master bath and for the second time in less than a minute, checked herself in the mirror.

Stop acting silly. He's just a man.

The thought alone made her almost laugh out loud. Troy Morgan wasn't "just" anything. Another knock and Gabriella soon heard room service setting up their breakfast in the dining room. She made a spontaneous decision about the no makeup and reached for the mini-makeup bag that Tiana had put together for her. After brushing her naturally long lashes with mascara and dotting her lips with gloss, she left the room.

She noted how Troy's eyes narrowed slightly as he turned and saw her, and how he immediately stood as she approached. Um-hmm. Nothing sexier than a man with some home training. "Good morning, Troy."

"Good morning, Gabriella. You look lovely."

"Thank you."

"I like your tank top. The struggle continues, huh?"

"Unfortunately."

"The table is set, Gab," Carol stated. "Do you need anything else?"

Gabriella glanced over at the table laden with a mini-feast. "No. Everything looks great. Thanks."

"All right, guys. I'm out. Holler if you need me."

Both Gabriella and Troy watched as Carol made her exit. The atmosphere seemed to shift as soon as they were alone. Gabriella grew uncharacteristically shy as she tried to control the raw attraction she felt for this man. She watched as Troy seemed to also struggle with where to put his eyes and hands. Could he be feeling it, too?

She broke the sex-induced tension. "I'm starved. Let's eat!"

"I guess we'd better," Troy said, moving to pull out the chair for Gabriella to be seated. "Looks like Carol ordered everything on the breakfast menu."

"Right?"

"I'm not naturally a breakfast eater," Gabriella stated as she reached for granola, yogurt, and fresh fruit. "But my PT says it's the most important meal of the day so . . ." She shrugged and took a dainty bite. Troy stared at her, and then at the plate. "What?" she asked.

"I know you're not calling that breakfast."

"Why not? This is a healthy way to start the day."

"Yes, if you're a bird," Troy sarcastically replied. He generously loaded one plate with an egg white frittata, breakfast potatoes, and chicken sausage and another with a bagel, cream cheese, corned beef hash, and fruit. Gabriella stared at him, and then at his plate. "What?" he asked.

"I know you're not calling that breakfast," she mimicked.

"Look, I'm getting ready to eat a meal, not an appetizer. So," he continued after taking a few bites, "to what do I owe the pleasure of this meeting?"

"Thought it would be a good idea," Gabriella answered. "We're going to be working very closely together for the next few weeks. I'd rather not do that with a stranger."

"You read my bio. It's purposely rather extensive. What else would you like to know?"

"It's one thing to read a story. It's another thing to hear from the subject."

"That's fair."

"So . . . a little about yourself."

Troy ate a couple more bites from each plate before washing it down with fresh-squeezed orange juice. "As you read, I was born and raised in Long Beach."

"What was that like? Growing up in California?"

"Well, for starters, it wasn't like *Boyz 'n the Hood* or a Snoop Dogg video," he explained. "At least not on my block. My dad died when I was thirteen, so instead of one, I had like, four, five fathers. Basically every adult male on the block. Mom had three hardheads, and after he passed, she went to her neighbors and basically gave them license to whip our butts if they saw us misbehaving. We didn't like it, but it's probably what kept us off drugs and out of jail."

"Sorry to hear about your father."

"Life goes on," Troy said with a shrug. "But I miss him."

Gabriella nodded as she reached for a small amount of the frittata. There was nothing she could offer to this statement. Her father was her life, the sun that rose and the moon that set, and even with all of their disagreements she couldn't imagine one day without him.

"I'm sure your mother held it down," she said, after a bite. "But I find it hard to imagine you not getting into trouble."

"I didn't say that there was never trouble," he corrected. "I just said that if caught, there were consequences. Growing up, I was a bona fide knucklehead, wreaking general havoc, getting into fights. A friend of my father was a police officer, and after I had a close call with the law, he began to mentor me. Taught me a few self-defense techniques, piqued my interest in operating within the law."

"If I'd seen you just out and about, I wouldn't have pegged you as a guard," Gabriella stated. "I would have said you were either an athlete or maybe a model."

"Model?" Troy assumed this was a compliment, but his face held its frown.

"Yeah. Don't act like you don't know how you look in the mirror. You could very easily grace a magazine. Matter of fact"—she sat back, perusing him carefully—"you'd be perfect for a certain act in my show."

"Oh, no, wait a minute." Troy held up his hands to underscore the sentence. "I'm here to protect, not to perform."

"You're on my payroll, Mr. Troy Morgan. You're here to do what is asked of you."

Troy sat back with his glass of water. In spite of his self-imposed mandate to stay professional, a bit of sexy seductiveness crept into his voice. "Is that right?"

Gabriella swallowed, aware that the tension from earlier had reentered the room. "Yes. I might put you into my show."

"Don't do that."

"Do you dare me?"

Troy leaned forward. "I double dog dare you. My job is on the sidelines. Do not drag me onstage."

Carol interrupted their conversation, and as this was the morning of her first West Coast performance, an organized chaos soon ensued.

All during the last-minute meetings and interviews

and sound checks and photo ops, Gabriella thought about Troy and what he'd said. "Do not drag me onstage."

Troy thought about her and what she'd said, too. "You're here to do what is asked of you."

For both, these words would have consequences. Only question was . . . were either of them ready to handle them?

6

The night was electric, and so was the energy in the back of the Hummer limo that held Gabriella, Troy, Carol, Alex, Gary, Gabriella's mother, Yvonne, and her younger, USC-bound sports star brother, Garrett.

"You might want to think about a hotel downtown," Yvonne said, checking her immaculately manicured nails. "This traffic is murder, and an accident might have you late taking the stage."

"I thought of that," Gary responded. "Which is why we're heading to the Staples Center an hour ahead of schedule."

"You know, Mom," Gabriella said, sensing the chance for her moment of private freedom . . . among other things. She forced her eyes not to betray her by looking at Troy as she spoke.

"Earlier, Carol and I were discussing the exact same thing. I know we have the deal with the Four Seasons, but we're going to look into LA's downtown hotels and check out the possibilities."

"Gab," Yvonne sighed. "Part of the reason your father

and I jointly purchased a home in LA was for you to have a more comfortable base while you're here."

"Don't try and put that all on me, Mom," Gabriella easily countered. Their divorce five years ago had been painful, but that her parents had remained civil, cordial even, had helped everyone transition to their new, coparenting partners status. "You guys did that as much for Garrett and his new position with the USC Trojans as you did for me. Even more so, matter of fact."

"Stop trying to dim my shine, girl," Garrett drawled, his eyes never wavering from the face of the phone that was attached like an extra limb. "You're getting ready to not be the only superstar in the family."

"Do you have an agent?" Troy asked, having no problem with intruding on this family conversation.

"Naw, man," Garrett replied. "But I'm glad you asked, though. I want your brother to hollah at me."

"Garrett!" Yvonne said, cringing at her honor roll son's choice of diction.

"Aw, Mom," Garrett said with a boyish shrug of his shoulders. "Troy knows how we young bloods roll. Don't you?"

"No doubt," Troy said, with a wink at Yvonne. "I know that you're trying to be about handling your business, that you want to put your claim on a wad of ends and let the world see your swagger. Ya feel me?"

Gabriella settled back into the limo's soft leather. Not only had her knight in shining armor defused the light of suspicion off her, but he was reeling in her parents' affections—no small feat. She knew because her father, Gary, who was known to wear a perpetual scowl, was actually grinning, and her mother, in love with Gary Stone since she was nineteen and still smitten post divorce, was actually looking at Troy as though she wanted to get a cougar flirt on! As the innocent conversation continued Gabriella begrudgingly slipped on her headphones, knowing that it was time to begin preparing for the show and getting her head right for her performance. But as the beats to the first song of her performance spilled into her ear, she imagined making the man who'd promised to guard her body do exactly that . . . and more.

Four hours later, Gabriella stood in the middle of the stage, fist pumping in the air, legs wide rocking thigh-high boots with five-inch heels.

"P to the R to the O to the T . . .

"E to the C to the T to the O . . .

"'R' you going to still be my protector?"

"Come on! Sing it!" As the audience repeated the chorus, she strutted to the far side of the stage. The faux-leather booty shorts accented her round derriere; the fishnet stockings looked as sexy as sin. She held out her mike to the audience, put her hand to her ear. "I can't hear you!"

"P to the R to the O to the T . . .

"E to the C to the T to the O . . .

"'R' you going to still be my protector?"

Gabriella headed back to the other side of the stage. She was in her element and the audience was in her hand. The dancers were in a perfect groove around her—six men and six women—protecting each other amid flips, twirls, and midair splits. The band was jamming, perfect note for note. She could see those beyond the stage either dancing or bobbing their heads to the beat. All, that is, except one. Troy. *He's standing there looking like a superhero,* Gabriella thought, in his signature black from head to toe. Legs spread. Arms crossed. Dark glasses. Totally still. *And way too much in control,* Gabriella also thought.

Hmm. It's time for me to change that.

From the moment she'd first seen him in her hotel suite, she'd pondered how to get next to this affable yet somewhat enigmatic man. After their conversation this morning, a possible avenue had become clear. She executed a series of well-honed moves while thinking: *Are you actually going to do this, Gab? You just met him, barely know him. Are you really going to call his bluff?* She neared him and caught his cocky gaze. No, you're not, his stance seemed to say. *Yes* . . . Gabriella thought, flipping her hair back while seductively approaching, *I am.* As the backup singers continued the chant, and the dancers danced and the crowd pumped their fists, Gabriella strutted back to the side of the stage, directly up to Troy and, without saying a word, gripped his arm. With a barely perceptible nod to the stagehand, the spotlight hit them. Boom!

"Ah, yeah!" Gabriella said, walking backward with her hand on Troy. She threw back her head and laughed at his obvious scowl. "I told you that I'd do it," she purred; lips close to his ear, away from the mike. His expression became unreadable. "What, you didn't believe me?" She leaned out toward the audience. "Ladies, do y'all want to see my protector?"

"Yes!" was the massive reply.

"Are you game?" Gabriella leaned forward and whispered in his ear. "Or are you scared?"

At this comment, he relaxed his stance. Gabriella

imagined that behind those dark shades his equally dark eyes smoldered. She smiled, and began singing as she pulled him onstage.

"P to the R to the O to the T . . .

"E to the C to the T to the O . . .

"'R' you going to still be my protector?

"And my friend, and my lover, oh!

"Are you going to still be my protector?

"Tell me, baby, drive me crazy, sing it! Are you going to still be my protector? Break it down like this!"

Bam!

The music went to the bridge and the dancers hit the floor in a military-style choreographed number reminiscent of Janet Jackson's "Rhythm Nation." But this beat was about Gabriella: marching, twirling, dropping it like it was hot and bringing it back up all in one shot. All the while Troy stood there in the middle of the hype—a caramel-colored Terminator—in the same pose that had drawn Gabriella like a magnet toward steel. Even now as she pranced around, she was aware of him, taking in his nonchalant attitude of disinterest, and his stoic, professional face.

Uh-uh, baby boy, you've got to feel this right here! With a final kick of her leg straight over her head, she twirled, took a running start and jumped straight into Troy's arms. She saw his eyes widen behind the dark lenses. "I knew you'd catch me," she whispered, before clasping her legs around his waist and dropping backward toward the ground.

The crowd lost it.

But she was just warming up. She began to swing

from side to side, shimmying up and down. Then, as if they'd rehearsed this for hours, she came back up and whispered a command.

He slowly turned them in a circle and all the while, she sang:

"P to the R to the O to the T . . .

"E to the C to the T to the O . . .

"'R' you going to still be my protector?"

She gripped his waist with her strong thighs, fell back, slowly pulled herself up again, and threw her arms around his neck. In one fluid motion she unclasped her legs from around his waist and slid down his hard, lean body.

Couldn't have been more erotic were she a stripper and he a pole.

"Ladies and gentlemen, let's give it up for our real, live, sexy, security man . . . my protection . . . Troy Morgan!" She slid him a sultry glance and gave a soft push before walking back to the front of the stage— booty swaying to the tune of the music playing—for the song's dramatic ending.

For a man who never let anybody see him sweat, Troy was about to float away in perspiration. His heart was beating a mile a minute and, as unmoved as he'd appeared on the stage, he was a throbbing, heated mess. It had taken every ounce of discipline he possessed to not succumb to the whims and moves of the vixen who'd tempted him when her crotch rubbed against his, and to not lose control like a love-struck, snot-nosed teenager right in full view of the adoring public. Damn! *Her body is tighter than I'd imagined and softer than I'd dared to dream.*

He'd been caught off guard when she left the stage and came toward him. Even given their earlier conversation, he hadn't been prepared. During the afternoon sound check, she'd done this portion of the act with a dancer, one he now realized had been conveniently absent from the stage minutes ago. Troy took two steps, and then two more. Still hidden by the thick black curtain, but better able to see Gabriella, and all the dancers on the stage. Where is that skinny, metrosexual-looking dude? Angry now, Troy searched the stage for him, wanting someone, something, anything to take him away from the erotic thoughts he was having about Gabriella, his coworker's wet dream, the woman who was way too much trouble for him to deal with. A few more seconds of searching and he saw him, dancing with the others, making the crowd scream with every thrust and note. *This is what they do for a living, man; stimulate the masses, get people excited. What she did with you wasn't personal. Yeah, you're her bodyguard, her protector, but she wasn't really singing about you.*

Troy didn't like this likely reality, but knew that to her this was show business. He got that. He understood. But the next time he saw Gabriella, there were some things he wanted her to understand, too. One, he was a man, not a boy, and not into games. Two, he wasn't against surprises per se, but if she ever again performed a "spontaneous" act, she'd better be prepared for the consequences. Three, taking a page from his former-playboy brother Michael's playbook, he didn't get involved with his clients. Yeah, right. That's how Michael's former client, Shayna, had become his wife. Ignoring that uncomfortable reminder, Troy continued his train of thought.

Four: Gabriella needed to know in no uncertain terms that he wasn't a toy. That she was playing with fire. Right now, at this moment, he was aflame! And as any grand-mother in any area code would tell you . . . if you kept playing with fire, you were sure to get burned.

7

She was hot, sweaty, feeling a plethora of emotions all at once. Her first night on the West Coast was over and the response of the crowd at the Staples Center had exceeded her expectations. All of the hard work and sore muscles and long rehearsal hours had paid off. The new show was a hit! Even now, after two encores, they refused to back down. Chanting her name, they stayed put in the arena: "Gabriella! Gabriella! Gabriella!" She was past the point of exhaustion, but went back out one more time.

"Thank you, Los Angeles! Good night!"

Signaling for her dancers to join her midstage, she stood there, soaking in the limelight and applause. Twelve sweaty dancers joined her at the center of the stage where they took one final bow. To the beat of her stellar band with its infamous all-girl rhythm section, dreadlocked drummer, bleached blond guitarist, and preacher's daughter on keyboards, she strutted off stage. When she reached the edge of the thick, black curtain she turned and threw out one final kiss. The official kickoff of the West Coast leg of the tour was over. And it was a success beyond anything she'd imagined. The Stone Cold Sexy tour was in the building!

Yes!

Three steps past the first thick, black curtain and a strong hand enveloped her upper arm, pulled her between the folds of a second curtain behind the platform, out of the view of everyone scurrying backstage. Before she could let out a scream or cry of protest, the owner of the strong hand that had enveloped her slammed her up against his massive, hard chest and wrapped strong arms around her.

"Be quiet," he commanded.

As if she had a choice. Gabriella was literally scared speechless, even though the smell of his cologne had immediately alerted her to the identity of her captor. Troy's natural animal scent blended with the smell of the popular and expensive designer's cologne. She was shocked, but not surprised at this turn of events. She knew she'd pay a price for putting Troy on the spot, knew there would be a day of reckoning for her spontaneous actions. She just never thought it would come this quick, mere seconds after stepping off the stage.

"Let go of me!" Her voice was soft, breathless, and she wondered why nobody seemed to have noticed her immediate absence. That his authoritative handling of her body, both onstage and now, made her strangely excited was something that she chose to ignore.

"You're playing a dangerous game," Troy drawled into her ear, his breath hot and way too close. "Never do what you did again, unless you want to reap the consequences of such actions."

She turned her head to tell him off. It was just the move

he needed. He slammed his mouth against hers—cushy lips, thick, strong tongue that demanded she open her mouth to receive him. She groaned, her nipples hardening as if on command, her hot spot growing hotter against her will, every fiber of her being wanting this man inside her, deep and relentless, the way she knew he'd be. She pulled his tongue into her mouth where an oral dance of swirling and lapping and licking occurred. Something quickly came between them—Troy's big dick. It quickly rose up to make its presence and Troy's intentions known, pressing against Gabriella's sweating, bare middle and reminding her (as if she needed it) just how long it had been since she'd had an up-close-and-personal encounter with such a tool. Without a second thought or moment's hesitation she ran her hand up and down the length of it and knew something immediately. She had never encountered the type of ridge this man was rocking. As tired as she was, a surge of energy rushed into her core, causing a wetness that had nothing to do with sweat. The same arm that had tried earlier to push him away now wrapped itself around his neck and pulled him closer. Troy's hand crept up under her bralike top and tweaked her naked nipple, a move that let her know that their thoughts were running along the same lines. All she could think about was being with this man, in the most intimate way imaginable, and as soon as possible.

But that wasn't going to happen right now.

"Gab!" Carol's cheery voice pierced the veil of privacy that in their moment of unbridled passion had wrapped itself around the love struck birds. "Where are you?"

Reluctantly Gabriella pushed Troy away, straightened her top and caught her breath. She waited until he'd gone the opposite way, then pushed against the thick curtain that had kept them hidden from prying eyes and eased around to the other side. "I'm right here," she said, once alone and somewhat calm. "Just had a problem with my, uh, shoe."

When Carol came around the corner, Gabriella was hopping on one foot, the shoe she'd quickly pulled off in her hand. She pretended to examine the inside of the shoe. "Thought there was something in my shoe," she said to Carol by way of explanation. "It was bothering me for the last hour on the stage."

"Here, let me have a look at it."

"That's okay." Gabriella replaced the shoe. "I think I got it."

Carol fell into step beside Gabriella, who was walking to her dressing room. "Girl, you did your thing tonight! That impromptu moment with Troy was hot!"

Who was she telling? Gabriella walked on shaky legs, still trying to come to grips with the fire within her that Troy had ignited with a single touch. Her heart was racing, her coochie was throbbing. In short, she was a hot mess. She needed time alone, to think. Which is why when she turned the corner and headed down the hall that led to her dressing room, her smiling, glowing family was the last group of people that she wanted to see.

"Baby, you were great!" Yvonne stepped up and wrapped strong arms around her daughter. "As you know, it's been a while since I've seen you and . . . Wow! Looking at you up there on that stage, it was hard to believe that you came from my womb!"

"Thanks, Mom," Gabriella mumbled, her mind still reeling and all messed up.

"She was a'ight," Garrett said, coming up next to his mother to give his sister a one-armed hug.

"Whatever," Gabriella responded, thankful for her brother's playfulness. It helped her heartbeat to slow and her breath to return: two events that were necessary if she wanted to live. "You know you loved it."

"I did indeed. Was even trying to see where I could fit in on the tour."

"The only places you're getting ready to fit in," Yvonne said with brow arched, "are with those business books and the football coach."

"I still have the summer to live my life," Garrett countered.

Gabriella wrapped a sweaty arm around her brother as they continued to her dressing room. "Don't worry, baby brother. I'll find a place to work you in."

"Good job, baby girl," Gary said, coming up behind the trio and placing his arm around his daughter's shoulders. "The show was fantastic. Not sure how I felt about that bit with Troy Morgan, though. We need to talk about that."

Gabriella turned around to answer her father and lost her breath again. She'd been totally unaware that Troy had been walking a couple steps behind them this entire time. He looked the part of a professional bodyguard in his signature attire: black tee, jeans, shoes, and dark glasses, with an earbud discreetly plugged into his ear. Thankfully, it appeared as though he was talking on it, which meant he hadn't heard her father's comment. Good. *Hopefully Daddy will get preoccupied, too,* she thought. Totally in the moment when she'd pulled Troy onstage, she was now struck with all kinds of thoughts. Like how crazy she'd been to be so bold and dramatic, to basically hump him in public before God (translated, Gary) and everybody! *At-*

traction or no, what the heck were you thinking? Clearly, it wasn't about the consequences of her actions. She glanced his way once more. He was clearly engrossed in listening to whoever was on his earpiece. Hopefully her parents would give her space.

Had she taken a moment to look the other way, she would have seen the knowing look that passed between Yvonne and Gary, and how they'd noticed their daughter's strained expression after seeing Troy behind them. They reached her dressing room door and after giving her younger brother a playful punch and her father a hug, she, Carol, and Yvonne went inside.

"How did you like that last outfit?" she asked her mother, hoping to take control of the conversation and firmly lead it in the direction of her choice.

"I liked what Troy was wearing," Yvonne replied, cocking her head and giving Gabriella a knowing smile.

So much for a different direction.

"That Troy Morgan is one handsome man," Yvonne continued. "I didn't know you'd written him into the show. With the lyrics of the song, it totally worked."

"That was a spontaneous moment," Gabriella replied. "And I'll admit it worked perfectly. But you and Dad don't have to worry. His focus will continue to be on protecting me for real in life and not for show on the stage."

"Hmm, that's interesting. For myself, I thought you two looked quite cute together."

Over the years, her parents had often employed the "good cop, bad cop" tactic in order to try and direct their children's lives. Though now divorced, these tactics remained. Gary would lay down the law hard and fast, while Yvonne befriended you, gained your confidence, listened carefully to everything you told her and then took a great deal of said info right back to Gary. Even after knowing how they operated, Gabriella had taken the bait more than once. But not tonight. Gabriella knew the ploy her mother was selling. She wasn't buying it at all.

She pulled her hair into a ponytail and sat down so that Tiana, her hair and makeup artist, could remove the night's grime. "I'm exhausted, Mom, and need to decompress. I think I'll pass on a late night dinner and just go back to the hotel."

"You sure you don't want to come back to the house? You can sleep just as well there."

"No, I'm going to go back to the Four Seasons. I'll see y'all tomorrow."

Gabriella didn't say much after that. She told Carol to handle whatever else needed to happen, knew that her father was dealing with the band, dancers, and other staff. She left the room with Troy and the limo driver by her side. They entered the vehicle and still her emotions roiled. She was thinking thoughts that were foreign to her mind, feeling a side of her she'd never felt before demanding to be unleashed. Rational thoughts flitted across her mind, but for the life of her the irrational impulses would not go away. Like the impulse to lean over and kiss Troy again. Like the desire to feel his succulent lips all over her body. It was insane to be thinking the impossible, ridiculous to imagine what could never be. Troy was her bodyguard, nothing more. Her father would never approve of anything other than a professional relationship between them. And then there was the vow—the one she'd tried to break to have a serious relationship with Marlon, the hip-hop star. Her father had reminded her then of what she'd promised. But sometimes, like rules, promises had to be broken. And if the way Troy had made her feel after knowing him for less than a week was any indication . . . now just might prove to be one of those times.

8

Gabriella settled against the backseat of the limo, still deep in thought. She was not at all surprised at the text she got from Carol, the one she saw as soon as she pulled out her phone.

What's going on? Where are you?

She quickly texted her answer. Headed back to the Four Seasons. Meet me there and get your own room. Will explain everything later.

Her phone beeped within seconds. Girl, you don't have to explain why you're getting ready to hit it with your fine bodyguard. I saw the way you kept looking at him after the show.

Gabriella fired back a quick response. The only thing I'm going to hit is the sack.

Another text from Carol quickly followed. LOL! Right, with Troy in it I suppose. Don't worry. I saw it coming. Your secret's safe with me. . . .

She chuckled and shook her head. *Carol Robbins. My girl . . .*

"What's funny?"

Gabriella looked over at the beat of her heart. She and Troy hadn't shared five words since getting into the limo. "What?"

"You were laughing. What about?"

"Just at something Carol texted just now."

Troy took off his sunglasses, looked at her for a long moment, nodded, then gazed out the window.

Her stomach clenched. Her kitty purred. She wondered what was on his mind. *Damn, why can't I think about anything but being alone with this man in my hotel room?*

"You're awful quiet. What's on that—*handsome, sexy*—mind of yours?" She slid a side glance in his direction and wasn't surprised to see his lazy eyes, surrounded by long, curly lashes, fixed squarely on her.

"How do you think your show went tonight?"

Gabriella lay across the plush leather seat, fully aware that her scanty tee showcased her girls to their best advantage. "How do you think it went?"

"I meant what I said backstage, Gabriella. Don't pull that stunt that you did tonight again."

"Why? I told you I was going to do it. The audience loved it. I think it went great. I think we should work it into the act."

"Not a good idea."

"Why not?"

"I think it skews our professional relationship, and I'm not a toy to be played with."

"Is that what you think I'm doing? Playing with you?"

He looked at her another long moment before he

spoke. "What I think is that you haven't dealt with a real man before. And what I know is that if you keep messing around with this real man"—he pointed to his chest—"you're going to get a lesson on how situations get handled in a grown man's world."

"Ooh," Gabriella purred, feigning a shudder. "I'm all scared."

Troy snorted, even as he narrowed his eyes. "No worries. I plan to keep things strictly professional. But if you weren't my client, trust me, you'd have every reason to be afraid."

"Were you always so sure of yourself?" Gabriella asked, sitting up to face him.

"I guess so," he answered with a shrug. "Being the youngest, it seemed I always had something to prove."

"Why do you think you felt that way?"

Another shrug, as he once again covered his expressive eyes with his dark shades. "As the oldest, Michael seemed to command respect simply by being. He's a natural-born leader who ran the neighborhood. His money-making schemes—from delivering newspapers to running a lawn business at twelve to setting up female tutors for his male high school friends—set him apart. His good looks made him popular with both sexes.

"Greg always was the studious one, the introvert. His intelligence was obvious; from a young age everyone knew he'd be somebody."

"And you?"

"From an early age I was always beating up somebody!" They laughed. "I was a hard head who didn't take teasing, bullying, or losing well. I was also big for my age. People often thought I was older than Gregory, especially since I felt it was my job to protect him."

"What do you mean?"

"Greg doesn't have an ounce of bad boy in his entire body. He never wanted to fight, join a gang, do drugs, or anything else that is often required to be thought of as cool. He wore these studious-looking horn-rimmed glasses and while others carried guns, he carried books. Some of the boys thought this meant he was soft, which he isn't. Greg would rather walk away than be drawn into a fight. I felt differently, as most who dared go against my brother found out."

"It sounds like you love your family very much."

He nodded. "Looks like you do, too. I see how you are with Garrett. And you must know he worships the ground you walk on."

"He knows I'm no one's idol. But yeah, he's probably proud of his big sis."

Troy still wore sunglasses, but his eyes seemed to bore into Gabriella's soul as he answered, "So am I."

"Really? Why?"

"Why? Seriously?" She shyly nodded. Troy removed his glasses. "It's not because of the obvious . . . your being a rich, successful star. But because you had a dream and went after it. Because according to what I've read, you didn't forget where you came from, you try and reach back to help up others—the young girls you mentor, for instance, and the hospitals you visit. There are many young stars who don't look past their own fame. You clearly do."

His words pierced her heart in an unexpected fashion. Fans adored her persona; family and friends loved her unconditionally. Undoubtedly, her parents found the success she'd achieved gratifying. But for a near stranger to recognize that she was more than her stage presence?

And that said stranger was a very handsome man whom she'd gone after and not the reverse? Troy was unlike any man she'd ever met before. She believed that much like the world thought of her, he—Troy Morgan—was one of a kind.

They reached the hotel. The driver let them out and Troy kept would-be fawning fans away as they tried to approach Gabriella. A camera flash went off. He instinctively pulled Gabriella to his body. She buried her head into his chest as they walked toward the elevator. One immediately opened. Two excited fans and a paparazzi member tried to step inside.

"Get back!" Troy barked, before pushing a button to the floor two levels below where they were actually staying. Once the doors opened, Troy wrapped his arms around Gabriella's shoulders and headed for the stairs. Silently, they entered the stairwell and climbed up to the top floor and Gabriella's suite. Once there, Troy pulled out the card key, opened the door, and stood back so that Gabriella could enter.

She'd told Carol differently, but on the elevator ride up Gabriella had tried to rid herself of the shameless hussy now occupying her body and bring back the good girl with the common sense. Sexy persona aside, she was far from promiscuous—had only been with one other man her entire life. Surely if she had the discipline to become the world's favorite pop star, she had it to resist temptation. By the time they reached the door, she thought she'd accomplished it. Had planned to bid Troy adieu and head straight to her suite. Walking down the short hall to their room, she convinced herself that she really was tired and all she wanted to do was go to bed. Alone. *Yes, that's it. Unwinding in solitude. I'll have Li bring up a cup of tea and then run a bubble bath. By the time my head hits the pillow I will have all but forgotten that what's-his-name is sleeping only several yards away.* Now, with the door open, Gabriella's back straightened with strong resolve. She stepped inside. And damned if the shameless hussy didn't upstage the good girl before Troy could close the door shut.

Turning to Troy with a shy yet saucy stare, she cooed, "Thanks."

"For what?"

"Everything that happened tonight. I like the way you work. The way you protect me. I even think that deep inside there's a part of you that liked . . . our little show."

"I don't have to tell you that you're sexy," Troy answered, casually walking around and checking out the large open space even though one of his men had confirmed its security before they'd arrived. "And you don't have to tell me that you like me, too."

"Oh, really?"

Troy laughed. "Don't even try it, girl. It's all in your eyes."

"It is not." Gabriella crossed her eyes and made a face.

"Ha! It's all good. Two healthy, passionate individuals— one male, one female—are bound to stir up desires. But I don't do sexual harassment lawsuits. That threat is enough to keep me firmly in my lane. So if you don't need anything else, I probably should retire to my room."

It bothered her that Troy seemed so in control of his emotions while hers were all over the map. She was used to making the rules, calling the shots. Which might be why Ms. Common Sense, the woman who'd walked down the hallway and made plans for tea and bubbles after bidding Troy good night, left the building while Ms. Shameless Hussy decided to take it up a notch. She sauntered toward him, slow and easy. One watching would think that she'd done it a million times, but this was this pop star's first real attempt at seduction.

"So you want to keep things strictly professional, huh?" Shameless Hussy's voice was low, the sexy hoarse quality a product of tonight's full use of her vocal pipes. Throwing both caution and common sense to the wind, she took a step and brought them closer together. "What if I say I had other plans for us after hours?"

Troy took a step back. "I'd say that the after-hour activities you have in mind are not in the contract."

Gabriella took another step, virtually pinning Troy against the wall as she wrapped her arms around him. "I won't tell if you won't."

"Tell what?"

"That we couldn't ignore the attraction that exists between us and decided to do something about it."

Troy's face showed his skepticism. "Something like what?"

"Like this." She leaned forward for a kiss.

He placed his hands on her shoulders, halting her motion. "I'm serious, Gabriella. I don't allow myself to become involved with clients," he whispered, against the mouth now pressed—wet and warm—against his own.

"And I don't normally come on to men. But you're right. I like you and believe that you won't kiss and tell. It's been a long time," she implored, her eyes seeking, showing vulnerability. "Just once." Now she was whispering, too, and surprising the heck out of herself in the process. There had never before been a time that she'd been this forward, and truthful when it came to her feelings for the opposite sex. Still, in for a penny, in for a pound. She watched as a myriad of emotions played across his face. "Just once, and then we can both stop wondering what it would be like. We'll go back to being professional. Please."

"I can't. I've got to set an example for the guys who work under me." Even as he said this, his hardening shaft was setting an example of its own.

She kissed the side of his face before running her tongue over the mouth he'd clenched closed. "They don't have to know."

"Really?"

"Really."

Troy pulled his face away from hers and looked into her eyes. "So let me ask you something, and I don't mean to offend."

"Okay." The only offense she could think of right now was the fact that there were clothes separating their skin.

"How many other bodyguards have you seduced?"

Gabriella stepped back, surprised at the question. "None."

Troy had immediately seen the hurt in her eyes. "I'm sorry. It's just that . . ."

She took another step. "No, it's okay. You're right. I'm your boss. You're my hire. Professional, strictly business, that's how we should keep it." She turned and began walking toward one of two bedrooms the suite contained. "Good night."

A long pause and then, "Good night."

9

Gabriella reached her decadently appointed master suite and slumped against the closed door, more tired than she thought possible. The two-hour-plus show had nothing to do with this exhaustion. No, this was all about being emotionally drained. Seduction was hard work. Especially when one's overtures were rejected. "You're going to get a lesson on how situations get handled in a grown man's world." A joyless chuckle escaped from her lips. If this was any indication of how the "grown folk" lived, Troy was right. Gabriella had no idea how things played out in this world. With her first and only love Marlon Simmons, a/k/a Mr. President, the world's hip-hop darling, the love affair had begun with a lot of innuendos, back and forth flirtatious banter, and numerous games. It had taken him years, literally, to talk her out of her panties. And mere months for her parents to catch on to the love affair, put their feet down, and end it almost before it had begun.

And now another attempt at intimacy had stopped even before it got started.

She sighed, looking at the door to the bathroom, and trying to summon up the strength to start a hot bath. Instead, the thought only conjured up images of a hard, wet, naked Troy, joining her in the water. *Enough, Gabriella. Go to bed!*

A soft knock on the door made her almost leap out of her skin. *Has he changed his mind? Probably not. Probably just Li making sure there's nothing else I need before she calls it a night.*

Her heart beat a crazy rhythm as she cracked open the door and realized that her first thought was the correct one. "Yes?"

"I'm really sorry for what I said. I didn't mean to imply that you were promiscuous or anything. But I see a lot in this business, get all kinds of offers. I just didn't know."

"It's okay. I shouldn't have been so presumptuous."

"Can I come in? And I'm not being presumptuous either," he hurriedly added, less she think there was only one thing on his mind. "I just want to, you know, make sure that we're cool."

Gabriella stared into his eyes. The look coming back to her was anything but chilly; in fact, it was red hot. Her heart smiled when she entertained the thought that she might be the reason. But these sultry looking eyes belonged to the man who'd rejected her just seconds before.

She opened the door a bit wider, then crossed her arms. "Is there something that can't be said from right there?"

She watched Troy's eyes narrow and his pupils darken. "There's something I can't see from here. All of you."

Swallowing, she opened the door and let him in.

Instead of reaching for her as she'd expected, and as

she wanted, he walked over to the window, turned, and asked, "Why do you want me?"

"What do you mean?"

"What's up with what you did earlier tonight? Was it just for show? And just now in the living room—were you making a point?"

"I don't know, Troy." The sincerity of Troy's question made her suddenly shy. "I just like you."

"I'm feeling you, too. I can't deny that. But, baby, this goes against every rule I've ever laid down since being in this business. Things could go awry and for me present serious repercussions."

"I wouldn't do anything to ruin your career, Troy. And while it is totally unlike me, I did make the first move. If anything, you could sue me for sexual harassment."

"My mind is saying I shouldn't do it, but my body is screaming to give you what you want."

"Then why don't you?"

Several seconds passed. For Gabriella, it felt like an eternity. For Troy, crossing the bridge of no return had happened much too quickly. "What do you want exactly?" he asked her.

Dipping her head, she softly answered, "I want you."

Again, an unreadable expression came over his face as he crossed the room. He placed a finger underneath her chin, forced their eyes to meet. "You're going to have to do better than that, baby. I'm not getting ready to set myself up for rape. If you want this right here"—he ground his hard dick against her stomach—"you're going to have to let me know straight out."

"I want it." The telltale statement came out in a whisper.

"Excuse me? I didn't hear you."

She cleared her throat. "I want it."

"Want what?" He moved closer still.

"What you want," she mumbled.

"No, baby doll. You've got to be clearer than that." By now, he'd walked them over to the wall, and was performing a slow grind upon her person.

One that was driving her wild.

"I want you to make love to me," she whispered, and couldn't believe that the words had come out of her mouth. But they had. And as unlikely as it was for her to have uttered them, and as unexpected, she had no desire to take them back.

At this request made in her light, ladylike voice, Troy's dick jumped and grew by two inches.

"You want me to what?" he asked, his lips against her earlobe, his hand inching beneath the cotton top.

"I want you, Troy Morgan," Gabriella calmly explained. "I want to do the nasty, make love, have sex, bang, smash, bone, screw . . . choose your description. Are you going to keep me waiting all night?" She ran a firm hand down his hard chest. "Or are you going to show me what you're working with?"

This woman hadn't said nothing but a word.

With a groan, he lowered his head to the lips still implanted on the forefront of his mind from that first hot, intense kiss. He crushed their lips together; their tongues immediately taking up the dance where it was left off when Carol had called out her name backstage at the Staples Center. He sucked her tongue into his mouth, even as his thumb made lazy circles around Gabriella's areola and hardened nipple. She wrapped her arms around his neck, pressed herself even harder against his hardened shaft. After kissing for several minutes, he came up for air, placed his head against the wall and took several deep breaths.

Then, without warning, he ripped off her already ripped top.

Her breasts, pressed together as they were inside her black lace push-up bra, were like water to someone dehydrated, like food to a starving man.

He turned her around and hurriedly unclasped her bra. Her breasts swayed with joy at their unexpected freedom, the air in the room producing goose bumps on her smooth, hot skin. He immediately dipped his head and caught a nipple between his teeth, tugged and pulled, sucked and licked.

Gabriella shook with pleasure.

For Troy, this was motivation to not only keep doing what he was doing, but to take it up a notch.

He bent lower.

With her still pinned against the wall, he lowered his head from the breasts on which he'd feasted and swiped his strong, wet tongue across her abdomen, dipped it inside her navel and lowered his hands to the waistband of her jeans.

"You're so soft," he murmured, unclasping the metal button of her low-riding jeans and unzipping the zipper. "Are you ready for this, sexy?" He gazed at her with admiration, his eyes settling on an area below her navel. "I'm going to enjoy every second of giving you pleasure."

He rolled the jeans down over her hips, taking with them her barely there lacy thong. She stepped out of the pants and he cast them aside. Her pussy had been waxed, the lips smooth and inviting, and Troy immediately accepted the invitation. He licked the line between her folds—once, again—and was rewarded with a moan and the act of her legs widening. He dropped to his knees, placed his hands on her thighs, and buried his head into her heat. His tongue parted her folds and he lapped up her nectar, teasing her clit before sucking it into his mouth much like he'd earlier treated her nipples.

She whimpered.

Long, slow strokes; his tongue bathed every part of her feminine flower. He took a long, strong forefinger and teased her entrance before plunging inside.

"Ah!"

Obviously, she likes this. Let's make it two. And he did, two fingers, moving slowly in and out of her wet canal, even as he continued to suck and nip her nub, feeling her wetness on his finger and in his mouth.

Delicious.

But what he didn't know about were the thoughts rolling around in Gabriella's head, thoughts that said this dance was way too one-sided. She reached for the buckle of his black leather belt, fumbled with the clasp before commanding its undoing. Quickly, she unbuttoned the metal clasp and, much like he'd done minutes before, unzipped his pants. She pushed them down, along with his black boxers. His dick sprang forth: thick, long, hard, and beautiful. She faltered for a moment. Last year she'd made a trip to the Metropolitan Museum of Art, but this was the first time she'd seen a live masterpiece up close and personal. And all this time she'd thought that Marlon was packing. Brothah man had been sporting a carry-on bag where this man would definitely have to check this ish!

"What are you going to do?" Troy asked, his tone low, his voice raspy. "Stare at it all night?"

Truth be told, this very well could have been her

answer. She could have marveled all night at this piece of work. But she had to agree with Troy. There were better ways to put it to use. So much like he'd done, she dropped to her knees, opened her mouth, and welcomed it in.

Is this what ambrosia tastes like?

She could only take in so much of him, so she pulled back and ran her tongue around his mushroomed tip. She took her tiny hands, both of them, and held his massive weapon. As talented and well practiced as she was on the stage, this was new territory. Sure, she'd done oral sex with her first boyfriend. But it hadn't felt like this. It hadn't felt like her life depended on making someone else happy.

That's how it felt now.

Once again, she licked her lips and then touched her mouth to his manhood. She smiled at the hiss that escaped from his lips; felt pleasure as she looked up to see his eyes closed, his head back against the wall. Vaguely, she felt his fingers massaging her scalp as her head made circular motions around his shaft. But it wasn't enough. She wanted more. She wanted him inside her and she wanted it now!

"Come," she said, trying to stand on shaky legs. "Let's get on the bed."

"No," Troy countered, the word strong and decisive. "I want you right here. Right now. Take everything off." Even as he said this he stripped off the black tee and shook the pants and boxers from around his ankles. He quickly reached inside his wallet, pulled out a condom and put it on.

Gabriella's hands shook as she took off the remnants of the stripped tee and threw off her bra. She felt vulnerable yet womanly standing there naked and free, his eyes feasting on her like she was a Sunday buffet. But there was little time to ponder the moment. He lifted her against the wall and placed his body against her. She gasped, her legs wrapping around his waist of their own accord, leaving her open and exposed, feeling the air on her nub. Right before his finger flicked over it once and again.

"You're so wet for me." Troy rubbed his finger up and down between her folds. "Tell me what you want."

"I . . . ooh"—she felt his tip at the point of her exotic entry—". . . already told you."

"Tell me again, so that I know it wasn't a mistake, a comment made in haste."

Gabriella kissed his succulent lips and looked deep into his eyes. "I want that big juicy dick inside me, Troy, more than I've ever wanted anything in life." She rested her head on his shoulder and finished, "Please, don't make me wait anymore."

10

The pleading in her voice was almost his undoing. He wanted to plaster her against the window, drive his point home while observing the LA skyline. But he knew the strength of the wrong camera lens and the problems that could occur should a picture of Gabriella's backside pressed against a hotel window get into the wrong hands. So he turned them around and walked to the couch, turned her to face it and bent her over. She flipped her hair and looked behind her. He needed no further motivation.

Gabriella braced herself on the only thing she still wore: four inch stilettos. She placed her hands against the back of the couch, arched her back so that her glorious gluteus maximus was high in the air. She let out a sigh as she felt his finger running down the length of her crease, parting her, loving her, treating her body like the rarest of treasures. He once again positioned his tip against her. Then slowly—oh . . . so . . . slowly—eased his way inside.

It was heaven. He let out a long sigh.

Placing his hands on Gabriella's smooth, round hips,

he began a rhythmic thrusting, a relentless pounding that made his dick harder, longer, thicker. She rubbed her booty back against him, the friction becoming almost more than he could bear. He plunged in deeper, pulled out to the tip and then repeated the motion, over and again. He bent over, grabbed her shoulders and deepened the exchange, the slick, wet sounds of their bodies slapping together creating its own salacious component to this decadent dance. Soon, their bodies gleaned with a sheen of sweat, tendrils clinging to her neck and back, beads forming on Troy's smooth forehead as his hands reached around to grab Gabriella's swaying breasts. He tweaked them: once, twice, harder. She placed her hands over his as he continued to ride her, and she continued to enjoy it.

After a particularly forceful thrust her legs almost buckled beneath her. She placed her knees on the sofa, offering yet another delicious angle from which Troy could take and give pleasure. He pulled out, slapped himself against her, slapped her bubbly round ass on one side, then the next, and drove himself back in.

"Ah!"

Gabriella wasn't a virgin, but she wasn't a porn star either. She hadn't been poked or prodded this way ever in life. It was excruciating and ecstasy all at once. She widened her legs for better accommodation, groaning as his hand reached from her breasts to her heat and heightened their amorous interaction.

Troy leaned over, not missing a beat or a stroke. "You like this?" he asked, his mouth wet against her ear.

"Yes," Gabriella purred, rocking back against him. "Yes! Yes! Yes!"

"Didn't know what you were getting yourself into

when you hired me, huh?" he queried, placing his own knee on the couch so that he could show her what he was really working with. "When you pulled me on stage. How do you like me now?"

Gabriella couldn't speak, only moan, low and throaty.

"This is what I thought of," he continued, his strokes long and nasty as he twirled his hips to hit every side of her heat, to tap every spot. "When you pulled me on stage and wrapped those sexy-ass legs around my waist. Hitting this. Right. Here." A thrust punctuated each word.

"Ah!"

"I want to make this good for you, Gabriella. I want to give you what you asked for, and more."

He stood, pulled her flush against him and then lifted her up. Covering her mouth with his and initiating a smoldering kiss, he walked them to the bedroom and gently laid her in the middle of the bed.

"Am I making you happy?" he asked her, a hint of charming, boyish insecurity coating his words.

"Very," she said as she lay there, open and exposed before him.

"That's not good enough for me." Troy ran a finger over her nipples, down her stomach and into her softness. "I want to make you ecstatic." He grabbed his shaft and hovered over her briefly before plunging in again, his tongue searing her mouth with strokes equaling those of his manhood.

"Is this good for you, baby?" he asked, after coming up for air.

"It's . . . I . . . uh . . . ooh . . ."

"It's all right if you can't talk, darling. I just want you to feel. I want you to know what a real man feels like."

For several moments he was quiet, alternating his

pumping action between long, smooth strokes and short, staccato pounding. *Yeah, I'm here to show you how it's done, baby girl. I'm going to make you think twice before you play around with a player. Yeah . . . I'm going to blow your mind until you forget your vocabulary!* He swiveled his hips, and was not only surprised, but pleasantly pleased when Gabriella did the same. The friction was amazing, and Troy found himself working hard to hold on to his release. He thought to leave her speechless, but what happened next had Troy searching for words.

Gabriella pressed her hands against his chest. "Stop."

His eyes widened. "What? Did I hurt you? Baby, I'm—"

"Don't you dare say you're sorry about anything happening right now. Get up."

He moved his hips in a way that suggested he could change her mind.

She gripped him with her inner muscles in a way that suggested that two could play that game. "Roll over," she whispered into his ear. "I want to be on top."

He judiciously followed her command, until he was beneath her. "Where you belong, huh?"

"For now." Her face became serious, focused, as she hovered over his tip before sliding down, inch by delicious inch, until he was buried deep inside her, touching the core of her heart.

This is so good, she thought, *feels so right. And yes, baby boy. You're amazing. You've taken my breath away, but not my words. So get ready. Because I'm not going to talk to you. I'm going to do something even better.* She wrapped her legs around Troy's waist, locked heavily lidded eyes with his, and ground her hips to a beat they made together with rocking pelvises and swirling hips:

"P to the R to the O to the T . . ."

Pump, pull, pump, pull. She grabbed his butt and pressed him closer still.

"E to the C to the T to the O . . ."

Bump, grind, bump, grind. Sliding her hands over his broad shoulders and across his narrow waist, she then ran her fingernails over his thighs.

"Are you going to still be . . . ah . . . my . . . protector?"

For an answer, he once again grabbed her hips and rammed himself inside her, over and again, still grooving to the beat, as he'd been doing. Obviously, he'd liked her song.

She felt her core tighten and her body begin to shake. "Oh my goodness, Troy. I think I'm getting ready to . . . I think I'm gonna . . . ahh!"

She exploded. He pulled out before following suit. A perfectly choreographed dance with a flourishing finish.

That was good for a warm-up, Troy decided, as he rested his forehead against Gabriella's sweaty hair. *Now, it's time for the encore.*

11

The next morning, streams of sunlight dancing across Gabriella's face awakened her. She groaned, turned over, and upon noticing the soreness between her legs, groaned again. Images of the previous night began appearing behind her eyelids and her eyes flew open. She raised and looked around the bedroom. She was alone.

Did I dream it? she asked herself as she plopped back down against the fluffy down pillows. She ran a hand across her midsection and repositioned her legs, again feeling the pleasurable pain that was evidence of her night of torrid lovemaking. No, that nonstop smashing was all too real. She reached for another pillow and placed it over her face to muffle her laughter. She'd never been this happy in her life!

After a moment, she heard Troy's voice invading her space, his deep, throaty laughter as he obviously chatted with someone on the phone. She threw back the covers and got out of bed. Donning one of the thick cotton robes the hotel provided, she padded barefoot out to the living room and was surprised to see her wide-awake, fully dressed bodyguard looking exactly as he had before their midnight romp.

Gabriella pulled her hair away from her face as she walked over and plopped down on the couch beside him. *Dang, he looks as fresh as a daisy. How long has he been up?*

"Look, bro, I've got to run. Tell Shayna I said good luck." Troy ended the call and turned to give Gabriella a kiss on the nose. "Good morning, sleepyhead."

"Good morning." She prepared to kiss him back.

"Don't be coming at me before a shower and a toothbrush."

"What?"

"I didn't stutter. I haven't heard any water running. Get in there and wash that beautiful ass of yours."

"No, you didn't just tell me that."

"Yes . . . I did."

"You should have awakened me when you got up. I'm sure my parents are tripping right about now."

"Already took care of that. Called your dad and told him that we had a morning excursion and would join them for lunch."

Outwardly chagrined, inwardly amazed, she looked at him. "A rather presumptuous gesture, don't you think?"

"Maybe," Troy said with a shrug. "I guess when he called I could have told him that we'd spent half the night with your legs over my shoulders and me hitting that spot. I just thought that since it was your family and all . . . that that was a fact that you'd rather not share." His features softened. He ran an adoring finger down her face. "You were amazing last night."

Gabriella lay her head back against the couch. "I was, wasn't I?" She didn't have to look at him to know he'd reacted. "Ha! Thought that would get you." She looked at him. "I know how you felt about me after our interview—that I was this pampered little rich girl with an attitude."

"Was I wrong?"

"That's me sometimes," she said in all seriousness. "But not often." She lovingly cupped his cheek. "I never knew making love could make me feel the way you did. I know I said only one time, but . . ."

"Once is not enough?"

Troy's look was cocky, but Gabriella couldn't even be mad. He'd handled his business in the bedroom like she handled her show on the stage—being large and in charge. Whipped didn't even begin to describe how she felt. "Are you dating anybody?" Last night, she hadn't cared if there were others, but in the light of day and the thought of others enjoying Troy's immense . . . talent . . . a sistah wanted to know.

"I've been pretty focused on this one girl for the past few months," Troy answered, with a slow nod as he spoke. "We never said we were exclusive, but . . ."

"But what?"

"I'd only been with her lately."

"Do you feel bad that you slept with me?"

"No." There was a companionable silence, and then, "But I do feel bad about breaking my own rule. I've drilled it into my employees that no fraternizing is allowed, told them that they could be terminated if I ever found out. But like you, I don't want last night to be the only night."

Gabriella had another concern, but didn't voice it. Instead she asked, "What are we going to do?"

He looked at his watch. "Right now, you need to shower and dress. The driver will be here in an hour."

"I don't have anything to wear."

"Carol stopped by and dropped off some luggage: toiletries, makeup, and enough clothes to last through a major earthquake."

"That's my girl!"

"She seems like a lifesaver and that's no doubt. I hope she knows how much you appreciate her."

"Of course she does. Why would you even fix your mouth to say something like that?"

"If what you say is true, then you're getting a little too testy. I just know how easy it is to take good people for granted. Carol seems like good people."

Gabriella copped an attitude quicker than Bolt could run the one hundred. His casually delivered comment hit a nerve, took her back to days of being bullied, when she was often falsely accused of thinking she was better than. She jumped up from the couch. "Look, just because we fucked last night doesn't mean that you know me, or give you the right to judge how I am. You work for me. Remember that!"

Troy leaned back and gave Gabriella a stern stare. "And you requested my presence . . . on all fronts. I didn't ask to be here and I don't need to stay. You . . . remember that!" He repositioned himself on the couch and continued. "Gabriella, I respect you. I like you. As an entertainer you've got mad skills, and personally, there's definitely a strong vibe between us. But I'm my own man. I don't need a woman to validate or complete me. I won't kowtow, act hen-pecked, or be disrespected, not even by the baddest babe who ever rocked a mike." He noted the wisp of a smile before she set her face again. "So if I'm going to be the protector you sang about while

How does he drive me over the edge so quickly?

Didn't matter. This was where she was headed, over the edge. Apparently, he was right there with her, ready to join her for the ride. As they began to move faster, thrust harder, hold tighter, a scream bubbled up from somewhere deep in Gabriella's soul.

"Troy!" she cried, holding the name like a note as her body jerked and shuddered with the force of her orgasm.

"Briella," Troy sighed, adding three hard pumps before he enjoyed his own release.

Aside from family and very close friends who called her Gab, she didn't go for nicknames. But as she felt Troy continue to throb within her, she repeated the name on her lips: Briella. And she determined . . . nothing had ever sounded so sweet.

12

Shortly before one p.m. Gabriella, Troy, and Carol showed up at the Stone estate. To escape the prying eyes of her father, Gabriella grabbed hold of her mother just after the greetings and asked for the tour of their new ten-thousand-foot home that she hadn't been in the mood to see the first time they'd visited. Carol went to confer with Dana, the publicist, whom she'd asked to meet them there.

Troy walked over to where Alex sat in the living room, scrolling his iPhone. "Hey, man. What's up?"

Alex answered without looking up. "You tell me."

Troy immediately sensed the underlying tension. Alex had been in the business a long time, had guarded his share of cuties and slept with others not on his watch. He knew how the game was played. "Look, let's go out by the pool. I need to talk to you."

Alex swept his thumb over the phone screen, ending whatever he'd been doing. He stood and headed to the floor-to-ceiling sliding glass doors. He still hadn't looked at Troy.

They stepped outside, both men facing the pool, neither of them seeing it. "Did you do it?" Alex asked at last.

Troy knew what his good friend was asking. "Yes." He'd always been straightforward with Alex and didn't intend to stop now.

"I knew it was inevitable, but you could have at least let me carry the fantasy for a week."

"I didn't plan last night to happen," Troy said, turning to face his friend directly. "I didn't know that she was going to do what she did onstage, bringing me out there and bumping and grinding like that. We went back to the hotel and one thing led to another—"

"Yo, man, I don't need a play by play. Especially from the boss who demanded I not try and get down."

"I don't feel good about breaking my own rule."

"Yeah, I bet it's just tearing you up inside."

Several moments passed, as the men finally took in the relentless waves from the infinity pool reflecting huge cumulous clouds against a stark blue sky. A plane hummed high above and in the distance. Butterflies flitted around the peace lily plants that strategically dotted the terrain.

"I'm sorry, Alex. I know you had visions of her being your girl and all."

"I knew she was feeling you from that very first day."

"Yeah?"

For the first time since the conversation began, Alex looked at Troy. "Don't even stand there and act like you didn't know."

"She acted like such a spoiled brat at that meeting that honestly, I didn't know what to think."

But he did now. During their conversation following the morning's romp, Troy had learned about Gabriella's controlling father, and the short leash he kept her on when it came to romance. She'd admitted that trying to keep her dad from sensing her attraction is why she dismissed Troy so callously, when every fiber of her being had called for a different reaction.

"I guess I can't blame a man for doing what men do," Alex finally said.

"Are you sure? I wouldn't want to lose my top security man behind some female."

"Why would I care about a skank-ass bitch who gave up the pussy after knowing somebody less than a week?"

Troy bristled, but his voice remained calm. "I get that you're upset, Alex, but that talk is foul. As our client, and more so as a woman, she deserves respect. Please don't use that type of language to describe her again."

"You're telling me that? I'm the brother who was singing her praises when you were saying she was just all right."

"Like I've said, I'm sorry about how this went down, man. I know you had feelings for her and whatnot. I'm going to do right by her, Alex. She's a special girl."

"Don't I know it," Alex said, with a shake of his head. "Don't I just know." He gave Troy an unreadable expression, then looked away and continued. "Listen, I need to take care of something. Can I get an hour break right now?"

Troy looked at him. "Sure." Guarding someone as high profile as the Stone family was grueling since it was basically around the clock. "But just an hour though. Gabriella has a press conference at three and I'll need you back here to handle the family while I roll with her."

Alex nodded, giving Troy another look. "All right."

Troy eyed his ace employee. "Are we good?"

Alex smiled slightly, held out his fist to give dap. "It's all good."

As Troy watched him leave the pool area and walk into the house, he truly hoped everything was good, and that a solid friendship and business relationship hadn't been destroyed. Not much time to ponder it, though.

As Alex entered the Stone's great room through the patio doors, Carol came outside. "Troy, food's ready."

"Okay, thanks." He walked toward her.

"Here you go," she said when he'd reached where she stood.

"What's this?" He took the envelope.

"Tickets to tonight's show. For your family."

He turned to her. "How many are in here?"

"Eight. Along with backstage passes. Is that enough?"

"Should be. Thanks." He paused just inside the door, shot off a few texts, and then continued on to the food-laden buffet.

Gary came alongside him. "Enough food here to feed an army."

Troy nodded. "Looks good. I'm famished."

This comment caused Gary's head to whip around. "What has you so hungry, Troy?"

"I hit the gym instead of having breakfast," was Troy's easy (and somewhat honest) answer. Upon rising, he had indeed gone to work out in the hotel's gym. But he'd expended more energy hitting something else when he returned.

Gary eyed Troy for a moment before giving a curt nod toward the food. "Well, dig in, young man. It's going to be a long day. You'll need your strength."

After loading up his plate with glazed salmon, baked chicken, wild rice, mixed vegetables, and freshly baked rolls, Troy headed toward the great room. He hadn't seen Gabriella since shortly after they'd arrived, and with the way Gary looked at him after his famished comment, he decided that the farther away he stayed from her—at least in her overprotective daddy's presence—the better.

Noting that Melanie, the stylist, Tiana, Gabriella's hair and makeup maestro, and Gabriella's latest hire, assistant Li Yang, were sitting at a small table in the great room, he went to join them. Passing the dining room table where Gabriella's family and Carol sat, he could feel her presence. Eyes on him, though he knew she tried to hide it, desire radiating out from her, because it matched his own. Twice last night and once this morning and he was still as ravenous for her loving as a hungry dog was for a meaty bone.

As he sat with the pretty ladies, trying to tend to one appetite while ignoring another, he could only imagine how much crazier this whole situation was going to get before her tour was over. Alex tripping, Gary watching, Gabriella pretending, and him feening. It was going to be a long six weeks.

13

"Boss, they're here."

Troy turned to the employee who'd delivered this message, gave a nod of understanding, and sent him back to his post. He motioned for Alex to come over. Since the entire Stone family was in attendance for tonight's concert, Alex and several other members of Morgan Security were all at the Staples.

"Yes, Troy," Alex said, once he'd walked over. "What is it?"

"My family is here. Guard the stage until I return."

"Got it."

I'm sure you do. Aside from the brief conversation that afternoon, Troy and Alex had spoken no further about what had developed between him and Gabriella. But during the warm-up, Troy had seen how Alex watched Gabriella, had taken note of the admiring look in his eyes. A brothah couldn't blame him. Gabriella had that affect on all men who looked at her. Troy didn't have a problem with that. He was a confident man. As long as Alex and the long line of admirers looked and didn't touch, everything would be fine. But as long as they were together, if another man stepped over the line, things would get ugly.

He turned the corner and saw his family, some looking wide eyed and star struck. Even his sports agent brother Michael, who worked with star athletes all the time, looked impressed.

"Hey, family!" Troy reached the group, stopping short when he saw his mother. He held out his hand. "Uh, hello, sexy. My name is Troy."

Jackie gave him a playful swat. "Boy, quit playing."

"I'm serious. Do I know you?" He winked at Robert. "Who is this babe you've brought with you and where is my mama?"

"She cleaned up pretty good, didn't she?" Robert teased, playing along with Troy. He popped his collar. "I'm going to have to step up my game!"

"Mom, you look absolutely fabulous." Troy reached for her hand and turned her around. "Look at you, rocking a ponytail and everything!"

Jackie's shoulder length hair, which she commonly wore in a simple curled under style or swept back and held by a clasp, was now pulled up into an add-on ponytail that reached midway down her back. The look, and flawlessly applied makeup, emphasized the slant of her eyes, high cheekbones, and long neck . . . and made her look ten to fifteen years younger. Tonight this fifty-something could give any twenty-, thirty-, or forty-something a run for their money.

"Blame it on Shayna's friend, Tanisha."

"Talisha," Shayna corrected, before saying to Troy, "she has a wonderful sense of style."

"Yes," Jackie agreed, "after I calmed her down. If it

had been left up to her I would have showed up here in a skin-tight mini and five-inch heels." She gave Troy a deadpan look. "I told her that my name was Jackie, not Tina!"

The group laughed.

"What you're wearing is a great choice," Troy said, admiring the fitted navy dress accented with silver shoes and accessories. "You know Gary Stone is her heart-throb," Troy mumbled to Robert, continuing to tease. "You'd better watch out!"

Robert straightened and took off his glasses to clean them. "When we leave here tonight, Gary will be where he's been for the last forty years—in her rearview mirror. I'm not worried about a thing!"

"All right, all right." Michael stepped forward. "Enough of talking about my mom and the men she's juggling. Sheesh!" He leaned over to Troy for a shoulder bump. "This is nice, bro. Thanks."

"Yes," Jackie added. "This is all so exciting. Thanks for the tickets."

"You'll have a chance to thank Gabriella later. She's the one who made this happen. I didn't even ask her." He turned to his former part-time employee, now Jackie's gentleman friend. "How's it going, man?"

"Nothing to it but to do it," Robert responded, holding out his hand. They shook. "If you need another security guard, just let me know. I'll come out of retirement for this gig."

"Ha! I'll keep that in mind." He walked over to where Shayna now stood with his other sister-in-law, Anise. "Where's Gregory?"

"He had to work," Anise replied. "I hope you don't

mind that I brought Kim. You remember her from the gallery, right? One of my partners."

"Of course." Troy gave her a light hug. "Come on, y'all. Let me get you guys settled into your seats." They reached the center aisle, third row. Two handsome gentlemen, part of Morgan Security, were among those sitting in the row. "Michael, you remember Bryon, Curtis."

"Sure I do. What's going on, guys?"

The men stood, shook Michael's hand, and after they were introduced to the group and Troy made sure they were settled, he prepared to leave. "Right after the show ends, someone will be out to get y'all, all right?" Various responses that the group understood. "Okay, then. I have to get back to work. Enjoy the show!"

Two and a half hours later, one of the security guards came and got Troy's family and ushered them into the green room where Gabriella received her nightly guests. Michael saw a couple people he knew and excused himself from the group to talk with them. Robert and Jackie hovered close to the gourmet hors d'oeuvres snacking on this and that while Anise and Kim stood in the corner whispering about faces they recognized and trying not to look straight up star-struck.

An immediate buzz in the room announced Gabriella's arrival. Troy entered just behind her and her dad, scanning the room, focusing on his intuition. With all of the training he'd had, his sixth sense was what served him best. It was like he was born for this job, and could literally smell trouble. After sweeping the room a couple times with his eyes and noting two of his men already milling around, he relaxed and caught up with Gary and Gabriella.

"Gary, my mom is here. If it's not too much trouble, can I take you over to meet her? She's the one who's responsible for me knowing about your music." He added casually, "Of course, Gabriella, my family would love to meet you, too."

"Of course."

Instead of looking him in the eye, she looked just past his shoulders. He knew why. The hawk was watching. One eye-to-eye glance and their secret would be out. The two were in lust. As soon as they got back to the hotel it would be on and popping!

Jackie's eyes lit up as she saw Troy approaching. "Boy! Why didn't you tell me you were part of the show? When she pulled you onstage my jaw dropped to the ground!"

"It's my fault," Gabriella said, her smile genuine. "His being in the show was my idea. It happened last night in an impromptu moment, but the crowd loved it so much we decided to keep him in the show. You must be his mother. I'm Gabriella."

"Yes, Gabriella; I'm Jackie."

"Nice to meet you, ma'am."

Jackie was visibly impressed with her manners, evidenced by a slightly arched brow. "It's wonderful to meet you, too, Gabriella. Your show was fantastic!"

"Thank you. This is my father, Gary."

Jackie's smile widened as she turned to the tall, handsome man standing beside Gabriella. "I know who this is. One of the singers whose story should be on *Unsung*." Gary acknowledged her compliment with a slight bow. TV One's hit documentary show highlighted the lives of phenomenally talented performers who never got their due. "Hi." She held out her hand and Troy could have sworn a moment of shyness overcame her. "I'm Jackie Morgan."

"Gary Stone," he answered, taking her hand to his lips and kissing it. "You're as beautiful as Troy said you were."

Wait, when did I say that? Outwardly, he showed no emotion, but inwardly he was tripping at seeing a stranger trying to get his mack on with his mama!

A clearing throat brought Troy out of his musing, just in time to see a square-shouldered Robert step up next to Jackie. "And I'm Robert McCrary, Jackie's significant other, my brother."

The two men shook hands, with tension even tighter than the he-man grip each gave the other. Then Gary smoothly turned back to Jackie and acted like Robert wasn't in the room. "I was honored that you were a fan of the Starlights and flattered to learn that you remembered me. I wasn't in the game for long, but I tried to leave my mark."

"You did that for sure," Jackie replied, giving Gary a flirty smile even as Robert's arm came around her waist. "My friends and I played your father's albums constantly. Years later, we played yours, too." She named off several songs from the two albums Gary made before a change in the music scene made his sound obsolete.

"Wow, now I know you bought the albums. Only a true fan would know those songs."

Troy looked over in time to see Robert clench his jaw. Uh-oh. Time to break up this fawn fest. Once a police officer, always a police officer. Robert might be packing. "Gary, I think I see your son over there." He gave him a slight push in that direction before turning to kiss his mom on the cheek. "Time to work the room, Mom. Love you."

"It was nice meeting you, Mrs. Morgan."

"Please, Gabriella. Call me Jackie. I really enjoyed myself. It was nice to meet you, too." The words were said to Gabriella, but astute Troy didn't miss the fact that as she'd uttered those last words her eyes had flitted to the back of one Gary Stone.

Maybe introducing them wasn't such a great idea, Troy thought, as he and Gabriella stopped and chatted with Michael and Shayna before moving on to all of the other well-wishers in the room. *Man, I can't wait to run this by the brothers.* As it was with most children, to Troy, Jackie was just "Mom." Tonight, he'd very clearly seen her as "female"—no, make that "a sexy, vibrant, still-gets-her-groove-on woman." To say the thought was uncomfortable was an understatement.

So he was more than happy when Gabriella's inconspicuous hand slid slowly down his back, cupped his hard buttocks, and put a totally different sexy, vibrant, still-gets-her-groove-on woman on his mind.

14

It was three a.m. before a weary Troy and exhausted Gabriella climbed into the back of their Hummer limousine.

"I thought this night would never be over." She sighed as she cuddled against Troy.

He quickly wrapped his arm around her. "It was a long night." He kissed her temple, and felt something else begin to get long.

"And what was going on with my father and your mom?"

"You peeped that, too?"

"I sure did. And so did your mom's boyfriend."

"Yes." Troy chuckled. "Robert got a little hot under the collar."

"He shouldn't worry. My dad's a big flirt. That's why he and my mom aren't married anymore."

Troy decided not to touch that comment with a ten-foot pole. "At least it took the heat off us for a minute. You've hardly said two words to me all day."

She turned, kissed his cheek, and ran her hand down

the length of his toned chest, settling it lightly on his manhood. "Awww, was my baby feeling neglected?"

He placed his hand on top of hers, pressed it down on the hardening hump. "Something is feeling neglected."

"I can take care of that real soon," she whispered, her breath hot and wet against his ear.

Ever mindful of both his position and his client, he looked toward the driver and gently pushed her away. "I'll hold you to that," he said.

When they entered the Four Seasons suite, it was evident that Carol had more than done her job. White candles flickered throughout the open-concept space. A hot bubble bath was waiting and two professional massage tables were set up in the room.

Gabriella checked her text messages and saw where Carol had indeed sent instructions that included the number to call when she and Troy were ready for the masseuse. That she'd assumed Troy was going to be in the room, and that a couple's massage might be a sexy way to set it off, was just one of many reasons why Gabriella loved Carol like the sister she never had.

She reached Troy, who'd walked to the window and was now taking in the room from that angle. "Who did all this?"

"Carol."

"So much for keeping this on the low."

"What? You trying to have me as your side chick?"

"Don't even go there. We both know who'll put up the road block if he finds out we're"—Troy pulled Gabriella to him, wrapped his arms around her, and began grinding against her pelvis—"having sex, making love, smashing, boning, doing the wild thing . . . take your pick."

Gabriella turned into his embrace. "You know I'm way too busy to fall in love with you."

"And I'm way too busy to get a broken heart."

She pushed against his chest. "Like you've never broken a heart before."

"I probably have, a time or two."

"At least he's honest."

"Humble, too."

"Right." She stepped away, but kept the physical contact by holding his hands. "Tell me about the last woman whose heart you broke."

"Wow, really? You want to swap relationship stories this early in the game?"

"Chill out, man. I'm not asking to read your journal. I'm just wondering why with all the beautiful women there are in California, one has never totally measured up."

Troy eased his hands away from hers and walked over to a bar chair by the counter and sat down. "I've had only one serious relationship in my life, and I messed it up."

"How?"

"By being honest. I told her I wasn't ready for marriage and didn't know if I'd ever want to walk down the aisle. Sometimes, when you tell a woman the truth, she doesn't believe you."

"She thought you were joking?"

"No, I think it's more like she thought she could change my mind. We dated two and a half years. After that she didn't want to wait anymore." He shifted his gaze from her to a point a few feet from yesteryear. "Michael had tickets to the pro bowl game in Hawaii. She wanted me to take her. I took a couple of my boys instead. When I got back, all of my stuff from her place had been mailed back to mine; along with a letter telling me that it was over."

"Did you ever see her again?"

"Ran into her a couple times; kind of awkward, not much to say. Heard she got married a year or so later. Moved to Atlanta. Had a kid. Got what she wanted."

The last line was delivered so softly Gabriella had to strain to hear it. "So whose heart got broken? Hers . . . or yours?"

"Both, I guess." Troy sighed as he rose from the chair and walked to the window. "Before that breakup, I'd never failed at anything that I cared about." He turned abruptly, shaking off his melancholy as he spun around. "What about you? Hearts in pieces from coast to coast?"

"I have no idea."

"You know you're the type of woman every man dreams of having?"

"Perhaps, but I've only been with one."

"Mr. President?" She nodded. "So the tabloids weren't lying. Y'all were hanging out."

"For a minute." Gabriella joined him at the window.

"Why'd you end it?"

"I didn't. Dad did."

"Whoa, it's like that?"

"Yes."

"And your heart was broken?"

"Definitely. Which is why you and I won't get all serious and fall in love."

Troy closed the distance between them, brushed a lazy hand across her bottom, and ground against her again. "I see you have this all figured out."

"Yes, I do."

"You're the one who's in control."

"Yes, I am. I'm decisive like that."

"You are?"

"I am."

"You need to remember something, baby girl." He slipped a hand beneath her top and tweaked a nipple.

"What's that?" she asked, in a whisper.

"You're not the only one making decisions."

He looked in her eyes as he continued to stroke her softly: across her back, up and down her arms, across her breasts. He didn't kiss her. Didn't try and up the sexual ante. Just looked. And stroked. With a grind here and there, against her core, into her soul. And then came the kisses—soft, tender, almost reverent—against her temple, on her ear, along her cheekbone, across her neck.

Just this . . . and Gabriella's thong was soaked. Her pussy throbbed. She turned her head, seeking those lips to connect with hers, before their bodies followed suit.

"It's getting late, baby." Troy pulled Gabriella's top over her head. "What about the massage?"

In an uncharacteristically brazen move, she reached for his hand, placed it square on her heat, and said, "What about massaging this?"

"Oh, trust me. That's going to happen. But why waste all this right here?" He swept his arm across the room. "Why waste the hot water? Come on, baby. All that dancing, and moving and gyrating across the stage. I know your body's tired. Take your clothes off so I can bathe you."

Gabriella simply looked at him.

Without a word, he swept her up in his arms. "Never mind. I'll do it."

He walked them into the master suite where he laid her on the bed, quickly removed her pants and thong, then pulled her up to unclasp her bra. Picking her up once more, he walked into the bathroom and gently placed her into the Jacuzzi. He reached over for the bath pillow, placed her head against it. "Relax, Briella."

She did.

He took this time to shed his own clothes, pull out several Magnum condoms, and slide into the tub. Reaching for the loofah sponge, and the specially crafted organic soap that Gabriella used, he then began leisurely bathing the billion-dollar beauty.

He started with her toes.

One by one, he ran the loofah brush between each toe. He rinsed them off. And then did the same thing with his tongue.

Toes.

Calves.

Knees.

Thighs.

Gabriella was shivering. The water was still hot. By the time he reached her neck, she was putty in his hands, and the only person in control . . . was Troy.

He gently sponged every inch of her body and by the time he lifted her out of the tub, Gabriella was as limp as a noodle and all but asleep. He reached for the lotion, made from the same combination of organic tea tree oil, calming aromatic oils of frankincense, spikenard, and chamomile, and raw shea butter. As he rubbed it on her soft caramel body, he couldn't determine which was softer—the oil or her skin. His lidded eyes took in her toned legs, hard, round booty with dimples above the cheeks, narrow waist, and weighty boobs as he massaged the oil into her skin.

"That feels so good," Gabriella gasped, when he ran a stiff, long finger across her clit.

He refused to lose focus, was determined to stay the course until he was done taking care of her in the manner he felt she deserved.

"Briella," he whispered, after he'd finally finished, pulled back the covers, and placed her inside. He climbed into the bed behind her. "You going to leave me hard and hanging like this?"

She groaned, rolled into him, found a comfortable spot for her head on his shoulder . . . and fell fast asleep.

He didn't have much time to be mad about it. After being up for almost twenty hours himself . . . he zonked out, too.

At first he swatted at it, much like he would a gnat. The air had been the first he'd felt on his morning-stiff dick, followed by the gentlest of touches on his tip.

There it was again, but this time there was moisture added, and pressure, delicious, rhythmic licks on his shaft. Still half asleep, he turned fully on his back. If this was a dream, he wanted even his imagination to have enough room to work its magic.

But this was no dream. As soon as he felt a stiff tongue go from his tip to his balls, tickle them and follow the vein on the underside of his treasure back up to the top, he knew that what was happening to him was all too real.

He opened one eye.

And saw two twinkling ones looking up at him. "Good morning."

He straightened the two legs that he walked on. His third leg was already straight, in more ways than one.

"Umm, this tastes good." Gabriella spoke in a soft, breathy tone as she pleasured him.

"It . . . feels good," Troy added, between hisses. "But I'm kind of hungry, too."

Her laugh was music to his ears. She quickly positioned herself so that they could feast on each other, and that's what they did: his tongue sliding between her already moist folds, his hands massaging her juicy cheeks, his finger teasing her tight brown star. For Gabriella, it was a chance to act out a fantasy of sorts. Her limited sexual experience and equally compartmentalized education on erotic matters suggested to Gabriella that she was what others would label a freak. She preferred the term "free-spirited" to what her best friend Carol called "nasty." From the way Troy was playing her box like an instrument, it would seem she'd met a kindred spirit.

Life was good, and about to get better.

"You're up early," Troy said. They'd both come up for air after giving due oral diligence to each other's private parts.

"Not as early as you," Gabriella teased, her hand squeezing Troy's penis, amazed that she couldn't close her hand around it, more amazed that she'd been able to take him in. For as braggadocious as her former lover, Marlon "Mr. President" Simmons, was on stage, and for as much talk as he spewed about being "the man," he would have been more honest calling himself "the midget." Not that five-foot-ten was short, but the term definitely would have found a home inside his boxers.

Gabriella was amazed at how smoothly Troy was able to help her take him all in. It had happened three times already, so she knew without a shadow of a doubt that this phenomenon could occur.

She was ready for it to happen again.

Continuing in her role as lead, she rolled over on top

of Troy and motioned to the condom packets spread across the nightstand. "Give me one of those."

A lazy grin accompanied Troy's reaching over and grabbing one of the foil packets. He opened it, pulled out the condom, and handed it to her. "Handle your business," he drawled.

Here's where the fun began.

Gabriella had watched a movie or two where the woman, in a sexy move, placed the condom on the actor's dick and then rolled it down with her mouth. In real life? Not so easy. First of all, the datgum thing kept falling off the tip of Troy's dick. By the third time she tried to swing her breasts seductively while retrieving the rubber from between the sheets, it was no longer sexy, but funny.

But both were trying to maintain the mood.

He rolled his hips seductively, as once again she placed the condom on his tip followed by her mouth. Unfortunately, a sneeze chose this moment to tickle Gabriella's nose. She squeezed her eyes shut against the inevitable, but before she could react she had inhaled, sucked off the as-yet-unrolled condom into her mouth, and sneezed. Hard. The prophylactic hit Troy in the face.

For a few seconds there was no movement or sound. Then they melted into a sea of laughter that lasted for minutes. But when they stopped, fun and games were over. One look into Troy's eyes and it was clear that he was ready to get down to business—Morgan style.

15

After spending Sunday doing appearances and later the show it was finally Monday, Gabriella's first official day off in Los Angeles. She wanted to do nothing more than lounge in bed with Troy all day. But that wasn't an option. Her team—Carol, Melanie, Tiana, and Li—were spending the day riding around Los Angeles in a car that Melanie had rented. Gabriella and Troy were on their way to a luncheon at the home of her label's president.

"Hey, baby. Are you ready?"

"Just about." Gabriella turned and smiled. No matter how late they stayed up, how long they screwed, or how little sleep they got, she had never seen Troy look like less than a million bucks. His signature color and that of his company employees was black. Today, the uniform consisted of a black button down shirt, black jeans, and black Jordans. The understated platinum Rolex on his left wrist and the two small black diamond studs in his left ear completed the look. After more hours in four-inch heels than should be legal, Gabriella was rocking a simple, handkerchief-hem mini and three-inch wedgies.

After wearing heels almost constantly since she was a preteen, her feet actually felt uncomfortable in totally flat shoes.

She turned back around, reached for the stack of bangle bracelets on the dresser, and began sliding them on her arm. Before he reached her, she felt him. She could sense his presence from at least ten feet away, like the pull between two magnets.

His arms slid around her. He pulled her back against him and whispered into her ear. "You know you're wearing that dress, don't you?"

"You like it?"

He ran his hand over the silky fabric, reaching beneath it to the boy short panties underneath. "I'd like it even more without these on." He reached up and felt the strapless bra she wore. "Or this." He licked her ear and smiled at her moan. "I'd like to have you wearing it while I'm stroking deep inside you."

She turned around and soon they were swirling tongues and exchanging saliva. This intense attraction between them was crazy. It seemed the more love they shared, the more each wanted. Neither could ever get enough. The other crazy thing was that even though they'd been together less than a week, it seemed that they'd known each other forever—already finishing each other's sentences and eating off each other's plates.

The doorbell to the suite rang, followed by the lovers hearing the door opening. "It's Carol," Gabriella whispered, as she pushed away and started out of the room.

"Saved by the bell," Troy drawled, walking up on her and reaching behind to squeeze a cheek in his big, strong hand. "But later on, just so you know . . . I'm going to tear that ass up."

"Hello!" Carol called out from the living room.

"Hey, girl," Gabriella responded, walking out of the bedroom on shaky legs.

Carol gave her a look that said "I-know-where-you've-been-and-I-know-what-you've-done." "How are you, girlie?"

"Tired." They hugged.

"Uh-huh." Carol's eyes twinkled, but she said nothing further about the well-sexed sight that Gabriella presented. "Where's Troy?"

"Who's asking?" Troy came around the corner. "What's up, Carol?" He walked over and gave her a light hug.

"Drama in the lobby," was her response. "Fans have learned that Gab is here, so I need you to come with me and talk with the manager so that we can take her out the back."

"Okay," Troy said, reaching for his cell phone. "Hold on." He dialed up one of his guys and soon there was a member of Morgan Security posted outside Gabriella's room.

Once they left the suite, Carol directed Troy away from the elevator and down toward her room. "Where are we going?" Troy asked.

"I've got something to show you," Carol said in a hushed voice. "And I don't want Gabriella to know."

Troy stopped in his tracks. "Oh really, best friend. This is how you're playing it? This is how you roll?"

Carol's head whipped around so fast you would have thought it was on a spindle. "Don't flatter yourself, you arrogant asshole," she hissed, her eyes narrowed and hand on hip. "I don't want you. Yes, I am Gab's best friend. But even if I weren't, you couldn't even holler at my dog, player, player, let alone me. We received a package," she continued, lowering her voice even more. "A threat against Gabriella. Now get your presumptuous mind out of the gutter and back on your job." The last four words were emphasized by a poke in the chest: the five-foot-three, buck-o-five sistah backing the six-foot-four, almost two-hundred-pound guard against the wall.

"Sorry, Carol." Troy had his hands in the air as if he wasn't packing a weapon in the small of his back. "You're right. It was rude and presumptuous of me to say what I did."

"You damn right it was."

"I apologize."

If looks could kill, Gabriella would have been looking for another bodyguard. But instead of responding, Carol simply swung around and walked the short distance to her room, Troy following.

Once inside, she handed Troy the Priority Mail box that moments before had arrived at the hotel's front desk. "Place it on the counter," Troy said, wishing he had a pair of plastic gloves. "Has anyone else handled this besides you and the hotel employees?"

"Only the person who sent it, I guess."

"Do you have a scarf or something? I don't want to further contaminate this evidence."

Carol went into the bedroom and came back out carrying a sock. "Will this do?"

Troy nodded, forcing his large hand into the black cotton. He reached inside the box and pulled out a doll. It was naked, and a bullet wound had been painted square on its forehead. A glance passed between him and Carol as he looked in the box and pulled out a single sheet of paper. He read the two-word message, written with a red marker in crude print:

Whores die.

"How often does this happen?" Troy had placed the paper and doll back in the box and was now texting on his phone.

"Not often, but this isn't the first time she's received crazy mail. We had a pretty serious stalking situation two years ago. The guy was served with a restraining order and that was the end of it. Aside from zealous fans, it's been fairly quiet since then. It's part of the territory that comes with being a worldwide star and sex symbol," Carol said with a shrug. "Most of the time, we keep it from Gabriella. It's a level of stress she just doesn't need."

"I agree. We don't need to tell her. But I need to know everything you can tell me about any type of threatening correspondence or packages she's ever received. Where are the other documents?"

"Either with the firm that guarded us on the East Coast—the main guy is Edward. Or with the police."

"I'll have my law enforcement contacts check into the police files. I'm going to need Edward's number."

"Okay." Carol reached for her phone and gave Edward's number to him. "What are we going to do now?"

"I'm going to head down to the front desk and talk with the manager. You're going to go back to Gabriella's suite and do what you've been doing—act like nothing's wrong. Do you have another card for this room?"

Carol nodded. She walked over to where the second card key was, still in the envelope, and gave it to Troy. "I'll take care of this evidence and be back to the room in about thirty minutes. Does Gary know about all this?"

"Of course."

Troy nodded. "Then I need to talk to him, too."

Carol looked at her watch and then headed for the door.

"Carol." She turned around. "I'm really sorry for what I said earlier. You've never given me any reason to believe anything other than that you're one of the best things happening in Gabriella's life."

"You're right. I haven't."

"So you forgive me?"

"I'll think about it." Carol was not smiling.

"That's fair." Troy watched her leave the room, then turned back to the package with a frown on his face. It was hard enough guarding a celebrity; now evidence of a mentally unstable individual sending threats had been added to the mix. His phone vibrated. He sighed deeply as he answered. "Hey, Robert. I need your help, need you to put me in touch with some of your investigative contacts down at the police station. We've got a situation."

16

After spending what was for him a tense hour at the luncheon, Troy was on high alert as the bullet-proof SUV he'd secured and that they now rode in arrived at the Stone estate. They'd taken a circuitous route to get to their destination, determined to make sure that they weren't being followed. There were half a dozen cars in the circular drive, along with a pimped out Harley. The only car he recognized was Alex's GMC truck.

Upon seeing his good friend's ride, not-too-distant memories assailed him. Memories about how angry Alex was when he found out about him and Gabriella. *Was it mere coincidence that he found out that Troy had slept with Gabriella and this harassment started? Alex had been upset, this Troy knew with absolute certainty. But he wouldn't go this far, do something this crazy. Would he?* Troy's eyes narrowed as Alex's comments during yesterday's conversation replayed in his head.

"I knew she was feeling you from that very first day. Don't even stand there and act like you didn't know." And the statement where Alex came unknowingly close to being throttled: "Why would I care about a skank-ass bitch who gave up the pussy after knowing somebody less than a week?"

Troy checked his Glock before placing the weapon back in its hiding place, in a holster discreetly positioned in the small of his back. God knew that the last person he'd want to believe could harm Gabriella was one of his own employees. But Troy knew that infatuation—no, make that straight-out love-struck foolhardiness—could make a man stop thinking straight. He wasn't taking any chances.

"Looks like a party," he said casually, as the SUV pulled close to the door. "Do you recognize these cars?"

"Three of them belong to my family," Gabriella explained. "The others might be owned by employees: the chef, housekeeper . . . even the gardener perhaps."

"No worries," Troy replied. "I was just making an observation." He also made a quick mental note to log the license plate numbers of the Stone family's vehicles and those of their employees. A surreptitious look passed between him and Carol. Fortunately Gabriella's attention was on the opening front door, and her father exiting the house accompanied by another man.

"Who's that?" Troy asked.

"I don't know," Gabriella said with a shrug. She exited the vehicle with Troy hot on her trail.

"Hey, Dad."

"Hello, Gab." Gary hugged his daughter. "Gabriella, this is my new valet and assistant, Chauncey Pointer. His father is an old friend of mine. Chauncey, this is my daughter."

The average-looking man, with a short fro and a spray

of freckles across his red-toned face, held out his hand. "Nice to meet you, Gabriella."

"Likewise." Her tone was kind, but Gabriella barely broke stride.

Troy remained where he was, watching until Carol and Gabriella had entered the home and the door had closed. "Gary, can I speak with you for a minute?" The two men walked to the end of the drive. Troy gave Gary the short version of what had been left at the hotel, and what he'd done about it.

"I know it isn't the last guy who pulled this," Gary said, once Troy was done. "He's currently in a mental facility. Most of these blow over as isolated cases," he continued, taking in Troy's worried countenance. "Just some kid trying to work our nerves."

"Hopefully, that's the case." Troy furtively took in the area around them. "Still, I'm glad we're leaving tomorrow for Oakland. I'm sending an advance team to the Oracle Arena to double check the entire facility and its security. They're leaving tonight."

Gary held out his hand. "I appreciate that you're on our team, Troy." The men shook hands. "It makes me breathe easier, knowing that you're protecting my daughter."

"Thank you, sir." Troy turned to walk away.

"Oh, Troy, one more thing." Troy turned back around. "How's your mother?"

Troy didn't try and hide his surprise. "My mother?"

"Yes," Gary calmly replied. "Jackie, correct?"

"Yes."

"I really enjoyed meeting her. She brought back some fond memories that I don't often recall."

Troy breathed a sigh of relief. For a minute, he thought that Gary's thoughts were going in a different direction.

But he was thinking about her as a long-lost fan. Of course, it would make him feel good knowing that someone remembered his former fame.

"She's good, Gary. I haven't talked with her much since the concert, but I know she enjoyed it, and meeting one of her childhood idols was a highlight." He was sorely tempted to put emphasis on the word "childhood," but instead chided himself for once again being presumptuous, and told himself to quit tripping.

Gary took a step closer. "Jackie is quite an attractive woman."

Okay, maybe I'm not tripping.

"Is she married to the man she was with?"

Troy had been surprised at Saturday night's flirting, and this prolonged interest took him aback. He'd seen a couple of the women Gary favored. Most of them were young enough to be his daughter.

"Robert is an important part of our family," was his eventual answer. "And their relationship is serious."

"Well, next time you talk to her . . . tell her I said hello."

Troy's response was interrupted as his phone vibrated. He looked down at the screen. *Perfect timing, Robert.* "I've got to take this," he said to Gary, and walked away without waiting for a response. "What do you have for me, man?" He nodded his head as he listened, standing just outside the Stone estate front door instead of going inside. "I appreciate that. Just keep me posted. We're leaving on a chartered jet late tonight for Oakland. I'll be in touch."

As he entered the house, Troy was a bundle of emotions. So much was going on: threatening mail delivered to his client, troubling thoughts about his employee Alex regarding said client, the good man he'd introduced to his mother helping him handle the case of said client, and the father of said client pushing up on his mom, who for two years had been involved with the man he'd introduced! He knew when he accepted this contract that things would get crazy. But this madness had gone to a whole other level and where it would end . . . God only knew.

The day continued and Troy wasn't the only one dealing with problems. Gabriella was seething, waiting on the product she'd sent Li to retrieve. The spa that carried her uniquely formulated facial and skin crème was in Beverly Hills, not that far away. Gabriella understood that things happened, but to not only be late coming back but to also not answer your cell phone was inexcusable. Gary had encouraged her to hire Li because of her stellar educational background and financial skill, thinking she'd do well for the company overall. But if a girlfriend couldn't even run a simple errand, Gabriella decided, it might be time to rethink this choice.

Carol walked into the room. "Did you hear from her?" Gabriella asked.

Carol shook her head.

"Where is my father?" Gabriella demanded.

"Last time I saw him he was talking to Troy," Carol calmly replied. She'd been friends with the pop star long enough to know not to take her outbursts personally. "Why? What do you need?"

"I need to know what he was thinking when he hired that creepy looking dude as his valet!"

"Gab—"

"I know. I'm wrong for that. But have you seen that guy?"

"Have you talked to him? Or did you make a judgment based on looks? He seems really nice, Gabriella, and his father just died. Please be nice to him."

Gabriella's expression was one of true contrition. "Oh, I didn't know that. That's probably why Dad hired him. He said that he and Chauncey's father had been good friends. Now, I really feel bad."

"You should. I know that beneath that diva demeanor you wear sometimes lies a person who is compassionate, generous, kind, and more sensitive than one looking at you would suspect." She paused, considering. "I think he'll be a good addition to the team," she said at last. "Earlier, I saw him reading a Bible."

Gabriella nodded. "I guess connecting with a higher power is never a bad idea." Li walked into the room and for Gabriella, thoughts of God flew out. "Where the hell have you been?"

"I'm so sorry," Li said, a slight bow punctuating her contrition. "But I had to . . . uh . . . wait for them to finish making your formula, and when I reached into my bag to call you I realized that I'd left the phone here."

"Leave the bag on the counter and finish sorting the fan mail. And never, ever, be unavailable to me again. You got that?"

"I'm sorry, Gabriella. It won't happen again."

"See that it doesn't."

Carol noted Li's slumped shoulders as she left the room. She turned to Gabriella. "Was that really necessary?"

"Maybe, maybe not. But I'm not going to let someone shirk her duties and think that it's okay. What if it were something really important that I needed and time was of the essence? No, you've got to teach people how to treat you, Carol, and Li just got a lesson."

Carol sighed, and chose not to die on this hill. "I'm going to check with Dana, make sure the film crew is all set for the next show. Do you want me to send in Melanie to discuss outfits?"

"Yes." A pause and then, "Thank you, Carol. You're the yin to my yang, girl. Don't know what I'd do without you."

"Sounds like if I ever make the mistake of not having my phone, I'll be finding out."

"Was I really that hard on her?"

"You were pretty intense."

"Maybe you're right. I'll work on my attitude."

The day continued with everyone on Team Gabriella going about their business, preparing for the tour to leave LA. Bags had been packed, travel and show logistics had been further coordinated, and security precautions had been tweaked and updated. The last day in LA had proved basically uneventful, and all of the major tour players—Gabriella, Troy, and father/manager, Gary—felt that everything in their respective worlds was under control.

But feelings were one thing and facts were another. And the fact of the matter was that situations and circumstances that all thought safely managed were about to get way out of hand.

17

The crew arrived in Oakland around midnight. After hearing that threatening letters had arrived at the luxury hotel in San Francisco where they'd planned to stay, Troy suggested-slash-insisted, that they set up in a private estate. Thankfully, Gabriella hadn't asked too many questions about the choice of a private home versus hotel. During her many years of touring, she'd stayed everywhere from a five-star suite to a Scottish castle. The main concern to her most nights was the softness of the mattress and the thread count of the sheets.

Her personal crew—Carol, stylist Melanie, hair and makeup artist Tiana, general assistant Li, a chef and personal trainer, along with Gary, his new personal assistant Chauncey, Alex, and several more Morgan Security members, the band director, and ten other members of the entourage—filed into the twenty-bedroom estate located about twenty minutes north of the Oracle Arena. Troy quickly set up in a bedroom right next to the master suite where Gabriella would be sleeping, and on the opposite wing from where her dad would reside. He met with Alex, got the blueprint and confirmed where everyone was housed, and then the two men joined two more and scoped the entire premises of the ten-acre estate. Satisfied that where they stayed was a virtual fortress, Troy then met with the head of the reconnaissance team that he'd sent ahead of them to check out the arena. They talked strategy for the following night's concert and also for the two PR appearances also scheduled. Finally, at around two-thirty a.m., he walked to his room. He yawned and turned the knob to his room, hit the light switch, and stopped short.

Gabriella lay sprawled across the king-sized bed in his room, wearing nothing but the handkerchief mini that he'd earlier admired. "Well, are you going to stand there all night and keep me waiting?" she purred. "I thought you'd never get here."

Troy smiled, walking to her while unbuttoning his shirt. A bit of exhaustion left with each step and by the time he stood over this silk-covered vixen, his soldier had started to stir.

"You said that you were going to tear me up earlier," she cooed, throwing back the cover to welcome Troy in. "I'm here to hold you to it."

"I did say that, didn't I?" He removed his pants, boxers, and socks, and slid his toned naked body between the sheets, immediately taking Gabriella into his arms.

She nestled her head against his chest and began rubbing her hand across it. "What's going on?" she whispered.

Troy casually kissed her temple, forcing himself to remain calm. "What do you mean?"

"I saw Carol and Alex talking earlier. Looked like they

were pretty serious, but when I asked her about it, she said they were discussing transportation logistics."

"Have you seen how many people are staying here, woman? That's serious business."

"Maybe, but I got the distinct feeling that it was more than that."

"Even if it was," he said as he turned, nestled her closer to him, and began rolling her nipple between his thumb and forefinger, "it's nothing for you to worry your pretty head about. Your plate is full enough."

Gabriella reached between Troy's legs and grabbed what he was working with. "Here's a pretty head," she whispered, bringing her lips up to meet Troy's succulent mouth.

"Damn, girl. You've got me going." He rolled on top of her, reaching for the condom she'd placed on the nightstand even as he spread her legs. "I'd never want to be known for not keeping my word." He stroked the nub protruding from her wet folds, and on second thought, began working his way down so his mouth could see a different kind of action. "I completely meant what I said earlier. I'm getting ready to tear this up."

Downstairs, Carol padded into a stainless steel wonder in new house shoes, Stussy slippers that she bought en masse and donated to charity after wearing them once or twice. It was one of only a handful of quirks that she didn't like to wear the same pair of house shoes in a new location that she'd worn in an old one. She wasn't a waster, nor did she think lightly of money. She'd come up hard, on the streets of Detroit, and while she'd escaped on the wings of a girl group, she never forgot where she came from, never ignored her roots and those still struggling.

She reached the refrigerator and opened it up. Running a frazzled hand through her shoulder length hair, she sighed. The refrigerator was full, stocked the way she knew it would be. The chef was thorough like that. But she wasn't standing in front of the fridge because she was hungry. She was trying to distract herself because her nerves were on edge and sleep was elusive. While Troy was trustworthy and as experienced and capable as any involved in top-notch security, Carol was still worried. Scratch that, she was straight-out scared.

"Hello there."

Although it had only been inches, Carol felt as though she jumped three feet off the floor. She whipped around, clutching her soft cotton robe around her and gripping the granite countertop. "Dang, Alex. You scared the mess out of me!"

"I'm sorry. That was truly not my intention. I was just surprised to see somebody else up. Sorry that I frightened you. I'll, uh . . . I'll just come back later, after you're gone."

"It's okay. You don't have to leave. I just wasn't expecting anybody, that's all." He offered up a crooked smile and Carol dispassionately took in his boyishly charming face and the striped, beige pajamas that covered his tanned, stocky frame. "You want something from the fridge?"

"A beer if there's one in there."

Carol pulled out a bottle of beer, another of soda, and a small tray containing sliced veggies and dip. She placed Alex's beer and the veggies on the counter, pulled out a bar stool, and sat down. "What has you up late?" she asked, crunching on a carrot stick covered in ranch.

"Don't know, just couldn't sleep. Any chips in here?" He slid off the bar stool.

"Probably. Check the pantry." While he did so, she unscrewed the cap on her soda bottle and took a thoughtful sip. "Are you worried about the package?" she asked, once he'd returned to the large island with a bag of bagel chips.

"Of course," he said, bristling at the question. "I'm part of security. It's my job to worry."

"Don't sit over there getting all puffed up on me. I've seen how you look at Gabriella, just like all of the other millions of men with fantasies and wet dreams. Your concern goes much deeper than that she's your employer." Alex looked at Carol, his expression blank. She snorted, sank a celery stick into the dip, and munched loudly.

He took a swig of beer and sat back. "What . . . are you jealous?"

"What . . . are you crazy?" Carol looked at Alex and did not blink. "If somebody sent a crazy, threatening package to me, Gabriella would be acting just the way I am. She'd do whatever it took to protect me. I know this." She took a calming breath, a drink of soda, and continued. "The world sees her as this mega superstar, this pop icon, which she is. But I've known Gab since we were five years old. To me, she's like a sister, and my best friend. So no, Alex, I am not jealous of Gabriella. I am proud of her. I am happy for her. And I take offense at your suggestion that I am jealous."

Alex shrugged, took another swig. "My bad. I'm sorry."

"Yes . . . you are."

"Dang! I'm trying to apologize!"

"I don't have to make it easy. I'm sick and tired of

men assuming that sistahs have to always be on a hating game!"

"Sounds like I'm feeling the brunt of anger for somebody else now. Who are you mad at?"

"Nobody. Just forget it."

For a moment, only the sound of crunching chips and vegetable sticks was heard. "So tell me about you, Carol," Alex finally said, settling against the bar stool and crossing his arms. "I know that you were with the girl group the Haute Coutures. What happened to the other girls? And how is it that a woman as pretty and talented as you is really okay with living in Gabriella's shadow?"

"Why would you ask me a question like that?"

Alex smiled, Carol returned it, and the mood lightened. "Because I really want to know."

18

Now it was Carol's turn to lean against the bar stool's high back. While her face remained passive, she was inwardly impressed at a man who had the nerve to ask outright the question that often showed up on other's faces. Though her music career in the public eye had run its course, she still encountered the glimpses of recognition, and the various reactions that would follow. A third would hint around at the girl group, waiting for Carol to make it okay to talk about. She never did. A third would smile apologetically as if she should feel sorry for herself, and a third would act like they'd gotten amnesia and couldn't remember the faces of the female posse that rocked the world less than a decade ago. So the fact that Alex had put it out there, asking straight out, was at the very least refreshing. And at the most made Carol realize that maybe she'd underestimated the strength of Troy's number two man.

"I heard something once on an *Oprah* show," she began at last, her finger following the rim of her drink. She ignored Alex's doubtful expression and continued.

"Yeah, I know what you're thinking, that her positive perspective is not realistic, but this really rang true. Somebody asked her friend Gayle the same question, how she felt always being in Oprah's shadow. Gayle said that she'd never felt that she was living in her friend's shadow. Instead, she felt that she was living in her light. When I heard her say that, it was a lightbulb moment, because that's exactly how I feel.

"Believe it or not, there are women who can be proud of and supportive when one of their friends makes it. We're not all like crabs in a barrel, calling each other bitches and putting our sistahs down."

Alex nodded. "That's cool."

"What about you? How do you feel coming in second to Troy?" Alex scowled. Carol noticed and said, "Don't look at me like I'm crazy. You think I don't know that you have a thing for my girl? Or had one at least, until Troy stepped into the picture."

Instead of answering, Alex finished his beer, tossed the bottle in the trash, and then walked over to the refrigerator and retrieved another one.

"Oh, so we can talk about my living in Gab's shadow, but your rolling in Troy's shade is off limits?"

"Look," Alex said, placing the beer bottle on the counter with a thud. "I need to straighten you out on a fact or two. One, I'm not 'rolling' with Troy, I work for Troy. Yes, it's his company and I'm an employee. But two, I don't live in anybody's shade. Ever!"

"Sorry if I offended you."

"Hell, yes, it was offensive. What man do you know who wants to hear that he's coming in second to another man?"

"What woman do you know who wants to hear that?" Now it was Carol's turn to have attitude. For a few tense seconds, the two just glared at each other. Finally, Alex turned away and took another swig. "I guess you're right. I probably shouldn't have said what I did either."

"Exactly."

"What happened to the other girls? There were four of you, right?"

"There were five members in the Haute Coutures."

"What are the rest of them doing?"

"The sisters are back living in Detroit."

"Sisters?"

"Didn't we talk about this? Brandi and Brianna are sisters. Brandi is doing really well. She went back to school, received a masters in psychotherapy and opened a private practice. Unfortunately, one of her clients will soon probably be her niece, Brianna's daughter. Brianna has an addiction."

"Oh, man. That doesn't sound good. What is it, crack?"

Carol shook her head. "Worse. It's DeMarcus, her baby daddy." Alex chuckled. "He's physically and verbally abusive, but Brianna refuses to leave him. That's not the type of atmosphere in which to raise a healthy child."

Alex's expression became sad. "Not at all." He passed a hand over his face and leaned back with a sigh. "The chick I remember is the short, light-skinned one, the girl who had those fake-ass green eyes."

"Everybody thought they were contacts, but that is really Latoya's eye color. Anybody who saw her father would immediately know where she got them from."

"Is her father white?" Carol nodded. "Oh, my bad. So what is she doing now?"

"Last I heard she was living in Europe. I think she's trying to revive her singing career."

"Y'all don't keep in touch with each other?"

"We try. I see Brie and Bran whenever I go back home. But none of us have seen Latoya in years."

"Don't you miss being in a group? You were performing, traveling all over the world at what—nine, ten years old? That had to be the life!"

Carol leaned forward, fiddling with her now empty soda bottle. "Parts of it were fun. But it was also hard work. People like Gabriella are born to be in the business. I don't think I was."

"Why do you say that?"

"Because while we'd be at some cushy hotel, I'd want to be back at home sharing a bedroom with my sister and fighting with my brothers. I like what I do now, working behind the scenes. I get to live the life without all the stress of being the star." She stood and stretched. "I'm going to bed. With two appearances and the show, tomorrow is going to be crazy."

Alex stood as well. "I guess I should turn in, too."

They headed out of the kitchen. When they reached the second-floor landing, Carol prepared to turn down the hall to the suite of rooms she shared with Melanie, Tiana, and Li. Alex was headed to the third floor.

"Good night."

"Good night," Alex responded. "I'm glad we were able to talk through our little misunderstanding."

"Me, too," Carol said with a yawn. "Otherwise, I was going to have to kick your linebacker-looking behind."

"You could try," Alex replied with a smile. He was still smiling as he stripped off his clothes and stepped into the shower. When he crawled naked between the sheets and drifted off to sleep, he had a certain singer on his mind.

Carol went to sleep with somebody on her mind as well. If what she thought just happened had actually occurred, it was an unexpected development, to say the least. But if fate was dealing her a hand called love, she was up for seeing how the game would play out.

Love was indeed in the air in another part of the house, too, where two lovers expressed their passion. The night was long on sex and short on conversation. Before dawn, one lover left the other and crept back to his room.

And eyes were watching.

19

Team Gabriella and the star arrived at the mall for the appearance being sponsored by San Francisco's power station, KMEL 106. It was chaos, as Troy had expected. Members of San Francisco's police force were helping to keep the crowd at bay from the temporary stage that had been erected in the parking lot. Plus, he'd subcontracted with two private companies. The extra security was helpful, but Troy wasn't totally reassured. He'd talked to Robert, and learned that his forensics contact hadn't been able to lift any unknown prints from the package. The postal workers', a hotel employee's, and Carol's were the only prints found. Which meant the person who sent the threatening package could be anyone, anywhere. Even here. He scanned the thousands of eager faces waiting to see Gabriella. Especially here.

"How are you feeling about this?" Gary asked, joining Troy at the edge of the stage where he was watching the stagehands set up and scanning the crowd.

"I'm confident in my men and the other security teams," was Troy's less-than-direct answer.

Gary was well aware of the potential dangers in his daughter performing outdoors, in front of this large crowd. Not only because of the recent threat, which he'd been told about the same day it occurred, but because on any given day some crazed person could target Gabriella. It was his singular constant worry, ranking way higher than say, her being in an automobile accident or falling off the stage. He remembered his touring days, and the lengths female fans would go in order to try and get close to the men in the group. And that was over thirty years ago. People were even crazier now.

"I don't see too much security, besides the officers," Gary said.

"Then that means my plan is working." At Gary's questioning glance, Troy stepped closer and kept his voice low. "The men are dressed to blend in with the crowd. Don't worry, Gary. I'm not going to let anything happen to your daughter."

Troy walked away. Gary stared after him for a long time.

"Don't try and pull me out on stage today." Troy was in Gabriella's dressing room. Tiana was putting on final makeup touches while a well-known hair stylist messed with Gabriella's thick curls.

"Why not? Aren't you my protector?" She flashed a coy smile and surreptitiously ran a freshly manicured toe up the leg of his jean.

Troy moved his leg. "Yes, which is why I'm not going to be a performer this afternoon. I'm serious; I need to keep focused."

"Dang, Troy. I was just playing. Don't get an attitude."

He stood abruptly. "I'll be right outside the door."

Carol came in as he left. "Whoa, what happened?"

Gabriella tipped back her head as the makeup artist placed liner under her eyes. "Why?"

"Troy just brushed past me looking like a storm cloud."

"Maybe he got his period," Gabriella said with a shrug.

Tiana and Li laughed. Carol, not so much. "Be ready to go on in ten minutes," she said, looking at her watch. "And remember, keep it to just the two songs. We still have to visit the hospital before catching the helicopter back to Oakland, and have to head straight to the detention center once we're there."

"Where are you going?"

"I want to talk with the stage manager before he does his final check of the stage, and make sure all of what you need is out there."

"Okay." Carol began walking to the door. "Carol," Gabriella called out. She turned. "I appreciate you, sis."

For the first time since entering the room, Carol smiled. "I know."

Fifteen minutes later, after air personalities from the radio station had further hyped up the already excited crowd, Gabriella took the stage.

"How y'all doing, San Francisco?!" She pranced from one side of the stage to the other, waving and blowing kisses, sporting five-inch Louboutin glitter booties and a tight white dress. "Ladies, where y'all at?" The females in attendance erupted. "Fellahs . . ." She shielded her eyes, looking out into the crowd. "Which one of y'all is my protector?" It sounded as though every man in the audience—and maybe some women as well—shouted out that it was them. For the next several minutes Gabriella sang and swayed and laughed and flirted, and basically placed everyone watching under her spell.

"P to the R to the O to the T . . .

"E to the C to the T to the O . . .

"'R' you going to still be my protector?!"

Gabriella walked to the edge of the stage, dropping to her knees as she questioned the crowd. Dozens of fans surged against the restraining fence, aching to touch their idol. One stout woman waved a bouquet of flowers while screaming, "Gabriella! I love you!" Others held up CDs, posters, and signed head shots of the beautiful singer. Hundreds held up cell phones to record the moment. All the while security heads moved back and forth, a hundred men trying to watch a crowd of thousands. No small feat, even for the most trained of men who were determined to make sure that nothing bad happened.

Until it did.

So quickly that Troy at first missed it; he had only turned his head away from the crowd for a split second, to better hear what one of the men from the back was reporting. He heard a creaking sound, and then screams. When he whirled back around it was to see the woman with the flowers climbing over a falling fence and heading straight for Gabriella. The female fan jumped and clung to the seven-foot-high platform, swinging her body up and rolling over as if she'd trained for Olympic-style gymnastics. Troy hurried to place his body between his charge and her admirer, feeling sharp fingernails rake across his face as he shielded Gabriella while rushing her off the stage. Because he left, he didn't see the ruckus that followed: dozens of security men trying to ward off hundreds of fans clamoring to get on stage, police officers surging forward with tear gas in hand, the radio organizers desperately pleading for peace, several zealous attendees being led away in handcuffs.

"What happened?" Gabriella cried, trying to see past Troy's shoulder as he hurdled her toward the limo.

"The fence broke."

"Well, fix it. I'm going to finish my set."

"You're done, Gabriella." He opened the car door. "Get in."

"I will not. Some of those people have waited for eight hours. I didn't even get through one song. I'm not leaving."

She tried to go around him.

Troy blocked her path. "You're not going back on that stage."

Gabriella's eyes narrowed as she took two steps to stand toe to toe with one of the country's finest guards. "I'm going back on stage and you're going to do your job to protect me!"

They both were quiet as a chant wafted back to them on the day's troubled winds. "Gabriella! Gabriella! Gabriella! More!"

Troy took a breath, trying to calm them both. "I understand that you want to please your fans. It's just not safe!"

"The world isn't safe, Troy. Where most of these people live is not safe. Do they have the choice to run and hide at the first sign of danger? Can they leave their troubled, gang-filled, poverty-stricken neighborhoods because someone tears down their security or destroys their peace? No, they have to stay and deal with it. And so will I!"

Troy watched as Gabriella's chest rose and fell with the passion with which she'd delivered these words. At this moment, she looked like an African princess, a warrior going to battle for her people. Later, he would realize that it was in this moment that he fell in love with her.

"You're bleeding." She reached up, cupped his chin, and turned his face to see the long, fresh scar, and the blood oozing out of it.

He gently took her hand away from his face. "It's nothing serious. I'll be all right."

"Maybe I should listen to you, and stay here."

"No, you're right. For some in this crowd, this will be the best memory of their lives. We're going to go back out there and make it a good one."

"Thank you, Troy."

"You're welcome." Troy looked at her, his heart melting at the trust and something else indefinable that shone in her eyes. Love maybe? *Naw, neither she nor I want any part of that emotion.* "Let's do this."

She nodded, the poignant moment gone, replaced by utmost professionalism and steely resolve. She turned to the police officers and other security who'd been standing a discreet distance away. "All right, fellas. Let's do this."

While Gabriella sang, Troy's eyes scanned the crowd even more furtively than before. His was probably the only pair of eyes not continually on the superstar. Thousands of other pairs could not look away. And one pair in particular never wavered from his muse, his heart-throb, the woman who made him love and hate her at the same time.

20

It was very late at night after a very trying day. Troy and Gary had been busy with the authorities and the security staff who'd been directly involved in the day's unrest. Alex and four other security personnel had accompanied Gabriella and a small team on their visit to the hospital. The time spent at the detention center had been cut from one hour to fifteen minutes. The team had wanted her to cancel altogether, but Gabriella had told them in no uncertain terms that not going was out of the question. After a grueling day that had lasted almost fourteen hours, Gabriella was tired, but still wound up from the day's events. She'd prepared for bed and then asked Carol to have the chef prepare a light snack. Ten minutes later in walked Troy, telling her to put on something comfy and follow him.

"Where are you taking me?"

"Come on, woman!" Troy stood there looking as sexy as sin, the long scratch left by the woman who'd rushed the stage giving him a dangerous air.

"I asked where we're going."

"And I said, throw something on and come with me."

"Look, it's been a long day and I'm not in the mood. Now go away."

When she continued to lounge on the bed, he took three long strides until he was standing over her. "I see what it is about you. You're used to always being in control, always getting your way. Right?"

"Pretty much."

"When is the last time you didn't get your way, when you had to do what someone else wanted, instead of what you planned?"

Gabriella made a real show of thinking about the question. She cocked her head and tapped her finger against her cheek. The next thing she knew she'd been swept off the bed, was in Troy's arms, and was headed out of the bedroom courtesy of his long strides. She was only wearing a thong and a tee.

"Boy, are you crazy?" she hissed. "You've got my ass out here in the hallway."

"I told you to put some clothes on."

"You wh—wait, stop!" she demanded, squirming as she whispered. Trying to dislodge herself from his hard grasp was like wrestling a tree. "This house is full of people. What if my father sees us?"

"Don't worry. I'd spread my hands over those juicy butt cheeks," he whispered against her ear. "Wouldn't want your daddy to see all of the junk in the trunk that you're working with."

They'd reached a set of steps that Gabriella hadn't noticed before, stairs that went up instead of down. She'd thought that they were on the top floor. There were squiggles in her stomach. She felt scared and excited at the same time. "Put me down!"

This said even as she wrapped her arms around his neck.

They reached the top of the stairway. Troy set her down, or rather slid her against his long, lean body until her feet reached the floor. By that time she barely felt her toes because Troy had lowered his head to hers and stuck that stiff, magical tongue that she loved so much into her surprised mouth. He sucked in her tongue, squeezed her butt, and ground himself against her. After a mind-blowing series of kisses, he opened the door to a rooftop retreat.

"Ooh, baby, this is beautiful!" Gabriella's eyes lit up like a child's at Christmas as she took in her surroundings: the way the lights of both Oakland and San Francisco twinkled in the distance and how the stars in the sky seemed close enough for her to reach out and touch. She looked to her right and noted a small table for two had been set up, boasting a single white candle, two small plates, two wineglasses, and a covered wicker basket in the center. A knitted throw was cast carelessly across the back of one of the bamboo folding chairs, and once her hearing strayed past the thump of her suddenly pounding heart, she picked up the strands of the latest love song from Gabriella's fellow Detroit native, Kem.

She was touched and moved and felt incredibly . . . vulnerable. Unfamiliar territory that she covered up at once.

"This is all well and good," she said, making strong strides toward the table while trying to ignore the feelings that scared her. "But what have you brought to eat. I'm starving!"

"Sit, my sweet," Troy replied, pulling the afghan off the chair as she sat and placing it over her lap. "I've got a delicacy that not even Chef, great cook that he is, could perfect upon."

Her look was clearly skeptical, but Gabriella was enjoying the unexpected experience.

"Gabriella Stone: worldwide superstar, successful businesswoman, and triple threat entertainer, I present to you"—Troy made a big show of reaching for the linen napkin over the wicker basket dominating the middle of the table as he spoke—"P, B, and J, baby!"

Stop. Hold the presses. What did he just say? She wheeled around. "I'm starving. We have a three-star Michelin chef under our roof . . . and you're over there looking smug about a peanut butter and jelly sandwich?" Her arms crossed as she awaited a response.

"Don't knock it until you try it," Troy easily countered, picking up one of the sandwich halves in the basket and placing it on her plate. He leaned toward her and whispered in a conspiratorial manner, "The peanut butter is extra crunchy, baby, and the jelly is grape!" He then rocked his body in a b-boy manner, turned an imaginary cap to the side, with a "know what I'm sayin'?" look on his face.

Gabriella burst out laughing. "You are a trip." She picked up the sandwich half and took a bite. She closed her eyes, chewed, and then took another. "It's probably 'cause I'm starving, but this really is good."

"Naw, girl. It's because that gourmet bite you just experienced was assembled by these here hands." He reached for the meal's "side dish," a fresh batch of kettle corn, and piled some onto both of their plates before popping a handful in his mouth. "I can't take credit for the popcorn though," he said with a mouthful. "That's straight up Ghirardelli Square right there!"

"Ha! You nut."

"Not yet." Troy's voice and gaze immediately shifted the course of conversation. "But soon."

Gabriella felt her coochie contract, but chose to ignore it. Being around Troy did many things; keeping her off kilter was one of them. But if she was going to have an on-going relationship with him, she deduced, she was going to have to change that. She was going to have to continue to hang around him, to tease and be teased, until she felt the type of camaraderie where her panties didn't get moist at the sound of his voice, or the mention of his name.

She pushed forward with her Keep-It-Social-Sistah agenda. "The way you're devouring that sandwich, I'd imagine that this brings back memories from your childhood."

"As a matter of fact, it does," Troy responded easily, taking the time to pour sparkling water into two crystal goblets. "As I was growing up, both my parents worked. I guess my brothers and I were what you refer to as latchkey kids. Both Michael and Gregory learned to cook, but I was too impatient. So whenever I was on my own, PB and J was my meal of choice. I took my time and honed my craft, making my take on this particular sandwich the best anyone has ever tasted." His look was both boyish and bold at the same time, questioning and confident, accompanied by a silly smile.

"I don't know about all that." Darn it if she could help it, but her smile was silly, too. "You grew up in Cali . . . right?"

"I did, but my story isn't what I want to talk about. I want to know yours." He leaned back and took a sip of sparkling water.

"Please. Everyone knows my story. Child performer,

girl group, solo sensation . . . and here I am!" She tried
to shift the direction of things by leaning forward and
popping a couple kernels of popcorn in Troy's mouth.

He took them, along with her fingers, chewed the
corn, licked her tips, and sat back as determined as ever
to keep the focus. "I don't want to know what everybody
else knows. I want to know the Gabriella that nobody
knows about."

"I'm not sure such a person exists."

"You may not be," Troy easily replied. "But I am."
They both took in the beauty of the stars before he took
a long look at her and spoke again. "You all right?" She
nodded. "Are you sure?"

"I'm fine." She pushed an errant kernel of corn
around the plate. "You know, sometimes I wish I could
just hang out with them, let them see that I'm a person,
human, just like they are. Then maybe they wouldn't go
so crazy when I'm around."

"That's just it, Gab. You're not just like them." He
swept his hands in front of him. "You're . . . this: mansions
and private jets and designer clothes and bodyguards.
That's what you have to remember. You also have to remember the main reason why I'm here—to protect you.
If I tell you not to go back out on stage, I expect you to
follow my instructions."

"I went back out and nothing happened."

"Not this time."

"They're the reason I get to do what I love," she said,
her voice soft and wistful. "I owe them so much."

"Maybe. But I'm here to make sure that you don't pay
with your life."

21

Troy's eyes darkened as he watched Gabriella's unconscious, nervous chewing of her bottom lip, before she reached a shaky hand for the goblet, and drank deeply. She belched—another act meant to lighten serious moments and then requested more of the carbonated drink. He ignored the crass action, refilled her glass . . . and waited.

Silence wrestled with stars to fill the night sky. Gabriella reached over for a handful of kettle corn, watching the strong forefinger that ran up and down Troy's goblet. A silent war was being waged and for both, for different reasons, the stakes were high.

"I don't want to talk about what happened today," she said at last.

"Good, me either. Let's talk about you."

"What do you want to know that you can't read about?"

"Let's see. For starters, when is the first time you ate peanut butter and jelly?"

"Would you believe me if I told you that this was the first time?"

"No."

She shrugged. "Well, you'd be wrong. Of course I know about them, but I'd never eaten this type of sandwich . . . until tonight."

"Get out of here!"

"True story," she said, with another shrug as she ate the kernels of corn. "Mom was never keen on any type of fast food, at least not that I can remember. I was entered into my first contest when I was two. I won it. After that, my appearance was always a concern. I can remember being five years old, wanting Cap'n Crunch or Fruity Pebbles cereal like my cousins ate, and instead being given oatmeal, bran flakes with raisins, or on occasion, scrambled eggs with a hint of cheese, served with toast and jam. Eating junk food—how she'd classify this sandwich—was a rare occurrence and never happened on my mother's watch. Sometimes, when my father was watching me, he'd give in to my whining and I'd experience the luxury of a Happy Meal."

"Oh, I bet Gary forever got your heart with that move."

"In a way," Gabriella said, laughing. "Though I must admit I was never crazy about the hamburgers. I preferred the fish sandwiches, with tomatoes instead of pickles and an extra slice of cheese."

"As a kid?"

"Yep."

"Weirdo."

"Ha! I know, right?"

"What about as you became older? Did you go to public school, or private? Did you know famous folk from the area, like any of the Winans, or Eminem?"

He watched as her face first showed, then just as quickly hid a second of sadness, vulnerability, some strand of emotion that made Troy want to gather her up, place her on his lap, and kiss the unwelcomed memories away.

But before he did that, he'd have to know them. So he pressed on, lightly, hoping she'd feel comfortable in sharing the obviously uncomfortable. "Wait, don't tell me. You were either the class smart nerd or the class clown."

"Neither." Her reply was soft, somewhat wistful. She pushed a few remaining kernels of corn around her plate. "School wasn't a good experience for me."

Troy's reply was soft yet firm. "In today's terms, I would have been classified as the school bully. Tell me who hurt you, and I'll kick his ass."

"I bet you would."

"Damn right, I would!"

"Just like you used to take up for your brother, the doctor."

He nodded. "Exactly."

"I was bullied, although it wasn't labeled that back in the day. Mom always made sure my clothes were top quality and my hair was on point. It's always been thick and, when I was a young girl, Mom would wash it, braid it, put me under the dryer and then let it loose. The result was this wild, Chaka Khan-like bush that I absolutely loved. But my hair got me into so much trouble."

"Because it's all yours."

She nodded. "The girls hated me. Had it not been for Carol, I wouldn't have gotten through that mess."

"She was at the same school?"

"Yep. She's always been there. I literally cannot remember my life without that girl by my side."

"So what happened in school? How did you overcome the girls who were against you?"

"I accidentally beat one up."

"How do you kick somebody's butt by accident?" Troy reached over for her arm and began stroking it. He was obviously enjoying the conversation.

"I know it sounds crazy, but it's really true!" Gabriella tried to ignore the sensations being created by Troy's strong fingers massaging her arm. Tried . . . and failed. She also failed to squelch the sadness that these memories conjured up.

Especially when Troy kept prodding. "What happened?"

"I barely remember. It was so long ago."

"I believe to the contrary. I get the feeling that you remember it very well, as if it just happened."

A look of unease sped across her face. "A group of girls surrounded me after school. The leader, a big, chunky girl named Nita, rushed me. I didn't fight her, just reacted."

"How?"

"I swung my book bag and knocked out her front tooth."

"Ha! You went gangster on that bully!" Troy chuckled again.

"It's not funny!" Gabriella hissed, batting back tears. "The girl had eight siblings and a gaggle of cousins. Their harassing phone calls were relentless, their threats constant. Mom finally had to pull me out of school."

"I'm sorry."

"I understand why they did it. In their eyes, I had everything they didn't—new clothes, a nice home, a two-parent family that adored me. I had someone telling me I was beautiful from the day I was born, that I could go anywhere and do anything. A lot of them didn't."

"That's why you mentor girls, and go to the jails and detention homes?"

"Yes. I want them to know that if nobody else believes in them . . . I do. I'm where I am today because someone believed in me."

"What happened to those girls who jumped you?"

"I hear Nita ended up joining a gang and doing time; not sure about the others. After that incident I was taught from home. I loved going to school, though," she whispered, after a moment's thought. "It was the last time I felt . . . you know . . . normal."

Troy studied the wistful look on Gabriella's face. Her got-it-all-together mask had slipped. For the first time, he caught a glimpse of what the flip side of her life had been. Something seeped inside his heart—a desire to protect her, shield her, and make her smile again. "Come here."

Gabriella finished her sandwich, grabbed her goblet of water, and walked to Troy's side of the table. He watched the relief rise in her eyes, the thought that he'd use his masculine wiles to take her away from a place best forgotten.

He had other plans. He wanted her to embrace what had happened and then forgive herself. Only then, he believed, would she truly have overcome the experience and be completely free from its lingering effects.

"Our past prepares us for our future. One that's safe, because I'm in it."

"Really? For how long?"

He shrugged. "For now."

She got ready to straddle his legs, but he redirected her to sit down in his lap, snuggled securely against his chest, wrapped in his arms. He reached over for the afghan, and covered them with it. Together they watched the stars, and listened to each other's heartbeat. Every now and then he'd squeeze her, or press his lips to her temple. There was no fervent tongue kissing, no rubbing of one's flesh against the other, no penetration. And it was also one of the most intimate moments Gabriella had ever known.

Downstairs, one of the house residents was seething. Had he known that the two people up on the roof were just talking after sharing a simple meal, maybe he wouldn't have been so angry. But he imagined writhing naked bodies—cool breezes blowing over hot skin. He imagined Gabriella's face, with eyes closed and jaw slack from Troy's relentless thrusts of passion. He thought of their lovemaking and hardened, cursing his weak flesh.

Reaching down, he idly stroked himself, thinking about what it would be like to be with her, to be inside her. And knowing that he really wouldn't be satisfied until that question was answered.

22

After a whirlwind trip to Oakland, the crew was back in LA. The day was beautiful, and Gabriella planned to enjoy it by doing one of her favorite things: nothing. With the Vegas leg of the tour coming up, a busy one that along with hospital and detention home visits also included a photo shoot in the Grand Canyon, she planned to take advantage of this down time and do absolutely nothing at all. She'd given everyone the day off, including Troy, and planned to just hang out and chill with fam. Even the chef had been given a reprieve as Gary promised to dust off his grilling skills and BBQ a slab of ribs. That would happen later, though, and her stomach was growling right now. So she left her room at the Stone estate and moseyed downstairs.

On the way, she took her time and admired the grandiose home her parents had purchased. It was too formal for her tastes, but suited her mother to a tee. Yvonne had sacrificed a lot for her and her brother, including her own dreams of a career in broadcast journalism. One of the blessings of being a successful pop star was that her mother could afford the life she surely deserved, and have all the material things she wanted. That it was a Mediterranean-style villa with vaulted ceilings, inlaid gold, and winding staircases was fine with Gabriella. As long as it made her mother happy.

She reached the first floor and headed toward the kitchen. But after hearing the strains of straight ahead jazz coming from the study in the opposite direction, she delayed her meal once more. Growing up, she used to sit with her father and listen to him dissect the skills of Charlie Parker, Thelonious Monk, Jay McShann, and others. "This here is real music, baby," Gary would tell her, often while she sat on his lap, imitating how he bobbed his head to the beat.

"Realer than yours, Daddy?" Gabriella would ask.

"Yes, baby. Even more real than mine."

She smiled as she reached the room, glad that the family had decided to hang out alone. Times with just the four of them were very rare. It was going to be a good day.

"Daddy, I could hear that music clear down the—oh—I thought Dad was in here."

Gary's assistant, Chauncey, looked up from the book he was reading. "Sorry to disappoint you."

"Did he just step away for a moment, or what?"

"No, he's in the gym. Gave me the afternoon off. I'm waiting to hear from a friend of mine, and he said I could listen to a few of his CDs while waiting for the call."

Gabriella almost turned to leave the room, but words from a previous conversation with Carol drifted into her head. "Have you talked to him? Or did you make a judgment based on looks? He seems really nice, Gabriella, and his father just died. Please be nice."

She took a step toward the stack of CDs on the coffee table. "So you like traditional jazz, huh?"

"Yes. Besides gospel and classical, it's the only music I listen to. No offense," he hurriedly added.

"What, you don't like pop, hip-hop, or R and B?"

"Not really," Chauncey admitted, with a shake of his head. "Some of the melodies are nice enough, but I like music that inspires me to do better, to be a better person. Most of the music on the radio nowadays doesn't do that for me."

"I guess to each his own."

"I guess."

Gabriella continued scanning the CD covers while wondering what Carol thought was so nice about someone so judgmental. But she hadn't gotten to the top of the charts by giving up early, so she persisted, determined to be nice, as her bestie had suggested.

"What are you reading?" she asked, with a nod toward the book that he held in his hands.

"*Deliver Us From Evil,*" he answered, looking her straight in the eye. "By Sean Hannity."

"Who's that?"

"You don't know Sean Hannity?"

Gabriella shook her head. "I don't read much."

"Or watch TV, I presume. He's one of the leading commentators on Fox News."

"That's a conservative news station, correct?"

"Yes."

"Are you a conservative?"

"Absolutely."

"And you believe you need to be delivered from evil?"

"The world is evil. If you'd watch the news you'd know."

"Do you believe my music is evil?"

Chauncey looked down at the book. "Naw."

"Good, because it's not." Gabriella placed down the CDs she held. "I'll see you later." She headed toward the door and then stopped just inside it. "I have one more question," she said, while turning around. "If you don't like my kind of music, why are you working for my father?"

Chauncey placed down the book and looked Gabriella in the eye. "My father spoke highly of yours, said how when he and my mom were getting ready to lose their home, Gary loaned him the money to stave off foreclosure. Knowing how precarious the auto industry was, he gave my dad plenty of time to pay him back. When Dad died, I sent a note to your father to thank him for his generous actions. He contacted me and offered me a job. My father and I were very close. And my dad was close with Gary. So in a way, I guess I'm trying to pay back your father by working exceptionally and being the best. And, in a way, it also helps me stay close to my dad."

"That's very special, Chauncey." For the first time, Gabriella saw the humanity that she imagined Carol had noticed. "Daddy seems to be pleased with your work. Sorry for your loss."

"Thank you."

"Good-bye."

"Good-bye."

Gabriella was walking across the large foyer area that connected the various wings. She was almost to the hallway that led to the kitchen when a wad of paper hit her upside the head. She didn't even have to look up to know who it was. "Stop acting like my baby brother," she said with false hostility. Another zinger hit her in the back of the head. "You're stupid!"

"Babby!" Garrett raced down the stairs and caught up with her, wrapping his arms around her before placing her in a headlock. "It's Babby!"

Gabriella laughed at the name Garrett had called her until he was five. Since everyone called him "the baby," he thought that Gabriella was "the babby." No matter how they emphasized the "g" sound, he refused to budge from his own pet name until he was good and ready.

They walked arm in arm into the kitchen. "Did you go out last night?" she asked.

"Yeah. Me and my posse hit up this little party in Hollywood."

Gabriella gave him a look. "You don't do little parties."

"Well, you know, small by my standards." He popped a nonexistent collar and walked to the fridge. "Where's Chef?"

"He has the day off. Daddy's cooking."

"What the hell?"

"Ha! I know, right? Mama thought we could use some quality family time. So Dad's grilling, and she's making the side dishes."

"You mean I have to eat cereal for breakfast?"

"Unless you want me to cook for you."

"In that case, Corn Flakes here I come!"

The siblings talked, the morning passed, and by the afternoon Gary, Yvonne, Gabriella, and Garrett were enjoying a homemade feast of ribs, chicken, potato salad, and coleslaw. They were also enjoying each other.

Gary finished off a rib, then sat back and wiped his hands and face with a napkin. "Man, whoever barbequed these ribs knows his business. They are fiery, flavorful, and falling off the bone!"

"They are good," Gabriella agreed, dropping a clean

bone in the bowl that had been placed there for that purpose. "Partly skill, but also, probably, partly luck. So don't let it go to your head."

Yvonne used a knife and fork to cut her meat. "The chicken is good, too, Gary."

"Everything is good." Garrett pulled out his cell phone and began to text.

"Really, Garrett? You're going to text on your phone to someone on the other side of the city or the country instead of talking with the people on the other side of the table? And get sauce on your phone?" Yvonne reached for her tea as she looked at Gary. "Kids these days."

"Stow the phone, son," Gary said. "This is family time."

"Y'all killing me," Garrett groaned. "I need to handle my business."

Gabriella chuckled, completely unconvinced. "What business is that?"

"Business with Michael Morgan, one of the country's premier sport agents."

This got everyone's attention around the table, especially Gary's, whose managerial hat slipped on faster than you could say "signing bonus." "What kind of business do you have with him? I hope you're not talking to him without your own representation present—namely me—as well as legal counsel."

The comment had stirred Gabriella's interest, too, namely because it made her think of Troy and what would happen if things didn't work out and Garrett was working with his brother. She'd never deny Garrett the best in his field, but having a Morgan in his life if there wasn't one in hers would not feel good. And the thought of Troy not being around, or even not being around often, didn't feel good . . . at all.

Time to change the subject. "Garrett has always fancied himself the businessman. Daddy, remember when he made himself a middle man and was charging his friends to talk to you?"

Yvonne laughed. "Who could forget that foolishness?"

"I couldn't believe it." Gary smiled, warming at the memory of his entrepreneurial then twelve-year-old son. "I'd always been available to give kids advice about the music business and point them in the right direction in starting a career. All of a sudden I'm not talking to very many of Garrett's friends and since none of them had moved or become the next teen wonder, I thought that strange. Then one day, after . . . what was his name, Garrett?"

"We called him Dirty Dee."

"His real name is Duane," Yvonne offered.

"Yes, Duane! Duane came over to the house and asked to talk to me. That in itself wasn't unusual, but when he pulled out a notepad of questions and began writing the answers, I knew something was up. I have to give it to you, Garrett, you trained him well. The only explanation he provided to my question of his note-taking was that he wanted to remember everything I said."

"Not that writing things down had been part of the information contained in Gary's 'consultation' "—Yvonne used air quotes. "That advice had come from you, along with access to your manager father, for a mere ten dollars. I think that's when we recognized his athletic ability, right, Gary?"

"Him getting out of the house because he thought a whipping was coming was the fastest I'd ever seen him run!" Gary reached for another rib.

The family laughed.

"Whatever," Garrett mumbled, though it was clear that he was enjoying the attention. "I'm always going to be an entrepreneur. Already have an idea for how to capitalize once I turn pro."

Gary turned serious. "I often wear my manager hat more than my father one. And while I don't say this enough, I feel it every day. I'm very proud of both of you. Yes, y'all have put a gray hair or two where there didn't used to be one, but both of you have followed my and Yvonne's advice of setting high goals and then achieving them through dedication, hard work, and belief. Sure, I've guided your career, Gab, but you are the one who developed a brand that makes every man want to be with you and every woman want to be you."

"Bullshit," Garrett said, jokingly covering the word with a cough.

"Don't hate the player," Gabriella said, giving Garrett a playful shove. "Hate the game."

"Like your sister, Garrett, you've set your sights on being a top running back—"

"*The* top running back," Garrett corrected.

"The top running back in the NFL. I have no doubt that you'll achieve that goal. So know that not only do I love you guys, but I feel blessed to be your father, and I'm sure Yvonne feels like the luckiest woman in the world to be your mom."

"Dang, Dad, you sound like a Hallmark card!" Garrett joked to lighten the mood as Gabriella batted away tears.

"It's all love in the club," Yvonne added, clearly moved by Gary's words. She looked at him. "I guess we didn't do too bad, huh?"

Gary returned her smile. "For two people who didn't know the first thing about parenting when we brought the babies home, I think we did all right." He looked at his children. "And if y'all keep doing what you're doing, I see major success in both of your futures for years to come."

Gary may have seen a long, bright future for Gabriella, but at the exact moment that the family enjoyed their spontaneous love fest, there was someone somewhere else also thinking about Gabriella, and making very different plans.

23

The Stone family was still sharing stories around the dining room table when Gabriella's cell rang.

"Excuse me, family, but I've got to take this." She jumped up from the table before anyone could object and walked quickly to the sliding glass doors. "Hey," she said, quickly closing the doors behind her and walking over to a chaise in the shade. "What are you doing?"

"Thinking about you," was Troy's reply. "Are you enjoying a day without me?"

"Actually, I am."

"Ouch!"

"No, I don't mean it like that. You know I enjoy your company. But it's rarely just the four of us and for the last several hours it's just been my brother, my parents, and me." She gave a quick recap of their day, including what had been a delicious home-cooked meal. "What about you?" she said when finished. "What are you doing?"

"About to do a little family time myself. I'm on my way over to my mother's house."

"Tell Mrs. Morgan I said hello."

"She said to call her Jackie."

"I know, but considering how I was raised, that's hard to do."

"I hear you. So what are your plans for the evening?"

"I really don't have any. Why? Are you missing me like I'm missing you?"

"I'm missing that wet, tight coochie, that's what I'm missing!"

"Gee, thanks, Troy. Way to make me feel like a piece of meat."

"Oh, do you expect me to believe that you're missing my winning conversation and not this big dick?"

"Man, please. If you came over here right now, you wouldn't have to say a word!"

"Ha! Just make it do what it do, huh?"

"Exactly!"

"Do you really want me to come over? Oh, hold on, Gabriella, this is Alex. On second thought, let me call you back."

"Okay."

It was a beautiful day, and in the shade the temperature was perfect. So Gabriella shifted to her side, closed her eyes, and within minutes this nonstop moving diva, who'd done ten shows in three cities in just over a week, was getting some well-deserved sleep.

Troy clicked over. "Hey, Alex. What's up?"

There was a brief pause before an answer came through Troy's car speakers. "Hey, Troy. Look, I wanted to tell you something before you heard it on the streets."

Troy frowned, both because of a nonattentive LA

driver who'd just cut him off and at the fact that he didn't like the tone in his friend's voice. "What's that?"

"I've got a new gig, man. Beginning next week, I'm guarding Mr. President."

"Mr. President as in Marlon Simmons?"

"The one and only."

Troy was silent for several seconds, digesting this news. There was only one reason that he could think of for why the man he'd known for more than ten years would leave his company. But not wanting to assume, he pressed on. "What's going on, Alex? Talk to me, man."

"I got a better offer, plain and simple."

"A better offer, huh? I wasn't aware that you weren't happy with what you were being paid."

"Sometimes you don't know what you don't know."

"You do realize you're leaving the company at the worst possible moment—while we're guarding the number one pop and R and B sensation in the world who just happens to be receiving very threatening correspondence, and just before the start of a grueling overseas leg?"

Troy asked this question, but knew that Alex was more than well aware of the situation. He'd been the one who'd retrieved the maliciously typed letters that had arrived at the San Francisco hotel where Gabriella was supposed to have stayed, and the one who just days ago found threatening comments on the Internet. Troy hadn't even allowed himself to think about what could have occurred had he not switched them to a private, secluded residence.

"Sorry, man. Can't be helped."

Troy didn't think he sounded sorry at all. He decided to test the theory. "Okay, I'll tell you what. Whatever Marlon is paying you, I'll match it, plus twenty percent."

Troy heard Alex sigh before saying, "I've already committed to making this move."

"What about the commitment you made to Morgan Security? What about the two-week notice that's required before leaving your post?"

"Guess you'll have to take it out of my last paycheck, dog. My decision is final."

"But you hate working with rappers!"

Silence underscored Alex's last sentence. He was done.

Now it was Troy's turn to take a calming breath. Putting himself into his friend's shoes, as his mother would have suggested, caused his heart to soften and his frown to skate away. "I know this is about Gabriella, man," he said, his tone totally different than seconds before. "Maybe if the tables were turned I'd do the same thing. But we've known each other a long time, since college. We've been through a lot.

"When I signed the contract to work with the Stone Cold Sexy tour, hooking up with Gabriella was the last thing on my mind. After meeting her I was even more sure of that. But something happened, Al, and it's not just about what's between her legs. It's about what's between her ears. We connected on a mental level and after our unplanned first encounter, I couldn't walk away."

"Well . . . I can. And don't worry. No matter how you're dropped you always seem to land on your feet. You'll be all right."

"I know I'll manage, but you're the number two man. There's nothing I can say to make you change your mind, or delay leaving until we get settled in Europe?"

"I wish you two the best."

They said their good-byes and, like Alex, Troy wasted no time in moving on. He tapped a name on the screen of

someone he trusted as much as his blood brothers. He
wasn't as skilled as Alex, but he'd be as loyal as a canine.
Trust couldn't be taught. Defense skills could be learned.

"Curtis, it's Troy. Clear your schedule tonight from
eight to ten. I need to meet with you."

Alex stood looking out over the Pacific Ocean. After
enjoying a drive with a coastal view, he'd stopped in
Redondo Beach for a bite to eat and to settle his nerves.
He'd grown up in Philly, and on his very first trip to the
City of Angels he'd fallen in love with the deep blue sea.
It could calm him faster than a heartfelt hug, and better
than a drink. He took a deep inhalation of sea air, exhal-
ing ten years of friendship along with his breath.

*I didn't want to leave you hanging, bro, but really,
what choice did I have? You got with the woman I wanted,
then threw that shit in my face. And I was supposed to
stick around like that shit didn't matter? Like I was the
Tin Man without a heart?*

He did have a heart though, evidenced by the next
person he called. "Carol, what's up? It's Alex. You got a
minute? I need to tell you something."

24

"Yo, Mom!" Troy had stepped to his mother's front door and, finding it unlocked, had walked inside. After the conversation he'd just had with Alex, he was more than ready to spend time with his favorite woman in the world. He crossed over to the near life-sized image of his late father, Mr. Samuel Morgan, and as the sons always did, offered a silent hello.

It was an act that had started out as a joke soon after Jackie received the life-sized and very lifelike portrait of her late husband, created by a dear friend shortly after his passing. It was painted from a picture taken after Michael's junior high graduation, one of the few times their blue-collar dad had donned a suit. He was smiling and looking important, his eyes twinkling at something Jackie had said.

"Dang, Mama," Troy had commented, the first time he'd seen Sam's prominent position over the fireplace mantel in Jackie's new home. "Having his picture here makes it feel as though he's in the room."

"He is," his mother had commented. "Aren't you, Sam?"

Whether by coincidence or divine intervention, a vase had fallen off the fireplace mantel, below where the picture hung. While it had landed on the marble hearth surrounding the fireplace, the delicate vase—a gift to Jackie from Sam that had included two dozen roses—hadn't broken. From then on it was a given: Sam was there, and wanted to be acknowledged.

Jackie found Troy enjoying a moment with his father as she rounded the corner into the living room. "Troy! What are you doing here?"

"What do you mean, 'what am I doing here'?" he asked, grabbing his mother around the waist and spinning her around before gently setting her back on the floor. "Didn't you invite me over?"

"Yes, but I said a late lunch. You're early. Not that I mind." She kissed his cheek. "Come on back to the kitchen. Since you're here, I might as well put you to work."

They bypassed the dining area, suffused in scent by a gynormous bouquet of flowers.

"Robert is stepping up his game I see," Troy said in a teasing tone. "Where is he, anyway?"

"At the gym," Jackie replied.

Troy stopped in his tracks. "The gym?"

Surely, he'd misunderstood. There was no way his mother could have alluded to a workout location. The Robert he knew hadn't worked up a sweat since chasing down a burglary suspect five years ago, then almost having a heart attack in front of the Kentucky Fried Chicken food chain where the criminal was finally caught. This was three years before Troy introduced Robert to Jackie. He wondered if Robert had told her about the incident that the two men had later laughed about.

"He's started working out." Jackie's response was

calm as she reached into the refrigerator and took out cuts of chicken marinating in a Chinese-spice-infused liquid.

"Since when?" Troy was genuinely confused.

Jackie nodded toward the huge bouquet sitting on the table. "Since that." At her son's continued bewildered expression, she walked into the living room and over to the stereo. "And since this."

She pushed the button. The smooth R and B sounds of a soulfully skilled singer oozed into the room. One of his surprise hits, a B-side single that rivaled Teddy Pendergrass's "Turn Off the Lights," Marvin Gaye's "Let's Get It On," and Boyz II Men's "I'll Make Love to You," Gary Stone's flawlessly delivered melody pulsated from the stereo, feeling intrusive and sexy and scandalous all at the same time.

> *The other men better get in line,*
> *Because it's just a matter of time,*
> *That the love in our hearts will shine . . .*
> *And that's because I've got to make you mine!*

Suddenly everything made sense: his mother's exuberance, Robert hitting a gym that was probably hitting him back, and Gary's suddenly becoming more personable in the past week. Troy had thought Gary's change of attitude was because of how good he and Gabriella were covering their lover's tracks. Now he was finding out that it was because Gabriella's father was trying to become his mother's lover!

Did Gary think his ass was Prince or what?

Troy walked over to the floral arrangement. "Gary sent you all this?"

"And a pair of diamond drop earrings. But Robert would go into cardiac arrest if he knew that; and as hard as he's been working out, I'm already worried about his high blood pressure. I want you to return them for me." She walked into her bedroom and came out with a small blue box.

"Damn, Mom! What's going on here?"

Jackie shrugged, and Troy blinked twice. Hard. If he didn't know his mother better he would have sworn he saw a blush and a coy smile going on. But that would have been impossible. This was his mother! Sheesh!

After recovering his equilibrium, he walked back into the kitchen. "Please say that nothing's happening. I don't have to school you on the reasons for these extravagant gifts."

Jackie placed down the spoon that she was using to marinate the meat and straightened to her full height of five-foot-seven. That it paled in comparison to Troy's six-foot-four made her no less small, considering the expression on her face. "No one has to school me in anything, boy. Least of all you."

"You're playing the mommy card," Troy countered smoothly. "I understand that. I respect that. But let me throw the son card into the deck. I'm the one who introduced you to Robert. I'm the one who introduced you to Gary. For the record, I wouldn't have done so, wouldn't have given it a moment's consideration, if I thought that meeting your teenage heartthrob would lead to friction between you and your man friend. Is that what's up?"

Sighing, Jackie finished dressing the chickens, placed them in a roasting pan alongside carrots, potatoes, pearl onions, and Brussels sprouts, and put the pan into the oven. "I didn't ask Gary to send anything," she said at last.

"How did he get your address?"

"Probably wasn't hard. I'm listed. At first I assumed that you'd given it to him—"

"Me?" Troy squealed as though he'd been shot.

"That's what made sense. At first. When I received the flowers. I called you last week, but didn't get an answer, or a callback."

Troy remembered receiving a message from his mother, and texting her that he'd call her on his first day off. That day, however, Gabriella had made him forget about anything not related to her. "And then?"

"Then, a couple days later, I received the CD along with the jewelry. Every time, I hoped that there would be a return address or a phone number accompanying Gary's cards. But there wasn't." Jackie reached for the wild rice that would accompany the chicken dish. "Robert's a good man," she finished. "I would do nothing to disrespect him. But . . ."

Troy frowned. "But what?"

"But I'd be lying if I said that receiving flowers and gifts didn't make me feel good. Any woman would."

"What's that mean exactly?"

The doorbell rang, saving Jackie from having to provide an immediate answer. Soon Troy's brother Gregory, and his wife, Anise, entered the home, followed just minutes later by the eldest, Michael, and Shayna, his sports star wife. Robert returned, too, and headed straight for a date with a scalding hot shower. When he joined them at the table he looked refreshed and, Troy noticed, a bit more slender around the middle. Conversation regarding old school heartthrobs was replaced by that concerning present-day successes.

Anise wiped her mouth after a succulent bite, and took

a swallow of sweet tea. "Troy, I can't thank you enough for the tickets to Gabriella's Vegas concert you gave us to auction off along with my latest painting, *Melody*. It has proved a perfect pairing. We've received some of the highest bids ever offered for a noncelebrity artist such as myself, and because of Gabriella's stature have garnered more media coverage than in the two years past and probably five in the future."

"No worries, Spice," he responded, using the nickname he'd given her shortly after she became his brother's wife. "I've learned that a certain amount of an artist's budget is set aside for charitable donations. It's the least she could do."

"Still, she didn't have to. And I appreciate it."

"I'll be sure and let her know."

Anise's husband, Gregory, placed a surreptitious hand on his wife's leg before addressing his sis-in-law. "How's your collection coming, Shayna?"

Since being invited to show her upscale sportswear collection at Bryant Park's Fashion Week in the coming fall, Shayna's and Michael's already busy schedule had whirled out of control. "There's still a lot to do," she admitted, sitting back as if weighted down by the revelation. "I meet with Choice next week, and then we'll head to Bejing to meet a premiere fabric designer."

"She's the fabric designer?" Jackie inquired.

"No, the fashion designer," Michael corrected. "Chai Fashions, Mom. She designed that knit suit I gave you for Christmas last year."

"What's the difference?" Robert asked, cutting the fork-tender chicken breast and relishing a bite. "Fashion designer, fabric designer . . . it's all about clothes, right?"

"Don't try and explain it," Jackie cut in, placing a

placating hand on Robert's arm. "If it isn't denim, khaki, or cotton, he won't understand."

"I tell you what I don't understand." Until now, middle son Gregory had been paying more attention to the meat and vegetables than anything else. Now, after taking a long swallow of tea, he spoke. "I don't understand why I haven't heard you wax poetic about conquering Gabriella, and how she too has succumbed to your irresistible charm."

Michael reared back. "Come to think of it, you're right, brother." He eyed Troy with keen interest. "Any other time we would have already heard the inflated stories of how whipped you had the girl. Being closemouthed about your conquests is unusual. What's going on?"

"Nothing." Too bad his expression didn't back up the answer. He couldn't have kept the grin from his face if he wanted to.

"Doesn't look like nothing," Jackie observed. "She's a very pretty girl."

"And talented," Gregory added.

"And rich," Michael finished. "Don't leave that out."

Troy pushed away his plate. "None of that matters to me."

"Wait," Jackie said, a scowl suddenly appearing. "What happened to the lawyer girl? The prosecutor?"

"Oh, man." Gregory reared back in his seat and placed an affectionate hand on his wife's shoulder. "I totally forgot about her."

"How quickly we forget," Anise drawled.

"Life moves fast around here, sis," Michael said.

Shayna cut Michael a look. "Don't let it move too fast."

"Only thing moving fast between us, baby girl, is your

fine self around a track." He sealed the declaration with
a kiss.

"I owe her a phone call," Troy said, while trying not to
squirm.

"You sure do." Shayna reached for her water glass.
"The one and only time we met, I liked her. She seems
like good people."

Troy sighed. "She is."

Jackie's eyes narrowed. "Y'all dated for a few months
and she's met part of your family. I don't care about these
twenty-first-century rules you kids have adopted. If
you're going to break up with that girl, the least you can
do while letting her go is look her in the eye."

After a few more moments of grilling, Troy asked
Anise and Shayna which one of them was going to make
Jackie a grandmother. This got him off the hot seat. At
least for the moment. But he knew that once it was re-
vealed that he'd dumped Delores and chosen Gabriella,
he'd be in hot water again!

25

"Hello, Troy."

Not "baby," "handsome," or "lover," Troy noted, names Dee commonly used when he rang her phone like he did now, mere moments from leaving Jackie's home. Not a good sign.

"Hey, Dee."

Had he been a mind reader, which he wasn't, he would have known that her thoughts resembled his to a tee. No "sexy," "beautiful," or "baby girl" happening today.

Something serious was about to go down.

"I see you've been busy," she said at last.

Troy could tell that she'd put the call on speaker. He was hands-free as well, driving from Long Beach toward his home in Leimert Park, and hoping to see Dee before arriving there. "I know I should have returned your calls earlier. I'm sorry for being MIA these past few weeks."

"With someone as lovely as Gabriella the superstar as your client? I'm hardly surprised to have been kicked to the curb. Though I do appreciate your call now. It shows home training."

Troy didn't necessarily like being reminded that this particular moment of "home training" had been prompted by the woman who'd conducted the school. "Working with a worldwide talent has been all-consuming, as I'm sure you can imagine."

"Oh, since I heard about your newest client, I've imagined all sorts of things."

Ignoring that pointed statement, Troy plowed on. "So . . . what are you doing right now?"

"What's it to you?"

She's not going to make this easy, Troy thought with a sigh. Then, he could almost hear his mother's voice asking, "Why should she?"

"I'm in town for only a day. Thought I'd see if we could meet for a drink."

"Why don't we share a meal and call it 'the last supper'?"

"Huh?"

"Just stop with the bullshit, Troy. You're not stupid and neither am I. So let's not tarnish some pretty cool memories by insulting my intelligence." When he continued to be silent, she continued. "I attended the Gabriella concert here in LA, Troy, and caught your act."

He wanted to tell her that that act had been spontaneous, as much a surprise to him as it was to the audience who witnessed it. But knowing this truth would come off as the bullshit Dee was trying to avoid, he remained silent.

After a long pause, Dee said, "I hope it works out for you."

"I never meant to hurt you, Delores. You're a good woman. Some man will be lucky to have you."

"I'm so damned tired of being the good woman that

some man will be proud or lucky to have. I've had this speech delivered to me too many times from a man who then turned his back and walked into someone else's arms."

Troy found himself in a rare position—one where he was uncomfortable and not in control. "Let's just meet for dinner, or a drink at least."

"Why? Do you think ending the relationship or whatever it was that existed between us will feel better in person? Will it help ease your guilt in moving on from me without a backward glance? Don't answer that." He heard her sigh. "I'm really not mad at you, Troy. Really, I'm not. Who can blame you for being head over heels infatuated by someone *People* magazine calls the sexiest female alive?"

"I've got a job to do. . . ."

"Shut up, Troy. If you think I'm going to believe that a man who loves sex as much as you do hasn't hit that pretty punanny, then either you don't think that I'm bright or you're not that smart." When he didn't refute her statement, she continued. "For the record, you never promised me anything, never led me on to believe we had a definite future. Did I get my hopes up the longer we dated? You bet. But were my optimistic feelings your fault? No. You never promised me a white picket fence and two point five kids."

"Dee, can we finish this conversation in person?"

"Since it sounds like your swan song, your *sayonara,* your see-you-later-bye, I think this phone call will do just fine. This is good-bye, right?" she asked, after a slight hesitation. "Not that I believe my instincts are wrong, but just so that I'm left with no doubt as to assumption."

"Like I said, you're good people, Dee. I like you. Perhaps we can remain friends."

"That doesn't work for me. I know you mean well and I harbor no hate in my heart for you, but being your pal is not in the cards. I spend my life surrounded by male colleagues. I'm not looking for another friend."

"Okay. I can respect that. So . . . I guess this is good-bye, then."

"Take it easy, Troy."

"You, too."

Delores "Dee" Atchison wasn't the only one wondering about Troy's relationship status. Gary and Carol sat in the media room enjoying one of their favorite pastimes, NBA basketball. With Garrett enveloped in football and Gabriella caring less about sports than a homeless man for high thread-count sheets Carol, who for Gary was like a second daughter, had been the one with whom he shared this particular passion. Today, they'd screamed and cajoled and willed their choice through game four of the play-offs. Now, in the fourth quarter with only seconds left and their team enjoying a ten-point lead, Gary was ready to chat.

"Where's Gab?"

"Upstairs, getting a spa treatment," Carol replied, her eyes still glued to the large, flat-screen TV. After Alex's unexpected announcement and the long conversation that followed, Carol welcomed the diversion.

"Where's Troy?"

"I don't know." She gave him a side-eye. "He's not the one giving the massage, if that's what you're asking."

"What do you think about him?"

Carol shrugged. "He's fine."

"I'm sure every woman thinks that, but what about professionally?"

"Oh my God, Gary, that was so whack."

"Ha! Okay, I'll admit it. I understood what you meant." He turned to watch the final ten-second countdown, then reached for the remote to mute the TV. "How are he and Gab getting along?"

"You probably need to ask your daughter that question."

"I will, but right now I'm asking you."

"He takes his job seriously, from what I've seen. His men seem to respect him. And so does Gab, which is a rare thing among those we employ. I think she appreciates having a man around her who's determined to do his job to the best of his ability. And who isn't intimidated by her demanding personality."

"His right-hand man, Alex, seems like a good guy."

Carol remained silent, choosing to let Troy be the one to share the latest development within Team Gabriella.

"Handsome, too." Again, the side-eye, but Carol didn't respond. She'd known this man since she was a child and was used to being pumped for information. She'd also become very adept at engaging in conversation without revealing anything. "So far I'm pleased with Morgan Security," Gary continued. "But the true test will come week after next, when we head to Europe and Asia. Staying primarily in hotels instead of houses will require Troy and Gabriella to occupy the same suite of rooms."

"Why do you think that will be a test? Troy will ensure her safety from aggressive paparazzi and zealous fans."

"It's not somebody from the public getting to Gab that

I'm worried about. It's the dog who may be on the prowl right under our roof."

"Gab's a grown woman, Gary. I think she can take care of herself."

"Yes. I'm afraid of that, too."

Troy sat in his living room talking to a young man whom at Robert's request he was mentoring and the one currently house-sitting while he was on the road. They'd just finished watching the play-off game and were chilling with bottles of beer when Troy's cell phone rang.

He put the call on speakerphone. "What's up, Curt." During his earlier conversation with Curtis, he'd asked him to go over and check on the Stone estate before they met later that night. "Where are you?"

"I'm still here."

"At the Stone location?"

"Yes."

"Is everything all right?"

"Not sure. But I think you need to get back here."

Troy's body was on immediate alert. He put down the beer and picked up the phone. "What's going on?"

"I just saw some suspicious activity on the camera mounted to the gate by the alley. I want to check it out, but don't want to leave the house unguarded."

"Where is she?"

Both men knew who Troy was talking about. "She's safe; Carol said that she was in her room getting a massage or some type of spa treatment."

This bit of information brought visions to mind—

images of the hot body he'd missed when Gabriella decided to spend her last night in California at her mother's house, and Troy felt it best to handle his business and see his own family.

"Where's Gary?"

"In the theater room with Carol, watching the game."

"Who else is there?" Curtis told him. "Okay, give me thirty minutes to wrap things up here. Meantime, see how fast Reggie and Bryon can get over there. I want you and one of them to check out the surroundings ASAP."

"Will do."

"And keep me posted."

"Okay."

"Thanks, Curtis. You're going to do fine as my number two. I'm on my way."

While Curtis had reported that Carol and Gary were in the theater room, this wasn't entirely true. Shortly after the game had ended Gary had made a call, gotten into one of the family cars, and driven to a nearby hotel. He stood there now, naked and hard, staring at the woman— naked and soft—whose suggestive pose told him he was more than welcome to join her in the king-sized bed.

"I've wanted this for a long time," he said, stroking his swollen member.

"Me, too," came the soft reply. When he continued to stand there, this seemingly shy but now brazen woman rose to her knees, scooted to the end of the bed, and took him into her mouth.

"Ah, yes, baby, I like that," Gary said with a moan, his

eyes squeezed shut in pleasure. "We're going to make some very nice music together."

The woman continued sucking, licking, and nibbling until he was as hard as . . . well . . . stone. Then she fell back on the bed, spread her legs, and said, "Then let the song begin."

26

Troy pulled up to the Stone estate and parked by the limo. Not wanting to attract attention to what might be transpiring near the home, he walked around to a side door and went directly into the security room. Curtis was there, still scanning the eight TV screens that showed the mansion from every angle.

"What do we have?" Troy asked, taking a seat. "Anything else out of order since you called me?"

"I realized since talking to you that one of the cars was gone. Carol confirmed that Gary isn't on the premises right now. Other than that, there are no more star watchers milling on the corner. But the traffic in the alley seems to be more than usual. I've been keeping my eye on a white SUV that's been back and forth a few times."

"Did you get a hold of anybody?"

Alex nodded. "Reggie is scoping the perimeter. Bryon and I went out there by the alley when he arrived. He's still monitoring that spot in person."

"Anything else unusual back there?"

"Three sets of footprints. Though there's no way anybody can scale that fence."

"I'll go and have a look. Also, I want you and Reggie to go ahead of us to Vegas. During our meeting, I'll give you a file on our itinerary, locations, et cetera, so we have everything scoped out before I bring her in. We can talk before I leave here, matter of fact, give you time to make last minute preparations before we leave the state."

"Where will she be staying?" Curtis asked.

"I'll get all of that to you tomorrow. We might opt for private homes for the rest of the tour, even in Europe if that can be arranged. They're easier to guard." Troy stood. "Nobody else knows about what's happening today, right—this increased activity behind the home?"

"Only those on the team, man."

"Cool. I'll update Gary, who will decide how much to tell Yvonne. I'm going to recommend that we keep a man here, probably Bryon, and not tell her anything. Chances are this was just another overzealous fan who found out about Gabriella. Once she leaves, the neighborhood will more than likely calm back down."

"I'm still tripping on how people get in here in the first place. This is a gated community." An exclusive area with the likes of Kim and Kanye as neighbors, it was one of the most exclusive enclaves in Bel Air.

"No piece of real estate is totally impenetrable. There are workers, delivery people, all kinds of folk with access. You know how crazy these people can be, bro. Where there's a will there's a way." Troy slapped Curtis on the shoulder as he headed to the door. "I'm going to check on Gab. Let's meet again in about forty-five minutes. After that, you can have the rest of the night off. But be ready to head to Vegas in the morning. My assistant will text the travel information."

Troy exited the room. He pulled out his phone to call Gary, but before dialing, sent Gabriella a simple text message:

I'm here.

He then walked through the combined living/dining area, furnished in a combination of modern and antique pieces, the orange accent color blending perfectly with large green plants. He walked down a hall to the theater and peeked inside. Nobody there. He then backtracked, turned down a different hall, and went into the great room. Beyond it lay the immaculately landscaped back-yard, which was tranquil, quiet, and empty. *Where is everybody?* He shook his head as he walked to the opposite wing and reminded himself that no matter how much money one had, there was such a thing as a too-big house. While taking the steps to the second floor, his phone beeped with a response from Gabriella to the text he'd sent.

Who cares?

Troy chuckled. *You do, baby.* He determined to later prove this fact over and again, but right now there were other things on his mind. He found Chauncey in Gary's office and decided that it would probably be to Gabriella's advantage if her father's assistant knew at least a little bit of what was going on.

"Hello, Chauncey."

Chauncey glanced up. "Hello, Troy," he said, going

right back to filing or organizing or what it looked to Troy like he was doing—rummaging through his employer's paperwork.

"Where's Gary?"

"Said he had some business to take care of and would be back in an hour."

"How long ago was that?"

Chauncey looked at his watch. "He should be back any time."

Troy wasn't one to dislike someone immediately, but there was something about this mousy-looking dude that rubbed him the wrong way. Maybe it was the condescending smirk that scampered across his face just now. No matter, Chauncey wasn't his problem. Whoever was after Gabriella, and more specifically, whoever left the footprints near the back gate, was the one on Troy's mind. "Can you stop working? I need to speak to you for a minute."

Chauncey placed the file he was holding into a folder and shut the file drawer. "Yes."

"We're reasonably sure that it's harmless, but I wanted you to know that some fairly threatening mail has been sent to the hotels where Gabriella stayed or was supposed to have stayed." Surprise registered on Chauncey's face. "She doesn't know about it," Troy added. "And for right now, we want to keep it that way. Gary knows about it and my men are on it, but because of your close proximity to her and your working relationship with Gary, I wanted you to know, too, so that you can be on the lookout for any type of suspicious behavior you may see in the next few weeks. Will you be accompanying Gary on this next leg of the tour?"

Chauncey picked up a stack of receipts and reached

for another folder. "He's not sure. More than likely he'll make his decision while we're in Vegas."

"Decision about what?" Troy and Chauncey looked up as a relaxed and refreshed-looking Gary strolled into the room.

"Hello, Gary. I was just asking Chauncey if he'd be joining us for the overseas leg of the tour."

"I told him you hadn't decided, sir."

"That's right. I haven't. More than likely you'll be along for the first few cities at least. We'll see how it goes from there." He turned to Troy. "Were you looking for me?"

"Yes."

Gary looked at Chauncey. "Give us a minute." After the assistant had left the room, he continued. "How was the visit to your family?"

"Interesting."

"Oh? How so?"

"I was surprised to learn that you'd sent gifts to my mother."

"Only what she asked for," Gary smoothly replied. "While backstage she mentioned the desire to hear our old songs. I just threw together a CD that I thought she'd enjoy."

"And the flowers?"

"Every woman loves flowers."

Troy paused, assessing his feelings for a conversation he'd not planned to have while also trying to figure out the motives for Gary's actions. Between his conversations with Dee and Alex he hadn't had time to process what his mother had shared, let alone his good friend Robert's thoughts on an old school R and B star pushing up on his woman.

Maybe I'm overreacting. Let me stay focused on why I'm here. "You're right," he said at last. "Everybody takes a trip down memory lane now and then. But just so you know, my mother's taken."

"She and that fat dude backstage are married?"

Troy let the dig go unchecked. "She and Robert McCrary a retired decorated police officer, a good, decent man, and longtime family friend, are in a committed relationship."

"Then a bauble and a few flowers from a former heartthrob shouldn't be a problem. It was a kind gesture, nothing more," Gary continued into the silence.

"She appreciates your thoughtfulness, but doesn't want anything else from you."

"She told you that?"

"In so many words. In fact"—he reached into his pocket and pulled out a small jewelry box—"here are the diamond earrings. When only a hotel address accompanied the package, and she knew we'd moved on, she knew I was the only way to return them. She thanks you for the CD and the flowers, but feels this gift is too much."

Gary looked at the box and shrugged. "Then give them to the cleaning woman," he said with a dismissive wave. "It really wasn't a big deal."

Again, Troy chose to not react to what could have easily been considered an offensive statement. Nothing against cleaning women, but it sounded like Gary had just placed his mother in the same category. Troy knew Gary had no idea how dangerous was the ground he was tamping on.

Troy took a deep breath, placing the box on a table

while he reined in his anger. "I came to update you on a few things," he said.

"What's going on?" Gary walked from the pool table to the table where Troy had placed the jewelry box.

"Gabriella needs to leave for Vegas tonight."

This immediately took Gary's attention from the box on the table to the man who'd set it there. "Why is that?"

"For safety reasons." Troy told him about the increased foot and vehicle traffic near the back wall of their estate.

Gary shrugged his shoulders. "We deal with fans all the time. That doesn't seem like such a threat to me."

"As we speak, an advance team is headed to our next venue," Troy continued, totally bypassing Gary's statement. "Once again, a threatening letter arrived at the hotel we booked."

"So whoever this is knows our travel schedule." Gary rubbed his chin thoughtfully. "And where we've booked rooms."

"Which means that whoever is sending them might either work in the travel or hotel industries or have connections to someone who does." Troy watched as Gary absorbed this news. "A friend of mine owns a very secure piece of property in a gated community just outside the city limits, large enough to easily house the whole team. I've placed a call to him to see if it's available. As you know, it's easier to protect a private residence than one that's open to the public."

"I still think we can leave tomorrow."

"I don't." He also told Gary about the borderline threats that had been posted on the Internet, and how his company was working on getting the IP address of the computer from which the messages were sent. Lastly he informed him of Alex's departure and Curtis's promotion. "I love my country," he finished, "but since I believe these harassments are home grown, I'll be glad when we put an ocean between us and this bull."

"I agree, Troy. In fact, I think that—"

"There you are!"

Gabriella walked into the room and for Troy it was like the sun coming out after an afternoon rain. Her entrance immediately dislodged the rain cloud of this latest information threatening his good mood.

Belatedly realizing that her enthusiastic greeting might rouse her father's suspicions, she added, "Li is here and just came from downstairs. She thought she heard your voice."

Troy turned fully toward her. "You're just the person I was coming to see after wrapping up with Gary. If possible, I'd like for us to leave for Vegas tonight."

Gary immediately interrupted. "I thought I told you that—"

"That's a great idea," Gabriella interrupted her father. "Carol and I were just discussing how it had been a while since we'd been to Vegas. Having a few hours to unwind in the city before starting the shows would be perfect."

"Fine." Gary made no move to hide his annoyance. "What time should I schedule the plane?"

Troy looked at Gabriella, who asked him, "What time should we leave?"

Troy noted Gary's increased scowl as he answered. "I'd say around eleven-thirty. That way I can make sure everything is ready for our arrival. Can everyone be ready?" He'd posed the question to Gary, who silently nodded. Troy glanced at his watch. "Okay, then. Let me get things wrapped up and I'll meet you back here at, say, ten o'clock?"

This time it was Gabriella who nodded her okay. She and her dad watched him stride confidently out of the room.

"Your bodyguard seems pretty sure of himself," Gary mused.

Gabriella headed out of the room, but tossed over her shoulder, "That's why you hired him, Dad."

She walked down the same hall Troy had traversed, but instead of turning left and leaving the room as he had, she turned right for a last minute swim in the infinity pool. Shortly afterward Gary too left the game room, his face set in a speculative scowl as he went to find his ex-wife and relay the changed plans.

All three had been lost in thought as they went from one room to the other. Which is why none of them noticed the person holding their breath as they passed, lest their eavesdropping presence be discovered behind a not-quite-closed door. The person who now knew not only that Gabriella would leave tonight for Las Vegas . . . but also knew why.

27

It was three o'clock in the morning, but Troy's steps were as light and springy as those of a man who'd gotten eight hours of sleep. In fact, it was the opposite. With so much to organize, rearrange, and oversee, he'd barely slept in the past twenty-four hours. Had barely eaten either. He was hungry, though not for food, and more than ready to assuage his appetite.

He opened the door with the stealth of a cat burglar, crossed the room without a sound, and after removing his shoes, gun holster, and all of his clothes, slid into bed, snuggling next to the soft body already lying there.

Gabriella immediately spooned into his arms. "I thought you'd never come back," she sleepily said.

"Have to make sure you're safe," he whispered, his hand sliding down her back and between her legs, his finger immediately pressing against her folds. "That's always my first priority."

"And you're sure my dad's asleep, and on his side of the estate?"

"Let's just say he won the drinking contest. No one has

to tell him that his were shots of Tequila while mine were H-two-0."

"Ha! You're such a bad boy."

"I am. That's why you love me."

"I won't deny I like your body. But no one has mentioned the *L* word."

Lifting one of her legs for better access, he slid his finger between her now wet folds, while nibbling on her ear. "No one has mentioned the *L* word *yet*."

She turned to face him. "So you think I'm falling in love with you?"

"I know that what's happening here is about more than sex. Although that's all I plan to concentrate on right now."

To prove his point, he lowered his head and kissed Gabriella's shoulder, before placing her on her back and focusing his attention on her now pert nipples. He outlined one with his tongue, while pebbling the other one between his fingers. All the while, he kept playing with her pussy, sliding his hands between her legs, gently massaging her clit in the same circular motion as the tongue now teasing Gabriella's belly button. She purred, and rubbed his head, gently pushing him downward.

He chuckled, the confident sound low and throaty. "Don't rush me," he chided, biting the insides of her legs before rubbing his body against hers as he moved up to her mouth. "I'm going to take real good care of you, no need to worry about that."

Searing her with a kiss, he rubbed his hard dick against her stomach, delighting in the feel of her hands going down his back before they squeezed his hard butt cheeks. She returned the kiss with fervor, her tongue swirling against his, her body arching up with excitement, her legs spreading to make room. After long moments of languid kisses and subtle nips on neck and nipples, he again began his descent to her personal paradise, this time not stopping until he reached his goal. With no warning he placed his tongue where his finger had earlier been, using its stiffness to part her folds, licking her slowly and thoroughly before sucking her nub into his mouth. She gasped at the onslaught, twisting her body one way and then the other in the throes of passion. He grabbed her hips to hold her still, forcing her to take all of what he offered, making her crazy with the way he kissed her there. With a finger sliding beneath to play with her ass, he settled his face between her legs and continued the onslaught. Over and over he licked her: fast, slow, soft, hard. His attention to her nub was relentless; even her nails digging into his shoulders could not make him stop. He sucked and nibbled and licked her like candy, blowing air over the wetness and driving her wild.

And still he continued. Her undulating hips assured that he was on the right track.

"Troy!" His name came out in a pant, and was repeated once and again as Gabriella experienced an orgasm so strong she swore she saw stars. Before she could even contemplate the phenomenon of Troy's tongue, however, she had to give due consideration to the big, hard dick that had just been thrust inside her and was now making its acquaintance with every inch of her inner walls.

Oh my God, she thought, as he stopped just long enough to place her legs over his shoulders. *This man is a beast!*

They made love for almost an hour, with Gabriella sometimes on top and in control as she rode his body like a cowgirl handling a bull. When she alternated between soft sucking and hard fucking, he almost lost control. When she clenched her muscles and squeezed his dick, while lowering her body up and down on his shaft, he narrowed his eyes and said, "That's right, baby. It's all yours. Enjoy the ride."

After their bodies were good and sweaty, with more orgasms for both of them than they could count, they ended the marathon and stumbled into the shower.

"Damn, baby," Troy said, his forehead pressed against the cool marble as water ran down his back. "That was amazing!"

"We did just try and screw each other's brains out," Gabriella admitted with a laugh, as she ran the loofah sponge between her slightly sore legs, relishing the throbbing she still felt. "I've got to give it to you, baby. You can throw down!"

Back in bed, once again snuggled next to each other, Troy whispered into Gabriella's ear, "You still awake?"

"Uh-huh." This delivered in a tone that suggested she was barely so.

"I have a new man to introduce you to tomorrow. Alex resigned and is now working with Prez."

Gabriella yawned. "I know."

"Oh, Gary told you?"

"No, Carol."

"Carol? How did she find out?"

"I don't know."

"Hmm, that's strange. Did she tell you anything else?"

"Like what?"

"I don't know. I know you two talk all the time."

"Yes, and just like I wouldn't share anything you told me, I most definitely won't be giving up any info on her!"

"Calm down, woman. I didn't ask you to break a

confidence. Alex didn't come straight out and say it, but I know that you and me getting together is the reason he quit the firm. Shows me just how upset he was about it. I was just wondering if Alex may have said anything to her, that's all."

Troy only received soft snores for an answer. He couldn't blame baby girl. He'd sexed her just that well. He was exhausted, too. So after using his iPad to conduct a security check of all gates and locks, he placed Gabriella more snugly in his arms and soon joined her in Snoozeville.

28

Full-time publicist Dana, stylist Melanie, makeup artist/hair stylist Tiana, and Gabriella's second assistant, Li, all piled into a limo. They'd arrived at McCarran International Airport in Las Vegas a half hour earlier and decided to mark their day off by splurging on a Hummer stretch. Over the last few months Dana, Melanie, and Tiana had become good friends, but assistant Li Yang had only recently been hired and during any down time frequently went MIA. Something about studying for online courses, she'd said when asked. No matter the reason, all in all they liked each other. The women figured this would be one of only a few days off in the coming weeks and a rare chance to hang out and have some downtime fun. So while as much of their luggage as possible went into the limo with the remainder being transported in a town car, the ladies checked their makeup, e-mails, and Facebook accounts, all while planning the day.

"I'm ready to hit the strip," Dana announced. "There's a high roller blackjack table with my name on it!"

"Dana, don't." Li didn't look up as her thumbs raced

over iPhone keys. "All of these games are designed to do nothing but take your money."

"Oh, they give some back to me once in a while."

"You can't win if you don't play," Tiana offered.

"Perhaps," Li countered, with a shake of her slender finger. "But I work too hard for my money to throw it away."

"We all work hard for this paper," Melanie countered. "Li, you're a newbie and Dana's a valued employee and a pro. You'd do well to try and stay on her good side."

"I was just teasing you, Dana," Li said. "I'm sorry if I offended you."

"Naw, chick. You're all right."

"What about Carol?" Li asked. She was technically Gabriella's assistant, but sometimes felt more like Carol was her boss.

"Probably with Gabriella," Dana answered.

"On her day off?"

This pulled Dana's eyes away from the window to Li's quizzical face. "Gab and Carol are best friends. You didn't know?"

"I never thought too much about it," Li responded, taking in the ho-hum scenery that was Vegas outside the strip and downtown areas. "I knew that they sang together in the Haute Coutures, but that's about it."

"They were friends before that," Melanie said. "More like sisters, in fact."

"But don't think that means that Carol is a slacker," Dana said. "Girlfriend earns her check—believe that."

"I'll tell you somebody who earns his check." Tiana's voice had turned dreamy, causing all eyes to turn toward her. "The bodyguard."

A unanimous groan went up in the limo.

Melanie sat a bit straighter in the seat. "That brother is fine!"

"I'd do him in a hot wing minute," Tiana admitted.

"Don't even think about it," Melanie said. "You know Gabriella is hitting that."

"You think so?" Li asked, eyes wide with curiosity.

"It doesn't matter what she thinks," Dana answered, cutting off Tiana's reply. She hated potentially harmful gossip as much as she loved hanging with the girls. And when it came to her girl Gabriella? She didn't play. "The bottom line is that Gabriella is responsible for all of our checks, so it won't do us any good to be talking out of turn about her."

"Doesn't matter to me," Melanie said. "He's not the man who gets me going."

"Who does?" Li eagerly asked, making it clear that she loved hearing gossip, harmful or otherwise. "Oh, wait. You're going to say that Alex dude, the one who works with Troy."

"I personally think he's more handsome," Dana offered. 'I'm not down with pretty boys."

Li scrunched up her face. "I wouldn't call Troy a pretty boy. I'd say handsome, good-looking, or gorgeous, but when I think 'pretty,' my mind goes metrosexual. Troy is all man!"

"Of all of those around us, the one who is truly all man is . . ." Melanie drew out the answer, looking at each woman with a devilish smile.

"Who, dammit!" Li asked with a laugh.

"Gary." Melanie's chin lifted a notch, as though daring a rebuke.

"Gab's daddy?" The look on Dana's face mirrored one who smelled dog poo.

"He is kinda fine," Tiana said.

Dana smirked. "Yes, if you're looking for a sugar daddy."

"I am one of those who will eat dessert first," Melanie responded, sitting back in the seat and adjusting her shades.

"Ooh, look!" Li exclaimed. "The strip!"

"Girl, stop sounding like a Vegas virgin." This said by Tiana, who looked about to break her neck taking in the sights her darn self.

"Is this your first time here?" Dana asked.

"Yes," Li responded without one ounce of shame.

"Then let's get settled into our rooms and then, little sister, you need to come with me." Dana put away her phone and offered her first genuine smile of the day. "I'm going to teach you how to play blackjack."

"Thank you, Dana." Li's eyes continued to take in the tall buildings and neon. "But I've got other plans."

Gabriella was not happy. Gary Stone was indeed her manager, and yesterday had been filled with memories of when he was her hero. But all he'd managed to do this morning was piss her off. At first she thought that somehow he'd found out about Troy spending the night in her bed. But she knew that wasn't possible. She'd showered and douched, even washed her hair, so she knew she didn't smell like sex.

Given the fun of yesterday's barbecue, she was confused. Their family time had ended in hilarious fashion, with Gary announcing that they were going to a matinee. "Like a regular family would do," he'd offered to a sea of blank stares.

They'd had fun. Because of his rapidly rising stature, Garrett, too, had donned an alter-identity. With thick, horn-rimmed glasses, a fake mustache, and flood-water jeans, he'd looked like Urkel's cousin, had one existed. Gabriella had placed her tell-tale curls under a black paisley-print bandanna and her expressive eyes behind dark glasses. These acts alone may have not been enough to allay suspicion, but the baggy clothes, fake pregnancy paunch, and the temporary tattoo Yvonne had pressed on her left arm made her incognito. The movie was funny, but the family found being out with one of the world's most famous entertainers, chomping on popcorn and chocolate-covered raisins without one autograph request, was a stone cold comedy.

But sometime after the family had all gone their separate ways, her father's mood had changed, and Gabriella didn't know what that was about. Gary had commandeered Troy not only at the house but during the entire private plane ride to Vegas, causing Gabriella to wonder what was up. When she'd texted the question, Troy assured her there was nothing wrong. Then when they arrived at the private residence in Vegas, Gary made a big deal about the location of her room and taking a room near it. But this morning had taken the cake: convincing Troy to let Curtis guard her while they took in eighteen holes. The irony hadn't been lost on Gabriella. All she'd thought of since last night was how well Troy used his "putter."

Gary's overprotective behavior could mean only one thing: he knew about her and Troy. But how? Except for yesterday's slipup when she felt there'd been just a tad too much excitement in her voice when she greeted him, she thought she'd been appropriately nonchalant about her personal protector. And after a tour of the house, which was big enough to be a hotel, she was sure there was no way Gary knew about their latest romp.

I thought we'd been careful, extremely so. Gabriella grabbed a pillow from the love seat on which she sat, pushed it against her middle, and mumbled, "Obviously, I thought wrong."

Her phone rang. She snatched it from the table, hoping it was Troy with a place for them to meet. One look at the number and her heart sank. But just a little. At one time this caller had made her heart go boom.

"Hey, stranger." She jumped up, closed the door to the master suite, and placed the call on speaker.

"What's up, shorty?" Hip-hop superstar Marlon "Mr. President" Simmons's low, gruff voice had been known to make panties disappear in less than sixty ticks.

Gabriella repositioned herself, lying on the love seat with one foot on the floor. "Where you at?"

"Headed to Vegas, baby."

"For real? Why?"

"Why else? I'm coming to see your show."

"Quit playing."

"My boy Sho'Nuff is down there, too. He's doing a show at the Hard Rock. I hope you don't mind that I gave him your number."

"Not really." Gabriella didn't really know Shawn "SMB" Smith, but the couple times they'd socialized he seemed nice—intelligent, too. "Why did he want my number?"

"He's throwing a little party where he's staying, at the Aria. I told him I wouldn't get there in time, but that he should invite you over."

"Doesn't he have a girlfriend and won't she get jealous?"

"Naw. Tracy's cool; plus, she's pregnant."

"Really?"

"Yep. So she's already got her Benjamins stacked for the next eighteen."

"What about you and your friend—what's her name? Priscilla?"

"Listen to you trying to probe. If you're not careful you're going to have a brother thinking that you still care about him."

"I'll always care about you, Marlon. I just won't ever date you again."

"Wow, hurt a brothah's feelings."

"Just speaking the truth."

"I was a fool to ever let you go. Maybe while we're both in Sin City we can try and do a little sinning together."

"You haven't changed. Always looking for greener grass. That's why I had to keep it moving."

"Your secret-service-acting daddy is the only reason you're not with me. Hadn't been for him, I'd still be hitting that nice, tight—"

"Whatever, Marlon. We both know had we stayed together I would have caught a case."

"Ha! Guess you're trying to catch something else now, huh?"

"What are you talking about?"

"I heard about your bodyguard being a part of your show and what not. You bumping and grinding all up on him. Y'all smashing or what?"

"Dang! Why don't you try and get in my business a little bit?" Even as she said this, an *aha* moment flashed as brightly as a paparazzi's annoying bulb. Even with her denials, Daddy had probably been suspicious from that very night on stage with Troy. Her past with Marlon had taught Gabriella that Gary wasn't the type of father who confronted right away. No, he gathered evidence like he was the late Johnnie Cochran or somebody, and then hit you with more evidence than a prosecutor seeking death. There was no telling how closely her father had been watching her and her late night lover. And no telling how much he knew.

After ten minutes of catching up, Gabriella ended the call. By the time her father and Troy had returned from golfing, she'd made a decision. Reaching for her phone, she sent Troy a message:

> Hope you had fun playing, but it's time to get back on the clock. Meet me downstairs in an hour.

29

Gabriella's request fit perfectly into Troy's plans. They needed to put some space between them and her father until Troy could come up with a plan that kept all of them happy. He'd already determined to stay close to his client for the duration of her tour, and not be lured away by her father again. That Gary was a control freak was only part of the problem. Troy had managed to avoid his probing personal questions on the golf course by sharing with him the text from earlier that Curtis had sent. A package had shown up at the hotel where they'd originally been booked. Troy had immediately relayed the information to the private investigator now working the case, and the package and its potential forensic evidence had been secured in plastic before being delivered by personal courier to this same investigation firm. A conference call was scheduled for first thing tomorrow morning. Troy looked forward to it. And for now, he looked forward to hanging with Gabriella. Though a part of him determined that what was happening between him and the superstar was just the fulfillment of human nature that came with being human, another voice kept telling him that it was more to it than that.

Troy ignored that other conscious brother, stripped off his clothes, and stepped in the shower.

Just over an hour later, Troy and Gabriella used a side entrance at the Palms Hotel Resort & Spa and once inside were quickly escorted to a private elevator by the hotel's manager. The security guard near the elevator immediately recognized Gabriella and motioned them forward. They entered a privately owned penthouse suite that most of those visiting the strip would never see. The living room boasted floor-to-ceiling glass panes offering a picture-perfect view of the casinos stretching down the length of Las Vegas Boulevard as well as the distant mountains. The glass wall also provided a view of the balcony and spa just beyond the living room, where two dark-skinned, muscled men cavorted with four buxom beauties in various stages of undress. About a dozen other people, mostly couples, either milled around the space or chatted in small groups. Sho'Nuff was sitting at the modern, glass-top table with several other men, but stood as soon as Gabriella appeared.

"There she is!" He walked over with arms outstretched and, as soon as he reached them, enveloped Gabriella in a friendly hug. He then leaned over, offering a fist to Troy. "What's up?"

Troy gave the brother dap. "Troy Morgan. Nice to meet you."

The rapper nodded. "Sho'Nuff."

They'd been chatting casually for only a few minutes before a commotion toward the room caused all heads to turn.

Gabriella's heart sank when "commotion" turned the

corner. Marlon? *Dammit. I should have known there was more to the story than his simply wanting me to have a good time.* And as if that wasn't enough, his new bodyguard was right behind him.

"Hey, baby!" Marlon didn't even acknowledge the host. He headed straight to Gabriella and enveloped her in a bear hug that lifted her off the floor.

Gabriella chuckled, trying to keep the mood light. "Marlon! Put me down!"

Troy took a step forward. Marlon noticed. So did Alex, who stepped forward as well. One of the men seated on the couch tapped another one, who reached under his jacket and started to rise.

Sho'Nuff threw out a hand to stop his bodyguard from advancing or pulling out firepower. He looked at Marlon. "Thought you said you weren't going to make it, bro?" The two men clasped hands and shoulder bumped.

"Plans change," Marlon said. He looked at Troy and then at Gabriella. "I see you brought backup. But, baby, I wouldn't invite you if it were dangerous. You're safe here."

Gabriella stepped closer to Troy. "I know I am."

Marlon's smile didn't quite reach his eyes. "Why don't you run along," he said to Troy. "Try your luck at a few tables. I'll take care of Gabriella."

Troy said nothing; just stood there looking like Will Smith's *Men in Black* replacement, eyes hidden behind dark glasses, arms crossed over his chest, and a smirk on his face. One of his boys used to work security detail for Marlon and had told him how the rapper and his posse ate drama for breakfast and BS for lunch. He'd come prepared to put up with childish tomfoolery. But he didn't know how much patience he'd have for Marlon's hands all over Gabriella.

"He's not going anywhere, Marlon," Gabriella said. "And you need to stop tripping."

"You think you need protection from me?"

"You tell me. Look at your boys, all strapped and ready to rumble. Do you think you need protection from me?"

After another tense couple seconds, a genuine smile spread across Marlon's handsome face. "You've always been able to get my blood stirred, baby girl." He reached for her hand. "Come with me. I need to hollah at you for a minute, seriously." Looking at Troy he added, "Alone."

"It's okay, Troy." Gabriella placed a hand on his arm, figuring that the sooner she humored Marlon with her presence, the sooner he'd leave her alone. "I'll be right back."

Marlon looked from Alex to Troy. "You two know each other, right? Oh yeah. He used to work for you before I stole him. Ha!"

Gabriella disengaged her hand from Marlon's grip. He looked at her, chuckled, and led her into one of the master suites. After closing the door, he immediately tried to pull her against him.

"Stop it, Marlon," she whispered, spinning out of his embrace. "Why are you trying to start trouble? I came here to have a good time and you're not even supposed to be here!"

Marlon's eyes narrowed. "Now I have my answer for sure. You and old dude out there have something going. You're banging the bodyguard."

"What I'm doing is my business. Your business is not being disrespectful to the people who work for me."

"How was I disrespectful? Never mind that." Marlon plopped on the bed. "I didn't invite you here to talk about some other joker. I asked you over so we could talk about us."

"What about us?" Gabriella folded her arms, trying not to be stirred by the sight of this gorgeous, hunky man lying across stark white sheets.

"Why are you all the way over there? Come here." He held up his arm in invitation. "Come here, baby. I've missed you." Gabriella walked over to the bed, sitting down a few feet away from where he lay. "Why are you all the way down there? Come cuddle with me."

Gabriella sighed and stood. "Okay, I see where this is headed. You invited me here for sex? Marlon, you know it's over between us."

"Damn, baby girl. Can't we be friends? Why are you acting all skittish and everything? Come here." This time the command was delivered in a whisper, as he pushed himself up and back against the headboard. She walked over and sat. He took her hand. "Now, is this so bad?"

She looked at him and smiled. "No."

"You got a thing going with Troy, don't you?"

"Marlon . . ."

"Come on, now. You know we're friends. You can tell me." He reached up and slid a finger over her cheek.

"Yes," she answered, making herself more comfortable. "But I have to keep it on the low. You know how Daddy tripped out when he found out about us."

"Yeah, your old man guards the princess, no doubt."

"He had one thing right, though. You are a player."

"No, I'm not."

"Oh, really? So where is your girlfriend and how would she feel to know you're here with me?"

"It doesn't matter." At the mention of the A-list actress who he'd dated off and on for years, including while he was seeing Gabriella, he rolled his eyes. "Only reason she's around is because you're not."

"Oh my God. You are so full of it. Where'd you pull that line from, the player's guide to being unfaithful and not getting caught?"

"I got it from the truth table. Now come over here and give me a real hug. Your boy out there don't have to know I still make those panties wet."

"Please."

"Then why are you acting all standoffish and everything? Are you afraid of him? Or me?"

Nothing moved Gabriella like a dare. She scooted onto the bed and rested her head on Marlon's shoulder. He reached for his phone and after sending a quick text, shared the real reason he'd invited her up to his suite.

"Besides wanting to hit it?" she teased.

"I'm always going to try and do that," Marlon quickly countered. "Especially with you lying here looking all fine, wearing that halter jumpsuit like a second skin, titties all pushed together and smiling at me, booty nice and tight." She swatted his hand away from her cleavage. "But if you're open for this idea I have for us, we can sit back, relax, and grow our stacks."

If Gabriella thought there was a chance that Troy would be jealous and/or angry about what was happening in the master suite, it was just because she wasn't aware of what was happening in the penthouse's game room. After tersely greeting Alex and scoping out the people in attendance, he deduced that there was indeed no imminent danger for his client. So, relaxing a bit, he decided to hit a pool ball or two. When he entered the immaculate game room, there was a poker game in full swing and two full-grown men acting like kids while playing a competitive video game. Troy walked over to a case, checked out a couple pool sticks, and after deciding on one that felt good in his hand, busted the rack of balls and started playing.

He wasn't alone for long.

A woman with long, thick black hair, greenish brown eyes, red pouty lips, and a mini dress that emphasized long, smooth legs balanced on five-inch stilettos sidled up next to him. "You always play with balls by yourself?"

Troy's smile was as easy as his response. "Not always."

"Can I play with yours . . . I mean . . . with you?"

Troy gave her tall body an appreciative perusal. There was no getting around it; this girl was beautiful. And unlike many of the lovelies he'd observed during his tour around the suite, her beauty seemed God given, and not the work of a surgeon's skillful hand. "Sure."

While she walked over and chose a pool stick, Troy set up the balls. "What's your pleasure?"

"Ooh, you don't want to ask me that question. But then again, maybe you do. I think there's another stick in the vicinity that I'd rather work with."

"I was referring to the game. Is eight ball all right?"

"Hmm; I guess it will have to do for now."

"Ladies first," he said, once he'd removed the rack.

The sexy stranger slowly chalked her stick as she looked at him. She leaned over, concentrating on the cue ball. Her booty, perfectly framed in the tight black dress, caused Troy to concentrate on her. She broke the balls apart with more power than he would have given her credit, sinking two of them in the process.

"Very nice," Troy said, with a nod. "Solid or stripes."

"Solid. Like I like my men."

He laughed. "Okay!" She sank another ball. They bantered back and forth throughout the rest of the game. He won. Barely. After which he asked, "You're pretty good. What's your name?"

"Contessa."

Racking the balls again, he responded, "Troy Morgan."

"Oh, I know who you are."

"Oh, yeah?"

"Yes." She placed down the pool stick and in a bold move walked up to him, pressed herself against him and wrapped her arms around his waist. "And I'd like to know more."

"Sorry, sistah." Gabriella's voice was low, firm, and just behind Troy's left shoulder. "But that's not going to happen." She stepped between Troy and the woman, glared at him, and announced, "It's time to go."

30

Shortly afterward a ticked off Troy caught up with a fast-moving, livid Gabriella when she reached the open elevator door. She stepped inside. He was right on her heels. She turned away from him, faced the wall. An immature action? Maybe. She didn't care.

"Gabriella." Silence. "Yo, Briella, that wasn't cool."

"Shut up," she hissed.

With a firm grasp on her arm, he turned her around. "What was that about?"

She yanked her arm away. "Remove your hands from my body. And don't talk to me!"

"How am I supposed to protect you if you're running away from me?"

"I don't know. How were you going to do that with your tongue halfway down that woman's throat?"

"I didn't kiss her, Briella."

"You were going to!"

"No, I wasn't!"

"You wanted to!"

They reached the lobby, but instead of going toward

the front doors, he once again grasped her arm firmly and headed them in the opposite direction. Using one of the all-access cards the hotel manager had given him, he opened a small conference room door and led her inside.

As soon as they entered the room he let her go and quickly locked the door behind them. "Briella . . . calm down!" His voice held calm authority while his eyes shot fire.

"Don't tell me to calm down! You work for me, not the other way around!"

"Then let me do my job and keep you safe. Did you not notice the paparazzi in the lobby, a gaggle of cameras just waiting to snap you storming out of this building?" He watched her eyes dart toward the door. "No, you didn't. Because you were too busy trying to be a pain!" Gabriella huffed and if her eyes could shoot real daggers, Troy would have been all cut up.

He took a breath. "Look, baby, I wasn't doing anything with that girl." Gabriella rolled her eyes. "Playing pool, that was all. Okay, so she rolled up on me. So what? It was probably nothing compared to what was going on with you and your hip-hop buddy behind closed doors."

"Oh, so that's what it was about. You're mad at me and jealous of Marlon—"

"Do I need to be jealous of him?"

"—so you cozy up to the first skirt you see as a way to get back at me?"

For several tense seconds they eyed each other before Troy asked, "Look at us, baby. Having an argument about two people who don't even matter to us." She remained silent, but her shoulders eased a bit. Encouraged, he took a step toward her and lowered his voice. "When what we could be doing is making use of the room I secured for us earlier, the one where we can have a little privacy before going back to the mansion and Gary's watchful eyes."

"That's fine. But this discussion isn't over. We need to come to an understanding of what this"—she waved her hand between the two of them—"is: a relationship, friends with benefits, a convenient fuck"—Troy's eyes narrowed—"or what."

"Cool. We can talk later. But just so you know . . . I would never disrespect you or any woman enough to say you're just a convenient eff. There are too many women around who are comfortable with casual sex to use a woman who isn't. You and I were hot from the jump; there was no stopping what happened between us. But now, I need to know something." He took a step back, increasing the distance between them. "Do you want to put the brakes on us? If you do, just say so and I can go back to being what I was hired to be. If not"—he looked at his watch—"I suggest we head upstairs and make better use of this time."

One second passed.

Two.

Ten.

Gabriella's phone pinged. She didn't bother looking at it. "What time is it?"

Troy glanced at his watch again. "It's early. Just a little before seven."

"Then let's go."

Gabriella pushed past him and opened the conference room door. She didn't look back to see if he followed. He did, not knowing whether she was headed for the bank of elevators or the limo. More relief than he cared to admit flooded through him when he saw her head toward the private set of elevators they'd just used. They reached them. He placed his hand at the small of her back. She didn't jerk away from him; instead, she stepped closer. Good sign. Even as he kept one eye on her, his other eye scanned the hallway, quickly seeing the cameras, curious onlookers, and fans. There seemed to be an inordinate amount of brothers milling about, but he charged that to the fact that Marlon was at the hotel. Likely, that was why the paparazzi were there as well. But he knew from some of his well-placed sources in that part of the biz that sometimes the best pictures came from moments least expected. He didn't intend for this to be one of those times. Once the door had opened he followed her inside and pushed the button to the fortieth floor. Silence filled the space between them as they ascended to their tempo-rary love nest. The carpet absorbed their footsteps as they walked to the room. Troy did a cursory glance behind him, by habit mostly. Even though his heart was filled with Gabriella and her actions, his mind was on full alert as to what was happening around them.

They reached the room. As he stepped forward to open the door, she wrapped her arms around him and laid her head against his back. Both knew what was coming next. They entered. Compared to the penthouse suite they'd just exited, it was pretty ho-hum. But neither Troy nor Gabriella noticed that. They were too busy staring at each other, and even that didn't happen for long.

"Come here," Troy commanded. He pulled Gabriella into his arms and slammed his mouth against hers for a fervent kiss. Sliding his hands from her waist to the juicy booty he loved so much, he squeezed each cheek as he pressed her against him. She was hot for him, too, evidenced by the way she ripped at his shirt and fumbled for his belt buckle, all while swirling her tongue and enjoying the taste of Troy's mouth, luxuriating in the feel of her breasts smashed against his solid chest, and the bone of contention they'd recently shared being replaced by the feel of a different kind of bone.

He picked her up and walked them to the bedroom. Wordlessly they tore at clothes, and each other, until both were naked and burning with heat. If possible he would have gobbled her whole, but instead had to be content with sucking one nipple into his mouth and then the other, before sliding his tongue down her stomach, across her hips, and finally between her nether lips. Gabriella moaned loudly, her head thrashing from side to side as she squeezed fistfuls of bed covering between her fingers. Her body shivered and toes curled at his possessive, demanding assault. Placing a hand on each of her thighs, he spread her wider, drove in deeper, savoring her juices like pricey champagne, knowing that this time was different. This time, he was marking territory no other man dare tread. This time, he was making both a decision and a statement: Gabriella belonged to him. He belonged to her. When the time was right, they'd share this reality with those who mattered. Not now. But soon.

The fire in room 4700 burned hot for a long time. For the two lovers time stood still; they had each other, and their love was the only thing that mattered. After rounds of glorious lovemaking they talked, declared their love for each other, and their readiness to take the relationship to a whole other level. Both agreed that they wouldn't go public until after the tour, when Gabriella could put what she knew would be much needed space between her and her father. Standing her ground against him would be a challenge, she knew. But she was ready. Troy was worth it. Everyone would have to deal with it.

In the days to come they'd do well to remember this conversation. Because in less than twenty-four hours their illicit, secret love affair was going to be front page news.

31

"Gabriella, wake up!" After barely a knock Carol had raced into Gabriella's room and was shaking her awake.

Gabriella scrunched up her face and tried to pull the covers over her head. Just moments before, she'd looked at the clock and been relieved to see that it was only 7:30. Rehearsal and sound check wasn't until noon. After yesterday evening's romp with Troy, followed by his sneaking into her room for a quickie just after two a.m., she more than needed all the sleep she could get. *So what in the heck is wrong with her?*

"Carol! Stop it! What the hell . . ." She pushed away her friend's nagging hands and tried to pull the cover over her head.

That wasn't happening.

"Gabriella. Shit is about to blow up. You need to wake up. Now!"

Gabriella knew panic when she heard it and that was sure enough the sound in Carol's voice. She pushed herself up and back against the headboard, rubbing her eyes and stifling a yawn as she went.

"Okay, Carol. What has you more fired up than a cherry bomb on this Fourth of July?"

Carol threw down a tabloid. "This."

The picture that greeted her pushed away any vestiges of grogginess from her mind. She snatched up the magazine. "Oh my God!"

"That's who you'd better call, because when Gary sees this? That's who you're going to need."

There were a series of four pictures covering almost the entire front page: an angry-looking Gabriella followed by a determined-looking Troy; Troy grabbing Gabriella's arm and her indignant reaction; Troy and Gabriella waiting at the elevator in what looked like an intimate pose; (and this is the one that made her jaw drop) Gabriella hugging Troy from behind as they stood in front of a hotel room door. She'd been looking at the cover for several seconds before even noticing the headline: HER BODYGUARD . . . AND MORE!

Not even remembering she was naked, she tossed off the covers and leapt from the bed. "Who in the hell took these pictures?!"

"Does it matter? The question you need to be asking is what story are you and Troy going to have for your dad." Carol walked over to the closet, pulled out a robe, and tossed it at Gabriella, who put it on.

Gabriella walked to the sofa in the sitting room area and sat down heavily. She stared at the cover a few more seconds before leafing through the magazine to the feature story. Her eyes ate up the words as hungrily as a monkey would a banana. She read silently at first. The article stated what the pictures seemed to confirm—that Gabriella had a new lover. It gave Troy's name and included information about Morgan Security, even listed some of the big names his firm had protected. *How are they getting all of this information?* An answer came to Gabriella immediately. The Internet. For all the good the World Wide Web had done in making the world a smaller and more informed place, it also served to make it easy for people to get all up in your business whether you liked it or not. They mentioned Marlon "Mr. President" Simmons—she wasn't surprised about that—but became suspicious when the article began revealing her visit to the hip-hop star Sho' Nuff's penthouse before moving a few floors down and spending "several hot and heavy hours" the article said, with her "current lover."

"According to sources who only spoke on condition of anonymity," Gabriella read, "the twenty-five-year-old singing sensation began the afternoon in the penthouse company of her ex-boyfriend, Mr. President. While her bodyguard, Morgan, remained in the living room, she and Mr. President cozied up in the master suite." She looked up at Carol. "I don't believe this crap!"

Carol raised an eyebrow. "Is it true?"

"Is what true?"

"That you and Marlon hung out in the bedroom . . . alone?"

"Yes, but we didn't do anything."

"I'm sure it wasn't for his lack of trying."

"Look, I need you to be on my side right now."

Carol joined her on the couch. "Sorry, Gab. I'm always on your side." She motioned toward the tabloid. "Keep reading."

"When Gabriella exited the bedroom, it was to find Morgan making out with a stunning brunette, in view of the entourage surrounding him!" She clucked her tongue. "Such fricking liars." Sure, she'd basically accused Troy of the very same thing, but as she'd admitted during their after-sex chat, she'd seen the woman's arms around Troy, but couldn't say for sure that they'd been kissing, an act that Troy vehemently denied.

"Gabriella raced over and cursed out the surprised woman, who'd been flirting with Morgan for hours." Gabriella slammed down the paper. "I am so going to file a lawsuit." Being in the tabloids was nothing new for her; she'd grown a fairly tough skin since her first appearance when she was twelve and wearing a new set of braces. The photo they'd taken to accompany the article hadn't been particularly flattering, as she remembered, but the article hadn't been unkind. It hadn't been an out and out lie.

This isn't an out and out lie, either, she thought. Sighing, she continued. "Shortly afterward, the two left the penthouse, but not the hotel. After a brief scuffle in the hotel lobby, the two raced to the elevators, taking a room on a lower floor. Our sources confirm that their make-up session lasted for hours. 'I was in the lobby until almost dawn,' the source was quoted as saying. 'And never saw them come down.'"

Gabriella let out a string of expletives as she threw down the paper, then jumped up and kicked it. Recent conversations aside, she really wasn't one who cursed much. Or got that angry. A lot had changed since she'd met Troy Morgan. From the looks of things, that was likely to continue.

"Where'd you get that?" Gabriella asked, now pacing the room.

"Chauncey brought it to me."

Gabriella whirled around. "Chauncey?" Carol nodded. "That's strange." When Carol remained silent, Gabriella prodded. "Don't you think that's strange? That he was up this early and out grabbing tabloids?"

"Not really, Gab. He told me that he'd gotten up early to run an errand for your father, and stopped at a gas station for a bottle of water. When he saw the magazine he bought it, figured you'd want to know before your father did. I think it was nice of him to warn you when he could have taken it to Gary instead."

"You're right. He could have taken it to Dad first and then I'd be the one blindsided. Remind me to thank him later."

Gabriella walked over to the window. The master suite she occupied faced the meticulously landscaped back-yard that was its own private paradise. This morning, all of the beauty was lost on Gabriella. She didn't see the marble steps that led to the infinity pool, nor the flaw-lessly planted and thriving Bermuda grass—a rare sight in the scorching Vegas heat—that served as the base to vibrant bushes, flowers, and exotic trees. She didn't catch the strutting peacock as it spread its magnificent feathers as if jousting with the sun. All she saw was her father's face, and how enraged it would look as soon as that paper was placed down before him. She thought about the promise and felt a headache coming on.

32

By eight a.m., Troy had already worked out in the impressive in-home gym, taken a shower, and eaten a light breakfast prepared by the chef. When his phone rang, a little after eight, he'd just pulled up the office schedule on his iPad to prepare himself for the talk with the office manager that would happen later on.

He looked at the caller ID and smiled. "Good morning, Jackie."

"Have you seen the papers?"

Troy frowned and was immediately on guard. Calling his mother by her first name usually elicited a sarcastic comment if not a straight-out rebuke. He couldn't imagine anything in the morning paper that would cause her to totally ignore his jab.

"Don't read the news much, Mom. But I have a feeling you're going to tell me what's in there."

"You, that's what."

"Me?"

"Yes, and on the front page, too. How many times have I told you boys to be careful when you're out cavorting? Then again," Jackie continued, her voice low, as if speaking to herself, "as many times as you've been in and out of hotel rooms, it's amazing that you're just now getting caught."

"Whoa, wait a minute. Back up, Mom. What paper is it and what are they saying?"

"It's one of those tabloids, and they've got pictures of you and Gabriella."

Troy relaxed ever so slightly. He wasn't happy the paparazzi had caught him, but given all the cameras yesterday in the lobby, he wasn't totally surprised. "Oh, that's no big deal, Mom. Gabriella went to a function at the Palms Hotel. I accompanied her. That's all."

"Yes," Jackie continued, just as cool as a block of ice in the freezer. "I just finished reading all about your accompaniment. Don't even tell me how you were protecting her while alone in a hotel suite. I don't even want to know. They even have the number of the suite that they swear y'all were in, and pictures, too—4700."

Troy reached for his iPad, went to a search engine, and put in his name. Sure enough, a link came up with a headline that he wished he could blink and make disappear. He scrolled down and saw what no doubt his mother had peeped: pictures of him and Gabriella at the Palms Hotel. Though he wished he'd not taken her arm in public (one may have called it "grabbed," but Troy would have argued the point), it wasn't a scandal for a bodyguard to be with his client in a public place. What made him sit up and take notice, however, was the picture of them in the hotel hallway—the picture that had to have been taken by someone that Troy—with all of his talent and training—had not seen.

"Troy, are you still there?"

"Yes, Mom. I'm here. I just pulled the article up online."

"Well, you need to read it, baby. It's bad enough how they paint you with what they're saying, but how they've made Gabriella look is a downright shame."

Gary stretched and rolled his neck as he looked out on the amazing garden that was a part of the villa. The house boasted several suites, not just the master. His suite, on the other end of the property from Gabriella's, was as big as one in a hotel, complete with sitting area, walk-in closet, small eating area, and bath with sauna included. The colors were soothing, a mixture of gray, silver, and stark white. The marble floors were covered with an elegantly designed Persian rug, and the kid leather on the chairs and the eight-foot-high headboard was as soft as a baby's behind. Gary looked around him as he waited for Chauncey to bring him his standard breakfast—two boiled eggs, a bowl of oatmeal, four pieces of turkey bacon, and whole grain toast—along with a pot of coffee and several papers: the *Wall Street Journal, New York Times*, and *Detroit Free Press*. It had been a long time since his days riding bikes down a street near Eight Mile Road, decades since he'd had to worry about finding work or paying bills. It was true that living out his dreams of a musical career had been short-lived. But his daughter had more than made up for his brief time in the spotlight; in fact, she had placed him back in it in a spectacular way. While he'd loved the celebrity and all of the perks—translated, women—that came with it, his role as her manager had brought him a type of power and prestige beyond what he'd ever dreamed.

That's right, buddy. As the baby son of Otis and Jean Stone, you did all right. He only wished his parents and older brother, Otis Jr., could have lived to see and enjoy this success. Thankfully he was able to share the fruit of his labor with his sister, Belinda, older by two years. After the group the Haute Coutures had earned their third platinum album, and Gary became a multimillionaire, he moved his sister from her crumbling brick home in the hood. She now lived comfortably in Auburn Hills, Michigan, with her second husband, Rex, and their two Yorkshire terriers. Gary was thankful that Belinda's daughter, his niece, had also escaped the downside of urban living. She was married to an engineer, had three children, and lived in Chicago. Sadly her brother, his nephew, didn't fare as well. He was in a prison in Indiana, a drug war/street gang statistic.

Thinking of Dennis pushed Gary's thoughts toward Garrett, the pride and joy of Gary's fifty-one years. It was enough that one of his children had become so successful, but for Garrett to realize his aspirations and become a professional football player would ensure that Gary died a very happy and totally satisfied man.

A soft knock jolted Gary out of his musings.

"Your breakfast, sir," Chauncey announced, rolling in a tray bearing dome-covered dishes, a small pot of coffee, and a carafe of orange juice.

"Thanks, Chauncey." Gary walked over from where he'd been standing by the window and took a seat at the round dining table with its gilded, gold-plated edges.

"It's a beautiful morning! Are you ready for tonight's exciting show? It's going to help this city celebrate the Fourth of July! You can have the night off and attend simply as a fan."

"That's generous of you, Mr. Stone," Chauncey answered, in his normal low, monotone voice. "But I'm afraid the fireworks have begun already."

"Oh really?" Gary laughed as he removed the silver dome over his still steaming oatmeal and reached for the butter. He noticed that in addition to what he'd requested, the chef had also sent him a bowl of fruit and another of hash browns. "Have you eaten yet, Chauncey? There's plenty to share." For Gary, eating with employees was highly unusual, downright rare, but he was feeling particularly jovial this morning. And extremely blessed.

"I'm sorry to be the one to bring you this, Mr. Stone." He reached for a tabloid that was beneath the other papers. "But I believe you'll want to see this."

Gary took one look at the pictures splashed across the front page . . . and lost his appetite.

Li stepped out of the shower and hurriedly dressed. Ten minutes ago, she'd received a call from Gabriella with instructions on what she'd need from her in the next hour. Plans had changed, and Li was not surprised. When she and the girls had arrived at the Palms, she'd immediately spotted the license tags of the limo service that Gabriella normally used. After telling Tiana, Dana, and Melanie that she'd meet them inside, she'd gone over, talked with the driver, and had it confirmed that Gabriella was not only inside but attending a party thrown by rappers, whom she knew Gary despised. It served her right to receive fallout for going against her father's wishes. Gabriella was a spoiled, ungrateful person who needed to learn to show more respect. Gary Stone was a good man, who'd helped his daughter become a star. Li knew that if she had a father like that, she'd never do anything to cause him shame.

33

Gabriella swore she hadn't taken a deep breath until safely in the limo. After the initial shock of reading about her previous day's outing in the tabloid, she went into survival mode. There'd be time enough for damage control when it came to the public. Her first thought was avoiding the inevitable showdown with her dad.

"How are you doing, baby?" Troy hadn't stopped talking or texting on his phone since meeting with Gabriella after the call from his mom. They'd both thought to get out of the mansion as soon as possible. True, Gabriella wasn't ready to deal with Gary, but just as importantly, she had a really big show in about ten hours. Not to mention a short rehearsal, sound check, and a preshow press conference. She had to keep her focus and keep it moving. Tomorrow was another day.

"I'm okay," she said, finally answering Troy's question. "Carol, did you get in touch with the agent?"

"Hold on, Melanie," Carol said into the phone before muting it and answering Gabriella. "Yes. I just got the text that she's found a beautiful home in Henderson. She says it's in a gated community, very low-key. You're sure to have your privacy there, she said."

Troy pulled out his iPad. "What's the address?" Carol gave it to him. Using a computer application, he pulled up a real time picture of the neighborhood, the street, and the house. The day before, Troy had released Bryon to head back to the office. He called him now with an update on their location and, once he had a free moment from Gabriella, would find out if the private investigator working with their firm had any new information.

Carol wrapped up her phone call. "Melanie has packed the rest of your stuff that was at the house. She and the girls will meet us at the arena." After a short pause, Carol answered the unasked question. "She didn't see Gary."

As if conjuring him up, Gabriella's phone rang again. It was the third call she'd received since slipping out of the house like Houdini did his handcuffs. The first two had been her father. She looked at the caller ID and wasn't too surprised to see who was on the other line.

She pushed the speaker button. "Yes, Mom. I'm okay."

"I'm glad to hear that you're okay, Gab. But you know that your father isn't." As was normally the case, Yvonne's voice was soft and soothing. There was no anger, chastisement, or judgment in her voice.

"Did you read it?"

"Parts of it, but I stopped, Gabriella, because I'd rather hear it from you." A pause and then, "Are you seeing him romantically?"

"Who?"

"I have choices?" There was surprise and the merest hint of humor in Yvonne's voice.

It was the first time that Gabriella's mouth had turned

upward since Carol had knocked on her door. "I did go to the Palms, with Troy, and we did go to the penthouse suite where Sho'Nuff and his boys were hanging out. I didn't expect Marlon to be there. If I'd known that, especially given the fact that Alex now works for him, I never would have gone."

"What happened?"

Gabriella told her. "We just wanted to get out of the public eye," she finished, as a way to explain the time spent alone with Troy in another hotel room. "We stayed there until the hoopla died down, until we could sneak out of there without being seen."

During the silence that ensued, it was as if Gabriella could actually hear Yvonne thinking. "You need to take your father's calls, Gabriella," she said at last. "Gary isn't just your father. He's your manager. Your public persona is a part of his business, and his responsibility is in handling your brand."

"I know I need to talk to him, Mom. And I will. Just not right now. You know how he reacted when he found out about Marlon. I have a huge show tonight and before I perform it, I just don't need any more drama than I've dealt with already." Gabriella's eyes misted over unexpectedly. "Will you tell him that?"

"Sure, baby. He only wants what's best for you."

"I know."

"Do you need me to fly out there?"

In that moment, Gabriella felt she needed Mommy very much. Then she felt Troy's hand on her leg—soft, firm, reassuring. "No, that's okay. But you're still coming to London next week, right?"

"It all depends on Garrett's tryouts and how easily we can get his living arrangements all worked out."

"I thought that was already done."

"You know your brother. He's not trying to stay on campus and he's not trying to stay here. I'm working on getting an apartment for him and three of his teammates."

"An apartment? Seriously? Why'd you buy that humongous house if you knew that you'd be there alone?" Then realizing how that may have sounded to the woman who Gabriella sometimes felt was still in love with her dad, she added, "I mean, it's a really nice house, but I thought you'd live there with Garrett."

"I did, too. But he says it's too far away and I have to agree. With all of the practicing and studying . . . he needs to be close to his teachers. And his teammates."

The limo pulled up to a gated community. "Mom, I need to go. But I'll call you later, okay?"

"Okay, Gabriella. I'm sure Troy is there with you. Tell him that he'd better take care of my daughter."

"You just did, Mom. I love you. Thanks."

Gabriella's smaller entourage reached the new home. While nothing like the villa, it was still very nice: gated, secluded, with all the bells and whistles a seven-figure price tag could command. Again, Gabriella saw none of it. The swirl of activity as they settled in to what would probably be their home for the next five days, along with prepping for the rest of the day's events, knowledge of the swell of calls Carol was fielding from the press—plus the tension from the inevitable conversation-slash-showdown with her father—took all of the focus and energy that Gabriella possessed. She and Troy had yet to discuss what had happened in detail, or how to handle it. For now, her answer to the press was "no comment" and for her dad . . . the same.

After giving Carol and Li some final instructions, Gabriella and Troy retreated to the master suite. It was their first time alone in two hours and for the first few minutes all they could do was hold each other.

Finally, Troy gave Gabriella a gentle kiss on her forehead and asked her, "How are you doing, babe?"

"I'm okay." The shaky, timid voice in which this answer was delivered begged a different opinion.

Troy stepped back enough so that he could ease his hands from Gabriella's back to her shoulders. He gave them a squeeze. "My baby is so tight," he murmured, his face filled with concern.

Gabriella placed a hand atop his. "Really, I'm okay."

"No, you're not," Troy said, reaching for his phone. "Hey, Carol," he said once she'd answered. "How fast can you get Gabriella's masseuse down here?" He listened, giving a slight head shake to Gabriella's silent protest. "Okay, cool. Yeah, have her come here to the house." Troy nodded at what Carol said. "Excellent. Have her come, too. Thanks, Carol."

When he ended the call, Gabriella's look was tender. "You didn't have to do that, Troy. But it was a good idea. A nice massage will do wonders. Thanks."

"Not a problem." Once again, he folded her into his arms. "Taking care of you is my business. It's what I do."

Two hours later, after Gabriella and the crew had enjoyed a nice brunch and Troy had grabbed a bite before phone conferences with both company headquarters and the team who would be working the show, the entourage arrived at the MGM Grand Garden Arena. As expected paparazzi were everywhere. Thankfully, the MGM had the loading dock on lock. The nondescript SUV in which Gabriella rode was able to slip into the building without incident. The five shows that would take place at the arena had been sold out within days of their posting. Even though the space had a capacity of almost seventeen thousand, there was still an intimacy to its design.

Shortly after arriving, Troy and Gabriella split up to handle various duties. Gabriella had a quick powwow with the stage manager and then phoned Melanie. "Meet me back at wardrobe. I want to make a couple changes to the costumes for tonight."

Upon hanging up with Melanie, she saw Chauncey rushing toward the arena's front entrance. "Chauncey!" He walked over to her. "Listen, thanks for the heads-up." Silence. "Carol told me it was you who brought her the tabloid."

"Figured it was something you needed to know."

"Most definitely, and I appreciate it."

"If you'll excuse me, Gabriella, I have to check on something for Gary."

"Of course. Hey, do you get back to the Dirty D much?"

"No. With normally only one day off, that's an expensive trip."

"Well, the next time you want to go just let Carol know and I'll take care of the ticket. Family is important."

"You really don't have to do that."

"I want to."

"Okay," he said after a pause. "Thanks."

She had just turned down the backstage hallway, flanked by Carol, Li, and one of the arena employees, when she saw him. As expected, he lit right in.

"You know better than to dodge my calls, Gabriella," Gary said, his tone containing both anger and hurt. "We need to talk and we need to talk now."

"I know we need to talk, Dad. But not here, and not now. I have a show to do." She walked past him.

"Come back here, Gabriella!"

She didn't stop. Just kept walking. Had it been possible, she would have walked right out of the arena and into some peace of mind.

34

Still livid, Gary exited the backstage area of the arena and headed toward the box office area and the arena manager's office. On the way, he saw Troy.

"I need to talk to you," he said as a greeting.

Troy had been expecting this moment ever since Gary started blowing up Gabriella's phone. Unlike her, he wasn't going to run. Never had. Never would. Looking Gary in the eye, he simply answered, "Sure."

Walking past the front office area, Gary saw the manager and waved. "Be right back," he said without breaking stride. He and Troy exited the building. Both men walked tall—head high, shoulders squared. Troy wore his trademark black, today a casual black suit paired with a black, short-sleeved polo-type shirt and dress shoes. Gary, always the suit wearer, had chosen a tan double-breasted pinstripe for the day, with matching shirt and tie. As soon as they turned a corner and entered into a small enclave on the side of the building, Gary rounded on him.

"I just have one question for you," he said, his voice deceptively calm. "Are you sleeping with my daughter?"

Troy did something that he only rarely did, especially when he was on the clock. He took off his shades. "That's a very personal question, Gary, concerning your daughter. One that I think only she should answer."

"Don't play games with me, punk, especially when I'm just two seconds from punching you right now. I'm coming to you straight, man to man, Troy. And I'll ask again. Are you fucking Gabriella?"

"And I'll once again give you my answer, man to man. First of all, Gabriella is grown, an adult, something it seems that you tend to forget. I understand she'll always be your baby girl—"

"Damn right—"

"But she's not a baby. She's a woman. And what you've asked, in very crass fashion I might add, is something that no man would ever share with another man about a woman. Not if he's got any kind of respect for women in general or her in particular."

Gary was silent a moment, as if sizing up Troy's worth, or maybe, whether or not he could take this young blood down. "I take that answer as a yes."

Troy shrugged. "You can take it any way you want. But if you want any information on Gabriella's personal life, you'll have to ask her. Both as my client, and my friend, every aspect of our relationship is completely confidential."

"You arrogant asshole . . ." Gary snarled, and took a step.

Troy didn't budge, or blink an eye. In fact, if he were any more still he could have been placed in Madame

Tussaud's wax museum. "Getting physical with me is not a wise move."

"Getting physical with my daughter isn't too smart, either!"

Troy didn't speak and Gary didn't move. Even the wind had the good sense to stop blowing lest it add to the fiery fury, which, being ninety degrees and counting in the place called Sin City, was considerable.

"I'm not stupid, nor blind. So I know there's something happening between you and Gab. I've already put in a couple phone calls, just in case we have to change security companies."

"Do what you have to do, man."

"I'd rather not at this late date, especially considering all the prep work that's already been done for the hardest leg of the tour—Europe and Asia. So let this serve to put you on notice. When it comes to Gabriella, your one and only job is to keep her safe: from the public, from the media, and from men like you. She is a superstar, and when she decides to enter into a serious relationship it will be with someone of her caliber and her standing."

Troy shifted, ever so slightly. "What exactly are you saying?"

Gary smirked ever so slightly, checking his perfectly manicured nails before he spoke. "Well, let me rephrase it," he drawled, before finally looking at Troy. "And I'll use small words to make sure you understand." Gary watched Troy's eyes narrow, and took pleasure that although he couldn't see it—even with the punk wearing all black in hot weather—the self-assured upstart might be breaking a sweat. Otherwise, Gary begrudgingly admitted, he'd taken the thinly veiled dig with remarkable aplomb. "You need to remember your place here, son, need to remember that we sign your paycheck. And while she may have slipped up in the past, from this day forward, my daughter doesn't sleep with the help."

"Are you finished?"

"Just want to make sure we understand each other."

"Your small words enabled me to understand you quite clearly. So if you have nothing further to add to your diatribe, I'll get back to work."

Gary was left to watch Troy's retreating back.

In between meetings with the arena's front office and marketing team, Gary pondered on how to handle the situation with Troy and his daughter, one he'd long suspected and that had now been confirmed. It was a tricky situation, but Gary had attended this rodeo before. That fool Marlon "Mr. Piss Ant" Simmons had the same kind of misplaced swagger that Troy wore like a fake gold chain sold to a tourist in Chinatown. Gary might wear designer suits and pricey watches, he might sleep in five-star hotels, but at the end of the day, his smarts had largely come from the streets. In his old neighborhood, punks like Troy Morgan were a dime a dozen. That's why he'd worked so hard to get out. He hadn't put in a semi-truck's worth of blood, sweat, and tears to have his multi-millionaire, platinum-selling daughter end up with small change. In fact, Gary had his eye on someone he thought would be a perfect match for his little girl—a prominent entertainment attorney with several zeroes behind the first number in his bank account.

By the time he'd finished his tasks and was driven back to the rented villa for a relaxing meal, Gary had a plan. He made a few phone calls and put the ideas he'd thought out in motion. He'd also talked with Yvonne, and had re-strategized the approach he planned on taking with Gabriella. He agreed with both his ex-wife and Troy that his daughter was a grown woman, and needed to be approached as such. One thing about Gabriella, Gary knew, was that in many ways she was much like him. And when it came to her career, business came first. That's the deck of cards he'd play with when he approached her later that evening. And, as always, Gary would play to win.

Because of two standing ovations, the show had lasted almost two and a half hours. Still, Gabriella didn't feel too exhausted. She was dancing on adrenaline and riding a wave of excitement. The crowd's energy had been nothing short of amazing, and then Marlon had showed up and pleased the audience with his impromptu five-minute performance, leaving them in a frenzy. The buzz about him, plus the leaked information that he'd be returning the following night, had sent scalper tickets through the roof. Or so Gabriella had been told. She didn't like the idea of Mr. or Ms. Everyday America paying so much for her tickets. But scalping tickets had been a part of the performance landscape for longer than she'd walked the earth. And people were willing to pay the high prices. So what was a celebrity to do?

Troy's earlier gesture was also largely responsible for her relaxed yet energized state of mind. After the sound check, they'd returned to Henderson and a master suite that had been turned into a den of peace. The masseuse that she'd used for the last five years had greeted her, the room already prepared with various colored candles and marvelous scents. A yoga session followed the aromatic massage. By the time Gabriella had reached the arena, her mind had been like, "Scandal what . . . ?"

Gary was one of the first persons to meet her backstage. "You were great, baby girl!"

She fell into his arms. "Thank you, Daddy." Times like these reminded her of the old days, when she was unsure and he was encouraging—constantly reminding her that nobody was better, badder, or more beautiful than her.

"Even Mr. Piss Ant held it down," Gary whispered, his head close to her as if they were conspiring best buds. "I'm so proud of you, Gab. But you know that."

During this exchange, Troy had remained a respectful distance behind them, blending into the scenery in a way that only a skilled guard could do. But he was as alert as a greyhound on a blood trail. The brother missed nothing at all, especially Gary's tactical change. *What are you up to now, Gary Stone?* At the end of the day, Troy deduced that it didn't matter. Nobody was coming between him and his girl.

They reached Gabriella's dressing room. "Baby," Gary said, his dark eyes shining, "there's somebody I want you to meet. Someone who's invited us to dinner; that is, if you're not too tired to go."

"Oh, Daddy. I'm not sure I'm up to entertaining."

"You won't have to; more than likely he'll be doing most of the talking."

"Who is it?"

"Kendall Anderson." Gabriella's eyes widened. "Exactly." It was precisely the reaction for which Gary had hoped.

"He flew here just to see my show?"

"You say that like you're surprised. You know he's one of your biggest fans."

"And wants to be more than that," she mumbled.

"Of course he does. He's the top entertainment lawyer in the country. Of course he'd want you for a client."

"You know that's not what I meant."

Gary knew more than Gabriella could even imagine. From the time she'd turned twenty-one, Kendall had made no move to hide his interest in teaming up with Gabriella . . . professionally and otherwise. Recently, he'd added an attractive caveat—partnering with Gary to produce new and upcoming acts under Gary's own record label. Even before this suggestion, Gary had thought quite highly of the young man who'd graduated from college magna cum laude and became a millionaire before the age of thirty. Now, he looked to be an even more perfect fit into the Stone dynasty.

"As it turns out he's in town, having just finished meeting with another client. He wasn't able to make the show, but he told me he's available until noon tomorrow, when he flies back to Atlanta. That's why I suggested we meet tonight. This is an opportunity that doesn't come often."

"Okay, Daddy," Gabriella said, using the towel around her neck to wipe sweat from her face. "I can see this means a lot to you. Give me an hour."

Gary nodded, and smiled as his daughter flounced into her dressing room without giving Troy a second glance. He strolled over to where the proud guard was standing. "I'm relieving you of your duties for the night."

"I'm afraid that Gabriella is the only one who can do that, sir."

"Well, consider me my daughter's messenger. She and I have business to conduct. And you will not be joining us." Gary sighed. His features softened. "Look, Troy. If you'll remember, I was in your corner when Gabriella wasn't. Why? Because you're the best at what you do. I appreciate your dedication to protecting my daughter. Tonight, however, your services will not be needed as the businessperson who's joining us has a more than capable security team. So take the evening to do what it seems you have little time for . . . relaxing. In the long run that will prove beneficial for you . . . and your client. Okay?"

Troy nodded, fully intending to do whatever it was that Gabriella wanted, rather than take the advice of her scheming old man.

After forty-five minutes, Gabriella emerged from her dressing room with Melanie by her side. She looked vibrant, radiant, and as if she'd just returned from a vacation in the tropics, not like she'd just performed in four-inch stilettos for almost three hours straight. The black pencil skirt she wore showcased her beautifully long legs, and looked both conservative and sexy at the same time. The loose, peasant-styled, pastel-colored blouse gave peek-a-boo hints at what lay beneath it, and a wide, black leather belt put her small waist on display. The outfit was complemented with glossy black stilettos, a triple strand of black pearls, and dangly black-diamond earrings. Her hair was pulled up and away from her face, giving her smoldering eyes an Asian slant and emphasizing her smooth and kissable neck. She walked with the assurance of one who knew she had it going on, and was perfectly comfortable with this fact.

"Where to, lovely lady?" Troy asked, when she reached him.

"My father has set up a late night business meeting. He's handled the security. So believe or not, you're being treated to the rare night off. But don't get used to it," she hurriedly continued. "It will probably be one of the last ones for the next three weeks."

She winked, and placed a soft hand on his chest as she passed him. Had she pressed a little harder, she might have been able to feel the cracks appearing on his heart.

35

Instead of taking the car back to their Henderson spot, Troy opted to hit the strip. Walking. He needed fresh air and a fresh perspective. At one-thirty in the morning there were still tourists strolling about, but the sidewalks of Las Vegas Boulevard were nowhere near as crowded as they'd been when Troy had seen it earlier, on the way to the show.

He walked and thought about this new place that he found himself—possibly wanting someone more than she wanted him. That revelation in itself was enough to almost coax the rarely imbibing bodyguard to throw back a double shot. When the thought first hit him he tried to ignore it, refute it, act like it wasn't only not true, but that it was not possible. But the feeling he'd gotten once given the dismissal by the lady herself? *You can't deny what that left you feeling, dog.* And he couldn't deny that feeling was hurt.

Troy peeled off his jacket and flung it over his shoulder. This simple act brought the admiring glances of several women around him, and a loudly whispered conversation by an inebriated group. There were too many thoughts whirling in his mind to hear any of the comments around him. He was too busy trying to figure out what it was that existed between him and Gabriella. And when he lost control.

Stopping at the corner, Troy looked around him and took in the sites: everyday places seen in Any City, USA. Walgreens, CVS, McDonald's, and Ross, blending seamlessly with casinos. New York New York, Monte Carlo, Hard Rock, Planet Hollywood, and Mandalay Bay helped to shape the skyline, filled in with smaller casinos, restaurants, and shops. While nowhere near a snob, Troy realized how rarely he actually did this, hung out with ordinary people to do ordinary things. Like walk down a street and take in the scenery. For the past few years his job had taken him into the atmosphere of high profile athletes, politicians, and stars whose identity did not afford them the luxury of such mundane endeavors. And even though he lived in LA's Leimert Park, an area of the city that his brothers called the hood, he now realized that even that aspect of his life was insulated. His home's security system was one of the best in the country; nobody entered his gate without being buzzed in, and as in anybody's community, do-drop-in neighbors were all but a thing of the past. The people he socialized with were those in his circle and were, for the most part, upwardly mobile, financially secure, successful men and women. His older brothers were part of that group. With Michael owning a successful sports management company and Gregory being not only a renowned and respected doctor but the recent recipient of a prestigious research grant, he'd had some pretty big examples to follow. In his humble opinion, baby brother was doing all right.

His phone vibrated. He pulled it out and looked at the screen. "Hey there, big bro. I was just thinking about you."

Michael, the oldest, was on the line. "I meant to call earlier, but it's been nonstop all day. Mom called me this morning, about you in the tabloids. How are you doing, man?"

Troy sat on a stone wall surrounding a fountain. "I've been better," he honestly responded. "But you know how we do it. I'll be all right."

"No need to hold up that strong, nonchalant facade with me, baby brother. I heard something in your voice as soon as you answered the phone."

"You heard exhaustion, for one thing." Troy gave Michael a rundown of the past twenty-four hours. "To tell you the truth, I'm glad for the night off. Even though it's such a rare occurrence that I honestly don't know what to do with myself."

"Where's your girl? Where's Gabriella?"

"She's attending a meeting with her father."

"At this time of night?"

"They had to get it in where they could fit it in."

"Must be somebody important."

"Kendall A-List Anderson." A slight scent of sarcasm wafted between these words.

Michael whistled. "That's high cotton right there," he said, using a term that was one of his late father's favorites. "I heard he's so gangster he rarely takes on new clients."

"Trust me; he'll make room for Gabriella."

This time, Michael caught the scent. "So . . . there's trouble in paradise?"

Troy shared with Michael his earlier conversation with Gary. "I didn't even sweat it," Troy finished. "Just knew that Gabriella would have my back. When she up and sent me off like a schoolboy at recess, I've got to admit it, man—didn't feel good."

"Do you think her actions had anything to do with what went down in the papers?"

"It had everything to do with that. But she wasn't the only one whose name got blasted. My picture is in there, too. And I never left her side."

"Do you think she's left yours? After all, business is business, and it's no doubt that Kendall's stamp takes everybody to another level, no matter how big you already are."

"Thanks, man. That's just what I needed to hear—about the greatness of that muthafucka." Troy jumped off the short wall and continued walking.

"What's your schedule like tomorrow?"

"Depends on the princess. Why?"

"Because you sound like you could use some brotherly love. And I'm headed that way to give it to you."

"It's not that deep, man. I just need to clear my head, that's all."

"Maybe so, but Shayna and I need to go to Vegas anyway. It's been a while since we've seen her mom and baby brother."

"You need tickets to the show?"

"Let me talk to Shayna and find out what she wants to do."

"All right then. Just let me know how many you need so I can secure them and backstage passes."

"Okay. If our schedule will allow it we'll probably take the first plane out."

"Call me when you know."

"I will."

"And, Michael?"

"Yes?"

"Thank you."

"You're welcome."

"I love you, bro."

"Love you, too."

Gabriella took the linen napkin and daintily wiped tears from her eyes. Kendall was fine, that was a given: smooth dark brown skin, solid build, sparkling white teeth framed by an immaculately maintained goatee. But she hadn't expected him to be hilarious. For the past hour he'd not only treated them to a private dinner prepared by the chef who accompanied him on business travels all over the world reached via his private jet, but he'd also regaled them with behind-the-scene stories about a cast of characters that most people would only read about: kings and princes, ambassadors and heads of state. She noticed that there was very little mention of his A-list clients. To Gabriella it was proof that he didn't share others' business—always a good sign.

During the evening, she'd also learned more about the larger-than-life attorney whose personal life stayed amazingly private. Though he came from old money, his lineage traceable to the "free coloreds of Boston," he wasn't staid or snooty. Though he'd been a Rhodes scholar and received his higher learning degree from an Ivy League college, he wasn't boastful. In fact, he was refreshingly down to the earth, although nobody would ever mistake him for being a common man.

Eventually, over a flawless dessert of molten lava chocolate cake covered with real gold flakes, the conversation came back to business.

"I'd very much like to represent you, Gabriella," Kendall said, in a voice that was both smooth and authoritative. "I've developed stellar relationships with most of the Fortune Five Hundred advertising companies; any number of which would love to have you as their spokesperson. I also am involved with several charitable causes that you may also find of interest, including the Boys and Girls Club and several outreaches for at-risk inner city youth. From what I've seen, you love to give back. This way, you can make even more money for these worthy causes and play a part in their continued development by sitting on one or more boards.

"Lastly, several of my former classmates and associates are hugely successful investors. And while I've no doubt your bank account is quite healthy, I believe that one can never acquire too much wealth. After all, the universe has placed it here for our good."

"Making a lot of money is no longer my focus," Gabriella responded. "I already have more than enough. My dad on the other hand . . ." The men laughed. "But the charitable causes sound very intriguing, especially the ones dealing with at-risk youth. I'd like to know more."

After comparing schedules, the two agreed to continue the conversation in the next few weeks, in either England,

Germany, or France. Shortly afterward, Gary and Gabriella accepted the ride from his driver upon which Kendall had insisted, finding themselves couched in the luxurious leather only found in a Flying Spur Bentley.

"Please come with me to the villa, Gabriella," Gary said as soon as they got into the car.

"Dad . . ."

"No, wait, honey. I know it's late. I don't want to talk tonight. I'd like us to have breakfast in the morning. And I also don't want to preach to you, Gab, or tell you what to do. Today, your mother—and Troy—reminded me that you are grown, twenty-one plus!" Gabriella chuckled. "I want us to have a discussion about business, baby girl, and how we can lessen the impact of this latest situation."

Maybe it was the wine, but tonight with her dad felt just like the old days, when it was him and her against the world. Her mother had always been supportive, but she'd initially been less than enthused about her daughter following in Gary's show business footsteps, and even after Gabriella had gained success with the group, had wanted to remain on the sidelines. During the Haute Coutures' tours Yvonne had stayed home with Garrett. Gabriella and her father had become very close while sharing their common interest. Yes, she was grown. But Gary was right. He wasn't just her father; he was her manager. And he would always have her best interest at heart. Gabriella knew this for a fact. Always.

"I've been thinking about a game plan and I'd like to run it by you. I'll listen to you, Gabriella, and I'll ask that you listen to me. Okay?"

She thought about it for a moment and then nodded.

She had deep feelings for Troy, and believed that they would be able to weather this storm. They still hadn't had a chance to really talk about their appearance in the tabloids. *I'll do it tomorrow,* she thought. After she talked with her dad.

36

Gabriella slept in the next morning. By the time the housekeeper roused her out of bed, it was almost noon. It had been worth it. She'd slept soundly, and after a long, hot shower felt totally refreshed. After a detailed phone conversation with Carol, a short chat with Dana about publicity matters, and a conference call with Melanie and the rest of her crew, she joined her father, whom she'd texted earlier with the time that she'd be downstairs.

"Well, hello there, sleepy head!"

Walking over and kissing Gary on the cheek, she responded, "Hello, Daddy."

"I know we've got a busy day ahead, so I hope you don't mind that I've already put in the order with our chef."

"I'm starving, so anything will taste good."

"Still, I played it safe by choosing some of your favorites: glazed salmon, rice pilaf, and a large salad. Did I do okay?"

"You did fine, Dad." She sat down and, after the maid had served her tea and orange juice and left the room,

Gabriella dived right in. "So what's this plan that you want to talk to me about, the one that's going to erase my latest scandal?"

"That's a stretch, Gabriella. I'm not a magician after all. But I do have a plan that interestingly enough expanded once I received Kendall's phone call."

"I was going to ask how the meeting came about. He called you?"

"Yes." Said with a straight face and without one ounce of guilt at the little white lie. "He's been following your career (this was true) and thought that now would be a good time to enhance your brand."

"He saw the tabloid."

Gary nodded. "He did indeed."

"Funny that he didn't mention it last night."

"Like me, he probably didn't see a need. We all know what happened is unfortunate."

"It's part of this life, Daddy."

"True, and how we handle it determines how much impact it has on your career. Now, Gab, don't get mad at what I'm about to say. I asked Troy if the two of you were sleeping together."

"Daddy!"

"I know, but hear me out first. I'm not just looking at this situation as your father, but as your manager, and as a fan."

"What did he say?"

"He said to ask you."

"Good for him."

"So . . . are you two sleeping together, Gabriella?" No response. Gary sighed. "We've been down this road before, Gab. I don't want your face plastered all over the tabloids with a different flavor on your arm every week.

Everything you do reflects back on your career, and can have repercussions for years to come! Hence, the vow."

"What's so bad about me having a life, Daddy? What kind of repercussions can happen just because I might choose to date someone?"

"So y'all are dating."

"Good try, Dad. I said might."

They paused while their salads were delivered and then Gary continued. "No matter what's true, here's what the fans see: a woman who went from spending time in the master suite of her ex-boyfriend to a lower floor with yet another man. I know we live in a society where supposedly anything goes, but that type of publicity—true or no—will ruin your reputation after a while.

"You've always wanted to be a role model for young girls."

"I am a role model."

"Yet what kind of message do you think this article sends to them?"

"One that says not to read trashy tabloids filled with lies!"

Gary took a deep breath. "Okay. You're right."

Again, silence filled the room as they chowed down on their salads.

After a bit of small talk as they began eating the entrée, Gary continued. "Whatever your feelings for Troy, and I'll keep my opinions about that to myself, I propose this. For the next four weeks, the remainder of the tour, keep things professional between you two. Stay out of the limelight. Meanwhile, I'll work with Dana and Kendall's PR team—"

"Kendall? What does he have to do with this?"

"I think he would be a nice diversion; get the hounds

to follow another scent, if you know what I'm saying. The tabloids love a good mystery and if suddenly you're seen on the arm of Kendall Anderson, well . . ."

"I thought you just said it wasn't good for me to go from one man to the next."

"Yes, but this is different."

"How so?"

"Because you two would be interacting in a professional capacity."

"Troy and I work together that way."

"No, daughter. Troy works for you. Kendall will work with you." Gabriella pouted as she continued to eat. "It's a win-win, Gabriella. Being photographed with him, getting the tabloids and news magazine shows interested in what may be transpiring between you will ultimately be a screen for the business relationship that can truly be built underneath it all. Not only that but . . . you could do worse than a handsome, hugely successful, well-heeled, well-connected man like Mr. Anderson."

"I'll give it to you that he's handsome. But isn't he like . . . your age?"

"Not even close. He just turned forty years old."

"Forty! He's fifteen years older than me."

"And a very young forty at that," Gary continued, ignoring her outburst. "He plays tennis regularly and runs several miles a day."

"Oh, Dad, please. Sounds like you're making the case for a nice thoroughbred that I should buy."

"He's a gentleman who can give you the world either professionally, personally, or both. You decide." When Gabriella failed to respond, Gary added, "Just take twenty-four, no, forty-eight hours to think about it. Preferably . . . without the input of your bodyguard."

"Why are you against Troy all of a sudden? You're the one who strongly suggested I hire him!"

"I'm not against him, baby girl. I'm just for you. It's as simple as that."

Troy was in his sister-in-law's mother's backyard, chilling with some of his family. He hadn't seen "simple" in twenty-four hours, ever since it began with his mother informing him that he was a tabloid sensation and ended when his client-slash-woman had given him the night off.

This morning he was thrown even more off-kilter when he woke to a text message from Gabriella telling him that she'd meet him at the arena at six o'clock, for the sound check. Until then, she'd texted, she'd be at the villa with her father. Handling business, she'd explained. One question alone had ping-ponged in his mind. *What. The hell. Is going on?*

"Troy!" His sister-in-law's stepfather, who just happened to be only a few years older than her, walked out onto the family's air-conditioned patio. Ironically Shayna's mother, Beverly, her husband, Larsen, and their three-year-old son also lived in Henderson, about ten minutes from the gated home that Gabriella had rented. "Man, my wife and I can't thank you enough. We've been so busy, you know, between me building up my limo business and Beverly taking care of the baby. A night for ourselves, kicking it at the Gabriella concert, is just what we need!"

"No worries, man. Glad I could help. Y'all are sure to have a good time." Troy accepted the glass of iced tea that Michael, Troy's brother and Shayna's husband, offered, glad for the one thing that he'd been able to accomplish that day. Carol had responded to the e-mail he'd sent Gabriella about tickets and backstage passes, and said all she needed was a guest list. He tried to convince himself that Gabriella was busy, tried not to feel left out, shut out, tossed out. Hard to do, given the intimate role he'd played in the star's sold-out tour since day one. Even harder to deal with was the fact that he hadn't seen her since her late night meeting with Anderson, the man whom Troy refused to find intimidating.

"Hey, guys!" Shayna called out to the men from the patio door. "Lunch is served and we're having it indoors."

"Be there in a minute, baby," Michael answered. "You guys go ahead and start eating. Troy and I will be in momentarily." He looked at Larsen. "Can you give us a moment?"

"Oh, for sure, man." Larsen hurriedly got up from the patio table. "I'll see y'all inside."

Troy watched him go into the house. "I never thought I'd see the day where y'all got along."

Michael smiled. "I know, right? He makes Beverly happy and that's what matters to Shayna and me. His brother, on the other hand, is a class-A jerk."

That was putting it mildly. When Michael met Shayna, she was newly out of a relationship with Jarrell, Larsen's brother, and the relationship with her mother was strained. As Michael and Shayna grew closer, tensions ran high. Thankfully, once Beverly had a baby and the mother and daughter had several heart to hearts, healing began. Over the past two years, they'd continued the mending until these days Shayna and Beverly were friends, and Michael and Larsen were cordial. And while she harbored no hard feelings, when Shayna came to town Jarrell was not invited over . . . at her request.

"So . . . still no more word from her?" Troy shook his head. "What are you going to do?"

"The same as always—handle my business. No doubt Gary is pushing her buttons, feeding her a bunch of BS. He's a control freak who wants to manage everything about Gabriella, including her love life."

"She doesn't seem like the type who'd take that."

"Yesterday morning, I would have agreed with you."

"And now?"

"Now, I don't know what to think." Troy leaned forward, rested his elbows on his knees. "I'm going to be honest, Michael. I've got feelings for her. And I know for sure that she's feeling me, too. But then here comes Gary waving a man like Kendall under her nose: Wall Street contacts, private jets, Ivy League education, bank account as tight or even tighter than hers. I truly believe that I can hold my own against any man out there, but when it comes to how a woman looks at it . . . I just don't know."

"Come on, now. Where's my cocky, confident, baby brother? We came from the block, bro, the hood, around the way. Everything we got we earned, you feel me? You have everything to be proud of and nothing to be ashamed of. We don't have to bow our head for anyone."

"I know," Troy said, settling back against his chair with a sigh. "I guess I'm in new territory, you know?"

Michael smiled. "You mean the place where the woman isn't sniffing behind your heels, where you might actually have to work a little bit to get the girl?"

"Yeah, I guess so." It was Troy's first genuine smile all day.

"Don't sell yourself short, son. You're a Morgan man."

"No doubt." They bumped fists.

"And all the money and status in the world cannot compete with that."

37

Gabriella rode toward the arena with butterflies in her stomach. She knew why. There'd been no communication with Troy since last night, when she gave him the night off and went to the late night dinner meeting with her father. And Kendall. Throughout the night, as she'd tossed and turned, unable to sleep, she'd tried to justify why she hadn't asked Troy to come along, why for the first time since she'd hired him he hadn't accompanied her to her destination. As dawn neared, she rationalized that it was because the meeting was in a private dining room at an exclusive restaurant with Kendall's bodyguards in attendance. And if she was truthful with herself, she had ignored the real reason: she didn't want any drama going down between her father, Kendall, and Troy. But there was more. That little girl who always obeyed her daddy, even when his wishes went against her own. And even though he'd surprised her by being rational and thoughtful and not going ballistic over the tabloid snafu—the way he'd done when he'd found out about Marlon—she knew that her father was well aware of her feelings for Troy. And he wasn't happy about it.

Well, after not being able to sleep, not getting the good sex that she'd quickly become accustomed to, and not being able to shake the nervousness of what the day might hold . . . she wasn't such a happy camper herself.

Gary's message indicator beeped. Gabriella barely noticed as she turned her head to look out the window. His deep chuckle caused her to turn back and face him. "What is it?"

"It's Kendall," Gary said, his smile as bright as if he were looking at six winning numbers for the Powerball. "He's already run the European schedule by his secretary and says he'll see us next week. In London."

That's just great, Gabriella thought. "Oh, really?" is what she said. "I'm surprised he was able to get away so quickly, with his busy schedule and all."

"That just goes to show how special you are," Gary answered, as he used a single thumb to type a reply. "A man will rearrange his schedule when the woman is a priority."

"I don't know why he's making me a priority," she grumbled, even though she knew she was probably saying way too much. Then to try and put her comment into the right context, she added, "I won't be able to concentrate on any charity events until after the tour is over." Her father nodded, but said nothing. "Wait, Daddy, what are you texting to him?"

"I'm sending our lodging information, and telling him that we're looking forward to moving ahead with these plans. I'm also asking him to send over any preliminary information he may have on the various foundations and causes that might be of interest. The sooner we can get our PR team to leak information on this professional partnership the sooner . . ."

Gary kept talking, but Gabriella no longer heard a word he was saying. The limousine had reached the arena and Troy was standing outside talking to what looked like a bunch of female tourists. It had been less than twenty-four hours since she'd seen him, but her eyes drank him in like a thirsty man in the desert and her mouth watered like the burbling stream he hoped to find. His back was to them—broad shoulders highlighted by the black short-sleeved polo shirt that on him looked more like a muscle shirt, tucked into the narrow waist that she loved to wrap her arms around. He wore some cargo type pants that she hadn't seen before, the looseness of which gave him a thuggish air. As they neared the group she watched a pretty blond babe sidle up to him, place a bold arm around his waist, and spout what Gabriella was sure was a bunch of complimentary blah-blah-blah. Troy smiled at the woman, but turned to watch the limo approach. She fully expected him to bid his adieu to the group and head toward the tunnel leading to the arena's loading area where the limo would park, but when she hurriedly grabbed her compact and looked through the rearview mirror, she saw Troy's back to her once again, and several more females around him. Even more, she saw his arm around the raven-haired chick now cuddled by his side.

WTH?

She snatched her phone from the large designer bag at her feet and tapped his name once it appeared on the screen. The call went immediately to voice mail. Gabriella's anger went from zero to sixty, fast and furiously. She shot off a quick text: **Playtime is over. Meet me backstage.**

Troy had seen the limo even before it headed into the arena loading zone, had spotted it as soon as it turned on the boulevard, and had thanked his lucky stars for the timing. He could only imagine what Gabriella thought when she saw him surrounded by a gaggle of women, a group of young ladies from an online club who were enjoying their first trip to Vegas and who were excited about the Gabriella concert they'd see later tonight. There was no way that she could have missed the scene—girls acting like they'd never seen a caramel cutie before. He could almost feel the daggers she'd shot at him from the front, as the limo approached, and those she continued to throw once the car had passed. Good enough for her, Troy thought as he felt his phone vibrate for the second time. He'd pointedly ignored her first call and knew that she'd follow it up with a text. Ignoring the call was probably not the most professional move, but he wanted Gabriella to get a little hint of how he'd felt last night as he'd watched her, Gary, and one of the country's most prominent entertainment attorneys walk down the hall and out of the backstage area. As with most people connected to the industry, Troy knew Kendall, had met him on more than one occasion. So the fact that old boy had breezed by him with a dismissive glance, treating him like someone's employee or "the help," as Gary had labeled him, hadn't improved the situation. A conversation with his brother, Michael, had forced Troy to acknowledge that Gabriella's actions had bothered him more than he wanted to admit—had made him realize that when it came to his feelings about the superstar he was in deep . . . . maybe too deep.

After reading the text, Troy spent another few minutes with the group of women who'd done wonders to soothe his bruised ego before heading into the arena area. "All right, ladies," he said, after posing for yet another picture with an adoring fan. "I've got to get to work. But remember, two of you lucky ladies might receive a backstage pass to meet Gabriella. Be sure and text your number to my phone." After a final dazzling smile, he strode toward the room where Gabriella held camp.

When he walked in, Gabriella and Melanie were browsing through a rack of costumes for the night's show. Another assistant was busy on her iPad while Carol lined up a row of various letters, head shots, and other PR paraphernalia for Gabriella to sign.

"Good afternoon, ladies," Troy said, oozing confidence as he walked across the room and gave Carol a hug.

"Hey, Troy." Carol glanced at Gabriella, totally aware of how hard her best friend was trying to act nonplussed when she was anything but. Had he walked in ten minutes ago he would have heard a string of expletives that included Troy being labeled a conceited body orifice.

"Hello, Troy," Tiana answered, barely looking up from her iPad. Melanie shared a greeting as well.

Gabriella was markedly silent.

"Gab," Troy said casually, taking a seat in one of two oversized chairs that along with a love seat and coffee table anchored the far right wall. "Is there any chance I can get a couple backstage passes for tonight?"

"More passes? Who for now . . . your groupies?"

Instead of reacting to her snappy tone, Troy simply

pulled out his phone and began checking e-mails. There were at least a dozen new ones, all from the group of excited women he'd just left. The one he opened, however, was from Tara Montega's camp. Tara was Gabriella's stiffest competition, a raven-haired Latina with Kelly Clarkson's wholesomeness, J.Lo's body, and a voice like Celine Dion who'd been trying to pull him away from Gabriella since the day he was hired. *I wonder how much snippier you'd be if I dropped this little tidbit.*

"You're not being paid to entertain. You're being paid to guard me and the other members of this tour."

"My staff is doing their job and last night you relieved me of the need to do mine. Remember?"

"As soon as you saw that I'd returned, that was your cue that off time was over."

"I'm here now, so what's the problem?" Troy's veneer of cool was about to wear thin. He took a deep breath to regain control.

"The problem is that you seem to forget your job!"

"You mean my place? I don't do diva, baby. I thought you knew that by now."

"You know what? I don't need this right now. And I don't need you. Get. Out!"

Troy shrugged as he stood. "Fine with me. I'll be right outside . . . guarding the door in case Carol goes rogue or Melanie decides to slap you upside the head with a stiletto."

Carol snickered and even Melanie's perpetual scowl softened. Gabriella was not amused. Troy walked to the door.

"I don't find anything funny and I don't appreciate your smart-ass mouth." Gabriella shot daggers at his back as he sought to make his exit. "There are at least a dozen security personnel who would love to have your job."

Troy stopped as he opened the door. He did not turn around. And while he showed no outward emotion, his tone was chilling. "And there are other clients willing to double what you're paying me to go and work for them." He finally turned and looked at her. "So whenever you no longer require my company's services . . . just let me know."

38

Gabriella stared at the door that Troy had quietly closed behind him. How was it that while she was the one who'd sent him out of the room, she felt like the one who'd been dismissed? Gabriella threw down the jump-suit she'd been considering for the opening song of the second set. Oh, no he didn't. "I'll be right back."

She stomped across the room and snatched open the door, becoming even more incensed at seeing Troy's back as he walked down the hall. *Didn't I just tell him that his job was to guard me and at this moment he wasn't doing too well?* "Troy!"

He stopped and slowly turned around. She quickly closed the distance between them, her finger almost in his face. "We need to talk!"

"We sure do." He placed a firm grasp on her arm and led them down a short hallway that she hadn't noticed before.

"Where are we going?" Gabriella asked, trying without success to free her arm.

"Where we can have some privacy." They reached the

door at the end of the hallway. Troy opened it and didn't let go of Gabriella's arm until he'd closed the door and locked it. He turned around to feel the palm of Gabriella's hand connect with his cheek.

The slap stunned him. He reacted by grabbing both her hands. "Woman, have you lost your mind?"

"Who do you think you are, talking to me like that in front of my team?"

"I'm the man you've been dissing ever since you saw me today. I'm not going to stand for your high-handed antics, Gabriella. Respect is a two-way street."

"Let go of me."

Instead of releasing her, Troy pulled her against his chest. "Get a hold of your temper. Just like I won't be your whipping boy, I won't be your punching bag either."

Gabriella squirmed to get away from him, her soft breasts rubbing against his hard chest as she turned this way and that. "I mean it," she panted, still trying to fight him. "Let me go."

He pulled her tighter.

She tried to wriggle her way out of his grasp, but all that did was increase the friction between their bodies. Her nipples hardened right around the time his dick decided to make its presence known. She tried to ignore the tingling in the core of her belly, tried to stop her vaginal walls from contracting with desire.

"I hate you," she spat between gritted teeth.

"I'm not too happy with you right about now either," he shot back.

Her head was cocked to look directly into his eyes. His head was bowed to meet her glare. Their lips were inches apart.

"Let me go," she whispered. But she was no longer

fighting against his grasp. Instead she was ridiculously aware of the woodsy scent clinging to his skin the way she now clung to his body, more than a little turned on by how his chest scraped her nipples and his hardened shaft pushed against her pelvis. Her pelvis pushed back.

Dammit, body. Behave! But it was no use. He ground himself against her, allowing his arms to drop down until his hands could cup her booty and pull her flush against him.

"What do you think you're—"

He silenced her with a kiss: hot and demanding, wet and precise. He shot his stiff tongue into her open mouth, swirling it around as if it were his first time tasting her. The mini she wore rode up as he continued to explore her tempting assets, squeezing each cheek barely hidden by her silk panties.

Gabriella lost the battle to seem unaffected and moaned aloud. It was all the encouragement Troy needed.

With one fluid movement he turned them away from the door and over by a table collecting errant scraps of paper and yesterday's dust. He swept the papers to the floor and placed Gabriella on the table. Gently directing her backward, he knelt before the legs that were gapped before him, placed his hands beneath her butt, and pulled off the thong. This time, there were no soft kisses placed at her knee, no wispy licks across her calves or nibbles to her inner thigh. No, this time he went straight for paradise, burying his head between her legs, burying his tongue between her folds.

Gabriella almost came right then.

Instead, she reached for the edges of the table, holding on with both hands for dear life. When he sucked on her nub, it was all she could do to keep from crying out, from screaming the name of the only man who'd been able to totally and thoroughly please her. He made love to her with his tongue until her toes curled: nibbling, lapping, sucking, kissing her lower lips with as much tenderness and passion as he had the ones that were on her face. She felt her body begin to tremble. Troy did, too. And he had no intention of letting her ride the waves of ecstasy without him.

"Get up." He rose as he commanded her, and held out his hand to help her rise. "Turn around." She did. He could only imagine what she was thinking as he undid his belt and unzipped his pants, could only wonder why her legs started shaking at the sound of foil ripping and the whoosh of fabric leaving his waist and hitting the floor.

But when his hands grabbed her hips, he wondered no more. The only thing on his mind was the feel of her soft skin against his engorged head as he rubbed it between her slick nether lips, nothing in his ears but the sound of her mewling as she spread her legs farther apart to accommodate his massive girth. He gently pushed himself inside her in one fell swoop, stopping only briefly as he felt her muscles contract around him. He pulled out and pushed again to the hilt, loving the way she seemed to be custom built to love him, knowing that whatever had happened between her and Kendall last night . . . it hadn't felt like this.

He swirled his hips even as he pulled out and thrust in again, setting up a slow rhythm that Gabriella immediately matched. He smiled as she pushed back against him, trying to take him all in, trying to keep him in place. She reached behind her and grabbed his butt.

"Harder," she commanded.

"Uh-huh, I'm going to give you what you want," he

said, his hips keeping pace with his words, or vice versa. "This is what you want, right?"

No answer. For Troy, this was not an option.

He increased the pace, shifting his body left and right as he did so. At the same time, he took a strong finger and ran it down the length of her back, continuing until he hit the crease of her ass and then increasing the pressure to slide between her cheeks. He smiled at the goose bumps that popped up on her skin, renewed in his quest to banish all thoughts from her mind; including those of a rich attorney and that she could live her life without him around. He felt her reach between their legs and tickle his sac. He'd told her that this was one of his sensitive spots and he was pleased that she remembered. When she brushed her hands across his balls before sinking her nails into his thigh, he thought that he'd explode.

"Gabriella."

He stopped moving. *Shit, who could that be?*

Obviously, Gabriella didn't care. "Don't stop," she whispered, and began rubbing her butt up against him. He increased the pace a final time, reaching forward to pinch her nipples as he pounded against her, as if trying to stamp his ownership across her soul.

"Is this what you want?" he whispered.

"Yes," she panted, knowing she shouldn't.

Listening and hearing nothing outside the door, he asked, "Am I what you want?"

Not here, Gab! No! "Uh-huh."

"Then don't." Thrust. "Ever." Grind. "Ask me." Gyrate. Pump. "To leave you again."

He tightened his grip upon her hips and sank himself inside her with heartfelt thrusts delivered at a feverish pitch. He felt her muscles contract again and knew his release was fast approaching. As he licked away a bead of perspiration from her body, he pushed himself in to the hilt. And exploded.

She did, too, moaning his name in the process. They shuddered and groaned and continued to gyrate until the last vestiges of their orgasm had played itself out.

That's when they heard the knock at the door.

39

"Gabriella, are you in here?" The sound of Gary's voice cut through the last vestiges of their lovemaking, like ice water thrown on a just-awakened face.

Her eyes wide, she turned and looked at Troy. He placed a finger to his lips at the same time he gently, quietly pulled out of her.

Another knock. "Anybody in here?"

After a couple moments the sound of retreating footsteps were like music to Troy's and Gabriella's ears. But her relief was short-lived; she knew that someone had heard them, and that when Gary wasn't able to find Troy he'd correctly guess that wherever he was, she was with him.

"Damn."

"I know, baby," Troy said, placing gentle kisses on her temple, cheek, and lips. "But don't worry. It's time that I had another talk with your father."

"And say what?" Gabriella asked, fumbling to put on her thong and reaching for her bra and mini-dress.

"That my intentions toward you are sincere and genuine, and that I'll never do anything to hurt his baby girl."

Gabriella delivered a quiet snort, pulling her mini over
her head and slipping into her wedgies. "If you think
that's what matters, then you don't know my father."

"Oh, so he'd rather you be with somebody you can
never love just because of the zeros in a brother's bank
account?"

"Pretty much."

"Then . . ." Troy said, pulling Gabriella into his arms
and placing more kisses on her face. "Then it's about that
time."

"About what time?"

"About time for you to decide whether you're going to
be my woman . . . or daddy's little girl."

They waited ten minutes, until sure that no one was
nearby outside in the hall. Troy's phone had rung several
times: Gary, Carol, and two of Troy's men. Gabriella was
sure her phone was also being blown up, but in her deter-
mination to catch up with Troy she'd left it behind in her
dressing room. Now she was back there, doing damage
control. Or trying to. To hear Carol and Melanie tell it,
fixing this incident would be about as easy as putting
spilled milk back into the carton.

"Did he seem really, really mad?" she asked Carol as
they huddled inside the locked dressing room, the one
that was filled with so many flowers—sent from
Kendall—that Gabriella already had Carol working on a
local hospital donation. She could not appreciate their
beauty, or anything else right now. Her focus was solely
on gauging not whether or not Dad was upset, but just

how much. She'd refused a phone call from her father, and no matter that the show was starting in fifteen minutes, she'd ordered everyone out.

"No matter how many times you ask me, my answer isn't going to change." Carol reached for a blotting paper, then dabbed at the sheen of perspiration on Gabriella's face. Her sweating had nothing to do with exertion, and everything to do with nervousness and fear. "I've got to be honest, Gab. I've never seen Gary so angry."

Gabriella walked over to a mirror, fixing the corset and fishnet stockings that already fit her to perfection. "I'll just deny it," she said, critically eyeing herself in the mirror as Carol fussed with her hair. She was trying to be calm, but Gabriella knew that this situation had worked her best friend's nerves as well. "I'll tell him that I was . . . I don't know . . . out."

"One of the stagehands said he saw you going down the hall with Troy," Carol said, repeating what she'd already told Gabriella at least twice. "Denying it will only further anger your father."

"Then what should I do?"

"Tell him the truth."

"That's a sure way to get Troy fired, and I don't want that."

"From the way your father was going off, whether Troy stays or goes might not be your choice."

Gary walked over to where Troy stood conversing with two of his security guards. He made no attempt to hide his displeasure. "We need to talk."

"It'll have to wait until after the concert, Gary. My men have—"

"It will happen now!"

Having anticipated Gary's wrath, Troy's reaction to his outburst was imperceptible. The looks on his men's faces, however, showed their total surprise.

"Make sure someone guards the backstage door at all times," Troy calmly explained. "No wristband, no admittance. Period. Curtis, I want you to—"

"It doesn't surprise me that you're hard of hearing," Gary snapped. He turned to the men. "You're dismissed." They looked at Troy. "This isn't his call. As the manager of this tour, it's mine. A new security company and members of the Las Vegas Police Department are ready to escort you out of the arena. Your boss will soon be joining you in the parking lot."

To underscore Gary's words, two uniformed policemen came around the corner. "Mr. Stone, which of these men do we need to escort from the premises?"

"All of them," Gary replied. "But I'd like a word with this one here first." His look seemed to dare Troy to stay, which ensured the fact that he wasn't leaving.

One of the men who'd been with the company just over a year, hesitated. "Are you going to be all right, boss?"

Troy nodded. "Go ahead. I'll be fine."

The two officers left, along with Troy's two employees. Gary spoke, his eyes on the backs of the men and police officers now walking down the hall. "It's all I can do to keep from jacking you up right now."

"If not for how I feel about Gabriella, and the respect I'd show anyone who was her father, I'd welcome the fight. It's been a while since I've handed down a good old ass whoopin'."

"That big ego of yours is why you've just lost a client. I told you that my daughter didn't date the help."

"Looks like you should have told your daughter that."

The fist came out of nowhere, but Troy's reactive skills were well honed. He'd barely glimpsed the blow coming, just a flash in the corner of his eye, when he stepped back and threw up a defensive arm in the same fluid motion. The hit clipped Troy's chin, but he was otherwise unharmed. "Like I said," he drawled, rubbing the spot where Gary had hit him, "I'd respect the father of any woman I dated. That's the only reason you're not on the floor with my foot in your chest. But know this. If you ever try and hit me again, I'm going to hit you back. Trust me, player . . . you don't want none of this."

"I sure as hell don't," Gary snarled, still aching for a fight. "And after tonight, when she sees how well Kendall will take care of her, my daughter won't either. Oh, and don't worry about your money or our honoring the contract. So as not to get drawn into an ugly lawsuit, we'll put the check for the length of the entire tour in the mail."

"You don't have to do that. Just pay me what I've earned."

"To have you gone is worth the fee. We don't want to take the chance of your trying to stay in our lives by any means necessary."

"You've really underestimated me, man."

"And you've obviously not understood what lengths I'll go to in protecting Gabriella's image. I haven't worked this hard to have her end up with someone like you."

"What about the lengths you'll go to protect her life? Have you forgotten about the threats she's received?"

"Right now, I'm more concerned about the threat in front of me."

"You think I'd do something to harm Gabriella?"

"Not intentionally. But besmirching her image can sometimes prove worse than a physical blow."

"There's no way Gabriella's relationship with me will harm her image."

"I think otherwise. Now, either leave on your own or I'll have you escorted from the premises."

Troy stepped toward him. "You might live to regret this, Gary."

"I'll take my chances," Gary countered, taking a step of his own.

Several tense seconds passed as the two men eyed each other. Then Troy walked out of the arena, and out of Gabriella's life, without looking back.

40

"You did what?" Gabriella and her father were in her backstage dressing room, where she'd demanded to see him as soon as her show was over. She was still dressed in the skintight jumpsuit that was her final costume change—a creative piece with stars and stripes in strategic places to both honor the Fourth of July and keep Gabriella semi-modestly covered. The audience had loved both it and the simulated fireworks that marked the end of her North American tour. Only more than a decade of professionalism had kept her from running off the stage before the show was over; only years of training allowed her to sincerely thank her audience and all of America for their support, and to let Europe know that she was on her way across the pond. But truth be told, her mind had been elsewhere the entire second half of the show. It was bad enough the first half, when she noticed that Troy wasn't in his usual spot on the side of the stage. But during the fifteen-minute break between sets her father had been MIA and Chauncey had been vague about both his and Troy's whereabouts. Her first thoughts had been that violence had erupted, but after her dad's valet and assistant assured her that both men were okay, it was Gabriella's turn to insist that her father be in her dressing room—ASAP—as soon as the show was over. It wasn't often that she pulled rank on her dad, but she'd let it be known in no uncertain terms that if Gary Stone wasn't there when she walked through those doors, it was going to be a situation.

Given what Gary just said, it looked like she could still have one on her hands.

"Tell me I didn't just hear you correctly," Gabriella continued. "Tell me you did not just say that you—"

"Fired Troy and Morgan Security. Yes, Gab, I said it. That's exactly what I did."

"Why?"

"Are you seriously going to ask me that question? As your manager, it is my job to keep your best interests first and foremost at all times. As your father, even more so. Tonight made it abundantly clear that that man was not good for your image, or for this tour."

"That's bullshit, Dad. Troy's firm is one of the best in the country. He has taken very good care of me."

"Chauncey heard how well he was taking care of you."

"What?" *How did that happen? We heard his footsteps retreating down the hall!*

"That's right—screwing in an abandoned office like a two-bit whore!"

This comment unsettled Gabriella, but only for a second. "Oh, so that's why you hired an assistant? To spy on me?"

"I needed to speak with you before the show and when I didn't find you here, I sent Chauncey in search of you. I had to almost threaten his employment to find out how he found you and trust me, to say he was as embarrassed for you as for himself would be a major understatement."

Again, Gabriella was taken aback. Remembering the moaning and groaning before their illicit climax made her skin flush. But she was too angry to be fazed. "He had no right to run off to you, telling my business. Whether or not you want to accept it, Daddy, I'm not your little girl anymore. I'm a grown woman who wants to be able to live the life that I choose, whether you agree with it or not."

"Have you forgotten your promise?"

"How can I when it's constantly being thrown in my face?"

Gary took a calming breath. "I'm looking at the big picture, seeing our empire from all angles. Whatever I do, Gabriella, it's with your best interest at heart. To build our business, and this brand."

"That's just it, Daddy. I'm more than a brand. I'm a woman who needs more than a show. I need a life!"

"I know that, too, baby girl. It's one of the reasons I'm so excited about your partnership with Kendall—"

"I'm *not* interested in him like that."

"Baby, you haven't even given the man a chance. He cares a great deal for you, Gabriella, and unlike Troy, who went behind my back and continued seeing you against my wishes, Kendall let me know his intentions up front and asked for my blessing in his pursuing a relationship. I gave it without hesitation. Because a relationship with him would only enhance your life. I just want the best for you, baby. In everything. And when it comes to men I have no doubt . . . Kendall is one of the best."

"Troy is a good man, too."

"I'll admit that when it comes to protection, he's at the top of his field. But beyond his good looks, obvious charm, and stellar resume, what do you really know about him?" He didn't wait for her answer. "I'll tell you what I know. I know that he's quite the ladies' man, that he left several women dangling to come on this tour—the most popular one being a girl named Lisa with whom he's often seen around town."

"Sounds like you did more than a background check."

"When it comes to who's going to be in our inner circle, I pull out all the stops. I'm not saying that he doesn't care for you, but as a man I'm telling you, we don't easily change our stripes. You saw how he was surrounded by women when we drove in this morning. Don't think that was a rare occurrence."

"So what. Women like him. That's not his fault."

"I told you Marlon was wrong for you and what happened?"

"We're not talking about Marlon."

"He ended up with domestic abuse charges, and it very well could have been your swollen jaw plastered all over the Internet. You go behind my back to hang out with him again and what happens? A scandal."

"I'd hardly call an erroneous tabloid article worthy of a Shonda Rhimes script."

"This isn't just about your musical career, sweetheart. It's about your life. It's about positioning yourself not only as an icon but as a businesswoman. And not just as a businesswoman but as a philanthropist. And it's about not only those things, but someone whom everyone—no matter their race, age, sex, or station in life—holds in high regard."

Gary's tone softened as he took a step toward his

daughter. "Remember that time when you were like four or five years old? We were walking through a hotel and there was a wedding taking place. Remember?"

Gabriella nodded, her features softening as she remembered the trip she'd taken with her parents. Her father had worked double shifts at the auto factory the previous year and had gotten a substantial income tax return. To celebrate their anniversary, Gary and Yvonne had decided to splurge and go to Disney World in Florida. When they arrived at the hotel, a wedding party was in the lobby. The bride was wearing the prettiest dress Gabriella had ever seen.

"I said, 'Look at the princess, Daddy. Can I be a princess when I grow up?'"

"And do you remember what I told you?"

"You said that I was already a princess."

"Then you said, 'But I don't have a dress like that'!" Gary chuckled as he shook his head.

"And that Christmas," Gabriella continued, her voice filled with fondness at the memory, "you bought me a beautiful white dress, all lace and chiffon, with those white patent leather shoes. I loved that dress."

"You were a princess then, and you're one now. You'll always be my princess, Gabriella. One who deserves the finest of princes."

"But, Daddy . . ."

"Tell me this. In all the suggestions I've had, or decisions I've made regarding your career, have I ever been wrong?"

"No, Daddy. Not even once."

"And I don't think I'm wrong now. Just give him a chance, honey. If things don't work out, then I'll know that the union is not meant to be. But if things go the way

I think they can, then Gabriella and Kendall will be the new power couple and Jay-Z and Beyoncé will get knocked off the throne."

Instead of flying, Troy had hired a limo service to drive him the four and a half hours to Los Angeles. He needed the time to think. Not one to hold on to anger, he'd pretty much blown off Gary's words before he left the arena. Once back at the hotel, he'd waited to hear from Gabriella. He knew she'd call. But two hours after his conversation with Gary there was still no call. Finally, he'd phoned her. When the call went straight to voice mail, he'd hung up, given her another forty-five minutes while he joined his boys for a game of blackjack. When he returned to his hotel room yet again with no phone calls or text messages, he'd told his team to pack up and head back to LA. That was thirty minutes ago. Now, as he rested his head back against the limo's soft leather seats, he was left to wonder what happened, what Gary had said to Gabriella. And why she hadn't called him. In a rare moment, he began to second-guess himself. Should he have stayed in Vegas, waited until he heard from her? But no, she had to know that he'd be trying to reach her, that he'd want to know how she was and explain his side of what went down. He could only imagine what went through her mind when she looked over and didn't see him on the side of the stage he'd pretty much occupied since she'd strolled over, pulled him out of the shadows, and called him her protector. He remembered how she'd given him a private concert one night, sang that song as he thrust himself inside her, said that from then on when she sang it on stage she'd think of him.

If that was true, he wondered, why wasn't she thinking about him now? And why hadn't she called? At a little past seven a.m., the limo pulled in front of Troy's Leimert Park residence. He paid the driver, grabbed his things, and made weary steps to his door. Once inside he stripped, showered, and sighed as his naked body made contact with his soft cotton sheets. It wasn't until then that he realized how tired he was. As he went to sleep he realized something else. It had only been a few hours . . . but he already missed Gabriella.

41

Two days later, Troy's phone rang. His heart skipped a beat when he saw the number, but when he answered the phone he was the customer of cool. "Yeah."

"Troy, hey." Gabriella's voice was soft, and sounded far away.

"Hey."

"I'm sorry to just now be returning your call. Daddy decided we needed to head to Europe right away. We packed up and left right after that last Vegas show."

"You've got a satellite phone." Silence. "You could have called from the plane."

"I fell asleep shortly after takeoff and slept almost till we landed. It's been a whirlwind since we touched down here in London." A pause and then, "I'm sorry about what happened. About how my dad ended your contract. He said that you'll be paid the entire amount and I'm going to make sure that happens."

Troy left cool on the couch, jumped up, and exploded. "Do you think I give a damn about that job, or the check you owe me? I've been worried sick about you, wondering if your father found out about us, and what he said if that's what happened."

"I'm sorry. Daddy told me not to call you."

"And you listened?"

"There's something I need to tell you."

"I'm listening."

"When I was sixteen, I made my dad a promise—that I wouldn't marry until I was thirty, until I was well established in my career and my youthful days were behind me. Ever since then he's held that vow over my head, even though I made it when just a child! He said I gave him my word. He's reminded me of this continuously over the past two days. But I couldn't take it anymore. I had to call you. I had to hear your voice and know you're okay."

"Wow." For the first time since answering the phone, Troy heard the exhaustion in her voice. "I can't believe your father would do such a thing."

"Mom says he had my best interest at heart. But even she feels I can't be held to something I promised him almost ten years ago."

"Does he know you're calling now?"

"No."

"Will you tell him?"

"I don't know."

A moment of silence and then, "I'm sorry, too, baby. I didn't mean to snap at you, but I didn't know, had no idea why you weren't calling. How are you, Gabriella?"

"I'm okay."

"How'd the show go last night?"

"The fans seemed to love it."

"And you? How do you think you did?"

"You know how hard I am on myself."

"Exactly. That's why I'm asking."

"I did okay. Missed seeing you standing in the wings."

Troy hesitated only a moment before being truthful. "I miss you, too." A pause and then, "Who's guarding you?"

A longer pause before she answered, "Kendall's men are covering me until Daddy hires another team more familiar with this type of work."

"Sounds like Daddy is getting what he wants."

"Kendall can't have what he wants . . . not everything anyway. He wants my heart and that already belongs to someone else."

"Do I know this lucky man who has your heart?"

"Yes, baby. You know him very well."

The smile in her voice filled Troy's heart with joy.

"Troy, I'm upset about what happened. Believe me when I tell you that I want you here."

"Did you fight for me?"

"What do you mean?"

"What did you say when you found out I'd been fired, that my company had been let go. Did you demand I be reinstated, let your father know who was running things for real?"

"But that's just it. As my manager, my father has the last word when it comes to this side of the business. I let him know that I didn't like it, that I thought you were the best guard I'd ever had. Every time I thought I was getting somewhere, he brought up the promise I made, asked me straight out if I was in love with you."

"What did you tell him?"

"That I didn't know. But I do. I love you, Troy. There's just so much going on right now—dates being added to the tour schedule, changes in dancers and other personnel.

It's got me stressed out. Maybe things can be different after the tour ends."

"I want things to be different now."

"I do, too."

"Good. Tell me where you're at and I'll book myself on the next flight."

"Trust me, Troy. That's the last thing you should do. My father will go ballistic, take it as a personal affront to his manhood because he's the one who told you to go."

"Who gives a damn about his manhood? I can handle your father."

"But I can't. Not right now." Troy heard her heavy sigh through the phone. "You've seen how my schedule is, baby, how things operate when I'm on the road. We'd hardly have any time to see each other, and honestly, it would just create even more friction between you and my dad. I can't handle that right now."

"I see. So you're over there for what, a few weeks, right? And then"—Troy paused and scrolled through the itinerary on his iPhone—"then you have the two dates in Canada and the final show in your hometown. It'll drive me crazy to not see you for almost six weeks, but you're worth the wait."

"Gabriella!"

Troy frowned. "Who's that?"

"It's, uh . . . Look. I've got to go."

"Why are you rushing off the phone? Wait. Is that Kendall? In your suite?"

"I'll call you later."

"Gabriella, don't hang up!"

But she already had. And in this moment it was clear to Troy that the Atlantic Ocean was not the only thing that was between them.

Ten minutes later and Troy was on the 10 Freeway, smoothly weaving in and out of traffic as he allowed his sports car to live up to its name as one of the fastest cars currently being made. He was blasting Tara Montega's latest single, forcing himself to think about anything other than how much what he'd just learned had hurt him. He crossed three lanes and merged on to the 110, now slowed down by the lunchtime crowd going wherever. Once he hit another clear stretch, he resumed his cruising speed of eighty miles an hour, turned down the music, and dialed the number of the one woman in the world who would always have his back and never let him down.

"Mama!"

"Hey, Troy!"

Just like back in the day when a kiss could heal his booboo, hearing her voice through the speakers made him smile. "What are you doing?"

"Something I have no business doing."

"Watching those soaps, huh?"

"Worse—these crazy judge shows. I'd bust you boys upside the head if you ever thought to put our business in the streets." They laughed. "Are you still in Vegas, son? Or are you in Europe already?"

Instead of answering the question, Troy told her about all the shops that were at his hotel in Vegas, and how she and Robert should stay there the next time they came down. They talked for about twenty more minutes before she again queried, "Son, where are you?"

"At your front door," Troy answered, laughing. "Let me in."

He heard her mumbling as she walked toward the door, and knew it would open with a question. "Boy, what are you doing here?" he said, mimicking exactly what he knew she'd say. "Was in the neighborhood and decided to stop by," he continued, giving her a big hug.

"I thought you told me that I wouldn't see you for six weeks," she said, returning his embrace. "Not that I'm complaining, mind you." She stepped back to look at him. "So what happened?"

"Change of plans." He walked over to the mantel where a lifelike portrait of his father, the late Samuel Morgan, hung in prominent glory. "What's up, Pop?" he asked aloud, continuing to look at the eyes that seemed to stare back at him.

"What changed?"

Troy noticed the curiosity in Jackie's tone. *Might as well go ahead and tell her before something hits the news.* He turned and walked toward the kitchen. "I'm no longer working the tour."

"What do you mean you're not working it?" Jackie followed behind him. "What happened?"

"Got fired," was Troy's casual reply as he opened the refrigerator and began examining the contents inside. He pulled out a plastic container. "What's in here?"

"Gourmet tuna casserole, just made last night. Gabriella fired you?"

"Yep." He reached inside the cabinet for a plate, opened a drawer to retrieve a serving spoon, and heaped a large amount on the plate.

"Why?" She watched him place the plate into the microwave before turning to lean against the counter.

"Let's just say that Gary and I didn't see eye to eye."

Jackie's eyes narrowed as she crossed her arms. "Boy, don't tell me that this is Gary's doing. Is this because I spurned his advances? Because if he messed with you to get to me there aren't enough flowers or old-school jams in the world to put him back in my good graces. Trust me, he don't want none of this."

"Ha! That's exactly what I told him."

"I'm not laughing. He has some nerve. And how could he fire you anyway? Isn't that a decision that his daughter would make?"

"Apparently not." Troy retrieved the food from the microwave and dug into the piping hot concoction with gusto. "Mmm, this is good, Mama. Reminds me of when we were kids. Did you make some Jell-O for dessert."

"I haven't made Jell-O since y'all left home. Now, stop trying to change the subject. I can't believe that Gabriella would put up with her father getting rid of you. I thought y'all were . . ." Jackie shrugged and walked to the refrigerator to pull out some tea. "Never mind. I'm just your mama. What do I know?" She poured two glasses of tea and joined Troy, now sitting at the kitchen bar. She watched him eat for a while. "Still shoveling that food in your mouth like somebody's going to take it away from you. You were even a greedy baby." After a companionable silence, she said, "I guess Gary didn't agree with you and Gabriella seeing each other. Intimately, I mean."

Troy almost choked on the tea he was swallowing. "Who said we were dating?"

"Her eyes did, when I saw the two of you backstage after her concert. Everything she felt about you showed in her eyes."

"Damn. And here I thought we were being all incog-Negro."

"Oh, you were doing a pretty good job. I had to watch carefully, and the evidence was only there for a second or two. But I saw it—once when you were on the other side of the room and she looked for you. Then there was the look that came on her face when she spotted you. And then there was the frown."

"What frown?"

"That was when she saw you talking to Anise before finding out y'all were related by law."

"Wow, you saw all of this that night? Why didn't you say something?"

"Wasn't any of my business. Plus, I knew you'd share it soon enough. It's one of the things I love most about all you boys—that you feel comfortable about letting me in on what's happening in your lives. Sooner or later anyway."

"Gary wants to control every aspect of her life, including who she's seeing. He's trying to hook her up with Kendall Anderson."

"Who's that?"

Troy told her. "He's over there now; his bodyguards are protecting her until Gary hires my replacement."

"I'm sorry, son," Jackie said, her tone consoling as she patted his arm.

"It's okay, Mom. You know I've never let a female stop my roll. And that's not going to start now."

"So what are you going to do?"

"I'm going to keep it moving. One or two phone calls and I'll be right back on the road, with a star who's just as big as Gabriella."

"Who?"

"Tara Montega."

"I'm not familiar with that name." Troy started singing the chorus of the pop star's hit song. Recognition dawned. "Oh, I know who you're talking about now. I just saw her be a guest judge on one of those singing competition shows, just last week. Cute girl," she continued after pondering this news.

"Yes, she's pretty hot."

"Don't hold a candle to Gabriella though. That's a beautiful girl, inside and out."

"How did you become an expert on Gabriella at a ten-minute backstage meeting after a concert?"

"It doesn't take me long to spot good character, and a good heart. Didn't take you long either, and I can't believe you'd give up so easily."

"Nobody gave up, Mother. I was asked to leave. I left. It's not the first time a situation with me and a client hasn't worked out."

"When was the last time?"

"Don't remember."

"Exactly."

"I'm not about to be like all the other young bloods she's kicked to the curb and run after her like a love-struck pup."

"Nobody said you had to. But anything worth having is worth fighting for. How you strategize the battle is up to you."

42

A week later, Gabriella was in Greece for the Eighth Annual World Wide Wonders Music Awards, a show designed to recognize the day's most popular talent even as they raised money to educate children around the world, and particularly those orphaned by war. Gabriella hadn't wanted to take her day off to attend the event, but both Gary and Kendall convinced her otherwise.

"It will be a perfect time for you to comment on your own project," Gary had said.

"I'm hosting a dinner before the show," Kendall had further explained. "And there are several influential people that I want you to meet, including the prince."

So here she sat, dressed conservatively yet fashionably in a form-fitting couture gown, the golden silkiness of the fabric complementing the fresh highlights in her dark brown hair. Tiana had piled it high atop her head, and had applied her makeup in dramatic fashion: glittery bronzer, smoky eyelids, and exaggerated lashes. She looked exactly how the public believed a number-one diva should look, yet felt like crap. But she kept the smile fixed expertly on her face, working to look interested as Kendall a queen about his plans to partner with other organizations in building schools and day-care centers in poverty-stricken nations across Asia and Africa. It wasn't that she wasn't interested in doing her share of good in the world. It's just that at that moment she could think of several other places that she'd rather be. Like in the large, wrought-iron bed in the Parisian villa they'd rented for the French leg of her tour. Or feeling the third leg of the man she wished were sitting beside her. She'd never missed intimacy more than every day since Troy left her in Vegas.

"Gabriella and I are happy to lend our high profile to causes like this," Kendall was saying when she tuned back in. "I think hosting a televised benefit of some sort is a wonderful idea. What do you think, Gabriella?"

"I'm always happy to support worthy causes, but won't be scheduling anything until this tour is finished and I've had time to rest." A slight crease in her forehead was the only sign of chagrin. Kendall had obviously seen it though, evidenced by how he reached for her hand and squeezed it, under the table.

The dinner blessedly came to an end and Gabriella and Kendall were whisked to the auditorium where the awards show would take place. For someone who while Troy was around hovered over her like a mother hen, Gary had been remarkably absent since Kendall's arrival, and the busy attorney suddenly seemed to have all the time in the world. He'd returned home for two days after showing up in London and had arrived back in Europe just this morning, in time to accompany Gabriella to these awards.

She had to admit, a part of her was glad to have him around. It made missing Troy easier. Kendall was sophisticated, and when he wasn't busy impressing royalty by spouting complicated legalese, he could be fun. Being easy on the eyes didn't hurt him either. Tonight, he looked especially handsome in his dark brown tuxedo, which blended perfectly with his cocoa skin. Thrice-weekly workouts did his body good. He didn't sport the rock hard abs and toned muscles that Troy possessed, but he blessed a suit nicely.

"Isn't that Kanye?" Kendall leaned over and the scent of sandalwood tickled Gabriella's nose in a good way.

"Yes," Gabriella answered, after looking over to see the man wearing shades being escorted to a front row seat.

"Wonder where his partner is?"

"Probably on mommy duty."

"Please. That little girl probably has a couple nannies, an assistant, a publicist, and a stylist already."

"I wouldn't doubt it." Gabriella smiled, deciding that while a bit understated she liked Kendall's humor. "It still doesn't mean Kim isn't home with their little girl."

"Have you ever thought about it?"

"About what?"

"You know—the husband, the child, the white picket fence?"

"Not really."

"Sounds like you're one of those divas who doesn't have time in her schedule or lifestyle for being domesticated."

Gabriella shrugged. "There's plenty of time for me to think about that. Right now, I'm focused on my career."

"I think it's something you should give some thought to one of these days. You'd make a good mother," Kendall said, giving Gabriella a look that was serious and sexy at the same time. "And a good wife."

"How can you say that? You don't even know me."

"True. But I know enough about you to want to know more." He lightened the seriousness of his tone, and the moment, with a squiggle of his somewhat bushy eyebrows.

The unexpected move made her laugh out loud. "You're silly."

"Sometimes."

Gabriella gave Kendall a genuine smile. Maybe she didn't need fireworks, or the type of man who could wet her panties or send her heart into palpitations with a single glance. Someone like Troy. Maybe she needed someone who could take care of her kind of like her father did; someone who would love her more than she loved him. Like he'd said the other night, Gary had never steered her wrong. Maybe she could fall in love with someone sophisticated and successful, if she really tried.

A murmur through the crowd caused her to turn her head. What she saw caused her stomach to drop. Everyone else was probably talking about how fabulous Tara looked. The pop star was resplendent in a shimmering gold mini, her long, tanned legs emphasized by five-inch heels. Shimmering gold highlights strategically placed in her upswept do added to the allure created by the dress and the heels and her perfectly applied makeup. There was no doubt about it. Tara Montega was stunning. But she paled in comparison to the man walking beside her.

Troy.

It was Gabriella's first time seeing him in a tuxedo and the effect was nothing short of ground shaking. The tailored suit emphasized every delectable inch of the frame that had given her so much pleasure; designer shades hid the eyes she knew darkened when filled with desire. Looking at his lips, she remembered the feel of them against her skin, remembered the skill with which he could bring her to orgasm with one strategically placed kiss. The breath continued to leave her lungs as she watched him place a protective hand on the small of Tara's back. Jealousy—raw and primal—erupted as she watched Tara whisper something in his ear and touch him in a way that was far too intimate for Gabriella's liking. What in the heck had happened to get her here: watching the man whom she wanted guarding her, who should be on her team, lead someone else into the auditorium? And how could he possibly look so good while doing it?

"Are you all right?"

Gabriella was so caught up in staring at Troy that she didn't immediately hear Kendall's question. Further distracting her was the fact that Marlon and his posse of ten hangers-on—including the A-list actress on his arm—had just been seated in the second row in the next section. Alex was there too, on guard. More unnerving, Marlon had spotted her and was now headed her way.

Damn!

"Hey, baby!" Marlon reached where Gabriella sat and made a grand show of checking her out before bending down to kiss her cheek. "You're looking good, mami!"

"Hello, Marlon."

"Damn, girl. If I didn't know better I'd say that you were trying not to show love to a brother."

"Not much to show somebody who'd leak a story to the tabloids."

"Aw, girl. You know me better than to think I'd do that."

"Somebody from your party did."

"It wasn't me."

"Whatever, Marlon."

Marlon turned to Gabriella's escort. "Kendall Anderson! What's happening, my brother?"

"I'm not your brother," was Kendall's stoic reply.

"Damn, it's cool over on this side of the auditorium. I'm just being friendly—maybe even thinking about sending some business your way. I'm in the market for a new attorney."

"Good luck with finding one."

"You wouldn't offer your services?"

"No, my client roster is full." Kendall placed a possessive arm around Gabriella to underscore his comment's deeper meaning.

Marlon looked from Gabriella to Kendall. "Oh, so it's like that?"

"Why don't you have your people call my people?"

"Man, eff you! Gab, I'll holler at you later."

Gabriella didn't answer. She was frozen by what she knew to be deep-set eyes behind ever-present dark shades, eyes now boring a hole through the arm around her shoulders. It was all she could do not to react by shaking Kendall's arm off her so that Troy wouldn't get any wrong ideas. From the scowl on his face, however, she'd say it was too late for that. And just when she thought the night couldn't get any worse, it up and did. One of the organizers came over, removed the name of the actor and guest who were supposed to be seated next to her, and motioned for the escort to bring Troy and Tara over to their row.

She tried without success to take her eyes off the mass mound of perfection heading her way. But she couldn't. It was the first time she'd seen Troy in his element, up close and personal, guarding someone else. It was a sight to behold. His gait was smooth, like a panther's, and full of swagger. Even in this fairly well-secured environment, his head moved slightly from left to right. Gabriella imagined he took in the whole of the room in an instant, knowing all of the exits and noting any potential dangers. *I wonder if he realizes the jeopardy he's putting his body into by coming near me?* she thought.

"Gabriella! What's up, girl?" Tara swept into the aisle and sat next to Gabriella. She was hoping that Troy would have taken that seat, but should have known that Tara wouldn't let that happen.

"Hello, Tara."

"Girl, that dress is amazing. And I love what your stylist did to your hair!"

Tara's voice sounded sincere enough, but Gabriella had heard how this chick could be messy. Still, she decided to play it cool. "Thank you. Your dress is nice, too."

"I was going to wear a Cavalli original, similar to the fabric you're wearing, but when my bodyguard showed up looking fine and oh-so-fabulous, I knew I had to step up my game to look good on his arm. Isn't that right, baby?"

Baby? For the second time in less than ten minutes Gabriella had to tamp down jealousy. *I swear if Troy is having sex with this woman I'm going to . . . You're going to what, Gabriella? Just what exactly are you going to do? You're the one who wouldn't stand up to your father and fight for what you wanted. You're the one who's sitting here trying to convince yourself that maybe Troy is just another brother and you can always get another. And now you're the one who realizes that the man your dad let go is one of a kind.*

Troy spoke, bringing Gabriella out of her reverie. "If you say so," he said to Tara, with a smile. And then, "Hello, Gabriella."

"Hello, Troy."

"You look nice."

"Thanks. So do you." Gabriella continued to look at him, wishing she could see those hazel-tinged chocolate orbs hiding behind the dark glasses, wishing that she could know what he was thinking. Wishing that both Tara and Kendall could magically disappear, along with the other two thousand folks in the room, so that it could just be the two of them.

"Doesn't he look amazing?" Tara said, interjecting herself into an A and B conversation that Gabriella wished she could C her way out of. She leaned over to Gabriella, whispering so that only she could hear. "I really should thank you. If I had somebody like Troy in my camp I would have never let him go." Her voice dropped even lower. "I plan to keep him by my side for a long time."

Here's the messy mama that I was expecting. "Good for you."

"Yes, it is good for me."

Kendall must have been listening, because he reached over and took Gabriella's hand. Even though Tara sat in the chair between them, Gabriella could have sworn she felt Troy's shoulders tighten.

She looked at the large digital clock that sat just out of sight of the television cameras. Five minutes until the show began.

"I'm going to the restroom," she said to Kendall.

"Russell will go with you." Russell was the bodyguard discreetly sitting two rows behind them.

"No. That's okay. I'll be fine."

Tara simply moved her knees to the side, but Troy stood as Gabriella passed him. She could smell the familiar woodsy scent, could feel his chest with her arm as she brushed past him. Once she reached the stall she pulled her phone from out of the beaded Hermes bag that only held it, a compact, a tube of lipstick, and a package of makeup blotters. She tapped the envelope on the screen next to Troy's name and sent him a quick text: I need to see you. Tonight. Alone. Here's the address where I'm staying.

The answer came within minutes, so soon that Gabriella figured he had to have typed it while sitting next to the woman who'd just all but sworn that when it came to Troy, she'd be the last woman standing. It was simple. Just three words. I'll be there.

43

Troy had meant the text when he sent it. Tara had said she wasn't interested in attending the party, that she had a terrible headache and instead wanted to go back to the hotel suite and lie down. He'd then asked if it would be okay for one of his assistants to guard the floor while he took care of some personal business. She must have thought this business included Gabriella, because her migraine disappeared as quickly as it had come. Which is why instead of meeting Gabriella at her villa, he was in the middle of an after-party where the music was too loud, the dresses too bare, and booze and drugs flowed freely. One thing about the atmosphere however: it made him earn his pay.

"Give us space," he demanded, as he ushered Tara through a throng of paparazzi and fans crowded around the hotel's entrance in hopes of catching a glimpse of someone of celebrity status. Using his body as a shield, he deftly guided his charge and her posse into the lobby, through the crowd, and into the ballroom where the private party was being held. Of course, it could have been arranged for Tara to use a side door. But then it wouldn't have created the photo ops and the grand entrance that she'd intended, and obtained.

"You're good," Tara said, bringing her lips precariously close to his ear and taking advantage of its proximity by offering a little lick.

He fought the urge to jerk away and instead gave her a devilish grin. "Come on, now, Tara. You know the rules. I don't date clients."

"Bullshit. I saw the tabloids. I know that you and Gabriella had a thing."

"You should also know that you can't always believe what you read, especially in the tabloids."

"So are you saying it isn't true?"

"I'm saying that even as beautiful as you are, I want to keep this strictly professional. It will help me keep my job."

"What if I told you that keeping me happy, in every way, was a part of your requirements?"

"Then I'd say that I wasn't qualified to continue this assignment." An easy smile belied the seriousness of his tone.

A flash of anger showed in Tara's eyes before she dismissed his thinly veiled ultimatum with a laugh. "Don't worry about it, papi. There are plenty of men with guns who can keep me protected. But I'm sure not every man has a"—she paused and looked at his crotch for emphasis—"weapon like yours."

Troy's retort was interrupted by the sight coming through the private room doors. Gabriella and Kendall entered, surrounded by four tall guys with big chests and mean looks. As he was greeting several people, Kendall looked up. He and Troy locked eyes. Kendall placed a protective arm around Gabriella's waist and Troy could swear there was a smirk on his face as he did so. Having put most of his hothead days behind him, at the moment there was nothing more that Troy wanted to do than bust Kendall in his face!

"Ah, I see why my question went unanswered. Obviously, what I read is true. Let's go over to the buffet," Tara began walking and threw over her shoulder, "before I lose my appetite."

When Gabriella entered the room, Troy was the first person she saw. There was a sigh of relief mixed with the jealousy that came from seeing the smug look on Tara's face. It was enough that she'd plastered herself against Troy's arm like a sweaty tee, but when she saw Gabriella enter, she immediately led them in the opposite direction. *Witch! I know they're screwing. There's no way Tara is letting Troy off duty at night.* The thought made Gabriella sad, and this surprised her. More than once she and Troy had tried to act like their relationship was casual—that once the tour and his assignment was over they might go back to whomever/whatever they were doing in their regular lives. But long ago, she had stopped lying to herself. She not only lusted after the handsome hunk known as Troy Morgan. She was in love with him.

"Gabriella!"

Thankful for the interruption of her troublesome thoughts, Gabriella was happy to look up and see a friendly face heading in her direction. "Hey, girl! It's good to see you." Choice was a fashion designer whose company, Chai Fashions, was a hit among celebrities.

They'd met during Choice's showing at Fashion Week. Gabriella had marveled over a slew of her clothes that Melanie subsequently purchased, and they'd been good friends ever since.

"It's good to see you, too. Even if you're not wearing me and you know you should."

"You know I've got to change it up now and then."

"I know it. I'm just messing with you. And just to keep it going . . ." Choice looked around to make sure Kendall was still in conversation with another man. "Word on the street was that you and Troy were an item. What's he doing here with what's-her-name?"

Thankful to have someone with whom to vent, someone who was celebrity enough in her own right that she wouldn't gossip, Gabriella answered, "Don't get me started."

"I'm not trying to get in your business or anything, but then again, I guess I am. What happened?"

"Let's just say things didn't work out with him and certain members of my team. We had to part ways."

"You know I have a controlling father, too, right?"

She did. Anyone who'd ever picked up an *Architectural Digest* or traveled in upscale New York circles of society knew about Charles McKinley, partner in McKinley-Black Enterprises, one of the most successful architectural firms in the nation. "Considering the power he wields in the professional arena, I'd imagine he's used to getting his way."

"Let me put it to you like this. When I got with Trey, Daddy wasn't too happy. He had his own ideas about who I'd marry."

"Oh my God. Are you sure his name isn't Gary?"

The women laughed.

"Unfortunately, Gab, your dad doesn't have the market cornered where wanting absolute control is concerned. My father and others had their own ideas about certain decisions. But at the end of the day, it was my life. Nobody could live it but me. And I had to do what I considered the right thing, what made me happy."

"And how did that work out for you?"

Choice's eyes twinkled before she leaned in and whispered, "Don't say anything yet, but . . . we're having a baby."

Gabriella contained her joy. "I'm so happy for you," she said, her tone low as she squeezed Choice's arm. "Congratulations. I bet you'll make a great mom."

It was clear to Gabriella that Choice hadn't heard her last comment, that she was preoccupied with something taking place just behind her. This was confirmed with Choice's next words. "Uh-oh."

Following Choice's line of sight, Gabriella turned. Her heart, which had been beating at a steady pace, suddenly felt as though it would explode out of her chest. Kendall and Troy were over in a corner, with less than an inch of air between them. Their faces were stern; their stances defensive. Gabriella didn't know what they were talking about, but she'd place odds that it wasn't about the weather. She hadn't even noticed when Kendall left her side. But it was unmistakable that where he'd ended up could prove to be potentially hazardous to his health!

"Really, player? Is that all you've got?"

"I've got whatever it takes to keep you away from

Gabriella. Gary has made it clear who he wants in his daughter's life, and it's not you."

Troy seethed with anger but held himself in check. When he'd seen Kendall heading in his direction he knew there'd be drama. That was to be expected. But the insecurity that this multimillionaire attorney was now exhibiting was a total surprise.

"Why don't we let the lady make up her own mind? Since you're sure in what direction she's heading, I'm sure I can expect this to be the last time you come at me with some bullshit, trying to intimidate. If you're so sure you've got Gabriella on lock, then act like it. Go back to where you should be as her escort, which is by her side. And stop trying to block."

Kendall took a step toward Troy. "You don't have enough clout to tell me what to do, son. I can buy and sell you with what I keep in my petty cash."

"If her affection was about money I might be impressed with your statement," Troy countered, taking a step of his own. "But it's about more than that. And trust me, you'd be wise to recognize this fact."

"Why, you little arrogant motherf—"

"Troy!" Gabriella hurried to reach the two men, who looked ready to mix it up for real. "Can I talk to you for a minute?"

"What do you need to talk to him about?"

Three pairs of eyes turned to Tara, who for the first time tonight had walked up to a crowd where nobody noticed.

"That's none of your business," Gabriella retorted. "Last time I checked, slavery had been abolished. Every employee is entitled to a fifteen-minute break every now and then. Are you so scared of me that you've got to protect your protector?"

"Please, don't flatter yourself. I don't view you as competition."

"Good. Then you won't mind that we go and have a conversation. My guys can watch you if you don't feel safe, but honestly, considering the security that the hotel is providing, I think you'll be fine." She turned to Kendall. "Excuse me for a minute." And then to Troy, "Can we talk?"

"Sure," Troy calmly responded. "We can talk. But I'm not sure you're going to like what I'm going to say."

44

"It looked like you and Kendall were about to kill each other," Gabriella hissed as they stood behind a curtain on the far side of the room.

"Oh, so you pulled me away because you were afraid for your friend?"

"I pulled you away because I wanted to talk, and because I didn't like the two of you acting like gangsters!"

Troy crossed his arms. "What do you want?"

"You!" He snorted. "I've told you that I was into you, that you had my heart. I also told you that things would be different once the tour ended."

"So I was supposed to put my life on hold until that happened?"

"You could have at least not hooked up with one of the biggest whores in the industry."

"Tara's good people; you more than anybody should know not to judge."

"You're right. That probably wasn't the best choice of words. But do you know how it makes me feel to see you with her?"

"Yes, I do. I feel that way every time I look at you and Kendall."

Silence prevailed as the two caught their breath. The air crackled around them, even as applause for whoever was on the stage drifted beyond their temporary veil.

"Look, Gabriella. I have a job to do and you have awards to accept. Nothing that needs to happen can get done here. Because the bottom line is, no matter how we feel about each other, your father is the one who's calling the shots. And he obviously feels like I'm not good enough, that I'm not in your league and that Kendall is. Until that changes"—he shrugged his shoulders—"it is what it is. This moment notwithstanding, I won't hide behind curtains to be with you. And when it comes to your father's disrespect of me . . . I won't back down." He leaned forward, kissed her forehead. "Good-bye."

He took two steps and turned around. "Gabriella?"

"Yes?"

"Has Gary told you about the packages, the letters?"

"What letters?"

"Ask him about it. You need to know."

Gabriella was hurt, angry, and sad, with nobody to blame but herself. She'd been in a mood for the past two weeks, and was even more so now that both she and Troy were back in L.A. Sure, she would have liked to blame him for how she felt, had tried to in her mind, but it wasn't working. Why? Because she couldn't disagree with anything he'd said. He was a good man. He did deserve her and her father's respect. He shouldn't have to hide and feel like a best-kept secret. *So why can't I stand up to my father and rescind that stupid, ill-made promise?*

The answer was simple: she didn't ever want to lose her father's love. And again, Troy's voice, and what she imagined he'd say to this argument: *If your father truly cares about your happiness, you shouldn't have to.*

"I'm so confused," she whispered, her restlessness pushing her off the chaise in the hotel room where she now lounged and up to pace the room. Even after Gary told her about the threats, the ones that Troy had helped to keep away from her, and why he should still be employed by her, she couldn't hate her father. "I love both of you! I want both of you in my life!"

Walking into the living area, Gabriella plopped down on the couch, placing a pillow against her abdomen as she tucked her legs beneath her, and recounted past conversations with her father. Talks where he'd clearly stated why she shouldn't consider Troy, why someone like him was beneath her. He hadn't used those words exactly, but he might as well have because that's exactly what he meant. That was no more evident than when he tripped all over himself whenever Kendall was around. She knew that if he could have, he would have accepted a marriage proposal from this star lawyer on his daughter's behalf. *I owe Kendall an apology, too,* she thought, remembering the way things had ended with him in Europe.

And then a major question came to her mind: *What do you owe yourself?* The power of her answer once again propelled her upward. She walked to the closet, pulling off PJs on the way. Within five minutes she'd donned a simple tee and jeans. Moving to the bathroom, she pulled her hair into a ponytail and covered most of her mane with a baseball cap. Then she called Carol and asked that she come to her room.

"What's the matter?" Carol asked as soon as she'd entered the suite. As soon as she'd heard her best friend's voice, she'd known something was up.

"Nothing."

Carol crossed her arms, giving her a look in the process. "What's going on?"

"It's about Troy. I don't want to lose him. I need you to get the keys to the rental so that I can go talk to Daddy."

"Tonight?"

"Right now."

"I don't know, Gab. I mean, I agree that Troy is too good a man to lose and understand why you want Gary to see your point of view. But we're in LA, it's late, and I don't feel good about your venturing out by yourself. Let me wake the driver."

Gabriella shook her head. "I don't want to be driven over; I want to drive myself. I need time to think and gather my thoughts and I want to do that alone. Don't worry, nobody will be looking for me in a Hyundai." When Carol's frown deepened, Gabriella walked toward her friend. "I'll be careful, Carol. Promise."

"I don't feel good about this, Gab. Let me go with you."

"You're a good friend, Carol, closer than a sister for real. I appreciate your concern, truly I do. Even more so after finding out about the threatening letters and boxes we received."

Carol's head shot up. "How'd you find out?"

"Daddy told me, but only after Troy suggested that I ask about them. You should have told me, Carol."

"We thought it best that you not know until we had facts. Thought that it might just be some kids playing around. And it looks as though that might be the case. Did Gary tell you that we received no more packages, threats, or anything once we arrived in Europe? And nothing at all since we've been back?" Gabriella nodded. "See, there was no need to bother you with something that's over and done."

"I'm glad to hear that. I don't need another stalker."

Both women were silent a moment as they thought about her last tour and the young man who'd driven to New York from Texas claiming to be Gabriella's husband. She'd had to get a restraining order to keep him away.

"Where are the keys to the Hyundai? I want to drive to Bel Air. Mom's gone back east so this might be a good chance for Dad and I to talk. Now that the tour is over, maybe we'll both be more relaxed."

"Why don't you take the limo or simply call?"

"Why not drive? You said there were no more threats, right?"

"Right, but—"

"No 'buts.' Tonight I want to leave the superstar behind, in this hotel room. I want to go outside and just be Gabby Stone, a regular person, doing regular things like driving a car. I've got my cell and GPS, and Mom's house is not even fifteen minutes away. I'll call you as soon as I get there. Okay?"

"Call me the moment you get inside the house. Better yet, call me as soon as you get to the gate."

"I will."

"I know you're a big girl and all, but you know I'd feel better if you let the driver take you."

Gabriella leaned over and gave the girl she'd known for most of her life a big hug. "I won't let anything happen to me. Who'd you have to fuss over?"

"I'll come with you."

"You need a night off. And I need a break from your bossy behind."

"Oh no, you didn't call someone else bossy. Ha! You know what? On second thought, a break sounds good."

Minutes later, Gabriella had slipped out of the hotel and gotten into the rental. Without the flashy clothes, five-inch heels, flawless makeup, and silky long hair on prominent display, she barely drew a second glance from the doorman. The reading glasses Troy had once insisted she wear further helped in her disguise. She programmed her parents' Bel Air address into the GPS, turned the radio to Stevie Wonder's radio station, KJLH, and pulled out into the city streets.

During the drive over, Gabriella let her mind wander and her thoughts roam free. Or tried to. Inevitably they'd end up in the same place—thinking about Troy. In between them were memories of life with Gary: his putting a microphone in her hand when she was barely two, her watching and mimicking his dance movements, his teaching her how to ride a bike and drive a car, their late night chats about show business, his chauffeuring her and the girls around to talent shows, and him telling her that she was beautiful . . . over and over again. He was the first one from whom she heard these words, and without a doubt the first man that she'd ever loved. Until now, he'd been the most important man in her life, one whom she felt had flung the stars and hung the moon. These days, however, another man was making her see stars and hear bells. Another man was telling her that she was beautiful and making her believe that he meant what he said. Troy Morgan. A man for whom she no longer wanted to deny her feelings.

"I want to be with you Troy Morgan," she whispered, as she neared the wrought-iron gates to the huge estate. For the second time in as many weeks, Gabriella admitted to herself that she was definitely in love.

After punching in the gate code, Gabriella reached for her phone. "I'm here, Carol. No, it looks pretty quiet actually," she said in response to Carol's question. "Gary's Porsche is here, but I don't see Garrett's car. Mom told me that he had a new girlfriend, so that's not a surprise." She pulled up next to a sporty little red car. "There's another car here that I'm not familiar with, but it might be Chauncey's. He said he was looking at finally trading in that SUV that's been around since his college days." She exited the car. "All right, girl. More than likely I'll be spending the night here. Why don't you come over tomorrow for brunch. If all goes well, Troy will be here, too."

Gabriella punched in a set of numbers on the keyless entry and slipped inside the home. It had been a while since she'd been at the mansion, and for a moment she stood in the foyer and admired its beauty—the way the dimmed recessed lighting cast a soft glow across the marble floors, and the way the floor-to-ceiling windows invited in both the moonlight and the dimly lit courtyard. For a moment she stood there, taking in the beauty and serenity of the scene. And all the while she was watching the coordinated spray of the fountain . . . someone was watching her.

Her first stop was the east wing and Yvonne's suite. She went to the massive walk-in closet and got confirmation that her mother had taken the trip back east that she'd planned. *Perhaps it's to meet the real estate agent who'd help sell our Long Island home.* After seeing his picture on a business card, Gabriella had teased her mother about a potential hookup. Of course, Yvonne had denied it, said she wasn't interested in falling in love. But Gabriella would be delighted if her mother found a second chance at romantic happiness. For the past ten years she'd poured all of her time, attention, and devotion into her children, but now with Garrett grown and in college, it was time for her mother to pay attention to herself.

She walked to the area of the home her brother occupied. His bedroom was also empty. Gabriella shook her head and smiled. It wasn't easy to think of Garrett, her baby bro, shacked up somewhere and doing the nasty, but she had no doubt that that was more than likely exactly what he was doing. She walked down the hall and was just about to head to the west wing and her father's domain when she heard a giggle.

The sound caused Gabriella to giggle, too, suddenly having a different thought about who owned the cute red car in the drive. *Really, Garrett? You're going to demand your own place and then do a girl in the home of your parents?* As she crept toward the door where she now noticed a dim light shined, she realized that maybe she was being too hard on her brother. After all, her mother was out of town, Garrett shared a town house with three hardheads, and Gary's room was far enough away that no amount of noise would easily penetrate his domain. *What am I doing anyway, creeping up to the door like this? It's not like I want definitive proof of my baby brother doing the nasty. Go find your father, Gabriella. Stay focused on what you came here to do.*

She turned away from the door where the noises were heard and had only taken two steps when a two-word command stopped her in her tracks.

"Harder, Gary."

Gary? As in my dad? Gabriella's mind didn't even engage as she turned around; she was totally on auto-pilot, her curiosity stirred up beyond belief. Who was with her father and why in the hell were they screwing in the house where both of her parents lived? It didn't matter that her mom and dad were divorced and lived in separate wings of a home large enough one could go weeks without seeing the other. There was a thing called principle, and whoever was in there with her dad had crossed a line.

When she reached it, she almost didn't open the door. But anger overrode any sense of embarrassment. That was why she reached for the doorknob and, finding it unlocked, slowly turned it and opened the door. The sight that greeted her would forever remain etched in her mind. Not because she saw her father naked. Thankfully he was on the bottom and all she saw was his legs. No, she'd never forget this scene because of who was riding on top. Someone that Gabriella would never have suspected. Her father had drummed it into her continually: we don't sleep with the help. There was no doubt that this was her father and he was indeed sleeping with someone in their employ. The reality of the situation both shocked and angered her at once. Perhaps that's why she didn't turn and run, but instead stepped farther into the room and asked a rather obvious question.

"What in the hell are y'all doing?"

45

If a woman being seriously sexed could be frozen in the middle of a down stroke, Li made it happen. Upon hearing Gabriella's voice, it was as if she clenched her thighs on the middle of Gary's dick, her pert ass straddled as if impaled on his penis, her eyes wide, and mouth agape as she turned to look at Gabriella.

Gary's actions were a little more decisive. He flipped them so that Li was on the bottom, and threw a cover over them both. "Gabriella!"

"All this time you're telling me about not dating 'the help,'" Gabriella sneered as she made air quotes, "and you're banging Li!?"

"Gabriella, let me explain—"

"Explain? You really think you've got to explain what I'm seeing right here? No, Daddy, I think what's going on is all too clear. I'm not supposed to date the help, but you screw them to your heart's content!" Gabriella's voice broke as she began backing up. "You tried your best to ruin what I had with Troy, and I almost let you! But no more, Daddy." Gary began to rise but, remembering his state of undress, sank back on the bed. "I mean it. I'm no longer going to listen to your reasons for trying to control me, and who I see. Stay out of my life!"

With that, she turned and ran out of the room.

Gary was hot on her heels. After hurriedly donning the abandoned slacks at the foot of the bed, he raced after Gabriella. "Gab!"

Gabriella quickened her pace. "Leave me alone!"

Gabriella's strides were strong and sure, but no match for those of her six-foot-plus father. He reached her just as she neared the main hall leading to the foyer and grabbed her arm. "Gabriella, stop!"

"Dad, let me go."

"Not until you hear me out."

"Fine!" she spat, jerking her arm away before crossing both, batting the tears that threatened away from her eyes. "I'm listening."

Gary took a quick look back toward where they'd come from and lowered his voice. "Do you think that little bit of snatch means a thing to me? She's been coming after me for months. You just happened to stumble onto me finally giving her what she wanted."

At this very moment, Gabriella experienced being livid and feeling she was about to vomit at the same time. "Is that explanation supposed to make me feel better? Do you think I should be happy that instead of being in a serious relationship you're just banging Li?" She took a step toward her father, her finger pointing at his chest. "You gave me every kind of reason not to be with Troy. Over and over you talked about how he was an employee and as such, I shouldn't have anything to do with him outside a professional realm. And I listened to you, believed you, like I've always done. And all the while you were doing the very thing you insisted that I not do? Disgusting."

Again she turned to walk away and again Gary grabbed her. "Gabby, listen to me."

This time, when she turned and jerked her arm away, her voice was eerily calm. "No, Daddy. I still love you, even respect you, but I'm done listening to what you have to say. Now it's time to listen to my heart. And my heart is telling me to go to Troy and try and salvage what might remain of what's been the best relationship of my life."

"You're going to choose some knucklehead with an attitude over your own dad?"

"Look at it any way you want to, Daddy. Like I said, I'll always love you. But it's time I live my own life. It's time I do me. If it's not too late, I'm going to be with Troy. I'm going to rehire him to head up security on my team. For you to remain on my team, you'll give him the same respect you do me, the same kind that you afforded Kendall just because he fit your ideal of a son-in-law. And if you can't do that? Find someone else to manage. Because if you push me to decide between you and Troy Morgan . . . you might not like my choice."

Tears blinded her as she reached the modest two-door Hyundai and crawled inside. She fired up the engine and took a deep, calming breath before easing the car around the circular drive and heading toward the gate. She thought about calling Carol and reached for her phone. But then she thought about how hard Carol had worked the past few months. *She deserves this night off, and some time to live her own life.* She left her phone alone and after pulling up the hotel address and initiating the

GPS, concentrated on making the short drive to her suite back at the hotel.

She stopped at the gate, waited for the slow, majestic opening that would allow her to make a left on Sunset Boulevard and head toward Beverly Hills. She reached the road, put on her left blinker, and felt something cold and hard pressed against her neck.

"Do exactly what I say," a low raspy voice demanded. "If you don't, I'll kill you . . . and then your family."

Troy had tried everything to stop thinking about Gabriella. He'd called his brother Michael, and gone over to a gathering at his house. He'd thought about drinking his way to forgetfulness, but after half a beer, had poured the rest down the sink. He'd flirted with a couple cuties while dancing to a hip-hop groove, but nothing worked to improve his mood. That's why after about an hour of faking it, he'd gone to his brother, bid him and his wife, Shayna, good night, and was now headed toward his home in Leimert Park.

Except that something didn't feel right.

Ignoring the ominous sensation in his gut, he turned on to La Brea Avenue and pushed down on the gas pedal. His sports car leapt forward, quickly eating up the pavement on a street fairly vacated at one a.m. He turned up the music, tried to lose himself in a beat or two. But that thing, whatever it was, refused to let him relax, refused to leave him alone.

"It's on her now," he reasoned to the empty car. "I gave her the chance to keep me around, and she left! I'm not going to beg her ass to stay," he continued, to the invisible audience inside his car. "What else am I supposed to do?"

He didn't know, but as he neared Wilshire Boulevard, he knew that whatever it was would probably not happen tonight. Still, with a sigh, he turned around and began retracing his steps, heading to the hotel where Gabriella last stayed. "I don't even know why I'm doing this," he muttered. But he was. He picked up his phone and dialed her number. It went to voice mail. His heart sank to his stomach and "the feeling" intensified. He called Carol, and prepared to listen through his car speakers.

"Carol, it's Troy. Sorry to call you so late, but are you with Gabriella?"

"No." Carol's voice was crystal clear, evidence that she was wide awake. "She went over to her parents' house to talk to Gary."

"Oh, okay."

"Why?"

"No worries. I just tried to call her and got voice mail."

"Why were you trying to reach her? I thought y'all—"

"Broke up? Technically we did, but that doesn't stop my caring about her. She ran across my mind and I decided to call."

"Actually, Troy, I'm glad you did. She refused to let a driver take her over to the house and drove over by herself in the Hyundai."

This news caused Troy to almost back-end the car ahead of him. "What?"

"I know, I was upset, too. But she wanted time alone

and went out in disguise. Don't worry, she's okay. She called me when she reached the house, just after going inside the gates."

"So you talked to her?"

"Yes."

"When?"

"About thirty minutes ago."

"Okay, cool. I'll try and reach her later, maybe in the morning. Thanks, Carol. Good night."

"Good night, Troy. And can I say something else?"

"Sure."

"Gabriella is strong and proud and might not want to say it, but . . . she loves you. Thanks for being in her life."

Troy hung up the phone and tried to relax, but the fact of the matter was that Gabriella's safety had long been on his mind. When he'd last seen Alex, the two had exchanged words, including Troy basically accusing his old friend of being behind the tabloid fiasco. "You couldn't have her, so you tried to sully her reputation," he'd told him. Alex had denied any wrongdoing, and then cursed Troy out.

But if not Alex, who could it be? *Who is it that's trying to hurt you, Gabriella?* Troy thought back to his last conversation with the investigator whom he'd kept on the payroll even though he was no longer Gabriella's bodyguard. A couple of questionable letters had been mixed in with the fan mail, but during the entire time that Gabriella had been overseas, no boxes or blatant threats had appeared anywhere. *She's okay, man, quit worrying. Carol talked to her. She's inside the gate.* Troy had personally checked out every inch of the estate and knew how secure the people behind its walls were. *Then why do I still have this feeling?* He didn't know, but he was going to find out. He slowed, made a U-turn, and headed toward Bel Air.

"Why are you doing this?" Gabriella forced herself to remain calm, having taken several deep breaths to steady herself. At first she'd been shaking so badly she felt incapable of driving. But there was something about a knife and a threat that made her gain control of her nerves, and quickly.

"Shut up and drive."

"Where are we going?"

"Didn't I say to shut your mouth? That's why you're in trouble in the first place."

"Why? What did I ever do to you? I was always nice to you, Chauncey . . . always!" She felt the knife press against her neck, felt a quick jab of pain as the blade pierced her skin.

"You are a daughter of the devil, sending young people who idolize you straight to hell! You are a spawn of Satan, and you must be stopped. You must be—"

"What, Chauncey?" Gabriella felt that as long as they were talking he couldn't think about killing her. "What is it that you want? Whatever it is, I'll do. I swear!"

"As if you have a choice. Turn here!"

Gabriella's heart raced. She'd felt better being on Sunset, a main thoroughfare where she'd hoped a police car would be spotted. She'd already planned that if she saw one, she'd run right into it! But now he was demanding she turn into a residential area that was dark and looked isolated. If she obeyed him, there was no telling what would happen. But then again, only God knew the repercussions if she didn't do what he said.

She said a quick prayer, and turned the corner.

46

Troy reached the Stone estate and turned into the drive. All seemed quiet and serene. He imagined Gabriella inside the large house, maybe still talking to Gary or asleep in one of the rooms upstairs. "I'll just talk to the guard," he said aloud, "confirm that Gabriella is in the house and then take my butt home."

He reached the gate and flashed his lights, hoping that if a guard was on duty, he'd come that way. He waited, but after a few seconds with no movement, he dialed a number he hadn't used in more than two weeks.

"Gary, it's Troy." Silence. "I've tried to reach Gabriella and have not been successful. I'm just calling to make sure Gabriella is okay."

"Gabriella is no longer your concern."

Troy could hear the ire in his former employer's voice. "Sorry to bother you; I know it's late. And I know I'm not your favorite person. But I just couldn't shake the feeling that something was wrong with Gabriella. So I drove over here and—"

"You're here? At my house?"

"Yes. I was hoping to talk to a guard and—"

"You just don't get it, do you? Gabriella doesn't want you. She's moved on, and is now with a man worthy of her time and attention. You need to get a life, and move on."

"And you need to check and make sure Gabriella's okay. I don't get these feelings often and they're always spot on. You do have security guarding the house, correct?"

"Do you think I'd tell a former worker, one with good reason to have malice against me, how we're protected? I think not."

"Seriously, Gary, I mean you no harm. But Carol told me that Gabriella drove over here alone. It worried me deeply. Please, can you just make sure she's all right?"

Troy heard a click in his ear and, realizing he'd been disconnected, banged the steering wheel. "Damn!"

He was beyond frustrated, but there was nothing he could do. He turned his car around and for the second time that night, headed home.

Gary tried to remain calm as he reached for his phone, an almost impossible feat since Gabriella had caught him with Li. He'd known better than to bed her in the house, but from the first time that he'd had her, that tight body had been hard to resist. When he'd found out Yvonne was heading out of town he'd decided to treat Li to the high life by inviting her to Bel Air, knowing Gabriella was at a hotel with Carol and the new security crew. *Stupid, man. That was really a dumb move.* He tapped his iPhone, pacing the floor of his master suite while waiting for the call to go through.

Like Troy, Gary's phone call to Gabriella went to voice mail.

He disconnected the call and phoned Carol, putting the call on speaker as he continued to pace.

"Gary?" Carol's voice croaked with sleep.

"Go get Gab for me, Carol. Her phone must be off or out of juice."

"She came back here? I thought she was going to spend the night there."

"We had a . . . misunderstanding."

"Okay. Let me go check." Gary waited while Carol went from her side of the suite to the room Gabriella occupied. When she returned to the phone, she was yawning. "You need to check one of the rooms there, Gary. She's not here."

Gary dropped the phone and rushed out of the master suite, going from worry to anger at the thought his daughter would blatantly ignore him. She knew he'd get upset. "Gabriella!"

They arrived at a nondescript hotel near LAX, the Los Angeles International Airport. Chauncey was driving. After they'd turned off the main street, he'd forced Gabriella to stop, tied her hands and legs together, and secured the bands around the steering wheel. But those bands weren't what had kept Gabriella from jumping out of the car and running for her life. No, his continual threats to harm her family had done the trick.

"Don't do anything stupid," Chauncey hissed, parking

the car in the hotel lot. "I'm going to teach you a lesson, that's all. If I'm successful, you'll get to live."

As instructed, Gabriella kept her head down as they entered the lobby. Now that she was untied, her mind whirled with possible ways to escape, but every time she considered making a move, she thought of Garrett and how much he loved sports.

"He'll be the first one I'll go after," Chauncey had warned. "I'll use a steel beam to break every bone in his athletic legs so that he won't be able to run away . . . like Troy did."

"He didn't run away. He was fired!"

"Shut up!"

They reached the room. Chauncey secured the door, then opened the backpack she'd just now noticed. He threw what looked like a white dress in her direction. "Go in the bathroom and put that on."

"Why? What is this?"

"Just do it!" Chauncey's eyes bulged and spittle flew as he yelled. "You're dressed like a harlot and I won't stand for it! Not now that you've been given to me. Now, go!"

Without a doubt, Gabriella knew she was being held by a madman. Now, she was really afraid.

Troy was on the 405 when his phone rang. He looked at the screen on his dash. It was Gary. His heart dropped. "Morgan," he answered, his voice terse, his entire body on alert.

"She's not here!"

"Have you called Carol?"

"Yes, and she said Gabriella hasn't made it back to the hotel. Can you come back to the house?"

Troy had taken the first exit after seeing Gary's name. "I'm already on my way."

He reached the estate and hit the buzzer. The gate swung open almost immediately, and by the time he reached the driveway, Gary was out the front door. "She was upset when she left, but I just figured she'd calm down on her way back to the hotel."

"What was she mad about?" Troy asked.

"I don't see how that's important."

Troy spun around and got in Gary's face. "Everything's important, man! We're trying to find your daughter and everything's a clue. Now why was she angry?"

Gary told him.

"Let me see if I heard you correctly. You were sleeping with *the help*?"

"Now isn't the time for your sarcasm, no matter how well deserved. What if somehow the person behind those threatening letters intercepted her car on the way back to the hotel? What if he's holding her captive . . . or worse? We've got to find Gabriella! We've got to find my baby girl."

"Tell me everything that happened, from the moment Gabriella arrived."

Gary relayed the argument that broke out after Gabriella's discovery. "I tried to stop her, but she ran out."

"I need to know everyone who's in the house right now, and I need to make sure everyone is accounted for."

"No problem. I'll ring for Chauncey." Gary walked over to a panel, hidden by a plaque. He pushed a button. "He'll be here shortly," Gary said, before running down a list of the employees still there at that hour. With the tour completed there weren't many, only the chef, the house-keeper, a relative who'd just arrived that morning . . . and Gary's personal assistant. A slight scowl marred Gary's face as he finished the rundown. He looked at his watch, then pushed the call button again, the one that rang directly into the room Chauncey occupied. "He's a pretty deep sleeper," Gary explained.

"Where is his room?" Troy asked. After Gary told him, Troy raced to his room. For whatever reason, he wasn't surprised to find that it was empty. Troy reached for his phone. "Robert, I'm sorry to wake you, man. But I need your help, and that of your boys on the squad."

Across town, Gabriella shivered under Chauncey's malicious stare. The white cotton dress she wore was thin and flimsy, with her fiery red underwear clearly visible beneath. She watched as his eyes continued to flicker toward them and used her arms the best she could to hide them from his view.

"You are dirty, and have brought shame on our com-munity," he said, continuing to berate her as he'd done all along. "You say that you care about young people, but look at the example that you're setting for our young women—that it's okay to dress like a stripper in those disgustingly high heels, and to prance around stage with your private parts showing."

"I—I—I didn't know that was what I was doing," Gabriella pleaded, forcing herself to talk low and calm. "I didn't know I was doing anything wrong."

"I sent dolls and letters, posted comments on the Inter-net. I tried everything to stop this tour!"

Gabriella gasped. "It was you?"

It was as if Chauncey didn't hear her. "I lost a cousin because of women like you. She was a good girl when she was young. Before she came under the influence of rap music and drugs and hardheaded men!"

"Maybe you can still save her." She hoped to appeal to his ego. It was a tactic that worked for most men. "Where is she? I'll go with you to find her and we can make her safe."

"She is safe. She's in heaven now."

"Oh. I'm sorry for your loss. But how can you say I was responsible for her death?"

"She was killed by a young teen who was getting high and listening to rap music. He didn't see her step out into the street! His music was so loud he didn't hear her screams!"

"I'm sorry, Chauncey. Truly I am. But—"

"Shut up!" Chauncey once again paced the room. "I sent letters to make you stop the destructive behavior. You didn't stop. Sent threatening packages. You kept performing. Finally, when I heard from your father I knew it was my chance to end this for good."

"How?"

"By treating you like the slut you are to get you out of my system."

"What?" This bizarre nightmare was real.

"It's the only way to save your soul."

Gabriella started to try and make him see reason, but then peered into eyes that were lifeless and dark. There was no reasoning with this man. She wondered how a man who'd acted so normal for the past two months could suddenly turn into a raving lunatic, more dangerous than any fan or stalker could ever have been.

She thought of her father and the words they'd exchanged before she'd raced out in anger. Thought about Troy and how they'd just admitted to one another their love. She thought about her family and friends and how much she'd miss them. A lone tear trickled down her face.

47

Just over ninety minutes after Troy's call to Robert, the Stone estate was all abuzz. Most of the activity was in Chauncey's room, where a computer expert scanned his hard drive for recent searches and the like, and two officers whom Robert had personally recommended searched the room for any clue that might lead them to the missing assistant. Troy was convinced that when he found Chauncey, he'd find Gabriella.

The computer guy turned to Troy. "I might have something here." It took less than two seconds for Troy to be by his side. "One of his last searches was for hotels and motels near the airport. He may be staying in one of them and planning to board a flight tomorrow."

One of the officers who'd overheard the comment said, "I'll check the airlines, see if a ticket has been purchased in either of their names and put out a BOLO at the airport, as well as within a twenty-mile radius of this last search."

Troy nodded, thankful that he wouldn't be the only person who would be on the lookout for this fool.

He left the room and went in search of Gary, who'd almost had to be forcibly removed from Chauncey's room so that the investigation could get underway. To make him feel useful, Troy had set him to researching those close to Chauncey, and calling any relatives who lately may have heard from him.

Troy found him in the dining room, his head in his hands. "Any luck?" Gary shook his head. Troy placed a comforting hand on his shoulder. "Try and stay positive, man. We'll find her."

It was a statement that Troy was trying very hard to believe.

The buzzer sounded, and within minutes Robert walked through the front door. Later, the irony would not be lost on all involved that the same man Gary disrespected was the one with the contacts to now find his child.

"What do you have for me?" Troy asked, once he'd followed Robert back outside.

"Started making things happen right after your phone call," Robert replied, his eyes shining with the excitement of being back in action. "E-mailed Chauncey's picture to a couple buddies, who then put the word out on the streets. We've got a couple pimps who do business in that area. They know all the hotels up and down Century, La Cienega, and all the cheaper hotels that are close to the airport. That's where some of the girls service businessmen in town for just a few hours. I'm confident that if he's anywhere in that area, we'll find him."

"How can you be so sure?"

"Because money talks and bullshit walks. I told my contacts that the award was a cool hundred thousand."

"Thanks, Robert."

"Don't thank me. If one of them finds her, that cash is coming out of your account."

Troy welcomed the humor, however short-lived.

One of the officers met him and Robert outside. "You might want to take a look at this, Troy. We found it in a book called *Deliver Us From Evil.*"

Troy took a look at the lone sheet of paper, with what looked like errant ramblings on it. Typed in single space, they covered the page. Taking a closer look at the font, his eyes narrowed. "This style looks familiar. I'm almost sure it's the same kind that was used in at least one of the letters." He walked into the house, turned on a lamp, and read the contents. The more he read, the more the blood drained from his body. Checking for his keys and cell phone, he raced back outside.

Robert reached out a hand to stop him.

Troy shook him off.

"Where are you going, son?" Robert asked him.

"To find Gabriella."

"But you don't know where to look for her yet!"

"I don't want to wait here until you tell me. I want to be close enough to reach out and nail his ass!"

Until now, she'd done well in holding back the tears. But with her hands and feet tied to the bedposts, and Chauncey in the shower cleansing himself before "joining them together in marriage," as he'd vowed, Gabriella allowed herself to weep. And all she kept thinking was if Troy were still her protector, she wouldn't be here.

Pulling against constraints that she knew were tied solid, she chided herself for the umpteenth time, wishing she could take back just five minutes of her life. The moment when she'd decided to open the door, the moment when she took in her father and Li, the moment she had it out with her dad, the moment she decided to leave the house, and the moment she fled.

Troy! I need you. I'm so sorry that I didn't stand up for you to my father, so sorry that I let him tear us apart. I'd give anything for a do-over, would pay any amount of money for you to know how much I love you.

Instead, she was a captive, about to be sexually assaulted. Just the thought of Chauncey's slimy body on top of hers caused her stomach to roil. She'd convinced Chauncey to remove the spread and let her lie down on the "pure" white sheets. She didn't want to imagine what must go on in places like this, had never been in anything less than a three-star hotel. It was dreary and dank, with indefinable smells. Just placing her bare feet on the nasty carpet had made her skin crawl.

Carol always said how spoiled I was. Looking at the stained ceiling, Gabriella realized her best friend was right. At the thought of Carol, tears rolled again. *I'm sure she's worried sick.* She didn't even want to think about Gary, or her mom. *How will they ever find me? It will be morning before they even know I'm gone!*

When she looked up into Chauncey's maniacal face and saw the knife once again in his hands, Gabriella knew she had more immediate problems to worry about.

"What are you doing?" Even tied up, Gabriella tried to shrink into herself. But she was spread-eagled, totally exposed. Chauncey could do what he wanted and there was no one around who could do anything about it.

Chauncey stared at her for a long moment. "It's not enough," he finally said.

"What's not enough?"

"You have done too much damage, ruined too many lives. Only the taking of your life will be enough to right these wrongs."

In spite of her resolve to stay calm, Gabriella pulled against the binds. "But I've already told you. My heart has always been in the right place, to make people happy. To entertain. Please, Chauncey. I didn't think I was doing anything wrong!"

"But you were."

In desperation, she tried another tactic. "Chauncey, are you a Christian?"

"Of course," he said, as his scowl deepened.

"Me, too."

"Yeah, right."

"I am! And I know that God is a loving God, a forgiving God. That he'll forgive me if I repent and . . . become your wife."

"It is not I that you want. It's that sinner Troy, the man with whom you gyrated on stage, the man you had sex with in public!"

"I don't want him." Gabriella's words came out in a rush, as she fought against a panic attack. "I fired him, remember? I don't want him."

"Your father fired him."

"No, I run the show, remember? I let him go." Seeing her words gain traction, she hurried on. "I knew that what I felt for him was wrong. I wanted to break free, but didn't know how. Maybe that's why you came into my life, Chauncey, to be the light and show me the way. He's gone now, and we can be together. You've delivered me from evil, Chauncey. Don't you see?"

She watched as he approached her, infatuation and something else she couldn't decipher shining in his eyes.

"Maybe I have," he mumbled, taking the blade and cutting the thin dress fabric down the middle. Gabriella shivered as he used the knife to move the material and expose her bare skin. She swallowed hard as he looked her up and down, noticed as he began to get an erection.

But she noticed something else—the knob on the door that was slowly turning.

"Come to me, Chauncey. Let's be one, like you said."

He took a step.

"That's it, drop the towel and get into bed." Gabriella's voice shook ever so slightly as she worked hard to not again glance at the door.

Chauncey took another step, and untied the towel from around his waist. Once again, his face turned from calm to crazy. "Look what you've done!" he screamed, while pointing at the little soldier masquerading as an erection. "Your feminine wiles have caused me to sin. You must atone! You must sacrifice with your life!"

He lifted his arm, firmly clutching the knife. At the same moment, Troy burst into the room, grabbed his arm and twisted while putting pressure on his temple to make Chauncey pass out. It would be several long moments before he regained consciousness, having never even known what hit him.

Troy raced to Gabriella's side. "It's okay, baby," he said, hurriedly covering her body as officers raced inside the room. "I'm here, now. You're going to be okay."

48

Hours later, a weary yet thankful Gabriella linked arms with Troy as they left the precinct. Chauncey had been taken into custody, where he'd be held without bond on charges of kidnapping and attempted murder.

"I still can't believe you found me," she said, looking at Troy with something close to wonder in her eyes.

"I had help," Troy said with a shrug. "I owe Robert a debt of thanks. He knows some of everyone on the force and in the community. It was one of his boys who took the picture to the motel where the desk clerk recognized him. And a stroke of luck that it happened so fast."

Gary, who while talking to Yvonne on his cell had missed seeing his daughter exit with Troy, raced to catch up with them.

"There you are," he said, placing an arm around Gabriella. "Yvonne is taking the first flight out. I told her we'd see her later today."

"Gabriella is going with me," Troy said, in a tone that brooked no argument or discussion. "She can make her own decisions tomorrow, but right now I'm not going to let her out of my sight." He stopped and faced Gary, his stance like that of a warrior, ready to defend what was his.

"I understand," Gary said with a nod. "Look, Troy. I owe you an apology for how you were treated earlier. I can't tell you how much I appreciate what you did, saving the life of my daughter. If I had been in your shoes, I don't know if I would have stepped into the line of fire, not after all that I put you through."

"Well, Gary, let me try and explain it to you. And I'll use small words to make sure you understand." Gary frowned. He'd dissed Troy with these same words. "This isn't about you. It never was. It's about me. And Gabriella. That is all."

He put his arm around Gabriella and began walking toward his car.

"She's still my daughter," Gary called after them. "No one loves her more than I do. Remember that."

Troy didn't respond. Gabriella didn't either. As they turned the corner, Troy noted that Gary still stood where they'd left him, watching, he imagined, until the car was out of sight. No matter. Gabriella and her protector headed to Leimert Park, where Troy knew without a doubt that he could keep her safe.

They drove through the near-empty streets of South Los Angeles, the car quiet as both occupants were consumed with their thoughts. Gabriella looked without seeing streets boasting restaurants and wig shops, churches and nail salons. She didn't have a clue where she was or where they were headed. She only knew that wherever Troy was, that was where she wanted to be.

Troy was busy battling his own emotions. They were

all over the place. There was anger for what Chauncey had put Gabriella through, so much so that had it not been for the extreme discipline Troy had honed over the years, someone would have lost his life tonight. Sadness, because that someone had almost been Gabriella. Joy and gratitude, because everyone was still breathing, and even more that Gabriella was going home with him . . . where she belonged.

He pulled up to a well-kept home on a quiet street, using a garage that rarely saw action. Once inside, he disengaged the alarm, still doing a quick check of each room in the house. Chauncey was behind bars, but tonight Troy wasn't taking any chances. He'd come too close to losing Gabriella and he didn't ever want to feel that type of angst again.

"I like your place." They'd returned to the living room where Gabriella now did a slow turn around. "It suits you."

"It's not a mansion, but it works for this man. Do you want something to drink?"

Gabriella shook her head. "All I want is a shower, and a bed, with you lying beside me."

Twenty minutes later, Gabriella, wearing one of Troy's large black T-shirts and a pair of baggy shorts, sat next to him against the bed's cushioned headboard. She relished in the feel of his strong hand as it ran up and down her arm, warm and comforting, reminding her that she was safe. Still, she shivered.

He noticed immediately. "Are you okay? Do I need to get an extra blanket from the closet?"

"No, I'll be fine."

"I've never been as scared as when I learned you'd

been taken. All I could think of was how I had to find you, how there was no way I could live without seeing you again alive."

"Me, too, Troy," Gabriella said, turning to face him. "I thought of the time together that had been lost, when Dad came between us and you went to work for Tara. I was too proud to say it then, too confused. But I want to say it now. I don't want another day to pass without your knowing how I feel about you."

Troy shifted so that he was facing her, too. "And how is that?"

She placed a hand on his cheek, running her finger down the faint scratch line from the crazed fan still marring his face. "I love you, Troy. I think I've loved you from the moment I saw you, from the moment you came into the hotel room looking cocky and sexy in your trademark black."

"You know how I feel," Troy admitted. "Even though I tried not to. Alex was in love with you and I'd warned him about trying to get close."

"Have you seen him lately or talked at all?"

"I saw him at a party the other week. We spoke, but that was about it."

"You two seemed so close; seems a shame to let a disagreement ruin what looked like a solid friendship."

"I agree. But when I tried to talk about what happened, he wasn't trying to hear me."

"Maybe you can try again."

"Maybe. But right now"—he pulled her closer, kissed her temple—"I have more important matters to discuss."

"Such as . . . ?"

"Such as what type of diamond do you want on your finger?"

She gasped, and pushed away from him. "Troy! Are you trying to propose to me with us sitting in bed looking cray-cray, you in pajama bottoms and me in a tee?"

"What's wrong with that?"

"You haven't even told me that you love me!"

"Women," Troy said, shaking his head. "I love you. Okay? Now will you say yes to marrying me and tell me your ring size?"

She crossed her arms and glared at him.

He cleared his throat and began to chant. "P to the R to the O to the T, E to the C to the T to the O . . . 'R' you going to marry your protector?"

49

It was a stunning day on the island and a perfect day for a wedding. Life had been a whirlwind since Troy's proposal two months ago, and after many lengthy discussions involving bridal consultants and wedding coordinators and family and friends, Troy and Gabriella had decided on a medium-sized wedding involving two-hundred fifty guests, on an island in Fiji. People had arrived in Los Angeles from all over the country before boarding a chartered jet and landing in this tropical paradise three days ago. The first day had consisted of an informal picnic on the beach followed by a fireside tell-all where Gabriella's and Troy's friends swapped stories of growing up with these two powerhouses. Yesterday had been a day of pampering before a sit-down rehearsal dinner that included lobster tails and chateaubriand. After dessert, Troy and Gabriella had kissed each other good-bye, knowing that the next time they'd see each other would be at the altar. That time had almost arrived.

Michael, Gregory, and Troy were in the groom's temporary cabana, along with two of Troy's lifelong friends.

Alex and Troy had finally cleared the air. He'd just left to give the brothers their privacy. The atmosphere was casual, the mood was chill.

Michael walked over to where the barber was doing a last minute touch-up on Troy's immaculately sculpted close-cropped curls. He watched his brother scroll through e-mails, as if this was just another day at the beach.

"You look pretty calm," he said, sitting down in the chair across from Troy. "For a brother about to permanently turn in his player card."

Gregory walked over and sat on the edge of a wicker love seat. "I was just thinking the same thing. You sure you're all right with this, bro? No second thoughts?"

"No." Troy was careful not to turn his head and incur the wrath of his long-term barber. "Not at all."

"For a while we thought no woman out there would be able to tame you." Michael pulled out his iPhone and began checking e-mails, too.

"Gabriella hasn't tamed me," Troy stated. "If anything, she's made me more wild."

Michael and Gregory exchanged a look before Gregory answered, "If you say so."

"About her." The barber gave Troy a mirror and turned him so that he could see the expert cut from all angles. He looked at the style and then at each of his brothers. "I never thought a woman existed who could satisfy all my needs, keep me both interested and entertained, and curb my appetite for variety. But Gabriella Stone is that one woman. And that's why I'm marrying her."

* * *

Yvonne tapped lightly on the door before walking into the cabana where last minute touches were happening with Gabriella's hair and makeup.

"You look absolutely stunning, darling," she said, her eyes shimmering with unshed tears. "Just like a princess."

"Quite appropriate, since she got her prince." Carol sat on the chair and watched Melanie fuss over her charge, making sure every silk butterfly perfectly showed off its crystal wings and straightening every wrinkle in Gabriella's twenty-five-foot train. She'd been batting away tears all day. "Remember how we used to dream about this moment?" she asked Gabriella.

"When we were nine, ten years old?" Gabriella nodded as she replied. "Can't ever forget those days. I was going to marry Usher while you were trying to live *la vida loca*!"

"I remember that!" Yvonne exclaimed. "Girl, you loved you some Ricky Martin."

"And the twins were going to marry famous guys as well, remember? Brandi was all googoo-eyed over Bow-Wow while Brianna loved Justin Timberlake."

"When y'all finally met those men on tour I thought those girls would die." Yvonne shook her head at the memory. While she had focused on raising Garrett as he got older, she'd been involved with the girl group during their early days.

They continued in this vein, talking about childhood crushes and crazy ex-boyfriends.

"So how does it feel?" Carol asked, as the stylist stepped away and Gabriella eyed herself critically in the mirror.

"How does what feel?"

"Getting ready to marry the man of your dreams."

Gabriella's smile was bittersweet. "Just like that . . . like a dream." She then turned, deciding to pet the elephant in the room, the topic that everyone was thinking of but no one seemed willing to broach. "I wish Daddy were here." She'd promised herself to not cry over his absence, but her tear ducts apparently didn't get the message. Two tears rolled down her face.

Yvonne rushed over. "I know, baby." She pulled two tissues from the box and quickly dabbed Gabriella's face, trying herself not to cry. "I can't believe how selfish Gary is acting. This is your day, and he should be here regardless of how he personally feels about your choice."

"If it were Kendall, he would have demanded we move up the wedding date and would have pulled me down the aisle."

"That's part of why he's angry," Yvonne admitted. "Because you wouldn't wait, give more time to thinking about this decision."

"Troy is who I want!" Gabriella insisted.

Yvonne pulled Gabriella into an embrace. "Then that's all that matters."

Silence descended, and there wasn't a dry eye in the room.

A knock at the door ended the moment. It was the wedding coordinator. "Is everyone ready? It's showtime."

"You ready, Mommy?" Gabriella tried to keep her voice from shaking, but she could hardly get the last word past the lump in her throat.

"Are you ready?" Yvonne asked in response. Gabriella nodded. "Then let's go out there and show them the most beautiful bride that has ever walked an aisle." This comment brought what Yvonne most wanted to see right now—a smile.

Strains of Beethoven—Gabriella's favorite from her piano lesson days—could be heard as Gabriella and her mother exited the cabana and entered the garden. The setting was postcard perfect. Beyond them was a long stretch of white sand, the Pacific Ocean a sparkling turquoise blue. The wedding colors, various shades of blue and salmon, perfectly complemented the colors that nature had provided. Gabriella's white wedding dress, a Sophia Tolli ball gown-styled original with a plunging sweetheart neckline, dropped waist, and voluminous skirt beneath the massive train, bore blue, salmon, and iridescent crystals across the bodice, perfectly tying in to the sophisticated tableau. Yvonne's gown was deep turquoise, made of a shimmery satin, with large diamond buttons down its fitted bodice and deep pleats in the wide-flowing skirt. The bridesmaids' colors ranged from baby blue to navy, with Carol's maid-of-honor dress a standout in its multicolored showcasing of all hues of blue. Gabriella took it all in from the back of the garden, at the beginning of the petal-strewn pathway leading up to the man of her dreams, the one who when she saw him made all else fade away. The way Troy looked at her made her know that he felt it, too.

"He really loves you," Yvonne said, witnessing the exchange.

"I know."

"I love you, too, princess."

Gabriella spun around. "Dad! You showed up."

Yvonne turned as well, a look of gratitude and relief in her eyes. She wasn't sure what or who made him change his mind, but she was glad he'd gotten her text and showed up appropriately dressed in a navy single-breasted tux. "I've been a jerk," he said, face contrite, voice sincere. "Having you make that vow at sixteen, let alone holding you to it, was patently unfair. And I have no right to ask, but . . . can I join your mother in walking our baby girl down the aisle?"

Later, if not for the video, Gabriella would be hard-pressed to remember what happened after that moment. She floated down the aisle as if on a cloud, with two of the people she loved most in the world by her side. Troy wore all white—a rare event indeed. His tux fit perfectly and highlighted his darkly tanned skin. His brothers, Michael and Gregory, along with her brother, Garrett, each looked handsome and dignified in their navy blue suits. The parents beamed from the first row, family looked on with delight from the front seating, while friends and the few members of the media who'd been invited filled out the back. Love in the garden was palpable as Troy and Gabriella exchanged the vows they'd written each other. The minister pronounced them man and wife. The kiss was so long and filled with fire that the audience broke out in laughter, cheers, and applause.

"I love you now and forever," Gabriella had said, ending the vows that she had written. "And you will forever be the song in my heart."

"The words you penned have come alive," Troy had responded. "Yes, I am now and will always be your protector; but also your best friend, lover, confidante, soul mate, and whatever else you need. I'm that ride or die dude"—a comment that evoked laughter amid the serious tone—"the one who from this day forward vows to be your one and only. Yes, forever."

50

Gary entered the reception area, where Troy and Gabriella stood talking to Robert and Jackie. The wedding party pictures had all been taken, and Gabriella had changed from her fairy princess wedding gown to a less cumbersome gown—still bridelike with its array of crystals, silk, and lace—but better suited for dancing. They were enjoying a casual few minutes while the guests were being seated and before they entered the sit-down reception dinner as Troy and Gabriella Morgan.

"I'm glad y'all treated the family to such lavish festivities," Jackie was saying, in answer to Troy's question about his mother's pending nuptials. "Because Robert and I aren't planning anything nearly as fancy."

None of her sons had been surprised when shortly after Gary's momentary wooing of Jackie, Robert had popped the question.

"If I had my way we'd all get on a plane to Vegas, hit a chapel on the strip, and call it a day."

Troy gave Robert a fist bump. "I hear you, man."

"Well, I don't." Gabriella high-fived Jackie, who

continued, "Vegas is fine for those who want it, but I'd like something more personal and intimate. Perhaps a simple ceremony right in the living room of our home."

"All right, honey. I guess that wouldn't be so bad." Robert leaned over and kissed Jackie on the cheek. In the process, he saw Gary walking toward them and immediately straightened, the smile fleeing from his face faster than a criminal from the po-po. The group immediately noted the change in his countenance, which caused all of them to turn toward its source.

Gary approached, his hands up in mock surrender. "You all have every right to be angry with me," he said upon reaching the group. "I'm here to offer my sincere apologies to all of you, for everything, but mostly to you, Troy. I know it's customary for the groom to stay with the bride, but . . . can I talk to you for just a minute? There is something I need to say to you man to man."

"You don't owe me any explanations, Gary," Troy replied.

"I know, but I'd like to say it anyway."

"Then go ahead. There's nothing you can share that some of the most important people to me in the world can't hear."

"And you might want to make it quick," Jackie added, looking at her watch. "I'd imagine the coordinator will be coming to get us any minute. The reception will be starting soon." She looked at Troy. "If it's okay with your wife, son, I don't think it would hurt to hear what he has to say. No matter what has happened between you two, he's still your father-in-law at the end of the day. That makes him family, and for the Morgans, that means a lot."

Troy reached for Gabriella's hand. "I don't plan on

keeping anything from my wife. So she also needs to be a part of this conversation."

"Very well." Gary gave his daughter a tentative smile and was rewarded with a tentative smile back.

"We'll see you inside, Troy," Robert said, taking Jackie by the arm and leading them away.

"I've been wrong about everything," Gary began, as soon as they were out of earshot. "If these past few weeks have taught me anything, they've showed that I'm a horrible judge of character. All my life I've tried to keep my baby safe and to know that I'm the very reason why her life was threatened—"

"Daddy—"

"No, baby. Let me finish. I'm the man who brought potential harm into your life and Troy is the one who prevented it from happening. Even then I let ego and greed blind me to this truth." He looked at Troy. "I'll admit that more often than not I've been a controlling, overprotective asshole. As misguided as these actions were, they all were born out of love for my child, the daughter who is the apple of this father's eye. If you're ever blessed to have a baby girl, you'll see exactly what I mean. But no more. If you can find it in your heart to forgive me, Troy, I will welcome you into my family, and give whatever blessings you two will accept on your marriage. From this day forward, I promise to stay out of your business." He looked at his daughter, love apparent in his eyes. "I just want to be a part of your life."

"It's all good," Troy said, holding out his hand for Gary to shake. "I can only imagine how hard it is to let go of the woman you've raised from a little girl. But rest assured, Gary. You don't have to worry from here on out." He placed his arm around Gabriella. "When it comes to taking care of my wife, and the love of my life . . . I've got this."

Shortly after this exchange, the wedding coordinator's assistant called for the newlyweds to join her at the entrance to the outdoor dining room. The fairy-tale theme had been continued here, with thousands of tiny lights beaming like stars across the midnight blue "sky" created from yards of organza and silk. The guests were quieted, and the well-known DJ flown in from his club in Miami introduced the newlyweds.

"Ladies and gentlemen, we present to you Troy and Gabriella . . . Mr. and Mrs. Morgan!"

Toasts were made, dinner was served, cakes were cut, the first dance was applauded. After that, and countless flutes held under the multiple fountains spouting pricey champagne, the party truly began.

"Go, Gabriella, go, Gabriella, go!" Jackie, Carol, her new sisters-in-law Shayna and Anise, members of the former girl group the Haute Coutures, and all the other women encouraged Gabriella, who'd changed into yet another white outfit—this time a form-fitting crystal-covered top with sheer, wide-legged pants. The bride boogied down a spontaneously made Soul Train line, showcasing childhood dances like the Tootsie Roll, the Carlton, and the Bump and Grind.

Not to be outdone, Troy followed his wife with a respectable showing of his native LA's "Crip Walk."

"Get it in, bro!" Michael hollered, as his wife, Shayna, rolled with laughter by his side.

"A few more moves like that and you'll end up in emergency!" Greg teased.

Jackie and Yvonne looked on, their faces beaming as only proud mothers can. "I'm glad Gary showed up to walk Gab down the aisle," Jackie said, talking to Yvonne while never taking her eyes off her fun-loving sons.

"I'm glad Troy showed up in her life," Yvonne responded, giving Jackie a hug. "To give him the reason."

Soon the dance floor was packed with the wedding party and guests. Alex walked over to Carol. "I see you've been trying to avoid me all afternoon. Kind of hard to do on an island."

"Why would I be avoiding you?"

"Because after leaving Troy's employ I said I'd call. And I didn't. I got caught up, and I'm sorry."

"Okay."

"Do you accept my apology?"

"I'll think about it."

"I'll do the Running Man and the Cabbage Patch."

"And let me film it for YouTube?"

"If that's what it takes for you to go to dinner with me once we're back stateside."

"I'll think about it."

"That's cool for later. But can I get a dance for now?"

"I've got to warn you, I do a mean Cabbage Patch."

"That's all right, woman." Alex made an exaggerated move of rolling his shoulders. "I'll take my chances."

After two hours of so much fun that many heels were replaced with satin, rubber-soled booties that the bride had supplied, she and Troy led the wedding revelers down a grass-covered path that ended at the ocean's shore, and a boat that would take them to a private island for their two-week honeymoon. They reached the sandy shores, Gabriella clutching her bridal bouquet with one hand while grasping her husband's arm with the other.

"Okay, single ladies," she teased, as she feigned giving practice tosses. "I know there are several of you out there who want a good man! Here's your chance to be next!"

The unmarried females jockeyed for position, with Carol, Melanie, and a former girl group member trying hardest to stay in the front of the group. Various shouts were heard as Gabriella turned around to toss the flowers over her head.

"Throw them this way, sistah!"

"Girl, stop playing and help me get a husband!"

"Here, Gabriella. Over here!"

Gabriella closed her eyes and tossed the flowers. They sailed high in the air, toward the group of outstretched arms. The woman who caught them couldn't have been more surprised.

"Carol!" Gabriella yelled, as she turned around.

Carol tossed the flowers to Jackie who laughed and tossed them back. "I'm already engaged," she joked. "Looks like it might be your turn."

Troy looked at Alex and noticed a pleased expression. He raised a brow as if to say "Word?"

"Thanks, Gabriella!" Alex shouted. Everybody laughed. Except Carol, who gave him a feigned mean look.

Gabriella leaned over to Troy. "Looks like there might be another wedding in our future."

"You might be right," Troy responded. He took her hand and led her to the boat. "But that's not at all what I have on my mind right now." He helped her onto the boat, and allowed his hand to slide down and surreptitiously caress her buttocks as they waved to those on shore. "Right now, all I have on my mind is you."

"Stop groping me," she chided. "You're such a bad boy."

"That's why you love me, baby."

"Indeed I do." Gabriella reached around and pinched Troy's ass.

"Aw! Stop it, woman!"

"Hmm, I'm wondering. You're going to protect me from the world. But who is going to protect you from me?"

"I don't know." Troy wrapped his arms around her and pulled her close. "But I plan to spend a lifetime finding out."

Zuri Day turns up the heat with three sexy page-turning tales of unexpected love and introduces the Morgan men, three fine brothers who have it all, except what their mama wants most for them—wives. . . .

Meet Michael Morgan

In the world of sports management, Michael Morgan is a superstar. But his newest client, Shayna Washington, may be his most lucrative catch yet. The record-breaking sprinter with the tight chocolate body has a talent and inner light Michael knows he can get the world to sit up and notice. He's certainly paying attention—and suddenly the sworn bachelor finds his focus changing from love of the game to true love. . . .

**Pick up *Love on the Run*
wherever books and ebooks are sold.**

Meet Gregory Morgan

When artist Anise Cartier leaves Nebraska for LA, she's finally ready to put the past and its losses behind her. She's even taken a new name to match her new future. And she soon finds a welcoming committee in the form of one very handsome doctor, Gregory Morgan. Their attraction is instant. So is their animosity. . . .

**Pick up *A Good Dose of Pleasure*
wherever books and ebooks are sold.**

Meet Troy Morgan
Gabriella is a triple threat—singing,
acting, and dancing—and has always
lived the life of a princess.
Now, her father is determined to marry her to
someone who can help expand her brand
and the Stone empire, not some ordinary Joe.
Of course, Troy Morgan is anything but ordinary.
But can bad boy Troy take a backseat
to someone with more money, more fame,
and more of just about everything than him?

From *Love on the Run* . . .

Shayna eased off the gas as she reached the light at the famous intersection of Hollywood and Vine. She focused on the crowd of people crossing the street: obvious and not so obvious tourists blending with the obvious and not so obvious homeless, skateboarding teens, and harried businessmen, and a sidewalk preacher holding up a sign reading: JOHN 3:16. Glad for the diversion, Shayna silently mouthed the crudely written words: FOR GOD SO LOVED THE WORLD THAT HE GAVE HIS ONLY BEGOTTEN SON, THAT WHOSOEVER BELIEVETH IN HIM SHALL—

The blaring horn from the car behind her propelled Shayna into action. Switching from brake to gas pedal, she looked into the rearview mirror and threw up an apologetic hand in the process.

What—or more specifically, who—she thought she saw behind the car that had blared the horn sidetracked her once again. Screeching brakes and another long horn blare, this one accompanied by curse words, filled the air as the SUV changed lanes to pass her, holding up the universal digital symbol to underscore his displeasure.

Yeah, buddy, I feel you. After everything Shayna had gone through in the past month, it was a wonder that her attitude wasn't eff it all! But having that outlook would have been shortsighted because Shayna had things to be thankful for. Yes, even though her ex-personal-trainer-slash-former-classmate-slash-former-best-friend had turned into a playa-playa-play-on-slash-harassing-fool-who'd-lost-his-mind and turned her world upside down. But on the flip side, life was calmer since she'd paid a personal visit to his mother and pleaded her case, and his mother had told him to leave her the hell alone. Thank God that saga was over. *Wasn't it?* Then why was her heart in her throat because of what she could have sworn she'd seen in her rearview mirror. A shiny black Beamer belonging to . . .

Calm down, Shayna. How would he know you're in Hollywood, and why would he follow you even if he did? Dude is many things, but a stalker isn't one of them. Girl, there are thousands of black Beamers in southern LA. Millions, no doubt. It was likely that a fair percentage of said black Beamers were driven by dark-skinned black men with squinty eyes and short hair. And what was that about everyone having a twin? Yeah, that's it. Her crazy ex's worldwide twin just happened to be on Hollywood Boulevard, just behind the impatient SUV whose driver had performed a flip-the-bird drive-by.

Then again, she could have been hallucinating because now, despite glances into the mirror every nanosecond or so, not only did she not see a black Beamer, she seemed not to be able to find any Beamer of any color anywhere. She was tripping, plain and simple. What other explanation could there be?

The GPS instructed Shayna to make a left at the next corner. She switched lanes and also changed thoughts, from exes who might stalk her to the saint who would save her: Michael Morgan, the hotshot sports manager for whom she had just two words.

Day-yum!

She fought the thoughts that assailed her as she expertly navigated the curved, narrow streets leading to his place in the Hollywood Hills. Not too far from the Hollywood sign, he'd told her. Better to think of the house than the man inside it. It would do her no good to let her imagination run wild, as she had from time to time since being approached by Michael's assistant and having the "my people will call your people" convo before the first face to face meeting. Having done her homework, she was totally prepared for his confident presentation and astute knowledge of her storied career. Googling his image had even steadied her for his classic good looks. What had thrown her when she'd actually met him was the raw masculinity, the steaming sexuality that fairly radiated from his body and, more importantly, her body's reaction to it. Her attorney had handled the bulk of the conversation during that and subsequent meetings. She'd played it cool and calm when she was actually hot and bothered. Her mind had been focused on simply remembering to breathe and trying to appear unaffected when she was anything but. Thank goodness that was all behind her. According to her roommate-slash-busybody-slash-good friend Talisha, Michael Morgan and his brothers were notorious womanizers who fancied exotically beautiful women with long hair and even longer pedigrees. Now that she knew this truth, there was nothing for her to worry about. He wouldn't come on to her and she most definitely was not going to flirt with him. Just thinking of the last tidbit her roommate had shared, about Michael and his brother Gregory having famously dated twins at one time or another, maybe even swapping and/or sharing them, made her stomach roil. This information nipped all romantic attraction and fanciful imaginings in the bud. Granted, adults were free to do what they wanted but from Shayna's point of view, some things were just plain nasty!

Then why is your kundalini still tingling when you think about him? Because in spite of what she'd heard about him, there was something about Michael that she liked. He'd not only been the perfect gentleman during their meeting, but a very astute and intelligent one as well. She'd been more than a little impressed.

But she'd give Halle Berry, Whoopi Goldberg, Hattie McDaniel, and Octavia Spencer a run for their Academy Award–winning money before Michael would ever know how she really felt.

As if on cue her cell phone vibrated, reminding her of why she'd never cross the line when it came to her relationship with Michael Morgan. It was hard enough to end a strictly romantic liaison, let alone the kind she'd had with her ex, one with history and professional career and other strings attached. She reached over and silenced the phone. Within seconds, the vibration returned.

Looks like my mama-reprieve is over. Her ex was back to blowing up her cell.

Shayna almost grimaced as she ignored yet another call. *Please get a life and leave mine alone.* Talking with *his* mother now seems to have only been a temporary deterrent, and calling *her* mother was absolutely useless. Not only did Shayna's mother, Beverly Powell, view Shayna's ex as a son, but Shayna's ex was now also her brother-in-law. Confused much? Then you know how Shayna felt when she received the mind-altering and life-changing news: that her forty-three-year-old mother had married her ex's thirty-two-year-old brother. By this time, Shayna's relationship with her off-and-on boyfriend of ten years was more off than on, and when she'd ended things for good a few months back, her mother's situation had thrown a serious hitch in the breakup giddyup. Shayna realized she was frowning and tried to relax. Hard to do when her mother was such a trip. *Why'd she have to go and make things so complicated?*

"Your destination is on the right."

Shayna gave a silent thank you to her GPS genie. If not for the advanced technological device, she'd have had no idea that this was in fact her destination or even that a house lay beyond what looked like a tropical jungle. She pulled into the driveway where more of the yard was visible. Large palm trees anchored an ivy-covered fence and just beyond that was a water feature and a profusion of exotic flowers, though bird of paradise was the only one that Shayna recognized. A curved, cobblestone walkway could be seen beyond the wrought-iron gate with steps hinting that more beauty lay beyond what her eye could presently see.

Impressive.

For the first time since the celebratory toast with her attorney, Shayna allowed herself to get just a little bit excited. Until now, she'd held on to her glee. Why? Because for Shayna Washington, life had had a way of showing her that not only was all that glittered not gold, but that what often held the dazzle of a ten-carat diamond was actually some cubic zirconium madness. How excited had she been when her former best-friend-slash-PT-slash-boyfriend had told her about an iron-clad, no-risk, pinky-promise-really-I-mean-it investment where she could double the twenty-five thousand dollars—her life savings—in six months and they could move in to the condo she wanted.

Very excited.

So much so that when the money disappeared two months later she still moved her now penniless but still credit-score-strong foolish self into a rental apartment with the man who'd squandered her life savings. "More money's coming, baby," was his mantra for months, as the bills mounted and the rent, when paid, was usually late. Then came the wake up call: returning from a track meet to see a yellow-noted greeting from the sheriff's department. Congratulations on your gold medal. You've got forty-eight hours to get the bump out. Okay, she'd imagined the congratulations part, but the eviction notice had been all too real. Thank God for her USC college buds, track mates, and good friends Talisha and Brittney. They'd moved her into their place without one I-told-you-so. Though both of them had. Many times. And when their lease was up shortly thereafter they'd suggested getting a place large enough for the three of them. That was the Culver City apartment where Shayna now lived. Their friendship and unwavering support had given her the courage to finally kick her first love to the curb for good, and to put up a permanent roadblock to her heart.

Like now, as she ignored the phone that vibrated for the third time in less than three minutes. She'd known her ex for more than half her life and while he'd acted crazy before, it had never been like this. *What's up with dude?*

Determined to focus on her future instead of her past, Shayna took a deep breath, a last look in the mirror, and stepped out of her pride and joy, the top of the line Hyundai that was a part of her last winner's package. It was one of the few "luxuries" that remained of the past two years' modest yet ever-increasing success. *Okay. Admit it. You are excited about this partnership with that manly mass of muscles masquerading as Michael Morgan.* As she unlatched the gate and walked through the Garden of Eden that was her newly acquired sports manager's front yard, Shayna reminded herself to keep this shred of excitement under wraps. She rang the doorbell at the same time her phone vibrated. Again. No problem with dialing down her thrill meter. Her ex was making sure that she ix-nay the green light that beckoned her to a fling with Michael Morgan, and keep her eyes firmly on the caution light that was flashing *business only*.

From *A Good Dose of Pleasure* . . .

Almost six weeks to the day from when she received her acceptance letter from The Creative Space, Anise landed at Los Angeles International Airport. Her aunt, Aretha, met her curbside, just outside baggage claim. "Hello, Shirley," she said, giving her niece a heartfelt hug.

Anise hugged her back, and after they'd placed her luggage in the trunk and settled into the car, she said, "Aunt Ree, please call me Anise." At her aunt's questioning look, she continued. "Mommy named me after my grandmother, and while I loved her dearly, I always hated that name. Shirley never fit me. I've done a lot of soul searching since my mother's death. Her passing taught me how short life is and caused me to think a lot about how I want to live the rest of it . . . on my terms. It's time to mark a brand new chapter, to live my life a whole different way. That began with changing my name. It has legally been changed to Anise, Anise Cartier."

"Cartier?" Aretha asked with raised brow. "Like the watch?"

"You could say that," Anise replied with a laugh. "But

when the idea came to me to change my first name, it's not what I had in mind. Carter sounded too plain to go with Anise so I just spiced it up a bit."

"No pun intended, huh?"

"Ha! That's right, auntie. No pun intended."

"Hmm." Aretha looked at Anise with an unreadable expression. After turning from Sepulveda Boulevard and merging into the parking lot otherwise known as the 405 Freeway, she shrugged and gave her niece's leg an affectionate pat. "I think Shirley is a pretty name. Changing it sounds extreme to me. But I'm happy that you're taking control of your destiny, baby, so make no mistake, I'll support you every step of the way." There was a sparkle in Aretha's eye as she continued. "Welcome to Los Angeles, Anise Cartier." She pronounced the last name with a haughty accent and elaborate sweep of her arm, causing them both to break into laughter. Anise's heartbeat increased as she took in the sights whizzing past her. *I'm in frickin' Los Angeles, California, baby!* Just as she thought this, a warm breeze swept across her face and settled around her shoulders. This had happened several times in the past few weeks. *Mommy.* Anise batted away tears at the knowledge that her mother was indeed with her, and seemed to approve of this journey to a new life.

The next morning, Gregory Morgan turned onto his street, having just finished a rare twenty-four hours straight at the hospital, almost half of them in surgery. His usual grind was twelve, twelve-hour shifts a month, but last night a seven-car pileup during rush hour traffic had occurred on the 10 Freeway, leaving one person dead and a dozen critically injured. UCLA's emergency room had been filled to capacity and beyond, with him and a team of four other doctors working round the clock to save lives. Fortunately, they had. Aside from the young man who'd died when his vehicle had spun out of control and been broadsided, no one else had died as a result of this unfortunate accident. Yawning deeply, he rubbed his eyes, already envisioning at least eight uninterrupted hours of deep, dreamless sleep on his king-sized memory foam mattress.

He was four houses away from his own home when he saw her: a darkly tanned treat, all legs and booty with shoulder-length hair pulled back in a simple ponytail. Beside her was a dog that could have doubled as a Shetland pony. Gregory couldn't ascertain whether she was walking her dog, or the dog was walking her. *Hello, neighbor!* He slowed to watch how her butt cheeks seemed to wink at him with each long stride, how the muscles in her calves became defined when foot met pavement, and how her arms and legs flowed in effortless synchronicity. As his pearl white Mercedes cruised alongside her, she tugged her huge dog to the side of the road and glanced over at his car. Their eyes locked. Gregory's breath caught in his chest. *Wow.* She was as beautiful from the front as she was from the back: big eyes, pert nose, big juicy lips that had him licking his own. Without realizing, he'd slowed his car almost to a stop, temporarily mesmerized by the bewitching natural beauty now half smiling, half frowning as she once again neared his car.

He was straight-up busted and too tired—and interested—to care that she'd peeped his stalkerish behavior. Also missing from action was his recent decision to lay off the ladies and put all of his attention to his medical research. Right now, Gregory was interested in researching something else. Pressing on the brake, he pushed the button to ease down the window on the passenger side and blessed her with a grand piano smile. "Good morning."

"Hey," she said, with about as much enthusiasm as a nun in a porn store. The beast growled. Gregory frowned. *Great. You can ride it in a rodeo and then have it guard your house.* Both owner and dog kept it moving.

Undeterred, Gregory released the brake and pressed down on the gas pedal. He glimpsed a hint of a smile before she turned her head. "Oh, it's like that? You're going to just throw a 'hey' over your shoulder and keep running?"

"Yes," the stranger replied, her eyes slightly narrowed and daring as she answered. "It's *just* like that." She broke into a sprint and cut through a neighboring yard, her four-legged protector right on her heels.

Gregory turned the corner. Beauty and the beast were nowhere in sight. He peered further down the street before turning into the alley that led to the detached garage at the back of his Hancock Park home. *That was fast. Where could she have gone?* After parking the car, he walked through the rarely enjoyed backyard that had been meticulously landscaped and into the two-story traditional home he'd purchased for a steal when the housing market collapsed several years ago. The back door opened into a hallway with the laundry room on one side and a mud closet on the other. A short walk and a turn landed one into the updated gourmet kitchen, which anchored the open-concept living space next to a mahogany staircase. Gregory didn't notice any of this as he retrieved a glass of orange juice from the refrigerator before mounting the stairs and heading for the master suite. He didn't think of his marble-encased shower with the dual rain forest showerheads as he undressed and stepped into the soothing water stream. As he washed away the tension of the stress-filled shift he'd just finished, Gregory was only vaguely aware of his surroundings. He was too busy thinking about sun-kissed skin and a dazzling smile from the stranger who'd told him it was "just like that."